ROSA GUY was born in Trinidad but raised in Harlem, New York. Bored and feeling there was little point in carrying on as a student, she left school at fourteen and started factory work. Realising that she got the worst jobs because she was Black, she became involved first with the unions at her workplaces and then in the larger struggle for Black freedom. She also started to write and had a play performed off Broadway but her stories and novels were rejected repeatedly until her work for young adults was taken up. These novels, amongst them *The Friends* and *Ruby*, have gained wide critical acclaim both in America and Britain. In the 1950s Rosa Guy was one of the founders of the Harlem Writers' Guild to help Black writers develop their craft. She lives in New York and in *A Measure of Time*, her impressive and captivating first novel for adults, she recreates the life of the city, from the 1920s to the '50s, with astonishing vividness. The life of her central character, Dorine Davis, is based on that of her step-mother who, arriving in Harlem in the '20s, also worked as a 'booster'.

A MEASURE OF TIME

Rosa Guy

Published by VIRAGO PRESS Limited 1984
41 William IV Street, London WC2N 4DB

First published in USA by Holt, Rinehart
and Winston New York, 1983
Published simultaneously in Canada by Holt,
Rinehart and Winston of Canada, Limited

British Library Cataloguing in Publication Data
Guy, Rosa
A measure of time.
I. title
813'.54[F]   PS3557.U93
ISBN 0-86068-512-7
ISBN 0-86068-516-0 Pbk

Designer: Lucy Albanese
Printed in Great Britain
The Anchor Press, Tiptree, Essex

In Memory of My Family
Audre Gonzales, Henry, Reginald
and Ameze Cuthbert,
and Corine

Prologue

Like a lady. That's how I stepped onto that train. Then this sudden push of hot flesh from behind sent me flying, knocking me one way, my suitcase the next. Naturally I got hot—most of those same folks scrambling over me to get seats had been on the Jim Crow train, and for the last couple of days I had been forced to listen to: "Sure'll be glad to change to that 'freedom train.'" . . . "Ain't it the truth." . . . "Be a blessing just to be in a place where we can just spread out." Yet there they all were just a-pushing and a-shoving, damn near broke my back, all trying to squeeze into that one car like it was but one coach on the whole train—proving they didn't rightly believe in all that freedom they'd been running off at the mouth about.

Snatching my pocketbook, squeezed between two pairs of shoulders, making it up the aisle, I still kept hold of my ladylike way. "Look a-here," I sweet-voiced. "Ain't no sense in y'all taking on so. We all going the same way."

A fly pissing on cotton would have gained more attention. So I left off reasoning, bent to retrieve my suitcase just as this foot, belonging to the feller using my back for a brace, kicked it out of my reach.

"Damn feller . . ." I turned, and my eyes caught the knowledge that the few seats remaining had dozens of folks heading for them.

Hating the word backward (especially standing still and riding that way), I knocked aside some legs, snatched up my suitcase, and leaving the man for later, burrowed like a beaver through the lot of them. I made it too. Matter of fact, I had actually lowered my hindparts into the northward-facing seat when a shove from beneath sent me toppling into the seat opposite.

"Shit now   ." Turning, and forced to swallow my cussing, I satisfied myself by cutting my eyes at the hefty (I declare it had to be a miracle how she slid beneath me) midaged mama settling down into her folds of flesh. Too worldly to be humble, yet too young to be downright sassy, I leaned toward her from that backward-riding seat, trying to force her to read every dirty word thought up on my face.

Guilty, yet glorying in her victory, Moms kept fussing with her hat, her bag, her blouse, eyes fumbling every whichaway to avoid mine. Churchgoing Mama (I had already pegged her when we got on the train together in Montgomery), solid Baptist, join congregations wherever she'd go, giving herself rights, wrong or no.

Turning from fussing with herself, Moms pretended interest in folks roaming the coach—those folks looking in between laps, begging for space on already filled seats, sending a last prayerful look over shoulders before moving on to the next coach—hoping they'd be remembered and counted among the living when the train next stopped. The look of them got me to snapping my fingers humming Ma Rainey's jailer's song. All about getting a sucker bound and chained. A goddamn frame. What nigger would kill a cracker's son—excepting by accident. . . .

Lord knows, nothing about old Moms resembled Ma Rainey—except maybe they were both soot black. But Ma Rainey, dressed in white satin, diamonds blazing her pure black skin, her one-hundred-carat smile brightening the room when she got to laughing and singing, happened to be a lifetime away from this lump of clay setting in life's way. I kept snapping my fingers just a-humming.

When the last of the stragglers had gone by, I turned my attention to seeing how the rest of the brothers and sisters from the Jim Crow car were faring: comfortable now, talking, laughing, forgetting the dirt and soot, the sweat that matted their hair to their heads and had worked into their pores during that long ride. Many still held on to greasy paper bags—the last of the food for the long journey. Most I reckoned to be just town folks—they dressed like it—in their best Sunday-go-to-meeting clothes. Not so the three from Mississippi (I figured Mississippi because they were already on the train when Moms and I boarded in Montgomery, and because they looked backwoods). One of them wore a suit of bright green, with matching tie, shirt, and cap. It shouted country so loud that all the soot and grime from the back car hadn't been able to quiet it. The three sat hunched so close a breath of air would have had a tough time squeezing between them. They kept sipping from a jug of corn liquor, whispering humble-like, eyes turned to the floor; the meekest of the meeks, those supposed to inherit the earth—only while waiting, they took their reward in a jug.

Whites had climbed aboard, too. Crackers, and a few Yankees (we Southerners could always spot a Yankee). One evil redneck kept cutting his eyes around, hot at having been pushed onto a train full of niggers. The red in his neck kept rising to color his face, then settling back to his neck. But for the most part the crackers got to talking to their colored neighbors. (That's what we called ourselves back then, when we weren't calling ourselves niggers. Crackers called us darkies, nigras, or niggers, and I understand educated folks were demanding to be called Negroes. But to call a feller black back then, you had to be ready to fight.)

"Nigra, when you coming back home?" . . . "You ain't gonna like it none up north." . . . "Our darkies don't know when they well off. Ain't no sense in leaving your good home."

And colored folks answering: "Hee-hee, now ain't that the truf?" . . . "You's right, suh. You sho is right." . . . "I ain't thinkin' a stayin' up norf no time—no suh. Reckon'll be home long 'fore you gits back." . . . "Who me suh? Naw—ain't thinkin' a leavin' mah good home to stay nowhere . . . hee-hee. . . ." Grinning, laughing, lying in their teeth. Yankees, for their part, didn't talk much (two sat on the window side next to Moms and me). They didn't talk to crackers, didn't talk to colored folks, hardly talked among themselves—just sat there reading or staring out of the windows. (Yankees are some peculiar folks.)

The one next to me wiggled, right uncomfortable, when I looked past him, out the window, to see the underbelly of the cities and towns racing by. Seeing that, I kept the stretch in my back, sitting tall, and looked past him out the window: I didn't belong to the underbelly of any town, or any damn city.

The house where I was born happened to be a grand old house. Master Samuels had willed it to Mama—my grandmother—on account of he had outlived the rest of his kin. Mama—and her mama—had looked after the Samuels as long as he—or she—could remember (I do declare I never did know how old Mama was), so by rights it was due her.

That old house boasted one of the first inside toilets in Montgomery, which put my family ahead of most of the town's black folks and a hell of a lot of white folks too, in that Cradle of the Federation (we blacks bragged about that same as whites—no jive).

And when I left home to go and live with Mamie, I didn't live in the underbelly of Cleveland. Mamie—black, wiry, with short nappy head—had bulldozed her way into a high-class neighborhood where light-skinned colored folks were down on their knees praying to white folks to quit running (which of course they didn't, white folks not seeing the difference between black and black). They looked up, saw Mamie—handkerchief tied around her head, directing the moving men, then learned Mamie was madam and not maid. Those high-yeller niggers wept. They took to scuttling across the streets like warthogs when they saw Mamie coming, waiting until she passed before easing out—so afraid she might be polite and say good-day. Chances are Mamie never saw them. Mamie's mind ran to but two things—making money and keeping a fine house. And at Mamie's a feller could lick the floors and his tongue feel nothing but the grain of wood.

Chug, chug, chug—scraggly grass, broken-down houses, longing faces—poor folks waving us by. No—sure never lived in the underbelly of a living town or city—and wasn't about to.

Chugging of a train means different things at different times to different folks. It can mean different things at different times to the same folks. When I left Montgomery five years before, the chug was saying: Is you free sure 'nough? Is you free? Is you free, sure 'nough? But that time I had been running away from Master Norton. I loved Cleveland—had a ball there. But never had felt free enough to go back to Montgomery.

But the good Lord giveth and the good Lord taketh. He had

snatched up Master Norton (at least that's who folks gave the credit). And here I was. Chug, chug, chug. Good-bye Master Norton good-bye. Good-bye Master Norton good-bye. The gladness at that old man's passing went so deep it felt like downright sadness. Glad he had passed, and as happy as a chinch in a funky mattress he had remembered me in passing. . . .

Chug, chug, chug. Dorine and Sonny, Dorine and Sonny, Dorine and Sonny—and the good times. Sonnydorinesonny-dorinedorinesonnydorine—and only the good Lord to part them. That chug flip-flopped my heart. Needles of pain sprayed my stomach. Six months! Overstaying my time in Montgomery six whole months! One-half a year! What had I been thinking about—leaving Sonny alone all that time?

I breathed deep to still my heart. Of course when I told him about my inheritance . . . if I told him . . . No, no. No more ifs between Sonny and me. No more secrets. I intended to bare my soul—tell all. Tell him the two reasons I had for overstaying my time.

Dorine Davis, is you done took leave of your senses! Is you done jumped clean outa your simple head! Ain't we done decide we got times for such things—after I makes me some money? After we gets married?

Sonny's voice sounding so loud in my head, I turned my eyes— from pretending they weren't looking at the two Yankees, to pretending they weren't looking at old stiff-backed Moms. Of course they hadn't heard. So I leaned back my head, closed my eyes, and thought out my loud-mouthed answer: *Nigger, you say you intend to be an overnight millionaire. That can take a million years. Never mind that you here in—*

"Nuuuu York . . . Nuuuu York . . . Whoooooeeeeee!"

It took seconds of adjusting my mind to make out that the bright green shimmer before my eyes was Country stretching in the aisle and not part of the dream I had fallen into. A face-splitting grin dragged his lips from one ear to the other, and he raised his jug to include the coachload of us. "Nuuuu Yo-ork. Here ah comes!"

One of his buddies, Squinty (on account of he had one bad eye and squinted out of the other), kneeled in his seat looking up, waiting for Country to say lines to crack up over. The third sat with his back to us, preventing me from pegging him.

5

"Ah's gonna git on mah knees—dat's what ah's gonna do. Right down on dese here knees an' kiss—"

"What? What you gonna kiss, brother?" Squinty egged him on. But Country, taking his time, wrapped his thick, pink lips around the top of the jug, took a deep drag, did a jig to keep the jug out of Squinty's hands, and said: "Now—wha ah's gonna do is dig me a hole—an' ah's gonna bury mahself up to mah neck in dat dere hole—an' any Mama's chile what lays hand to uproot *me* is headin' straight as hell for that fiery inferno. . . ."

Colored folks got busy burrowing their behinds as far down as seats allowed. They got to staring out of windows, praying to the Almighty for Country to shut his big, black mouth, hide his pink lips, and fade out of sight (back then in 1926, town folks reckoned they were better than backwoods folks. Didn't matter they were all moving along the same road).

"Ah's one ba-ad nigger," Country preached. "Just let one somebody try to uproot *me* an' he'll be a-headin' straight for hell, be he nigger or be he cracker."

Embarrassment got Moms's eyes to feeling around for mine. Knowing that, I kept mine solid on Country. I even broke out grinning to show her where my feelings lay. She glanced at the man sitting beside me, then to the one next to her, then she muttered—just loud enough for my ears: "Sure God wasn't actin' all that big and bad a li'l while back."

I caught my lips between my teeth to keep from turning up laughing. Country and his buddies sure had been still and scared-looking all the while they rode below the Mason-Dixon. Pulling out of D.C. seemed to have started him. And the farther north we rode, the more rambunctious he got.

"Ye-ah, ah's gon' spout roots an' ah's gonna grow into one a dem lightpoles. And cold, rain, snow, or sleet—nothin's gonna stop me from greetin' all you all blackbirds what comes a-flyin' in."

All the blackbirds went to squinching even farther down in their seats. That's why Moms, looking around for one sympathetic soul to share her misery, saw only the tops of heads.

"Ah's gonna turn into one a dem lightpoles—the kin' niggers want to turn into, 'fore dey stays back in 'Sippi drivin' a automobile."

"Man," Squinty said. "When you ever see a nigger ridin' a automobile in Mississippi. Ain't you heard about what happen to Preach Duncan when he come a-ridin' into town in that new automobile a his'n?"

From the side of my eyes I saw Moms twisting, all itchy in that forward-looking seat. Then ignoring the fact that I was ignoring her, she whispered: "Only thing them Mississippi niggers ever drive's the wind, swingin' from them trees."

Lord, that's the worst thing for her to say to me. I had had my fill in Cleveland of colored folks looking down at me because I hailed from Alabama. I declare, the farther north colored folks came, the better they thought they were. Folks from Virginia treated all southern-born like dirt. Those from North Carolina looked askance at South Carolinians, who in turn put down folks born in Georgia. Those from Georgia didn't want a living thing to do with us born in Alabama—and the Lord help those poor black souls who happened to have sprung from the muddy banks of the Mississippi. Seemed like the worse white folks treated us, the more we felt called on to justify their treatment.

Yet the good Lord, and all those colored folks, knew that there wasn't one state in all of the South where colored folks were treated like folks, and where white folks didn't lynch our butts like they were scared to wait for tomorrow. So when Moms cracked like that I broke my sworn silence to reply—polite-like: "Ma'am, you mean driving in the wind like Old Man Witlow drove in the wind?"

Anybody boarding a train in our neck of the world was gut-bound to the knowledge of Old Man Witlow. It had nothing to do with him being lynched—lynching happened to be our way of life. Even toddlers knew that when whispering got hushed; when elbow-nudging and eyeballing and humming and shushing went on when white folks passed; when roads cleared of folks, and doors got shut and bolted, and in darkness grown-ups strained to listen to the outside happenings—that was lynching time. It was the way Old Man Witlow got his that caused him to be cut as deep as forever in folks' memories:

That morning when Old Man Witlow's kin braved the dawn to claim his body, there wasn't one thing left of the old man. The only thing proving he had been lynched was the burned-up rope swinging in the wind from the tree charred white—and on the big magnolia tree next to it, a big grease spot spreading to cover its mighty trunk.

Now Old Man Witlow had been a hefty man, which led to speculation about the big grease spot. We younguns went to look at that spot every day, and I do declare, that spot got bigger and bigger by the day. As time went on, folks got to putting the fear of the Lord in their children by warning: "Keep that shit up and I'll burn your hind-parts so's you won't be no mor'n a handful of grease to smear on the bark of a magnolia tree." I swear niggers can sure joke about anything.

Payback, even when it's accident, brings joy. Seeing that she hadn't wiped me out with her hell-and-damnation stare, Moms glared out of the window. And not wanting my big grin to break into out-and-out laughing, I called to Country: "I know what happened to Preach Duncan when he got that new automobile." Country looked up the aisle at me, scared I might be trying to steal his thunder. "What?"

"They lynched his butt, that's what," I said.

"No, they ain't." Country grinned his relief over my ignorance. Yak yak yak, he got to loud laughing. And knowing the loudness kept churchgoing Moms's back getting stiffer and stiffer, I thought to give it one more shot of starch: "I sure 'nough thought they hung his black butt," I said.

"Might have at that," Country speculated. "Last time ah seen ole Preach, he was hightailin' it outa 'Sippi on dem size thirteens. Mas' Talbert was way behind—but he was a-gainin'."

"Nigger, shut your mouf up and set down." I had paid Redneck no mind until he had shot out of his seat and stood, hot breath blowing down on Country. "If you ain't setting in two seconds, ah'm gonna take your ass and shove it right off this goddamn train."

The chugging of the train grew loud as nappy heads commenced to popping out of shoulders where they had been hiding. The quiet in the train suggested folks calculating what to do if called on to take sides. True, black folks outnumbered whites three to one on that coach—even that fool redneck had to have seen that. It was equally true that we Southerners had been used to letting one white ride herd over a dozen of us. But here on the "freedom train," on the north of the Mason-Dixon?

Right off, Squinty stepped in the aisle to stand shoulder to shoulder alongside Country. And while the rest of us worried over what we might do, the third buddy got to standing, or unwinding—seemed he might never stop. By the time he had pulled himself to his feet, every head in that coach had bent as far back as necks allow—Redneck's right along with the rest.

Whatever Redneck saw on Lanky's face, though not visible to the rest of us, affected us. He looked around to see how many crackers he had encouraged to follow. He hadn't. So he eased on away, slinking back to his seat.

"That cracker must think he's still down home." Moms's voice sounded right agreeable. "It sure's gonna take them some time getting used to things ain't what they used to."

"They sure is, ma'am. They sure is." I smiled, leaning back, happy that I had acted the lady all along.

"Yes suhree, ah's free. No more Jim Crow car for me." Country marching up and down the aisle, hugging his jug. "Yes suhreee, ah's freee. No more crackers lynching me." Marching and brushing Redneck in passing and Redneck looking just short of snatching him, Lanky be damned.

But Lanky had decided on enough. When Country came abreast he plucked the bottomless jug out of his hand, took a swallow, then passed it on to Squinty. And just like that Country sat down. Then they got to whispering—sitting so close a breath of air couldn't squeeze between them. That was nice. A team. They needed to be. They had already hoed a long row to make it this far from the backwoods, from the look of them, and they sure needed to pull together to make it the rest of the way.

And just like that I missed Mamie, and Cleveland, and her house where all of us blackbirds passing through—singers, hustlers, dancers, and musicians—pulled together, offered one another encouragement. I thought of Mamie, sitting at her gaming table, black coffee at her elbow, cigarette hanging from the side of her mouth, smoke curling past the squint in her eyes. What kind of life would I have away from her in the big city?

"Weights, baby," Sonny's voice sounded in my head, "don't do nothing but drag a feller down. . . ."

I sighed thinking of the little fat, black weight I had put on Sister Janie's shoulders. Yeah, Sonny'd be mad.

Well—wasn't nothing for him to do but get glad. Hadn't I paid his way to New York? And wasn't I bringing more to sweeten up the pot? Talk about weights! What the hell did he have to complain about. . . ?

> Lord, Lord, Lord.
> Let's talk about the blues.
> Lord, Lord, Lord,
> I got more blues than I can use.
> Young, brown, so lovely
> Got this fine brown frame.
> Yet I got a man, makes a fool
> Of me just the same.

Jumping unbidden into my mind like that, the song got the tears to starting (I cry at the prick of a pin). A bad sign—a real bad sign. . . .

BOOK ONE

1

"Dorine Davis!" Sonny had polished up that anger to blind me. I knew it. "What the hell keep you in 'Bama so long?" he growled, his brow furrowed. He had to be glad to see me. I figured he didn't want to show it so I hid the good feeling I got in seeing him.

"Was it that long sure 'nough?" I spoke careless-like. But Lord, he did look good. So good, every speck of soot and grime I had cultivated on that long three-day journey doubled in weight.

I dug Sonny's style. His close-cut hair (I hated stocking-cap slick), his pressed look—a tack in all its sharpness had a hard time competing with the creases in Sonny's pants. Conceit like a high-gloss varnish smeared over him as he led me out of that wide-open Penn Station into the darkening evening, his head bobbing pridefully, inviting the once-over. I obliged.

The new fedora—he hadn't had that in Cleveland. Nor the gray pinstriped suit. The diamond on his pinky (Sonny had it enlarged whenever he touched money) had grown to finger-breaking size. That got my mind to buzzing—the money I had given him to get to New York had to be made of rubber to stretch for all those trimmings, along with an apartment and furniture. He led me across the street to a brand-new red roadster shining at the curb, and six months of planning on sharing all secrets changed to lockjaw.

Letting me in the car, he got behind the wheel and sat tapping it, impatient for the oohs and aahs to gloat on, the questions to start him to lying. Tap-tap-tap, went the fingers on the wheel. I sat natural, like sitting on a toilet seat, looking out onto the street like at a blank wall. That eased the air out of his balloon-head and left him stuck with his simple temper. "What in the hell was you doing all this time in that hellhole?" he said. "Damn, you had enough time to make a baby."

Which got onto the right track for me to confess, clear the air, get our lives to rolling like they ought to. But all that prosperity! In six months! No suh. I knew my Sonny. No way for him to have done what we had planned and all the sporting too. My teeth wedged together, my prayers that he hadn't messed up my money steamed heavenward.

"Sure is surprised at you," he kept on. "Talk, talk, talk, plan, plan, plan, and you had to go and mess up. Ain't you known that by staying away so long you could mess up my hustle?"

No, my man wasn't mad. He was scared. Scared, and talking to keep my mind away from what my eyes were seeing. The excuses he had ready depended on me defending myself. Well, if he thought that, he sure had another thought coming. . . .

Finally he eased the car into the traffic, and stepping on the gas swelled his head up again. Sonny could no more help being a show-off than he could help breathing. Impressing folks pumped his lungs. Without one thought of my three-day journey—which could have made a mule tired—he headed downtown. "Got to show you *my* town," he said.

Lockjaw prevented me from talking, from explaining that a three-day trip did to me the same as it did to ordinary folks. So I sat back to let him prove to me how New York had become *his* town.

But a feller had to have hardening of the arteries, and gall-stones, too, to sit stone-faced indifferent at the first sight of New York. Streetcars clanging, sparking the night, cars—more cars than I had ever seen at one time—their bright lights bearing down on us on all sides, brought out the oohs, the aahs that Sonny had been waiting to hear. And more lights—lights, lights, lights, stretching out the roadway for us to drive. Coming from Cleveland, it did more than dazzle—it petrified me.

Sonny headed downtown to the Wall Street area. He had to show me "the tallest building the world got to offer."

"Is that the one?" I kept asking at every building we drove by. "Is that the one?" All of them were taller than any I had ever seen. By the time we pulled up before the Woolworth Building, lockjaw had changed to hangjaw. Looking up, up, up, I declared, "These fools don't know what they about. They challenging the Lord!"

"Ain't nothing compared to what *we* gonna build," Sonny bragged.

"Sure 'nough?" Too big-time to catch the put-down, he answered, "Hell, this one's touching the sky—the next'll be straddling God's front porch."

God's country. I accepted that. Sonny had swung the car uptown, and we cruised Times Square. Alabama had never been my town. Now even Cleveland faded before the force of all that glitter: lights running around the Times Building, smoke coming from the billboard cigarette smoker's mouth, water falling down the sides of buildings, splashing out onto the avenue, sparkling in the lights. Electricity had changed night into day, and folks stood out enjoying it. In such numbers! Talking, laughing, crowding streets and eating-places, lining up to enter glittering showplaces. Colored folks, too! Right out there in that brightness—wearing bow ties, boaters, slick-looking spats, sporting canes—laughing, talking loud, belonging—and sounding free. . . .

Right then and there I fell in love with New York. I never stopped. Years later Ray Charles was to sing: "When you leave New York you ain't going nowhere"—that ran true for me back there in 1926.

Heading home, we stopped for a red light somewhere in the Fifties, alongside a chauffeur-driven limousine that must have been a half-block long. Sonny got to grinning, nodding, tipping his hat. Dirty, gritty, I hated being exposed. But Sonny kept up that face-splitting grin. The man tipped his hat. "Hi-ya, Sonny." The car drove off.

"Hey Jimmy!" Sonny shouted after the moving car, loud enough to be heard for blocks. I looked around, thanking God no one had heard. Sonny looked around too, still grinning, wanting folks to have seen him. It had to be a sin for one man to be so proud just saying "hey" to another. I stilled my hand to keep from reaching out and pulling his thick lips together.

"Jimmy Walker," he explained.

"Who's that?"

"Whatcha mean, who's that? Girl, that's the mayor of New York!"

Sonny kept the simple, proud grin going all the way as we drove up under the el tracks with the train rattling overhead, deafening us. At 110th Street we turned east, then north onto Seventh Avenue. "Baby," Sonny said, "we in Harlem now—our natural destination."

The car had started rolling smooth. Seventh Avenue was asphalted. Double-decker buses went up and down the avenue, tops rolled back.

The tree-lined avenue boasted buildings with doormen standing guard. In the marbled lobbies, I caught glimpses of uniformed black and white elevator men talking to white swells dressed to go nightlifing. A grand place, Harlem! Fabulous! An elegant avenue, Seventh Avenue.

I hardly noticed when we crossed the border into black Harlem, but suddenly we were there. An excitement rose around us. Folks. Folks standing out on the avenue, talking, laughing. In the cool evening air, away from the bright electric lights of downtown, the stars shone, the sky gleamed a deep, clear blue, and folks were out enjoying it. They stood alone, in pairs, in clusters, agreeing, disagreeing, laughing in whispers, laughing out loud, splitting their sides. A feeling of folks reached out to me, and I dug that too.

We stopped for a red light at a corner where a crowd had swelled out, spilling off the sidewalk onto the avenue, blocking traffic. They were listening to a heavyset black man with an angry mustache who stood on a podium, sweating in a dark wool suit. I heard his loud voice, and not understanding, I asked Sonny, "What's happening here?"

Sonny honked his horn and drove on, a little too heavy on the gas. "Ain't nothing but them fucking West Indians," he said. Cusswords from a feller who prided himself on his smooth talking?

"West Indians? Who they?" I asked.

"Folks what comes from them islands."

"What islands?"

"West Indian islands."

"They looks like niggers to me," I said, turning to see better.

"That's what the hell they is," Sonny said, "but they swear they better than other folks. Always bitching about things ain't good here. Raising hell about what white folks do and don't do. If they don't like it here, why they just don't get the hell on back where they come from?"

"That what they talking about? White folks?" I asked. "What they talking?"

"They say it's English," Sonny said, "but they talk so damn bad, ain't no understanding them. And it don't make no difference how long they here, they always talk like they just got off a banana boat."

"You mean you ain't understood what the man said?" I asked.

"I ain't heard. But I know he bitching on account of that Marcus Garvey they done put in jail."

"Who he?"

"West Indian son of a bitch, conned folks out of money to buy some rotten ships. Ought to keep his ass in the pen—else ship him the hell on back where he come from."

"Oh—that's what the man's mad about. On account of being conned. . . ."

"Naw—on account of white folks putting their leader in jail. Oughta be thanking them folks, but no, they out there raising hell."

Sonny and I were born to disagree. But then, he hailed from Baltimore. Folks from Baltimore had blind spots when it came to whites. Nothing that white folks did was ever wrong, and nothing black folks did was ever right. I always figured it was from being born so far north and yet being considered southern that tended to confuse them.

But seeing that man, hearing him out there shouting, impressed the hell outa me. In all my days in Alabama, the only one somebody who I knew to speak his piece above a whisper against white folks was Big Willie Hopkins. Big Willie happened to be tetched. And in the South, nobody, black nor white, messed with crazy niggers. Now for the first time I saw a black man shouting on the street corner against white folks. It had to be a damn sight better than talking behind locked doors with the lights out, afraid to whisper.

We pulled up in front of a building on the west side of the avenue. A uniformed doorman came running at the blast of Sonny's horn. Bowing and tipping his hat, he took my bags. Then he saw me. With a deep frown, he pushed his cap up and back (black folks wasted more time trying not to waste time on poor black folks). Knowing that my long trip had rubbed off all my hard-won polish, I forgave him. I stuck my head up, pushed up my shoulders, and swept past him. I had to let him know that even if I didn't look like an Astor, nonetheless I just might be a family member.

I never knew whether or not I impressed him—or the elevator man who took us up. That fool stopped the elevator two inches past the floor (I declare he did it on purpose). My first step brought me to my knees. Sonny never blinked as he helped me to my feet. Without a backward look at that grinning black clown, he held my arm, walking me down to the door. My lover boy sure had class.

He rang the bell, and that alerted my buzzer system. Why ring the bell to his own place? I stood listening for sounds from the other side of the door. And it came to me that I ought to tell Sonny how glad I was to see his black, good-looking self—because depending on who owned those footsteps, I might never get the chance again.

I opened my mouth to tell him. But then heard myself saying: "How come you ain't using your keys?"

"Keys?" Never had a word been spoken so dull.

"Yeah." I tried to match him for dullness. "They open doors—things like that."

Whatever his comeback, the door opened and this big, rhiney—I declare he was as red as could be even to his hair—stud stood rearing back, filling the doorway. His playground—started beneath his chest and draped over his belt—broad enough to please a dozen chippies, the real young, real greedy kind. "Well, well, well." Brown freckles danced in the sweat on his face. A laugh exposed a mouthful of gold (niggers worshiped gold back then).

"Yeah," Sonny said, "this here's Dorine. Dorine, Tom Rumley."

Big Red eyed every inch of me that clothes allowed. "She purty, Sonny-boy. You ain't tole me just how downright purty she is. And a handful, too—just the way I likes them."

Being a little plump in those days didn't move women to tears. But the look that went with the words got my back to crawling. I stepped into the apartment with an attitude, swaggered down the long hallway into the high-ceilinged living room, my mind racing on the kind of hand I had to deal them—Big Red for the suggestion in his eyes, Sonny for allowing it. Putting men in their places had become one of the things I did best.

Tom Rumley's living room sported some expensive furniture—stuffed down couch and chairs, carved wooden table, elegant lamps, crystal chandelier—if it could be found in between the collected junk. Newspapers and magazines were piled in the corners, collecting dust. Gadgets of all kinds took up space. The walls were covered with pictures of motion-picture actresses and family portraits of people fading into the past.

Tom Rumley stood back, inspecting me, his thumbs hooked into his vest. So I brought my eyebrows together in deep puzzlement: "God, where does a feller get to sit around here?"

The gold disappeared. "Make a place," he snapped. "You'll be staying a spell."

"Who says?" My eyes shifted to shifty-eyed Sonny.

"Tom is let—"

I stopped him. "Let's get the hell outa here. Home is the only place I wants to be." Dealing it easy was not my intention.

"You can do a lot worse." Big Red's freckles got dark. Sweat flashed on them like specks of silver over his face. Good. That's the way I wanted the old nigger. Nerve. Assuming rights I wasn't about to give.

I looked away from him to Sonny and pretended right along with him that the shine in his shoes was the one thing in life worth my time. Then I forced him to follow the trail my eyes were following. They rested first on the eye-busting diamond. Sonny tried to hide it with his hat. So I made the fedora the most conspicuous thing. He pushed it behind his back, giving me a clear view of the pinstripes running up and down his suit. And seeing he hadn't yet learned to disappear, I pinned him to the spot with a stare into his big eyes. They went to blinking, blinking, blinking. . . .

Sonny and I looked alike. He was black to my brown, his features were broad where mine were fine—but around the forehead and eyes, we looked a family. Our eyes are what some folks call frog-eyes; others call them bedroom eyes, snake eyes, dreamy eyes. They pop out, forcing the eyelids to stay halfway down over the eyeballs to give a normal look, and have to be damn near closed, like a frog's, to shield secrets. Between Sonny and me, the secrets had been mostly mine, and I had long practice in shielding them.

Sonny had been a hustling man when I met him in Cleveland. He bragged about it. That first night at Mamie's, I had been serving food when he came to unload the bootleg whiskey. Someone had called to him: "Hey Sonny, do you know you got a sister working here?"

"Ain't got no sisters," this deep bass voice had answered, "and ain't looking for none."

"Well, if you trust your ma, it got to be your old man who ain't told it straight." Then someone had led this thickset, broad-built black stud across the room. Skit-a-dat, my heart had gone slipping and sliding over my chest.

"Where you live?" were his first words to me.

"Right here."

"At Mamie's? Good. Mamie's my buddy. Pick you up to-morrow."

He had been my first date. The first man I ever loved (the second man I ever laid with). I lost my reason for the first time in my life. But more to the point, Sonny lost his. Whatever happened after never changed that.

Losing our reason when we had no such intentions caused fighting between us from the first. I chased that man like a fox chases turkeys. He put me down: "I ain't got time for no simple broads," he said. "I'm a hustler—a hard-hustling man. If a broad can't give up some money, I ain't got no use for her. There's but one thing in life I need: money."

I stopped chasing. Then he came around, whipped. He had to have me. So we stuck: him not wanting to, and me too simple to quit, yet knowing I'd do myself good by quitting.

Sonny was a parrot about his dream. "I'm gonna get to New York and bust that town wide open. Baltimore might be the town where hustlers are born, but New York, baby, is where they're made."

But Sonny's style kept him a fool about money. He made a lot, and spent more. So I ended up having to send him to New York.

20

Sister said that I came into the world tightfisted. She declared I gave one shout and went to nursing with my fists balled so tight no one had been able to open them. Changing had never been my strong point. If Sister did exaggerate, it wasn't by much. My first cultivated saying has always been "Money spent is money gone." If loving was against Sonny's religion, giving money to anyone was dead against mine. But my greatest failing has always been my superstition: "Bad luck dogs a feller who turns his back on family," and Mama's saying: "The Lord moves in mysterious ways, His wonders to perform."

Well, there I was, eighteen, going with Sonny for four years. He loved me in spite of himself. And I was sitting on money I had no intention of giving or sharing with a living soul.

My getting "caught," and Master Norton dying at the time he did, had to be the mysterious workings of the Lord: "Go ye, my children, and sin no more." A curse surely had to follow me the rest of my days if I didn't give Sonny that money and us a chance for a better life.

Now here was this popeyed, love-me-no-more lover, true to type, showing me that his ass had not been the place to cultivate my seed.

"Look, Dorine . . ."—he already had a New York twang thick enough to cut, and it cut through my foggy thinking—"I told you I had things I had to do in New York. If you had come like we planned . . . but six months, baby! Six damn months! Look, Tom says we can stay here long as we want. If you don't want that, you can start looking for yourself a place."

Look for yourself! That polluted the fog in my head. Big Red added his two bits: "Hell, if she don't want that, she knows what she can do."

No use letting them go on even thinking. Stretching myself way past my five feet four inches, I wiped Big Red out of my way to stand eye-to-eye with Sonny. "Where's my money?"

Sonny was nothing but a bag of tricks, a coward to his backbone. Worrying about his looks—meaning his way of life—kept him at arm's length away from trouble. My determination to make him lose both looks and life took meaning in my eyes. He blinked. Kept blinking.

"You hear me? Where-is-my-money-Sonny? Now don't you go

stretching my mistake into your fucking tragedy." Low-pitched, mean, and meaning every word. "On account of that's what you 'bout if every damn cent I gave you ain't down on this crappy table in two seconds." I banged hard on one of Big Red's carved treasures. Dirty, greasy, my hair matted and nappy from my long ride on that never-ending trip, I looked bad enough to put fear into the heart of the Lord, never mind behind those blinking eyes.

"Dorine baby, you must be tired." The New York twang gave way to pure Baltimore bullshit. "Ain't been in the city five minutes and here you is cutting up. . . ."

"I ain't started yet, nigger. When I do, it will be like nothing you ever seen. I'll raze them clothes off your back, take that car and pot it so you can spread it on bread, and I'll hand you your head in your hands so you can hear yourself holler!"

"Whooooeeeee." Big Red's attitude jumped respectful. "You sure that li'l gal's from 'Bama, Sonny? Sounds more like one a them high-spirited Georgia broads. Hot dog! Woman after my own heart."

And Mr. Big Shot: "Bay-bee, how you sound? Your money's safe. Sure, I had to spend some—on togs, the car—you known I had to set myself up a front—"

"You ain't heard?" I had gone past listening. "Just put the money here." I banged the table again.

"Tom, talk to this woman," Sonny pleaded, easing away. " 'Splain to her what I'm about. Everything's straight, bay-bee." He eased right out of the room. That confused me. Should I stop him, or let him leave? "We got it made, bay-bee. We got it made."

Listening to his footsteps rushing away up the hall, I let him go. Tired in more ways than one, my love had been having a hell of a battle with my tightfisted habit. My habit proving right had been more of a letdown than a surprise. Still, when the door slammed, I sank into a chair and got to crying (I cry at the prick of a pin).

"Whoa, whoa. . . ." Big Red patted my head. "Ain't no sense in you taking on so. You made of good, strong stuff, gal. Ain't no man in the world worth them tears."

He patted my head, massaged my neck. That soothed me but made the tears flow even faster. "You know Sonny," Tom said. "He ain't doing nothing out there but trying to make money. Don't you go worrying. Things'll work out." He sounded like an old father, the way he was supposed to. I relaxed a bit, and as he kept massaging, his hands working on my spine (what might have happened if that kept on?), I relaxed even more. But then my pores stirred and leaned toward the door. Sonny had come back. I knew even before the shine of his shoes pulled my eyes.

"Look, Dorine"—Sonny's voice had settled into that tricky huskiness I dug—"ain't no sense in you acting so tough. Got us barking at each other like yard dogs. How you know you ain't gonna like the room Tom's fixed up for us? It's big. Come on back here and let's talk. Come on an' tell me whatcha been up to."

It's not measured in seconds how sad can change to glad—nor how a right smart woman can change into a fool. I took Big Red's handkerchief, blew my nose, and let Sonny guide me up the hall.

"What I been up to? I been up to missing you, old simple nigger. And I ain't lying about that worth a damn. . . ."

I was tough. Not in the street sense, like I made out, but more in the way of folks who have worked all of their lives, are still too young to have reached their stride, and have a long way to go before reaching their prime. Mama had seen to that, from the day light first shone in my eyes to the day when she took me out of school and took me with her to work in Miss Elizabeth's kitchen. I was eight years old.

Mama had never been one to take kindly to foolishness. She had never had to—we kids minded her. Tall, straight as a tree, black as darkness, with her mouth a trapdoor barking orders. We kids followed the line that she ruled straight, never wavering. We just listened and grew.

Don'ts were Mama's pride. She didn't talk about our father, and hardly opened her mouth about our mother. I declare, if Sisters Janie and Mildred had not known our mother I might have suspected that Mama had fashioned us from dust and ashes, as the Good Book said, to do her bidding.

Mama worked hard. Leaving the house in the darkness of mornings, she never got back home until we kids were in bed. That kept her happy. That woman loved hard work. She had three loves: God, cleanliness, and hard work. Whatever love she managed to salvage for us children had no chance competing against those three things.

"Cleanliness is next to Godliness," she preached. And we

stayed as close to God as soap and water allowed. We left for school weekdays, and for church Sundays, with the hand-me-down clothes from white folks cut down to size and starched out a mile around us. And although our feet were going from bad to misery with those too-small shoes stretched to get around them, we shined those suckers up to reflect the sun.

Mama too. Mornings she stepped—stiff as starch, with that white straw hat the air was scared to breathe dirt on set straight on her head—into the horse-drawn buggy Miss Elizabeth sent to fetch her. Nights she stepped down just as immaculate. I always reckoned that pride in that old house had made her so stiff and unbending.

My first remembrance of anything was of being on my knees, scrubbing those wooden floors with a stiff brush, buckets of water, brown soap and lye (the worst-looking things about me have always been my rough hands). That had been my chore—keeping the floors white. Janie's, outside of looking after us younguns, had been washing down the walls, ironing, and making sure we did our part of the work. Mildred had to take the beds apart, wash and air the springs, put them together at sundown, and wash and hang out our clothes. Even Little Brother, the day he began to toddle, had been handed a broom to sweep out the backyard. And we all got together to clean the old iron stove.

I do declare, that old iron stove will always be the strongest chain tying Mama to us in memory. Every day we took that stove apart, scrubbed it, burnt it so that not one speck of anything that resembled grease remained. At night when Mama came home—made no difference the time—that was inspecting time. Her first move upon arriving home was to take off that white straw hat and toss it onto the stove. Picking it up, she squinted, always seeing a speck. One speck, and into the washtub it went. Then we all had to be tumbled out of bed to commence scrubbing and burning. . . .

"Janie," Mama liked to complain, "ain't I told you to clean this here house?"

"We did, Mama. I swear God we did." Poor Sister—her brown skin yellowish-pale right down to her fingertips—had always talked whining to that old woman.

"Then how you 'count for this here dirt messing up my hat?" We took turns squinting at that white straw—damn near needed a magnifying glass. It didn't matter if we did or didn't see, so long as Mama had. Every piece had to be scrubbed over in that brown soap and lye. Then we got to holding our breath as that hat slid over the stove again.

Everything outside of the air we breathed had to be inspected that way: sheets hanging out on the line all day—one speck, and back in the tub. Taking a clean, white handkerchief, Mama wiped the floor, and there we'd go, holding our breath again (the greatest miracle I own to seeing is that we kids survived suffocation). After the house had been inspected to Mama's satisfaction, she allowed us to go back to bed. Then, no sooner had we closed our eyes, there this old woman would go, waking us up again. School time. I declare, that woman never slept.

I always reckoned that being tired from snatching at sleep had been the real reason school never held my attention. I don't rightly remember spending one full day at school. One of my chores had been taking Brother to school. I took him in the front door and I went out the back, and the rest of the day I spent playing around and snatching sleep in the woods. The teacher might have complained to Sister. But Sister didn't see school as important. After all, Mama had taken her out of school to look after the rest of us when she was no higher than a pup.

I'll never forget that day when my little nap turned into a full day's hard dreaming. I awoke to a darkening sky, and when I reached home, a search had long been under way. That was the night that Mama made her longest pronouncement: "Dorine Davis, I got more troubles than I can support on these old shoulders. If you don't want to go to school, I got no brief against it. But you ain't gonna be causing me no grief." The next day she took me with her to Miss Elizabeth's.

The work I had done in that old house had been play compared to what I had to do in that white woman's kitchen. I scrubbed floors, scrubbed walls, scrubbed springs, made beds, peeled vegetables, cut meat, washed and wiped dishes, served lunch—sometimes big lunches—then had it to do all over again for dinner (I swear I'll never figger how Mama had made out before I came). Still, I did it all with a willing heart: Miss Elizabeth had promised me pay. But at week's end she handed my money to Mama. And Mama, without one look my way, tied that quarter in a handkerchief and stuck it deep in her bosom.

Up to that day, I had truly believed that all Mama's grandchildren had been one big idea formed to do her bidding. That night, my mind got to changing. Bumping along on that buggy, a fretting got to taking place inside, and when we finally arrived home, it came out, freeing her hand in midair as she was about to toss that white straw: "Mama, can I hold my own twenty-five cents, please, ma'am?"

"What for?"

"On account of it's mine." I might have been born with courage, but that was the first I had been called upon to use it. "I worked for it, ain't I?"

"Lord, from out of the mouth of one I done fed." The words and that look were designed to silence me. But for the first time, the Lord and I listened in different ways.

"You mean I ain't getting my money, Mama?"

"You asking again?" Her lips sucked into a line to put an end to the subject.

The next morning I didn't get out of bed when she woke me. "I ain't working no more, Mama." During the night, I had had a revelation: Mama didn't have it so bad. She had taken Janie out of school to look after us. We kept house so all she had to do was sleep in it. It had become clear as selfishness would allow that those who worked outside gave the orders. As long as Mama had been bringing home clothes and food from Miss Elizabeth's kitchen, I had had to be satisfied to listen. But now it was the same with me. I could bring home hand-me-downs and food and money. The only reason I had to take orders was if I willed to.

Mama finally collected her senses to ask, "Why ain't you gonna work, gal? You sick or something?"

"No, I ain't sick. It just ain't no sense in working when I get the same thing staying home."

"Git outa that bed, gal!"

"Mama, I swear if you make me go to Miss Elizabeth's, I'm gonna break her best china, cut her tablecloth, and put pebbles in her soup."

"You'll do no such a thing."

But she didn't know! Truth was, for all my eight years, Mama

26

didn't know what I was subject to do—no more than she knew any of us, given a change of situation. My situation had changed, and forever after I've never been confused on how money can change a feller. I hadn't changed enough to look her in the eyes—that would have been sassy. But hugging my pillow and staring at the floor, I was seeing deep in her mind without understanding how I could look so deep, only knowing that the sight of Miss Elizabeth's possible broken china had cut to the core of her heart and had to change her mind.

"All right. I'll give you a li'l something if you behave." She gave me ten cents and I settled for that.

Ten cents gave me power over the rest of my family. Every week I gave Sister and Mildred and Brother one penny each. I saved the rest. It made no difference how they begged: I never gave them more. Nor did it matter how much Janie teased about my being tightfisted. I didn't care. They were better off with me working than before.

I had only been working for Miss Elizabeth a few months when I chanced to overhear one of her men guests say, "Is that Jane's grandchild sure 'nough? My, she sure is purty. You see them legs on her?"

"You been looking too?" Someone else laughed. "Round and plump. Sure don't look like no eight-year-old."

Mother wit? Instinct? Or downright brassiness? From that day I took pains to put big hems in those hand-me-downs, and everytime Miss Elizabeth had company, I pulled my belt so tight my skirt hitched up on my rump; then I'd get to switching.

"My, ain't she something!" women laughed. "Elizabeth, you got to lend her to me sometime."

It never crossed white folks' minds that black folks might not want to work for them. If they wanted you, they asked your madam, and we were supposed to be pleased. But if the truth be told, it never crossed my mind either. I was pleased. That crackers thought me smart just made me pull my belt tighter and twist all the more.

The men liked to tip me, and when I showed all my teeth, they just tipped that much more. Got so that on days when I was borrowed, I made way over the twenty or thirty cents promised. I gave Mama the promised money and kept the rest.

Hiding money became a problem. First I tied it in a cloth and hid it in the blousing part of my pants. When it got too awkward, I wrapped it in brown paper and stuck it in a shoebox at the top of the closet. But that kept me worried. Sister would surely find it. So I brought home an old cracker tin, put my money in it, and buried it under a tree in our backyard.

I had never been a dreamer, always a doer. Still, I recall going around as tight-lipped as Mama (although Mama was tight-lipped about everything and I only about money), planning on filling up that box, then another, and another.

One Sunday our Uncle Lofton came to dinner, and I asked him, "Uncle Lofton, how much do you think it would take to build a house as big as Miss Elizabeth's?"

"Don't rightly know," Uncle Lofton answered. "But I reckon it must cost a heap. Maybe seven hundred, even a thousand dollars."

"Is that right?" Even back then that kind of money didn't sound like much to me. I knew that soon I had to be able to build a bigger and better house.

When I was ten Miss Fanny borrowed me for the first time. Miss Fanny and Master Norton were rich, the richest of Miss Elizabeth's friends. And because she was the richest, the day I went to her I put on my shortest dress and switched my hardest. At least, I did until I looked into Master Norton's eyes. Then I pulled myself tall—my ladylike best. Scared. But it was too late.

Master Norton was not like the rest of the crackers who laughed and made my floor show a joke. Master Norton had gentle eyes and when he laid them on me, it was like a hand. He wasn't funny. Every time I bent over during that evening, I felt that hand on my behind. Turning, I would look into Master Norton's serious-as-hell, lean face, framed by that head full of white hair, his gentle smile, and knew something had to happen.

Three days later Mama came into the kitchen to say, "I hear Old Josh done come 'round to fetch you to go to Miss Fanny."

"I don't want to go," I told Mama. "Don't seem to me like it's time for them to be having no company so soon after the last time."

Mama liked to kill me with a look. "Gal, you crazy? Who you to be telling white folks when they can or can't give things? You should be right proud, getting asked by the Nortons."

And Miss Elizabeth coming in behind Mama, just a-laughing:

"Dorine, you sure went over big at Miss Fanny's the other night. Here ain't three nights passed and she send her boy for you. Ain't you the lucky one?" Even white folks liked to please the Nortons.

As it turned out, there was no party, and not much company—a couple had come to dinner. And when I went into the kitchen, the cook and parlor maid cut their eyes at me. "What you come for?" the parlor maid asked. "Ain't nobody here need you."

"You best tell that to Miss Fanny," I answered. "She the one sent for me."

But they wouldn't let me serve. The cook made me fix the platters while the maid did the serving. When the cooking was done, they handed me the pots to scrub. (Black folks working for rich whites are a mighty jealous lot.)

The evening was about to end when Master Norton came into the kitchen. "Dorine"—he was mad and showing it—"why ain't you been in to serve? What's happening in here?"

Cook and maid exchanged looks to conjure up the devil's idea of sin. The cook pushed a platter into my hand and whispered, "Don't you go telling Master Norton it was us kept you in here. Miss Fanny the one tole us keep you in here."

The company hadn't been gone two minutes when Master Norton backed his big automobile into the yard. "I'm taking you home, Dorine."

"What's the matter with the buggy?" Miss Fanny had come out—I thought to lay down the law, but as it turned out, she was only begging. "Ain't nothing wrong with the buggy, Charles, Old Josh ain't sick."

"Everything's all right, Fanny." That soft gentle voice was one that nobody seemed to cross, yet that smile didn't fool a living soul. "I just want to show Dorine what it's like to ride in a automobile."

Miss Fanny had to be screaming out loud from the way her neck strained; her face grew red and her eyes stared. But she only said, "All right, Charles. But hurry home. You know how I worry when you're out too late in that nasty old car. . . ."

I hated her. Hated her soft, fine lady self. Hated her worse than I ever was able the tightfaced bitchy cracker wenches who hated blacks for the pure pleasure. With all her money and a town respecting her, she still had to stand and take whatever this man had to give. She had the right to borrow me, but not the right to protect me. (At that age, I had read the soul of white America south of the Mason-Dixon line, and was raring to leave.)

The gut-glad feeling of satisfaction that smirked my face at the sight of Miss Fanny looking after us, like she wanted to send her eyes along with us even if she couldn't stop us, was because of my being young. Foolish. Beneath my fear—and I was scared—was the fact that I wanted more than anything for Sister and the rest of them to see me ride up to that old house in this big car.

How to get there without anything happening took up most of my thinking. But with all of my thinking and scheming, the best I came up with was putting my hands on my hips so that my elbow could act as a barrier. Master Norton never noticed. When he did stop on this stretch of wood-lined road, he reached over and pulled me to him as though my elbow had no bones.

"Come, come, Dorine." He kissed my forehead. "Ain't no sense in putting on. You been switching that li'l can of yours off like you ready for something. Ain't you known I'd give it to you?"

"I ain't been switching, Master Norton," I swore. "How you reckon I'd be switching? I'm only ten years old."

"Ten years!" He let go of me, put his hands on the wheel, letting them rest there. "Is that all how old you are sure 'nough?" I breathed with relief. But too soon.

All of a sudden he pulled me to him, and with one move pushed his hand up my dress, past the elastic of my bloomers, and grabbed hold of my little thing with his fingernails. To move was to get torn.

"Whatcha gonna do, Master Norton?" I whispered, scared, holding hard not to pee in my pants.

"Don't you know, Dorine?"

"I don't. I swear I don't, Master Norton. I ain't done nothing like that before. My grandma'll kill me."

"How she gonna know, li'l Dorine? Ain't nobody got to know 'cepting you and me." He kept playing, tightening then loosening his fingernails around my thing. Fear held back the tears that wanted to flow. My voice sounded weak:

"I want to go home."

"Don't that feel good, li'l Dorine?"

"No, it don't, Master Norton. You hurting. Ain't you gonna take me home?" The pinching got hard, harder. He held me to him. To stop the pain I said:

"Yes, yes. That feels good, Master Norton."

That worked. He took his hand away and opened the door on his side. As he eased himself from behind the wheel, I scrambled over the top of the door on my side and headed for the woods.

That might have been the smartest thing to do if I had been accustomed to woods at night. But that dark was the blackest of black. Blacker than any night I had ever seen before or since. Crawling things slid against bushes, trees, my legs, and the darkness, like a wall in my face, held me still. Things without shape—snakes? lizards? wildcats? all?—crumbled the leaves at my feet. Things hit against my face in flying. I stood still running, sculptured by fright. I was in that same pose when the light from Master Norton's flashlight fell over me.

I didn't even struggle as he dragged me out of the woods and threw me into the backseat of the car. Nor did he give me time.

Wedging himself between my legs, he tore away my pants and pushed into me like something wild. Pain burst from my pussy to my brain, scattered into a thousand tiny lights. I opened my mouth to scream, but it locked open with pain. My eyes strained out of my head. Breathing stopped. I was dying. He was killing me and didn't know he was killing me. Then he eased out and life and breath pushed back into my body. I screamed then. Screamed and screamed and screamed. But my screams were the same as the noise of the crickets, of the owls, the frogs, the wildcats on the road that night. No chugging cars, no bumping buggies passed that lonely road.

From a distance, I kept hearing this voice saying: "Don't move, Dorine. Don't move, Dorine. Don't move, Dorine. It won't hurt if you don't move."

I lay still. But he kept moving. Tearing me. Moving up and down, tearing me. Pain added to pain. I couldn't think. Yet I felt the need to pray. Couldn't pray. Waiting for my end. And then it came to me that this was my end. I was dead and in hell and the evil that was going on would go on forever after. Never, never end. Up,

31

down, up, down, plunging deep, as deep as I was deep, I tasted blood, gagged on my blood, and he kept plunging, plunging, nailing me to the seat. Nailing me. Nailing me. I lost consciousness.

"Dorine? Dorine?" Through a blur I saw him standing. I still felt him in me, but he was standing outside the car. "Dorine?"

He was scared he had killed me. I knew it. I didn't want to move. But then the thought came: if he thought I was dead, he might bury me out there in the woods. I tried to sit up. He sighed. (I believe to this day that that man would have buried me out there.)

As I sat up, he moved. I saw him in the headlights of the car, wiping himself. "You bleeding something awful, gal." He came, helped me out of the car, felt for the wetness on the backseat. Satisfied that there wasn't much damage, he put me to sit back in the front seat, pushed his handkerchief between my legs, and started up the car. I sat, not moving, feeling the blood pouring, wanting it to pour all out of me to the floor of the car, run out and drip in the road, drip all the way to my grandmother's old house. I didn't know if it relieved me to be alive. I knew it surprised me. Surprised to be able to sit, to see little insects in the headlights of the car.

We drove without talking. Drove for a long while before Master Norton said: "Well, li'l Dorine. Your grandma said you was a sassy one. Said all I had to do was pat your butt and you'd open up like a bud. I got to hand it to her, she ain't lied on you one bit."

"She said that?"

"Sure did. Why you think I tried you except that she asked me to?"

Mama's face rose like God Almighty before my eyes. Her hard-as-nails eyes, accusing. Lord, I should have died! Why hadn't I remained quiet and let that old buzzard bury me out in the woods?

"You gonna tell?"

"Sure thing. She the one want to know how easy you are. She got the right to."

Shame like fire burned through to my face. "Please, Master Norton, please don't tell. I ain't done nothing like that before."

"But if I don't tell, one of them others will."

"But I done tole you, ain't no other. I swear."

"I'm talking about them sisters of yours."

"How they gonna know?"

"You mean to tell, you do something like that, you ain't gonna let on to your kin? Sure you will. And 'fore you know, they'll tell Jane and she'll lose trust in me on account I ain't the first to tell."

"I won't say nothing to nobody, Master Norton. God strike me dead. I declare I won't."

He took my hand and put it on his open crotch. "Now, I don't know," this gentle man said so softly I had to strain to hear. "Your grandma got a lot of confidence in me." My hand slipped away to his lap and he reached down to put it back on his crotch. "Whatcha gonna give me if I don't tell?"

"Whatcha want, Master Norton?"

But I knew. Under my hand his shrunken part had begun to swell and I let my hand stay, afraid if I moved it he would know I felt it.

"You want to give me what I want?"

Right then the pain in me grew sharp. I longed to say no. Go tell. Do what you want but leave me be. But the feel of that bone-hard shaft under my hand told louder than words it wasn't any use. Saying no would only be for the sake of saying it. "Yes, suh. Anything, suh."

"Well open it up yourself and let me in."

This time I did open my legs to his. This time it was worse. Rubbing on that raw open wound was the worst thing I had had to bear in my life. But I bore it. Never whimpered. Just lay back while he rubbed and rubbed my raw, open flesh. Later he stopped at a creek and washed me good with his handkerchief. Washed my legs, my thighs, my pussy. "You sure are a sweet li'l thing, Dorine," he kept saying. Kissing my wound and bathing it. "A sweet, sweet li'l thing. I ain't gonna tell Jane." Back in the car, he slipped five dollars into my hand. "And here's something you don't have to tell her either."

Mama came out to the car when he pulled up. "Jane," he said in that respectful, gentle voice. "I brought home your li'l gal same's the way she left. But you better keep a sharp eye out for them niggras 'round here."

"What she do?" Mama's hard-as-nails eyes tried to pierce through the darkness into my head. It was the wrong place to look. I got out of the car and walked into the house—and believed from

33

that day on that there was nothing I couldn't do if I wanted.

"She ain't done nothing wrong. But it don't hurt none to keep a sharp eye out."

"You don't have to worry none, Master Norton. I keeps me a strong hand on my girls." The strength of that will that helped me into the house was the same strength that helped me, after I had gotten into bed beside Sister, to listen without vomiting when Mama said: "You mighty lucky, having a nice, rich white man like Master Norton looking after you. Praise the Lord." I covered my head with the sheet, knowing that Mama didn't know about nothing 'cepting a whole heap of work.

That knowledge kept growing as my fight to stay out of Master Norton's hands became a one-girl struggle against the world. Whenever I looked up to see Old Josh driving up, I got sick unto death. Both Mama and Miss Elizabeth, always anxious not to offend Master Norton, would insist that I was well and send me on my way. Then I learned to vomit at will and took to staying home more and more. One day I heard Mama complaining to Miss Elizabeth: "I declare, I don't know what come over that gal of mine. Used to be strong as a mule, but here lately she's doing right poorly."

But Master Norton wasn't fooled. When he got tired of not seeing me, he came right to the house, and brushing by Janie, walked into the bedroom like he owned us. "I want to know what the hell's going on here. Every time Miss Fanny sends for Dorine, word comes back she's sick."

"See for yourself," Janie said. "Poor girl's been laid up all day."

I had pulled my head under the covers when I heard him coming. Now he touched my head. "Dorine? Dorine?" And when I didn't look out from under the sheet, he said, "Dorine, I sure God hate to hear about your being sick. It must be on account of what happened the last time. Reckon I'd better talk to your grandma. It ain't right that you be sick and she not know what you been up to."

I pushed my head out and looked up at that soft-spoken, gentle-looking evil old buzzard. "It ain't nothing to do with that, Master Norton. I'll be up and about directly."

"Good, good." Turning his polite gentlemanly smile on Janie: "Miss Fanny will sure be glad to hear that. She's mighty fond of our li'l Dorine."

34

After he left, Janie asked, "What's he talking about? What happened the last time?"

"I don't know what that fool man was talking about, Janie. You know how white folks don't make no sense at all."

"They sure don't," Janie agreed. But she was still puzzled. "They sure God don't."

And so I kept going to the Nortons, every week and sometimes twice a week. And the five dollars, and sometimes ten, kept coming in. And every cent of it went into that box under the tree. I had lost my guilt of holding out on Mama. If she had so much trust in Master Norton, let him give her five dollars. The fifteen cents a week plus the promised fee when I was borrowed was all I gave her. All I ever wanted to give. I never changed. I never had reason to.

2

The feeling that things had changed between us kept slipping and sliding beneath our laughing. We laughed a lot. But sensing the change kept me from telling him how much I hated living in that one goddamn room. Then, too, Sonny kept taking me out, showing me *his* town.

He took me to Starlight Park. We rode on the merry-go-round, on the Ferris wheel, playing at a childhood we never had. We walked around sightseeing, eating ice-cream cones.

At Coney Island, we rode the merry-go-round, and the roller coaster, then we walked on the boardwalk eating hot dogs and ice-cream cones.

At Rockaway, we rode the merry-go-round, and the roller coaster, then we walked on the boardwalk eating hot dogs and ice-cream cones.

At Far Rockaway, we rode the merry-go-round, and the Ferris wheel, and stood on the beach while the breakers rolled over our naked feet. The water pulled the sand from beneath our feet, stealing our support. And we ate ice-cream cones and hot dogs and laughed more than we had ever laughed together, even while our eyes kept gliding past each other's.

Sonny parked his car to take me for a subway ride (something he never again did). "The scuffler's pullman," Sonny called it. We rode down to City Hall, took a street car, working our way to midtown, then took the double-decker bus back up to Harlem. Driving up Fifth Avenue, looking down at shoppers going in and out of stores, Sonny said, "Here's where the rich white folks do their buying, baby."

His voice, so proud, made me bite down on my tongue to keep from asking which one he thought he was: rich? white? both?

Going out to the Statue of Liberty, standing on the ferry, salt water spraying my face, and hearing folks, foreign folks, around me talking: "Ay, but is goot, goot. Yass. It's symbol. We see her in a liddle, liddle while." It seemed fitting when seeing the lady, her arm pushed in the sky, to say:

"There she is, there she is." Shouting to the boatload of foreigners oohing and aahing and crying. My throat got right tight. "She sure is grand, Sonny, just like you said she'd be."

"What else? We Americans," Sonny said, "builds the best."

"But who thought of building her?"

"Dunno, baby."

"Who thought of putting her way out here?"

"Dunno, baby."

"Why they put her so far out?" I asked.

"Search me," he said. "All I know is that our lady's out here welcoming them foreigners when they comes in."

"Should put one like her in the Penn Station to welcome folks coming up from the South," I said.

"You crazy, woman? We ain't no damn foreigners." That twisted my heart. More than the words, the feeling that even our thinking about things together had changed.

And the sick feeling played around my heart, when standing on the roof of our seven-story building, we looked out to see the orange-red ball of the late sun, sinking fast behind the low buildings where clotheslines—sheets, dresses, shorts, drawers—strung out against a sky bright enough to blind a feller with tomorrow's promises reduced everything to shadows—the Power and the Glory—the Lord making of man's necessities shadows flapping in the wind. And then darkness. The sun going out. Electric taking over, stretching darkness for miles. Such excitement! Knowing that beneath the darkness, promises were being kept. Folks were dancing, or about to; going to shows, or getting dressed to; girls, guys getting set to take on the whole town. What a joy! If water had brought Jonah to the belly of the whale and darkness, electric had brought folks to the center of the world and life. And what about me in this new life?

"New York," I sighed.

"Yeah, one hell of a city," Sonny said, not understanding my deep-down, sick feeling.

When we went downstairs and Sonny got to dressing, it didn't surprise me. He had been feeding me knowledge right along. He had been doing the "right thing" by me, but sight-seeing time was over.

Back in the little room sitting by the window, I got to filing my nails, pretending not to see the way he matched the stripes of his pinstriped suit, untied and retied his tie so that it looked the same, brushed his heavy eyebrows trying to look like the devil himself, wiggled his pinky to catch the light on his diamond, splashed toilet water over his face—overdoing, sure I'd try to stop him, try to keep him home. But if he thought that, he had another thought coming.

I kept on filing at my nails. From the corner of my eye I saw him turn to give himself a last look, and the admiration stinking out of him for the life of me made the words slip out:

"If a whore didn't have more confidence," I said, "she'd best give up the trade and go to hog calling."

"What's that?" Sonny had always been deaf to all but compliments. I looked through the curtains, out into the air shaft. "I ain't heard," he said.

"I ain't said a word."

I examined my fingernails. One more shave and I'd have to grow a new set. My hands dropped to my lap. To keep my eyes away from the slime of having the right answers on his face, I examined the curtains separating me from the brick of the next building. Trapped. I had to start marking the days until I freed myself from that room. Upstairs on the roof, looking over the city, at the sunset, the wide-open space about me, I had for a second been free—even happy. . . .

Six months! Six months ought not to have made that kind of difference. We had been too close. Had I changed? Babies do more to women than make mothers of them. That thought brought me to the mirror where, standing beside Sonny, I let my robe fall to my waist. I examined my titties. Still firm. Plump. I threw my kimono up to look at my backside. I prodded it, searched for telltale stretch marks. Smooth as peaches, round.

"Whatcha doin', baby?" Conceit blinded Sonny to my kind of reasoning. He smiled, put his arms around me, pinched my nipples. "Ain't got time," he said.

I hunched up my shoulders—I didn't care. Then I heard myself say: "Where you going?"—and wanted to stick my fingers in my ears to shut out his lies.

"Got to meet a man."

"How come you ain't taking me?"

"Business, baby." He smiled a soft, sorry-I-must smile, blinking all the while. "Business. I'm already over an hour late on account of looking at them stars." So—even if he wanted to, he didn't have time to wait.

I sat on the edge of the bed listening to his footsteps up the hall. The door slammed. I put my head in my hands. Lord, it had happened. Was happening. I couldn't take it. I needed to get to bed and cry and cry and cry—get it all out.

Ten minutes later, my high heels clicking down the hallway, I went into the living room where Big Red knelt, trying to fix a Victrola that hadn't worked since a slickster had palmed it off on him. (I kept puzzling on how this big-time sport kept getting "took" by every small-time hustler. But then Tom Rumley thought he was still down home, the way he liked to "do things myself.") "If Sonny gets back, tell him I stepped out, will you?"

Freckle-face looked up. "If Sonny gets back, I reckon he'll see for hisself." A fourteen-carat wisecrack. "Tell me, pretty lady, where you off to?"

"That's for me to know and for you to find out."

Giving short answers happened to be my specialty, but it had to be a sin how that golden smile turned them out of me. A decent word from me would have sent him to the nuthouse.

On the avenue, my feet knew better than my head where they were heading. Sonny had been keeping me clear of the West Indians, so of course that's where my feet led me. And they led me to the right corner. The crowd stood looking up at the same tall, handsome black man with his shaking mustache that I had seen on my first day. His sweaty face shone in the glow of the streetlight as he shouted: "I tell you the white mahn wicked. . . ."

"Yes, he wicked, wicked," folks standing near to me agreed.

"The white mahn is criminal. . . ." The hot flannel suit he wore had to add to his discomfort. He took off his hat, wiped the leather band inside, wiped his head, then his face. For a moment his face looked clean, calm—then the sweat commenced again, the mustache commenced to shaking. "You say he ain't criminal?" he asked those folks who had done nothing but agree. "Then let me ask you—how come this mahn thief we ships? How come, I ask you? How come he stick we leader—the honorable Marcus Garvey—in jail on a bogus charge!"

"True, true" from the crowd. "The charge bogus—bogus as hell. . . . Bogus, I tell you!" He said every word to its last letter. "And I will tell you why. Is because he think that by jailing we leader, he can stop we from leaving this country! He think that by so doing, he can force we to remain here—to live like pigs and to work like slaves! But he lie!"

"Ohgod, he lie. He lie." The woman standing in front of me spoke in an angry voice that went up at the end surprised-like. She looked around, her wide face with its high cheekbones expressionless, as though set in stone. Tall, narrow hips and broad shoulders, she stood as solid as a pillar. His pillar. She looked at me from small beady eyes, and I tried to ease away from her. But the crowd had thickened around me. I couldn't move. That scared me—being alone in Harlem surrounded by a bunch of foreigners! The woman looked down at me. She nodded.

"We ain't come here to live like nobody pig," she said. "We ain't nobody slave."

I half smiled, keeping my eyes on the speaker. I didn't want to get entangled with that bird-eyed, nonmoving force of a woman.

"Life is one big struggle," the speaker said. "Never forget that! So if the white mahn want struggle, we'll give it."

"You bet your life," an American voice said from behind me.

"We gon' gi' he in he teeth," Stone-face said.

"We. Shall. Endure! Struggle! We. Shall. And we shall endure!" Something about that shining, sweaty face, the shaking mustache, his feeling, entered me and grew. The crowd heaved. Excited. "Yes. We shall endure in this struggle. We shall free our leader—the honorable, the glorious Marcus Garvey!"

"Hear! Hear! Hear!" the crowd shouted. Sweat pushed out on my brow. "Hear, hear," I echoed them.

The preacher raised his arms, hushing the crowd. "The white mahn strong," he whispered. "Don't forget that!" Then raising his voice again: "But we blacks are strong. . . ."

"Hear! Hear! Hear!" we shouted.

"We must not forget that! And so we must be—all for one." He raised a fist over his head. Hundreds of fists went up in the air. "All for one!" the crowd echoed.

"And one for all!"

"And one for all!"

"And one for all!" I joined in.

"We. Shall. Be. Free!"

"We shall be free!"

"Or die!"

"Or die!" Lord, I had never been together with so many folks.

"What good if we ain't stick together?" Stone-face said in her singsong, surprised voice.

"You said it, sister." A broad smile spread out my face. "You just about said it."

"We shall be free." Our handsome leader promised. "Our honorable Marcus Garvey shall be free. . . ."

"Free! Free! Free!" the crowd chanted.

"We shall make good our vow. And we shall sail from these shores, back to the motherland. Africa! Africa for we Africans!"

"Africa for we Africans!" the crowd cheered. But they had lost me.

Africa? What damn Africa? Here I had just got to New York and loved it, and these folks talking about leaving? I looked around at the hot faces, the thrown-back heads, the mouths tight and determined. I had come to find West Indians, and instead found a bunch of Africans.

I eased my shoulders, trying to get through the crowd. But folks stood still—an unmoving wall. Stone-face turned, her face friendly. But I was ready to go. "I-I-I come out here to-to look for West Indians . . ." I said.

"How you mean?" she asked, her face still unmoving.

"I-I-I mean—I don't know nothing 'bout no Africans. . . ."

"What you talking?" she asked.

"I come looking for West . . ."

"And what you think we is?"

"That man up there says you all is Africans."

"And what you think you is?" She looked so far down to me, I swore I had shrunk to the size of a maggot.

"I—I—I'm American," I whispered.

"How you mean?" Her smooth-as-stone brow cracked into wrinkles.

"I—I—I—don't know nothing 'bout no Africans. . . ."

The wrinkles faded, settling her mouth into folds at the sides. She hunched her shoulders and turned from me, digging herself deeper into her footsteps.

"We must work together like one mighty fist!" my lost leader kept on as I fought to get through. The man behind me smiled kindly. And knowing he had heard me, I said, "You see—I come out looking for West Indians."

"Most are West Indians out here," he said. And recognizing him as the American who had spoken before, I whispered to him: "That man up there says they's Africans."

"Like you, like me, sister."

"Mister, I come from Alabama."

Stone-face spun around. "And where you think your ancestors from?" she asked.

"Alabama, ma'am. All my folks come from Alabama. I can prove it."

Her mouth dropped. "But the woman a fool?" she said in a loud voice, then resettled herself in her footsteps, adding: "But then, what you expect from the children of slaves?"

"Ma'am," I shot back, "I'll have you all know that I was born in the Cradle of the Federation." (I swear we used to brag about that.)

Hot out of my mind, I pushed my way through the crowd and made it back home, still steaming. Marching down the hallway into the living room, I found Tom still kneeling over his Victrola.

"What ails you?" he asked after one look at my face.

"Them damn West Indians—or Africans—or whatever in the hell they is—they can go to hell—"

"Whoa," Tom said, sitting back on his heels. "Who done gone and got my brown gal all lit up?"

"Tom, I declare, I ain't even met this woman, and she come telling me about my folks."

"How's that?" he asked.

"Got a damn nerve, saying my folks come from Africa."

"Oh, you been out there with them Garvey folks," Tom said.

"I declare that woman looked at me like I was dirt."

"Pay them monkey chasers no mind," Tom said. "They always blowing hard. Never did figger why they come here in the first place if Africa was where they wanted to be."

"I ain't never seen her before. And there she go. . . ."

Tom went on with his tinkering. "Was a time I hung out there listening—near every night," he said. "Not lately—not since they put Marcus Garvey in jail. I got tired of hearing the same thing night after night. Way I see it, Marcus Garvey ain't Jesus Christ. He can't walk them waters to get back to Africa—and they ain't gonna sell no black man decent boats. . . ."

"Tom Rumley, it ain't Jesus Christ what walked them waters. It was Moses."

"Moses? That right?" He looked up, thoughtful for one second. "You sure? Seems Jesus Christ's the one done all them things."

"Goes to show you ain't no good Baptist."

"I ain't no good nothing 'cept a hustling man." He had dropped a screw and went looking for it on all fours. "Anyhow, the way I see it, so what if we comes from Africa? We here to stay now. I ain't thinking of ever leaving New York—except one way. . . ."

"Tom Rumley! Don't tell me you believe that shit?"

"Shit? What shit?" He kept searching for the screw.

" 'Bout us coming from Africa."

"Makes sense," he said. He found the screw and sat back on his heels to look at me. "We had to come from someplace."

"Ain't you from Baltimore?"

"Sure thing. But where was we when this whole shebang belonged to them Indians? We had to belong to someplace."

"What shebang?"

"This country, Dorine lady. This country."

"This whole country!"

"Sure."

"Belonged to them West Indians?"

"Naw. American Indians."

"American Indians!"

"American Indians!"

Education comes in drips and drops to a feller who never went to school. Sure, I knew about us being slaves. Mama had been born to a slave (but only years later did I hear black folks bragging of their Indian blood, trying to prove they weren't out-and-out niggers or bloodline to slaves and white masters). Up to that time, I and lots of black folks took it for granted that but two kinds of folks lived on these shores: white folks and black folks.

"All I know is them West Indians is a simple bunch," I said. "Trying to make out a feller's dirt on account of he's from the South. Tom, you ain't heard nothing till you heard that woman say to me that I was the child of slaves. If it weren't for all those folks being around, I declare I'd have gone upside her head. . . ."

"Why you wants to get all riled up over that?" Tom said. "They was slaves, too."

"They was. . . ?"

"Sure they was."

"Tom, you putting me on? How you know?"

"Well, now . . ." He stopped his finagling and looked at the mess of magazines and newspapers all around the room. "Sure is enough wrote about it. And they know it. I heard Marcus Garvey hisself talk about it. We all was slaves, Dorine. We got brought to these here parts on ships. Only some got dropped off on them islands. Others got brung over here. Sure—we all was slaves."

"You swear to that, Tom Rumley?"

"A hell of a lot quicker than I'd swear to Moses. . . ."

I hit the streets running, all the way to that corner. But the speaker had gone, the crowd had thinned. Stone-face had disappeared. I searched the streets. . . .

Nights Sonny went out, and one minute later, I'd be out there, standing on that corner, waiting as the crowd formed, looking into each face. Up and down the surrounding streets, or streets I heard West Indians lived on, I went. . . . But Lucifer himself had sent that woman to try my soul. Succeeding in tormenting me, he had recalled her.

Then one night we drove down Fifth Avenue on our way to Small's Paradise. Driving past a cluster of people talking with their arms and hands, West Indian style, I looked them over careless-like, as had become my habit. There she stood—tall, broad-shouldered, narrow-butted, like a statue of stone, looking down on them. My sworn enemy.

"Stop the car!" My tone forced Sonny's foot down on the brake. I jumped out. Ran to the crowd. Pushed my way through. And standing, hands on my hips, foot tapping, I shoved my face up to hers. "You all was slaves, too!" I shouted. "You all was slaves, too!" Running back to the car, I jumped in. "Let's get the hell on, Sonny." Sonny stepped on the gas and we roared down the avenue.

"What the hell happened back there?" Sonny asked, looking back over his shoulder. I looked back, too.

The look of old Stone-face, staring after the car, had to last me till I turned one hundred. Grinning, strutting into Small's Paradise and hanging on to Sonny's arm, I heard the band playing Charleston and right away, I got to swinging my shoulders, snapping my fingers, and laughing out loud. Flying high.

"What's ailing you, gal?" Sonny grumbled, looking around to see who might be looking at me acting the fool. "You been sipping a li'l something?" Thinking of how he'd crack his sides laughing when I explained to him after we got seated—seeing how he hated West Indians—only made me laugh louder.

We followed the waiter through to ringside, where our table had already been set up with ginger ale and ice. And as we went Sonny kept nodding, smiling, blowing up to double his size, impressing folks already impressed by him going to ringside. But no sooner had we sat down than the beat of the music had me jumping up and pulling him out of the chair and onto the dance floor.

White couples were dancing, or using up energy to the music. The high cellers, who were naturally better dancers, could hardly dance for trying to look ritzy. So I joined the dark sisters out there showing how rugs were supposed to be cut to the Charleston—Charleston. Celebrating. It wasn't every day a feller got the chance to put down a monkey chaser. . . .

Charleston, Charleston . . .

Sonny didn't go in for dancing. He had bad feet. Most places he went just for the show. Keeping up with me made him sweat. He hated sweating. "You sure you ain't been smoking reefers or something?" I kicked higher. "What's the matter with you, woman?"

"Happy."

"I'd take you out more, baby," he apologized, taking it for a compliment. "But you know how it is."

I didn't. But neither did he. I kicked higher, exposing my teddy. It was black lace with pink ribbons, matching my black lace dress trimmed with pink ribbons. Folks had a hard time seeing what they were looking at. And suddenly I knew that I had been dancing for someone special—someone with nice eyes, warm eyes, appreciating eyes. So I added a bit of snake hips, a little Black Bottom, then went back to kicking, showing my appreciation for being appreciated.

"Cut out that kicking," Sonny growled, looking around ringside, scared others were seeing. Of course they were. That's why they sat at ringside. "Come on," he said, taking my arm. "Let's sit." But the band had gone to jam-time:

Charleston, Charleston . . .

I took off. I had never taken to drinking and smoking as tools. But when it came to dancing, I was a dancing fool.

The other dancers went to the sidelines, to clap, to stomp in time with the music, Sonny along with them. Sweat poured. The floor belonged to me. God, it felt good to be out on the town, to steal the show, to have put down a simple-talking, simple-acting West Indian. And it sure was a ball having on a pretty black lace teddy.

Back at the table, Sonny kept up his frowning. "Sure wish you

45

come down. Quit acting like a hussy." He pulled a solid-gold flask out of his breast pocket and poured out a thimbleful of whiskey. "This here's a classy joint, baby. Pull down your class. Pull down your class. . . ."

The sight of the gold flask sobered me up. "I hope you ain't brung me here to put on the dog."

"No, but I don't like the woman I takes out to act like no nigger."

Which brought me to looking the club over. The room was small, so tables were close and folks had to sit hunched over not to touch their neighbors. And as usual in Small's Paradise, it was paradise for whites. They sat at ringside, high yellers were sandwiched in between them and the darker folks nearer the door, and white-coated waiters, towels over their arms, stood at attention in the back to keep the order. Which brought my eyes around to the other dark brother who rated ringside at the other side of the room. And I found myself looking into some nice eyes, warm eyes, appreciating eyes. . . . The woman with him was pretty, if older. She had to be twenty-six. She had an ivory complexion. Her hair, black, shiny, had been shingled into a V at the back.

Sonny raised his glass to their table, but the warm-eyed man kept looking away. Scalp cut, brown, round face, clean-looking, boyish but portly, he had to be almost forty. I liked his look. Where most wore tuxedos, he wore a dark suit and looked at ease. And he rated ringside.

"Come on, let's dance, Dorine." Sonny pulled me up when the band started. Knowing he had no interest in dancing, it was no surprise when, paying no attention to the steps that made for dancing, he worked me around to their table.

"Well, well, well, look who's here," Sonny said.

My lovely gent looked past Sonny to smile at me. Sonny didn't notice. He slapped the man on the back. "Big H, how is it going, my man?"

Big H's eyes said he didn't go for backslapping. Nevertheless, he stood up. "How are you, Sonny?" He spoke quiet, polite.

"Great, great, Big H, just great. Got myself this great pad on Seventh Avenue" (the difference between thinking and being had always confused Sonny). "A real moneymaker. I been meaning to stop around to talk . . . got a li'l proposition. . . ."

The man's gentle smile said no. "You always know where I can be reached," he said.

"At The Club. Okay, be dropping by."

Sonny took my arm to lead me back to the floor. But my gent held out his hand. "My name is Big H," he said, smiling.

"Oh, yes," Sonny said. "This is Dorine, Dorine Davis."

"Dorine? Dorine Davis. What a pretty name," he said, still smiling. "Miss Davis, may I introduce you . . ."

I never caught her name. This awful heat had risen from my chest to consume my face. My heart pounded so I stumbled when Sonny pulled me onto the dance floor. I buried my face into his shoulder as we slow-dragged toward our table. "Sonny," I murmured. "Who's that man?"

"That's Big H."

"The man done told me his name, Sonny. What I wants to know is who the hell is Big H?"

"Mr. Kingpin of Harlem—of today." Sonny's voice meant *he* was the kingpin of tomorrow. "A big-timer. Got a slew of racehorses upstate. Owns that place called The Club. Girl, that's the biggest numbers banker in Harlem." I looked into the greasy smile skidding over Sonny's bragging face. "The only thing short about Big H is his hair. He's damn near bald—because of his head full of sense. Calls hisself working for black folks' causes. But he damn sure ain't made his millions that way."

"But Sonny," I whispered, just for his ears. "Ain't you heard that man talk? He's West Indian. . . ."

3

I broke the news of our apartment on the morning after we moved in. I dealt it the only way I knew how: underhanded. I tipped the elevator man to tell me of the first vacancy. When I got the place on the top floor, I spent days shopping and fixing it up. I waited for Tom to get out of town (he spent more time out than in), then lifted Sonny's keys, telling the doorman to tell Sonny which apartment he had moved to. Sonny came home at five that morning.

"What the hell is this?" he came in cussing. "All this money? Seventy-five bucks each and every month! How the hell you 'spect me to turn over that kind of money?"

Living in a room supported Sonny's style—the fine clothes he wore, the flashy car, the rolls of money he liked to flash. But one whiff of the doorman, the elevator man, the big, luxurious apartments with the maid's room and the butler's pantry, had given me the notion that they were indispensable to *my* style. What's more, I had a bank account that gave substance to my notions.

"Sonny, you been telling folks you got this great spread," I said, following him as he stomped through the seven rooms, red-eyed mad, foaming at the mouth. "Looking as good as you looks, they been believing you. Seems to me you ought to be glad."

He stood, breathing hard. From the look of the furnishings, it was permanent. And I had fixed it well. Heavy mahogany beds in the bedrooms, parquet floors polished to blind, curtains, ruffled in the bedroom, straight in the living room—I had spent hours in the hanging. Everything spoke of time spent, weeks, even months.

"You ain't known how good you had it at Tom's," he raged. "We ain't had to buy nothing."

"But this here's ours, honey."

"Ours? You know what's gonna happen, don't you? One day you'll be walking up the block and you'll see a pile of junk stacked up on the sidewalk. When you get to looking, it will be this here shit. What you gonna do then?"

"You ever known me to be put out of a place in your life?" I asked.

"You know why, don't you?"

"No, I don't!" I stared, daring him to speak his mind.

His eyes slicked over. But their shiftiness had already signaled what he had in mind.

"Why you want to get mad, bay-bee? Ain't nothing you ever done you got call to be 'shamed of." It ain't measured in speed how a slickster's mood can change. But I had followed his twisted thinking and it led to no surprises. "Now—just think of it." He looked around at the furnishings he had just down-rated a moment before. "This place mightn't be no bad deal. You know we can—"

"No, we can't!"

"You ain't hearing me out, bay-bee."

"But you gonna hear me out," I said, locking eyes with him. "We ain't renting no rooms. We ain't giving house rent parties. We ain't running no joint. And my house ain't gonna be no fucking meeting place for your out-of-town friends to come calling. You got that? You told me you wanted to make me a duchess—well, I made it easy for you. This here's my palace."

"Dorine bay-bee, all I'm saying is . . ."

But seeing knowledge of him hard in my eyes, he backed down, smiling. I knew he was leaving persuading me for another time. I had been there before. Lordy, I sure had been there before.

I'll make you my duchess. . . . Even then it had been jive. Although not at first. He had been a slick twenty-five and I a wise-cracking fourteen. There had been no dive, horse race, or just plain friendly visit where you didn't see the other when one of us appeared. Dorine 'n' Sonny, Sonny 'n' Dorine. Sounded so much together that folks swore out it was one name. The next step sure had to be marriage, folks said. But that notion had been doomed from birth.

Sonny was a born hustler—a two-bit hustler—always ready for an easy buck. Hustling was as much a part of him as his hands, his eyes, his thing. No matter what he might be doing—playing cards, joking with friends, making love—his mind ticked, ticked, ticked away like a clock, figuring his next hustle.

"How much money them white folks pay you?" he never got tired of asking.

"Ten bucks a week."

"Ten bucks? You crazy or something? Leaving your house every day to slave for them white folks for ten bucks?"

"That's more money than I ever made scrubbing floors before."

"Baby, you ain't lived so long. Don't play your life cheap. The only folks supposed to work for that kind of money is old folks, dumb folks, or ugly folks. You ain't none of them. You got too much class."

"Man, I got folks to support." Sending money back home was an obligation before God to us from the South.

"You working at Mamie's, ain't yer? You got me, ain't yer? What you got to worry 'bout? Them white folks'll squeeze you so's you'll lose your looks—just like Mamie. You'll lose your health, then all you'll have is an end stone at the head of your grave which says: Here lies the body of a damn-fool kitchen machine."

Yet Sonny never gave me a cent. Sure, he took me out, showed me a good time. But all his money went to keeping up his front: fine clothes, working car, and bigger diamond in his ring. His answer for a home: a two-by-four room in an attic. Oh, he was sharp.

But I had no intention of giving up the first job I had in Cleveland. The reason I did, in the long run, was because of Mr. Ogden. When I first had dealing with the family, it was only with Mrs. Ogden. Mr. Ogden ran his own business and never stayed home. Mrs. Ogden loved me. "Oh, what pretty teeth you have." Those had been her first words to me. Which meant that in a few more years and a bit more fat, I'd make the ideal Aunt Jemima: honest, happy, a good cook, and just love white children. She had two: a four-month-old baby girl and a four-year-old boy. My work had been to clean the house, do the laundry, cook, and take care of the children.

Then one day Mr. Ogden came down with a cold. Like most men, he proved a nuisance sick. "Dorine, Dorine," he kept complaining. "Dorine, bring me aspirins." "Give me some water." "Help me to the bathroom." "Bring a towel for my head." I had to damn near be a machine to do all that and care for the house and his kids, too. What did his wife do? She tried to stay out the whole time he was laid up.

After a couple of days he felt better. Then it was: "Dorine, I'm hungry." "Dorine, the soup is cold." "Dorine, give me something better than this to eat." On the third day he sat up. Could have gotten out of bed, but it had gotten good to him: "Will you fetch me my paper?" "Mix me a drink." "You didn't make the steak rare enough." "Come straighten this sheet out on the bed."

I went to the bed and leaned over, trying to pull his weight with the sheet. That didn't make him sit up. Instead, I felt this thing crawling up my leg, and when I looked down, it was his hand.

I jumped away. "Look here, Mr. Ogden, I get paid for cleaning your house, washing your clothes, cooking your meals, and caring for your kids. If there's extras, the pay goes up."

"We can talk about that," he snickered. "What's a good price?"

"Two hundred bucks!"

He laughed. "You think that's worth it?" He pointed between my legs.

"I reckon your wife makes more. She got this house, this here furniture, all them fine clothes, and lives in grand style. I'm the one what looks after the house, the clothes, the furniture, and I look after you kids. Now, if I have to lay down on my back, it goes without saying the price goes up."

His hair-filled noseholes tugged up his lip. "You think a nigger bitch is worth the same as a white woman?"

Hell must be a wall streaming down fire. I waited till that scene cleared my eyes before I said, "They worth more, Mr. Ogden. If they ain't paid more, it's because white men have thieving souls."

"What do you mean?"

"Just that if we weren't worth more, white men wouldn't be always sticking their noses up black women's assholes."

Walking through that fire meant my end, but I was ready. He didn't reach to touch me. "Get the hell out of here, you black bitch!" Screeched like a woman.

I went. Out of the room and out of the house. Flying. Tearing down curtains, opening drawers, scattering things all over. It was a mess when I found it, it had to be worse when I left. The little boy came out running: "Dorine, what you doing?"

"Go ask your pappy."

Rage sustained me until almost to my door; then I got scared. I didn't put it past that fat, hairy-nosed son of a bitch to call the police and swear I had robbed him. Instead of to Mamie's, I went on to Sonny's. "You got to find me a place," I begged him when I explained what had happened. He lost no time. In less than two hours, I had rented an entire top floor of one of his friend's homes. It was a great place. I even took money out of the bank to furnish it. But that apartment brought a change in Sonny's and my relationship.

All the while I had lived with Mamie, Sonny had taken me out nightly, to eat, to ball. Our lovemaking we did in snatches. When I moved into the apartment, he took to dropping in, staying for dinner, spending the night, always swearing that he couldn't live with no women. But one night became two, then weekends. Next he had moved in.

Living like married folks stopped him from talking about marriage. Stopped him from taking me out. Stopped him from buying little presents as had been his habit. He got to complaining about money as though he did the spending. Next the hint: "Bay-bee, I sure hate to see you living this way. I wants to set you up. I wants to make you my duchess. I'll be your duke." From there it went to: "Baby, I got a friend. Ain't nothing but some money. He's passing through town tomorrow, and I thought you might . . ."

It hurt me bad that he wanted to use me. "Sonny, I'm only one somebody's woman. And that's yours. I ain't no whore."

Right before my eyes, with me not able to stop him, he went from lover to wanting to be my pimp. It was time to cut him loose. But when it came to Sonny my actions never matched my intentions. I studied him because I thought to change him. Studied that broad, black face, saw the smile when he thought up a scheme, learned the shift of his eyes when the game was low-down, the blinking when he lied or cheated, knew when he got nervous by the twitch in his cheeks. Learned all about him, and still didn't cut him loose.

Then two things happened that caused a change in my thinking: Mamie had to lie low on account of the law. Within a week of her closing a letter from Janie told of her husband, Joseph, losing a leg in the sawmill (both Janie and Mildred had married, Sister to a sawmill worker, and Mildred to a schoolteacher, Morris. They both had one kid apiece—girls: Sister's was named Jennie Mae, and Mildred's, Lil). For every newborn I had sent more money. I couldn't see my kin strapped in the poor-trap we had been stuck in. Now I had to send even more. Going into my "rock money" would have unhinged me (I ain't giving that as any excuse—that was a natural fact). So I approached Sonny: "That friend . . . your friend . . . whoever friend he is . . . from out of town?" That greased smile made me come as near to hating Sonny as I had ever.

"Bay-bee. . . ."

"But I ain't no two-bit whore, Sonny. You best know that. And the feller you bring to me better be . . ."

Dicty whoring, we called it: high-class. Always particular men—usually white—with money, and always passing through. I hated it! Laying a man I had no feelings for kept me evil for days.

Then one day, sitting at Mamie's, evil, watching her play a game of solitaire, she squinted at me from the other side of curling smoke. "Seems to me that money you making don't make you happy." Mamie sure had a way of knowing things.

"I hate turning tricks!" I burst out. "Seems I was born with men messing over me."

"If you hate turning tricks, don't. There's other ways of making money."

"Tell me one. And before God and the grave of my mother, hell will turn to a fucking igloo 'fore I turn another."

"Go back to housework."

"You done jumped out of your mind?"

"If you don't want to lay on your back to make money, then you got to be where money is, honey. You a nigger gal, living in a white man's town. What else you gonna do?"

What else? In those days black women didn't work in factories, nor at lunch counters, except those few in the black neighborhoods. We didn't work as nurses in hospitals, not even as attendants, nor as salesgirls in department stores. And we hadn't begun to dream of being clerks in office buildings. I hitched up my shoulders. "I declare I swore off working in white folks' kitchens," I said.

"But white folks the ones what got the money, Dorine."

"That ain't all they got. They got nerve."

"That they has," Mamie agreed. "They done found long ago that it takes all kinds of nerve to live. So they's the ones you got to learn from."

Up to that time I thought I had known all Mamie did to make money. But sitting there, looking at her deal herself hands of solitaire, squinting, chewing the tips of cigarettes to a soggy brown, I learned how wrong a feller can be. When I walked out of her place that night, I had made peace with myself, with God, and with the bones of my dearly departed mother forever turning in her grave on account of promises I kept swearing to. The next promise I made, I sure didn't intend for it to be made for promises' sake.

Patience might have changed Sonny's entire life. But with Sonny, when an idea stuck in his thick skull, pulling it out was tougher than prying crabs from funky pubic turf.

"Dorine," he said as we walked along 125th Street, "you sure is some looker. You know how proud I gets to be seen walking beside you?"

All that charm, and Sonny sure knew how to use it. So much so that, even knowing the thinking that forced it, and the words hovering not one second from his tongue, I loved it. "I don't see how I come getting somebody as good as you is," he said. "I sure don't deserve you. What you see in me, anyway?"

If the truth was told, nothing. I only had feelings for him. "I loves you," I said.

Holding my hands, playing tricks with my fingertips to get me feeling prickly inside, ought not to give such pleasure. Walking the streets in broad daylight. "Look at this, Dorine." Sonny pulled me to look at a lamp in a window. "Can't you see that lamp right next to our bed?"

Cheap lamp. Ugly. But anything to keep the courting going. "Sure is pretty," I said.

"Come on, let's buy it."

"Not now, Sonny. Save it for my birthday."

"That is right. You got a birthday coming up soon. But I don't want to get you no lamp for your birthday. I wants to get you something snazzy—a fur coat. . . . Yeah, we'll go stepping out—the Cotton Club. That's what we gonna do for your birthday."

The Cotton Club. Sonny had taken me there once. We had been the only two black faces in there. Sonny had been so proud.

Playing with my fingers again, walking, strolling, feeling relaxed, almost—and then he turned into this restaurant. "What you doing, going in there?"

"We got to eat, don't we?"

I might not have been in New York as long as he, but I did shop on 125th Street. I bought food at Wisebecker's, household goods at Blumstein's, and little things at Woolworth's. But I knew better than to go into Child's. "They don't serve us in this place, Sonny."

"What you mean, they don't serve us?" Sonny looked all bigtime. "Dorine, this is New York. I eats anywhere I wants."

"You been here before?" I asked.

"Sure, plenty of times. Trouble with niggers, they never try, and always bellyaching about prejudice. Me and my buddies always eat here."

"They white?" I asked. Sonny nodded.

"That don't make no difference. These people here are used to big-timers. And we ain't small-time, is we?" He nudged me and laughed.

"Them racketeer friends of yours will be responsible for your death, Sonny."

"Ain't no cotton fields in New York, Dorine."

I reckoned because Sonny had never known cotton fields was why he didn't see how we had drawn every eye in the place when we walked in—like magnets. And maybe he was thinking, Enough of that courting, let's get down to business, so he took no notice of the waiters turning from us. I had to lead the way to the table. And while we walked, we pulled every eye along with us.

We sat down. I heard his simple mind ticking away. He reached over the table to take my hand. "Dorine, I'm in a jam. I needs me some money in the baddest way. . . ."

Being a slickster is okay, if being blind didn't go along with it. Conspicuous as two fleas in a glass of milk, and about as welcome, is not time to be getting down to talking trash. "Now it ain't no sense in the world for me to have to go to strangers begging when we got this great layout. Now I been think—"

I snatched my hand from his and turned to call a waiter—who ought to have turned his head, instead of looking through me. That gave me a funny feeling. So I touched my face, worked my hands over my dress. Hell, if flesh disappeared it didn't follow that man-made goods went along. I stared at Sonny, waiting for him to use his pull. But like most Baltimore folks, Sonny's antennas were none too good. That made me mad enough to look him in the eyes.

"How come you broke? What happen to all that money I give you?"

"That li'l ole grand? Dorine, that ain't no money."

Seeing that I had spent up a lot of my time and energy accumulating it, I said to him: "I know one thousand people that thinks one grand is a heap of money." I stared at him until he blinked. "And I'm one of them." I turned and snapped my fingers at a waiter.

Nothing happened.

"What's that clown putting down?" I asked. "If he can't see us, you'd think he'd be curious as to why this table is empty."

The other tables were filled. Folks stood on line at the door, waiting to be seated. Sonny snapped his fingers. The headwaiter turned to look, then snapped his head away so fast I waited for it to fall off his shoulders.

"Come on," Sonny said, getting the message. "Let's get the hell outa here. Damn if I wants to spend my money where I ain't wanted."

"No. We ain't going nowhere," I said. I hadn't wanted to come, but seeing I had, life lost importance to me if I left without being served. Sonny looked around, uncomfortable, wanting to get up to run, but not having nerve enough to leave me.

"Hey," I said to him loud as I could, seeing the headwaiter leading an old woman, shaking so from an affliction she had trouble walking. "Sonny, you reckon them monkeys them West Indians chase around them islands look like that?" I pointed at her.

Poor old Moms, she turned her floury-powdered face, shaking. Who were we? Why were we there? Why had I insulted her? Well, I was only starting.

But my loud talking brought the headwaiter to our table. "What do you folks want?"

"To eat," I snapped, " 'less you can show me signs hanging what says colored ain't allowed."

"What do you want to eat?" Stiff. Proper.

"Two hamburgers and french fries," Sonny said, talking fast. It sounded to me like a promise: I'll order the fastest thing cooking; please feed it to me and I'll hurry to leave.

"Hell, no," I said. "Ain't waited this long for no hamburgers and 'taters." I looked over at another table where a waiter was serving. "Bring me some of that there chicken with that white sauce on it." (White sauce! The thought like to made me want to vomit.)

"We have no more of that," Poker-face said. "You'll have to settle for hamburgers and french fries." (Peculiar Yankees. A cracker would have just said, "Git the hell on out.")

"We'll take it," Sonny said. I stared through his eyes into his soul. This piss-and-sell con artist, ready to trick me out of my style, yet too scared to talk up to a goddamn waiter.

Seconds later, the waiter brought two plates of hamburgers and french fries. He set them before us. The potatoes were cold, the meat burnt. Even Sonny had to say: "Man, looka here, this food is burnt."

"That's all we have," Poker-face said and turned away.

"Then throw the goddamn shit out and bring us some decent cooked food," I said. He turned, tried to stare me down. But crawling is a matter of nature. And it took a strong wind to get my popping eyes to flutter. "It's all right," I told him, to prove it was no hard thing to read his shallow mind. "Take all the time you wants. That's all we got lots of."

"Madam," this straight-backed Yankee said, "if the food is not prepared to your satisfaction, I suggest you try elsewhere." (Two blocks from black Harlem and showing his ass. White folks didn't scare easy back then.)

I lowered my voice to keep our talk private. "Motherfucker, if you don't put some decent food on this here table in five minutes, I'm gonna start from the top of your head and split you down like a fucking string bean." I reached for my purse (white folks thought that all blacks naturally carried knives).

The waiter backed off. Sonny stood up. "Dorine," he whispered, all hoarse, "let's get the hell out."

I grabbed his arm. Held him to the table. "That's all right, baby," I said. "Don't get your gun. I can take care of this simple mother with my knife."

Sonny sat. His skin went from black to gray. His big eyes stared so far out of his head I almost reached out to catch them.

"Okay, okay," the red-faced waiter said. "Tell me what you people want."

He had no way of knowing that Sonny's eyes were popping from being scared, not from being crazy. Then, too, a crowd of colored folks had gathered outside and were looking over the half-curtain at the windows. Chances are, they were out there laughing at us—two black clowns with no more sense than to be sitting in a white folks' eating-place. I reckon he thought they were Garvey folks, ready to march in and take over.

"I'll tell you what we want," I said. "Now, if you can get us that there chicken with the white sauce on top. . . ."

I declare, if white folks got to shame black men, I wish they'd do it in private instead of in public where folks can see. It sure would make life easier on black women. Of course, Sonny got to blaming me. "Ain't nothin' I hate worse than a loud-talking woman what acts like a nigger. No class. . . ."

"Sonny, I ain't the one who wanted to eat at them ofays. I only went along to support your intentions."

"Don't support me no more," Sonny said. "How you know you ain't messed up my contacts—fucked up my business?"

"I ain't the one what done all them things, Sonny. Them white folks did."

His popping eyes hot on me told me he intended that I be the one who suffered.

But I wasn't about to do that. When he slammed out of that house, I got to cleaning my big, beautiful apartment. I wiped down the bathroom tiles, fixed the little big-eyed figures squatting naked and naughty on top of the shelves. In the bedroom I stood out the ruffles of my white organdy curtains, the ruffles of the matching bedspread, and those on the skirt of my dressing table. In the living room I pulled out a stuffed chair to set it more comfortably by the unused fireplace. Made sure the starched doilies were straight on the back of my green velvet couch, emptied cigarette butts from the coffee and side tables, then went to the joy of the apartment: the windows with a view looking down on Seventh Avenue. Darkness set in, and I still stood there, looking out—looking at the spot under the lamppost where Sonny kept his car parked, and wondering if, after all, the view was such a damn joy. . . .

Back in the bedroom, I lay on the chaise longue, fell asleep, woke up, turned over, fell asleep again. The next time I awoke, I knew my punishment had begun.

I suffered that night, and the next, and the next. I kept looking out at that empty space beneath the lamppost. Going to bed, I lay listening for his footsteps out in the hall. Going to sleep, I kept pulling myself awake because I had dreamed of the shower running in the bathroom. I got up knowing that I had lost my bargaining card—the apartment. Even to me, it had lost importance.

Which didn't stop me from sleeping the day away to get to night on my birthday. Sonny and I had spent every birthday together since I was fourteen. And he had promised. . . .

Seven-thirty, I put the crimping irons on the stove. I went to the window. Eight o'clock, I went into the kitchen and took off the white-hot irons to let them cool. Eight-thirty, I went to put them back on again. At nine o'clock I stayed in the kitchen to regulate them—and me. Crimping and bouffing my hair, braiding the back to look as though it was cut, I tied it and slipped into my perfumed bath. I spent a long hour soaking. At eleven, after laying out my lavender chiffon dress with the matching stockings, I sat at the dressing table staring at my sad face in the mirror. With determination I set about to brighten it. I put oil on my eyelids to sparkle my eyes, bright red rouge to my cheeks, and wicked, red lipstick. Then added a mole here and a mole there, to add to the wickedness.

I polished my nails—first my toenails, then my fingernails. Buffed them. Pulled on my stockings, taking time to admire my shapely legs. Then I went to the window. The lamppost looked lonelier than ever.

At twelve o'clock I thought of Big H. I kept my mind on him while I dressed. Slowly. I put on a veil over my eyes, pinned a lavender flower to my hair, then slipped into my dress. Pretty—goddamn lovely, my mirror said. Wicked and looking it. I walked to the window. . . .

Cheating had never come easy to me. It didn't then. But I thanked the Lord there was a man around who admired me, might even want me. And there was but one way to find out. "Never again, Dorine Davis," I said, staring at the lamppost, "will you spend a birthday in New York City—the busiest, happiest, the craziest city in the world—alone."

Then at five A.M., when the red roadster slid into place under the lamppost, I tore off my clothes, dived into bed, glad of the stink of my perfume, the rouge bright on my face.

He came in loud. Dropped his keys, pushed against a chair so that it fell over. Then he went into the bathroom. Going into the bathroom, he left the door wide open and turned on the shower. He wanted me awake. He wanted to take off where he had left off, raise hell, give himself excuses: me, for being responsible for his being broke, his being ashamed. Let him wait. I kept my eyes closed, my back to his side of the bed. His horns had to change into a fucking halo, his knees grow callouses as hard as his head from begging, before I'd give him the chance.

Cold from his shower, he jumped into bed, twisting and turning, pulling the covers off me, trying to shake me awake. I kept my back to him, kept my breathing even. Let him try. If the one thought in his big head was to shake me awake, rile me so he could get those simple excuses off his mind, by morning folks would be calling him barrel-headed Sonny. He kept wiggling, wiggling, finally moving against my back. I heard this voice saying:

"Where the hell you been, nigger?"

"Oh," he said. "You ain't 'sleep?"

"You hear me? I ask where you been."

"Out with folks what appreciate me."

He sounded the way *I* had planned to sound: like I don't give a damn.

"What's that supposed to mean?" I said.

"Nothing. Just been out with folks willing to stake me to the good life."

"Nigger, you living better now than ever before."

"How you figger?" he complained. "Spending money? All going out? None coming in?"

"Who? You?" I hated answering to obvious baits. "I'm the one doing the spending. . . ."

"Hell, Dorine," Sonny said. "You don't call what you doing spending. You call that dribbling. You know me. I got to be where the money is. Where I can touch it. Roll in it."

Seeing where that talk was leading, I changed the subject. "You been out with another woman. Think I don't know?"

"Woman? Why it got to be a woman? I'm talking about me, baby. Me, hating to feel poor. I'm talking about this here place. The money to pay the rent."

"You ain't yet offered," I said.

"What's gonna happen when your li'l bit of money runs out, Dorine? Ever think of that? You ain't been looking for nothing to do. And here I got this money-making proposition, and you turning up your ass like you some Miss Vanderbilt."

True. I hadn't given much thought about what next to try my hand at doing except to keep it off my "rock money." Sonny had kept me so busy worrying over him.

". . . Well let me tell you one thing. You ain't Miss Vanderbilt. You can't grow money between your titties by hugging this here apartment to your bosom. And if that's what's on your mind, don't expect me to sit around waiting, growing roots on my foot or moss on my ass. The name is Sonny, baby. Sonny—remember me?"

"Don't wait," I said. "Go on, get another woman if you think they come better than me. See if I care."

"If that's the way you feel about it," he said. "Don't you worry, I will." The next time he went out, he stayed.

Crying did nothing for me but wash away my good looks, I saw when Sonny had stayed away one week. "Dorine, baby"—I spoke to my reflection in the mirror—"you got yourself this great spread. A fistful of money. You got you. Now go for yourself." So I went and bought this big, black Buick.

That new car did to me what new hats do for some folks. It gave me a sense of myself. Money going out, none coming in, and killing all chances of running out of my mind before I ran out of money, I had to have bought a mortgage on luck. I did.

Strutting out to the car, ready to burn through the streets, I heard this voice as I took out the key: "May I give you a lift?" I looked up smiling at the man smiling out at me from the chauffeur-driven Duesenberg that had pulled up alongside.

"I'd been walking these streets waiting for you to drive by and ask," I said, and jumped into the Duesenberg, settling down beside the brown-faced gent with his caring face, his warm, brown eyes.

Big H reached beyond me to close the door. "I had hoped to see you long before this," he said. "If I had known where you lived. . . ."

Certain men pull certain things from certain ladies. Big H pulled the coquette out of me. I batted my eyelashes, blushed, played cute. "Right there," I pointed. "But I heard about your club. . . ."

"By all means," he said. "When can I expect you?"

"Not right through this time."

"Busy?"

"Sort of. But when I have the time. . . ."

"You have it. As much as you need." He looked a gentle he-wasn't-rushing-me look. I smiled my thanks. We had gone a few blocks when he asked: "Where can I drop you?"

"Back where you found me."

"Oh—I am so sorry. I'm taking you out of your way."

"No," I said. "We're going the same way. . . ."

He made the chauffeur turn and they drove me back. Seeing me go to the door of my car, Big H laughed. He leaned out. "Remember—anytime."

They drove off. I stood looking after them. New York gents. Elegant. Class. In all my life I had never known anyone fatherly. Someone who might take care of me? Why the hell not? Go on, Dorine Davis, grab it while you can. This is your life, your one time to be young . . . . Then I jumped into my big Buick and drove around town, looking for a red roadster.

Up streets and down avenues, all over town. Red is not the hardest color to find. I spotted the red roadster easing into a parking space in front of a restaurant on Lenox Avenue, and racing up to it, pulled up alongside honking my horn. Sonny looked over, and seeing me, his eyes bucked. I waved, stepped on the gas, drove home, and waited. Two minutes later Sonny walked in.

"Hey, Dorine," he said. "Whatcha putting down?"

"Whatcha mean, what I'm putting down?" I smiled, hard, cold. I had planned it that way. Keep the old fool guessing. Make him beg. I had a big, black Buick. If I wanted, I had a chauffeur-driven Duesenberg to show off in. Who needed him? I looked hard into that good-looking black face with the word slickster spread over it. Simple nigger, I thought. You got to be born brand-new to keep up with a young thing like me. Young, a pile of money, a car, and good to look at. Simple old fool, you done lost out. So let the door hit you where the white man kicked you.

"Whose car you driving, baby?"

"Whose do you think?"

"Holding out on me, huh?"

"Who you for me to hold out on?"

"Where you get the money to buy a new car?" he asked.

I always holds me some money, nigger, I thought. I said, still with that hard smile, "You eating in or out?"

"In, baby. You know ain't nobody cook good as you."

"That why you been eating out?"

"I'm out there trying to find a way for us, baby. That's what I'm doing. But I'll tell the world—you can really stir up some grits."

Fool praise. Game-playing. Before I knew it, I had gone into the kitchen and had found his favorite beefsteak, just where I had put it, and had started frying it along with home fries.

Sonny sat watching me, trying to stare secrets out of me. But fortune-telling had never been his strong point. So he came and stood behind me, put his arm around me, and commenced to teasing my titties. He turned me around and pushed his stomach flat up against mine and it came to me that, after all, that's where I wanted to be.

I had planned it that way when I left Montgomery. Sonny and me, together. No secrets. I had planned to bare my soul so we could start off living right. If it hadn't been for my secrets. . . .

"Sonny, I got something to tell you," I said when we sat down to dinner.

"Well, I guess you have," he said. "Where in the hell you get enough money to buy a car?"

"Mamie lent it to me." The lie slipped out—habit.

"Enough money to buy a car?"

"Yeah, I asked her. She lent me. Mamie knows I'm good for it. She says she'd let me have more—if we get into business."

"Business? What the hell kind?"

"Numbers? Banking them. We can start small, Sonny."

"West Indian shit."

"And we can build. Before you know—"

"Shit, I tell you! Mamie ain't gonna give you or nobody else that kind of money. Nobody gives that kind of money—or lends it neither."

"We can start with five grand."

"Five grand! Peanuts. Who in the hell can do anything big with five grand?"

I had heard that the big-timers started with less. Alex Pompey—the one called Cubano Loco—had started in a little cigar shop. Wilfred Brunder, Henri Miro—all kingpins, all with big money. There were even women calling themselves queens, driving around in their big cars, living in big mansions, flashing gilt. And here was this big-acting stud who had never held on to a dime shouting:

"I ain't no beggar. We can have five times that in a month if you listen to me and let me run this place."

Sonny wasn't listening. He didn't want to hear.

"Trouble is, you ain't used to living decent," I shouted back.

"Living decent! Woman, the way you act you think making money is a sin."

"It ain't no sin. But what you trying to do to me is."

I had planned to play it calm, stay cool. But my brain and mouth seemed never to work together. "My money sent your black butt here. Listen to you. Your goddamn lies! You wants to get married. Lies. All you want is to hustle me—hustle my house. You ain't nothing but the son of a low-down whore. A two-bit whore who made a—"

Sorry is already too late. Sonny would kill over his mother. I wanted to cut my tongue out for having said that. Sonny choked on his steak. I got up and hit his back. He shoved me from him.

"We ain't got nothing to talk about, Dorine. You don't know a damn thing about business. And you ain't never laid eyes on my mother." He got up and went to the door. Seeing him going, I shouted: "She is a whore. And a cheap one at that. Yes, son of a bitch, your mother is a cheap two-bit whore who—"

He turned, his hand hitting out. He slammed me up against the wall, then rushed from the kitchen. I ran into the hall after him, wanting to stop him, to tell him that if he walked out of that door, my life walked with him. But a cow running scared is a simple mother. . . . Lock-tongued, I watched him leave, knowing I had no intention of letting him go. I had invested in him—from Alabama to New York City—and I had no intention of losing out.

Turning the screw to give pain is the born knowledge of a hustling man. Sonny didn't come back for days. And for days I stared at the walls, lay awake, looking up at the ceiling and into his blinking eyes. For days I drove around Harlem, my eyelids peeled so far back from searching, my thyroid seemed to be misfunctioning. The day I got back to find his clothes gone from the closets, a lifetime of sharp thinking went dull.

I ran down the stairs, rang Tom Rumley's bell, banged on his door. "Tom, Tom open this door!" Shouting, sounding frantic scared Tom so bad he barely cracked the door open. "Where's Sonny?" I asked. "Where the hell is he holed up?"

Tom, not one to harbor secrets, nevertheless took his time answering. He studied my face, saw that I was about to lose my mind, then said: "Well . . . now . . . Sonny's been doing a li'l hanging at the Cotton Club."

"Cotton Club!" How to get in? They sure didn't welcome folks my complexion.

"Yeah." Tom shook his head. "You know Sonny. Crack open a door where white folks be, and Sonny goes scooting in. Hell, that damn fool even roots for them goddamn Yankees."

I went back upstairs and got dressed fit to kill, then, getting into my car, I drove to the Cotton Club, honking my horn and making such a racket that every drunk who made two bits shining cars came running.

All this to impress the big black bouncer (black women driving big cars back then naturally impressed folks) who made his reputation from cracking open the heads of black folks trying to crash.

I stepped out of the car, swept into the club, a twenty-dollar bill folded in the hand I held out. "Hey, handsome," I said to the bouncer. "Seen Sonny? He's expecting me."

The stud took the twenty, thought one half-second, then pointed with his chin. I followed his general directions. But two steps into the room, this thickset Irish separated himself from the shadows. I walked by him—one second's eye contact would blow twenty bucks. I swaggered. But his suspicious eyes still bored through my back. So I stopped at the first table and gave a pat to a bald-headed gent smiling into the eyes of a frizzy blonde. The cat looked up, looked me over. I winked, gave him the "come on" look. He smiled—a real sport. I switched, keeping him and the big feller guessing. Working my way around the side of the room to the front, I pretended to be gaga over the high-kicking high-yeller dancers doing their thing. But I was searching, searching.

Gay haughty laughter kept busting, along with popping bottles of champagne (Prohibition?). Half-drunk red-faced guys staggered around, handling laughing broads. Beads, diamonds flashed as folks shouted at each other across the table. I spotted Mayor Walker, his head bowed, almost touching the blonde he was speaking to, and knowing that Irish Mike still stood in the background watching, I walked in the direction of the table, pretending to stop. But my eyes had seen two blemishes standing out in that all-white room.

Cubano Loco—just dark enough to be different—sat with five men a short distance away from Mayor Walker's party. Beyond him, the darkest thing in the room, talking to someone in the shadows at the far side, sat Sonny.

I sauntered in his direction, trying to see who his words—like piss too hot to hold—were streaming to. I had to keep moving almost in a circle before I saw her. A white woman with black Sonny in the Cotton Club! Shock didn't hinder me. I kept straight.

The woman saw me first. She sat facing me. Looking up as I came, fright flashed across her face. But Sonny's antennas never picked up. Everything in me pushed me to go. Leave. At once. Dorine Davis, get the hell on out of here. No one in this place is in your corner. Not even a waiter. And that black bouncer—forget about him. "Hey, mother, what you putting down?" I said.

Sitting right there, Sonny jumped three feet in the air. He turned his big head around, slow . . . slow. He looked up, blinked once, twice, then: "Dorine." Sweat squirted out of him like someone had squeezed an atomizer. He scuttled around in his chair—a rat trying to find a hole. One way out through me. He took out his handkerchief, mopped his head.

"Hey, honey-bun. Sure am glad to see you." What else?

"I-I—I just been telling uh-uh—uh, Linda here that it—it's time I um-um—um got by to see old Dorine." He winked the eye farthest from the broad like he had me in a con against her.

"What you mean, *old* Dorine?" I said. "You old enough to be my daddy, nigger."

Calling this big-time stud "nigger" in front of an ofay was the same as cutting his thing off and shoving it in his mouth to smoke. Every muscle of his body twitched as he fought for control. A waiter brought a chair. "Will you have a seat, ma'am?"

"I ain't sitting." Sonny snatched the chair, pushed it hard against the back of my knees. I sank down. Easing back into his seat, he blinked that eye again.

"Dorine here's an old friend," he said. "My oldest in New York." His greased smile picked up his heavy, shaking cheeks. "She and me—we's gonna do business together. . . ." I felt a sharp pain on my shin. "Ain't we, Dorine?"

The blonde smiled, shifting watered-down blue eyes under blue-lidded, mascaraed lashes. I ignored her (never blamed women for what my man did). "All I wants to know, Sonny, is why you ain't been home." Another kick to my shin under the table had me shouting: "Stop kicking and start talking, nigger!"

"Don't you pay Dorine no mind," he said to the broad. "She—"

"Goddamit, talk to *me!*" I said. "I'm the one talking to you. That broad ain't split her lips since I been here."

"What you want me to say?" His fat head got to turning, scared somebody might be looking, listening.

"Say where you been keeping your cheating black butt, and say it now or I'll take this goddamn place apart piece by piece and let you have it with every goddamn piece."

The quiet in the place spoke of his reputation going up in the smoke of that smoke-filled room. He stood. "Okay, Dorine, we'll talk—at home." He bent to whisper to the broad. I exploded:

"Don't do that to me! Don't whisper in no broad's ears when I'm around, mother!"

"Can I be of some help here?" Mayor Walker had come up behind me.

"Yes, you can," I said. "You can get out of my fucking way."

Sonny spun around, grabbed my arm, and hustled me toward the door—bowing and smiling, smoothing his way all the way.

Having to drive back home in separate cars saved both our lives. Sonny wanted to go upside my head, and I wanted to drive my fingernails through to the other side of his eyeballs. As it turned out, we outraced each other, going through red lights, braking to avoid crossing cars, sideswiping fools crazy enough to get in our way. We cussed out of our windows like fools, or like fools on the way to getting crazy. By the time we reached home, the miracle of getting there alive had shaved the edge off our madness. Riding up on the elevator—with the elevator man listening—reduced me to cutting my eyes. By the time we got into the apartment, Sonny had honed down to his natural slick self:

"What the hell you mean, coming to my bread-and-butter joint to raise hell?" he said, leading off to shift the blame to me. "What you trying to do to me, woman?"

"Trying to make something to own out of a sack of shit. What you think you putting down, nigger?"

"You the one what wants to get married," he said.

"Married?"

"Shit yes. Married. That's what I done said."

That blasted a hole through my mind. My tongue fumbled.

"How come you want to act up?" he said. "How come you ain't letting me find my way? Hell—what I'm gonna do if every time I try something you jump bad?"

"Tell me how a ring will jump on my finger by you jiving 'fay broads?" But hope had crawled into that space he blasted. It sounded in my voice.

"How you sound, bay-bee? You knows I loves you. You got to know that. What other woman you know me to be around long's I been with you?"

True. Sonny's reputation had been that of a loner—until he met me. That's why I knew he loved me. And I never doubted his love—when he was with me.

His big eyes worked over my face, my mouth—a man thirsting for a kiss—my face puckered against its will, inviting him.

"Bay-bee, all I think about is you. What I'm gonna do for you. But no sooner I gets into something, there you go—shouting, getting on my back. Lord, woman, why you think I got to be alone? To think. To plan. Every time I step in this house, you got your mouth poked out. You jinxing me, baby. You putting weights on my back."

"Sonny, you ain't talked marriage so long—it sounds right foreign "

"Woman, is you a fool?" He came to me, pulled down the top of my dress, kissed my nipples. I struggled to say no, I ain't no fool. But I was too happy.

The smell of him, his body heat through his clothes, his big, hot face between my titties. . . . "Bay-bee, ain't nobody into me more than you. You got to know that." Feelings gets a feller weak, weak, weak. Sonny picked me up and put me on the bed. He undressed me, kissing my shoulders, my titties, my belly button. Too excited to undress, he unbuttoned his pants and entered me.

That night, we loved. Sleeping, waking, going for each other, sleeping, waking, taking each other—making up for nights we had missed. Me trying to use him up, leave nothing for the next feller. Talking, laughing about times we had had, times we were having, times we were about to have, made me glad I hadn't spoken about Son. Glad I hadn't brought weights, hadn't trapped him, jinxed him. All hell could wait for the day we got started doing whatever we were going to.

I ran naked around the room to have him catch me, love me—to prove he loved me. No weights, no jinxes, no traps . . .

Showering, perfuming, dressing in frilly things, easy-to-tear-off things, to start all over again, to love all over again. We fell asleep and slept right into the next evening.

"God, but I sure am hungry, baby," Sonny said, turning to me. "What say we have some fried steaks and home fries the way only Dorine Davis knows how to make 'em?"

Looking into his big bedroom eyes, his tired, wanting-to-sleep eyes, I said: "Ain't no steaks, but we can have a heap of eggs and home fries."

"Got to have some steaks, baby. What say I run out for a whole gob of T-bones? Then we can have T-bone steaks the whole week."

God, I loved that man. He sure made me happy. I kept grinning at him in the mirror while he slipped on his shirt. While he reached for his jacket, never even bothering about his tie. We had each other, love and money enough to keep us in T-bone steaks for a long time to come. I had my secrets—but then, we had nothing but some time.

Ready to leave, Sonny leaned over the bed. He bit my ear and snuggled his face in my belly. "Dorine, did I ever tell you that you was sure 'nough one hell of a woman? I ain't never really and truly loved no other woman in my life but you—and my old lady." He kissed me. "Now tell me what you want me to bring you."

"T-bone steaks."

"No—I mean something for you—something special."

"I don't need nothing."

"But I wants to—what say some perfume?"

"Okay, perfume."

"What kind?"

"Any old kind."

"Perfume it will be."

I pulled him back to me and we rolled over and over on the bed laughing. He pulled himself away, gave one last look in the mirror. Then he went out.

"Hey line—wanna line? Hey line. . . ." The call of the line man. . . . I kept my back turned to the pillow beside me, my eyes closed. During sleep, I had dreamed that space was empty. I awakened with the gut-taste of emptiness spreading through me, worse, the feeling of having been a fool. I kept trying to force myself back to sleep to begin the dream where I had left off, but "Hey line—wanna line?" forced my eyes open. They moved to the brightest window of the brightest day, then to the clock: ten o'clock. I had slept far into the day.

I looked over to the dressing table. No perfume. A white hand-kerchief—a soiled one. When had he thrown it there? Getting up, I went into the kitchen, looked into the icebox. No steaks. I walked to the kitchen window where I stood looking out at the line man stringing the line from the pole that stood in the center of the back-yard, for the apartment beneath mine.

"Wanna line, lady?" he called up to me.

I shook my head no, then went to search through the icebox again. Still no steaks. So I went back to the window. "Line man," I called. "Need a line—apartment 7-D."

I went into the living room and stood looking out of the win-dow at the empty space beneath the streetlight. Fool, fool, fool. Goddamn fool. What had I thought the empty closets, the empty dresser drawers had spoken of?

The bell rang. I rushed to open it. The line man. Old man who risked his bones climbing poles and leaning out of dozens of win-dows dozens of times a day. I almost heard those old bones creak, protesting. Sunbaked skin, rough hands, swollen joints, stiff with age and work in all kinds of weather and all the things that made poor souls suffer.

He knew his way to the kitchen. He knew his work. He walked down the hall while I stood listening at the door. Was the elevator climbing? Going down? Going down, down.

I walked to the living room to stand looking out at that empty space again. Then I sat in the stuffed seat near the never-to-be-used fireplace, holding my hands.

"Finished, lady." He stood in the doorway, faded gray eyes watering, knots for fingers twisting a ragged old cap. Baggy pants—and those knotted fingers. Don't go, old man. Sit and talk about climbing poles and stringing rope.

"Sure it will hold?" I asked.

"Oh, that it will, lady. That it will. Now, is there something more?"

Fifty cents for his trouble, a quarter tip for knotted old hands. I sat on, not thinking. Then thinking. Had I the right to be such a fool? No. I went for smart. Then I sat not thinking. A horn blew, disturbing the graveyard quiet of the room. Graveyard? A picture of Sonny, unconscious over the wheel of his car, flashed before my eyes. Had that been a dream? A warning? Lord, here I sat about to believe the worst, when Sonny—poor Sonny . . . Relief like a cold shower revived me. I laughed. I had thought my man had done me wrong, when he all the time was out there dying, maybe dead.

Happy, I dressed and went down to Tom Rumley's. "Tom," I said to the freckle-faced man peering out of the door, "something done happen to Sonny."

"Something like what?"

"An accident—I think. He ain't been home."

Tom's mouth dropped open—staring. When he managed to close his mouth again, he said: "This sure ain't the first time."

"No, but this time I knows he would have made it back if something awful hadn't happened."

"How's that?" Tom scratched his nappy red head.

"Don't stand there asking them simple questions, Tom," I said. "Folks who loves knows things like that."

Big Red shook his head, laughing. "Well, if anything done happened to Sonny, it sure ain't happened to his car. But then Sonny looks after that car better than he do his face."

"I ain't here to joke, Tom Rumley. Only to ask your help."

"Well—didn't look like nothing was wrong when I last seen Sonny."

"When was that?"

"Fifteen minutes ago, parking in front of the Cotton Club. If something happened, he ain't known about it. 'Less he thought he had managed to sneak that ole red car into heaven with him."

God, I hated that old freckle-faced, gold-mouthed clown. I went back upstairs, went back to bed, and slept for one week.

And in all that week, not one person rang my bell. I had no friends in New York. No one cared. Sonny didn't. He, who I had done so much for, would just as soon have seen me dead.

Lonely, but too young to die, I finally got up and looked in the mirror. I had lost weight, dark circles ringed my eyes, sweat matted my hair. No man living or dead ought to bear the blame for Dorine Davis looking that plain. Nor of her being a fool. Being young had never been a drawback. The only reason I sometimes acted young happened to be because of my years.

Powder and rouge put me back in business. I dressed in black, pulled a floppy black hat over my nappy hair, and put on sunglasses to hide my eyes. Then I went out and drove to the Cotton Club. It was cold, a light snow was falling, the streets were slippery, forcing me to drive slow. No drunk ran out to wipe down my car when I pulled up before the club. And if my intentions had been to take the joint apart, the opening door had two reasons—one black and one white, standing shoulder-to-shoulder—to change them. Sonny's car was parked out front. But raising hell on that block might get me shot, stabbed, beaten, or, worse, thrown in the nuthouse. I had been hurt enough. The next somebody to get it wouldn't be me.

Driving toward home, my mind churned for ideas for my next move. I saw this short, stocky guy who hung out on my corner, hunched down from the cold and wind, hands deep into his pockets. "Hey, feller." I stopped beside him. "What about a lift?"

"Sure thing," he said, getting in. "It's cold out there."

Easing the car into traffic, I asked him, "Know my man?"

"Ain't he the stud what drives that red roadster?"

"The very one."

"Sure, I know him. Sporty cat . . . only I don't see him around much as I used to."

"He hangs out at the Cotton Club, the Lenox Club, or on the avenue sporting—know what I mean?"

"Sure, sure."

"I need a tail on that sucker."

"On him!"

"Yeah—him."

"Hey, that stud's big-time. He's in with them white folks. Nobody go messing with them types, sister."

"Buster, I ain't asking for nothing I ain't willing to pay for—and good." Always out of work, his kind were never hard, only wiggly. "There's but two of us in my family," I said. "And I'm the one what calls the shots." Reaching into my bag, I pulled out the note I had had ready for the doormen at the Cotton Club. "It's worth twenty a day, every day that I know where he is, and when he is where he is."

Shorty looked at the bill. "That's all I got to do? Let you know where the stud is?"

"That's all—and you got your twenty. Got me?"

"Gotcha, lady. Gotcha."

From that night, I knew where to find Sonny, and I went. The first night, I walked in on him at Yeah Man's, sitting alone, eating fried steak and home fries. I sat near the door, my eyes boring through his back. He kept moving his shoulders, uncomfortable. Then he looked around him. After a spell, he looked over his shoulder to the door. His fork dropped on its way to his mouth. His eyes did just what I had expected. His heavy-with-grease mouth hung open.

That's right, old nigger, run. Keep running. You used the hell out of me, of my money. That gives me rights. If I had to live in hell, then you damn sure got to suffer its tortures right along with me.

The next night, his searching eyes lit on me walking through the door of the Hole-in-the-Wall.

"Seek and you shall find" went on for a week. I had expected it to go on forever. But one night, no sooner had Shorty walked out of the door when Mr. Big Time himself walked in. He came right into the bedroom where I sat at the dressing table, making up, and laid a package down. "Here," he said. "I brought it."

I kept on with my face. "Perfume, Bay-bee," he joked. "Ain't that what I promised? Perfume? That's what I brought."

I got up from the table to slip into my dress. "Look at you," he said. "You the one what forgot. But you know me, when I promise a thing, fire will get to burning the gates of heaven 'fore I forgets." He smiled. "That's a fact."

I had been offered a gun once. And suddenly I knew why I hadn't accepted it. I would have used it. Because Sonny thought me a fool. And because I was. The feel of him in that room put a weight in the pit of my stomach. I actually wanted to be smiling and sweet, instead of hard. I didn't have a gun. I kept looking around for a substitute, to put an end to my simple feelings by making a dent in his head. "What you doing using a key to my door?" I asked.

"Your door? Bay-bee, this is our home. Just because I ain't got my clothes here don't mean I'm gone."

I didn't believe what I was hearing. "Look, Sonny, if you got money for me, put it down and go."

"That's what's the matter with you black women. You wants to take away our manhood, always talking about money, money, money. Never giving yourself a chance to see what we black men about. Always trying to push us this way and that—like we some checkers on a checker-goddamn-board. Dorine bay-bee, I hurts to care for you."

"Then give me my goddamn money."

"See? You black women ain't got no understanding—"

"Of why you all goes out with high-yeller women and white bitches?"

"You jealous, Dorine!"

"And you gonna pay."

I stared into his staring eyes. Sonny tried to stare back—but when the air hit all sides of those big marbles, he got to blinking. "Okay," he said, his voice serious. "I see you ain't gonna believe me if I spit the truth in your face. But we into this white thing, Dorine. You is and I is. There ain't no getting around that. Look at you—the way you dress, that big car you pushing, them sashaying airs. That's all white folks' shit. All of it. That's where the money is. You know it. Mamie can't lend you no money for us to hit the style we wants. So I'm asking you to see me through—just this one time, Dorine. I got a proposition. We can make a bundle—a mill-ion."

"I don't want to hear."

"There's this man, Dorine. . . ."

"I don't believe I'm hearing you straight."

"He got more money than he knows what to do with."

"Sonny, get the hell on out."

"And have you chase me all over town? Naw. I ain't for playing them games. All I want is to make me some money. You know me. Now you can be in on it, or you can deal yourself out. But I got to have somebody. If not you. . . ." He hitched up his shoulders.

That was the straightest I had ever heard Sonny talk, to me or anybody. Not one line of jive sounded in his voice. "Now there's lots of houses around Harlem where white folks still live. But they got to go. Here's this white cat who's into block-busting. The way he got it figured, that section overlooking Central Park? That's got to go. Why not now? There's some town houses along that park front. He's looking to open up a string of them and I think he wants to ask me to be in as his partner. This is where you comes in, Dorine. This stud loves him some brown meat. . . . Yeah, yeah, I know you ain't into turning tricks. But it ain't that way. Just entertain the cat for one night." Seeing the expression on my face, he stopped, walked around the room. "Hell, Dorine, it ain't like you never done it before."

"I ain't about doing it again."

"Only this once." He hitched up his shoulders again. "Like I say, I'll get somebody. . . ."

"You running scared, Sonny. You just want to get me off you black ass."

"Sure I do. But then both you and me know you got to stop sometime. Yeah, you messing with my style. And no, I don't like it. But nobody does nothing forever." That made sense.

Mr. Millionaire, John (I never caught his last name), was a fake. I knew the minute I saw him (I had cut my baby teeth on men with money). His tan skin had seen some bad weather; his hands had handled hard times. No fires lit those flat brown eyes from inside. Even to my prettiest smile they stared, dull, plodding, like behind a plow, shouting that he settled for nickels because dimes took too much effort. I tried to signal a warning to Sonny, but never could catch his eye.

"If it ain't gonna be big, Johnny, count me out." Sonny kept talking, talking. It was hard for John to get a word in. "You see, I'm a big man—a man of business. If I didn't think you could help me grow—I'd say no in a minute." He flicked a big cigar (something he had never smoked), let a smile pick up his fleshy cheeks, and blinked. Seeing Sonny blinking, I got to wondering who was conning who.

"Well, Sonny," Mr. Millionaire said, in a no-class voice, "we ain't gonna have one bit of trouble buying up those brownstones."

My brain dinged. Brownstones? On Central Park? I let my mind travel up and down that street. Didn't see any, so I tried to signal Sonny again. When he kept his eyes on the joker, I got up, went to change the record on the Victrola from a Helen Morgan to a guy called Ted Weems (Sonny did the damndest things for atmosphere), crossed in front of Sonny for his eyes to follow me. But they did no such thing. Worse, my chiffon negligee with its ostrich feathers fell away to expose my plump, smooth knees and Mr. Millionaire never looked. And that feller was supposed to dig brown meat! I sure hated to think how he acted to types he didn't like.

"We have the first colored family set to move in. Then the entire block will buckle" (meaning blacks folks would be living there).

"All I knows"—Mr. Big Shot waved the funky cigar—"is that I'm in. I wants a rent-free ground-floor, for my joint, and my name S-O-N-N-Y up in letters so big that a blind man can feel it. And just like that, you won't have to worry, the money'll start pouring in."

"I'll see to it, Sonny," John said. "Your time is about due. In just a matter of months, One hundred and Eighteenth Street will be all ours."

One Hundred and Eighteenth Street! But Sonny had said the park! One Hundred and Eighteenth Street had nothing to do with the park! Not Central Park anyway. Somebody hadn't gotten the story straight—but who?

Confused, I couldn't keep up. "Money," John said, "is money. Those who came first naturally got the top of the barrel. Those who come after must make their own way—ha-ha."

"Oh, you wasn't born here?" I asked.

"Yeah, I'm born here." His eyes shifted to look over my ears, driving home the feeling I didn't fit his dream type. "But my folks came from the old country."

Ah, that accounted for it. The dark blue suit, cheap at any price; the hard-shined shoes, slightly worn at the heel. I had heard that foreigners didn't care about looks. They stashed their money while going around looking like paupers. It was a fact, Sonny looked like a million and didn't have a dime.

Alone with me, Mr. Millionaire had trouble unstrapping his tongue. He needed to drink my good Canadian whiskey (which wasn't easy to come by) to gain confidence. I noticed, too, that my cigarettes (I had put them around the room for show) kept disappearing. He had to be pocketing them—as good a way as any to hold on to money.

Doubts kept building. So I poured silence on top of his silence. Damned if I would say anything to help him, or hurt Sonny. If he was the fake I thought him, it would come out. I didn't mind waiting. Soon the silence got so thick, if he wanted to stay, he had to fight through it:

"Uh . . . uh, you sure got a swell place here," he said.

"You got around to noticing that?" Not making things easy for men is a natural gift.

"Huh? Ahem. Ha-ha . . ." He tried again. "Sure was a great day. . . ."

"Uh-huh."

"I . . . I . . . mean . . . um . . . um . . . It gets a hell of a lot colder this time of the year."

"Oh go on, you educated thing, you." Rich folks just didn't come that dumb. Not even the foreign rich.

"Well—I . . ."

Tired of his fumbling over words I said, "Look, don't you think it's time you leave?"

He left off trying for words and went to fumbling with my titties. I jumped up. Mad. My good whiskey was almost gone. "Look, I don't want to be rude, but . . ."

Blurry eyes looked into mine for the first time. "That fellow of yours, Sonny, he got a good head for business." That stopped me from putting him out. What if the sucker was shy and not a phony? What if I messed up Sonny's chances for making his million? What's to lose? As Sonny said, I had done it before.

"Let's get to bed," I said. In the bedroom I slipped off the dressing gown and got into bed. The stud brought along what was left of my good whiskey. I reached up and snatched the bottle from him. There had to be limits on how much I was supposed to take.

His drinking had done him no good in bed. He fumbled like a drunk, galloped all night to get nowhere, then fell asleep so that I had to push like hell to get his dead weight off me. Then I went into the bathroom and scrubbed almost through the flesh, drowned myself in perfume to get his smell off me, and went to lie down on the sofa, determined to run through my mind bits and pieces of the puzzle bothering me all evening. But fell right off to sleep.

The next morning I woke early and went into the bedroom to find Mr. Millionaire in exactly the same position I had left him. My first thought—slipping into bed to awaken him and make him think everything was as planned—I changed to snapping up the shades to let sunlight do my work for me.

His eyes opened to the light. He looked into my face and scrambled out of bed, reaching for his clothes—old, faded, wasted-out underwear. He dressed in a flash.

Ready to leave, he took out a billfold, pulled out a twenty, and handed it to me. Doubts knotted my brains. I looked at the money, then at him. "What's that about?" I asked. Handling money from a "night of love" had never been in any arrangement between me and Sonny.

"Isn't that enough?" he asked, flat brown eyes bouncing off mine. He seemed as anxious to leave as I was anxious for him to go. I felt awful, seeing him in the morning light, with his nothing-looking clothes and the blue stubble on his chin adding to his beat-up look.

"Was that the deal?" I asked.

"Yeah—that was the deal."

Still not liking it, I took the money, folded it, and pushed it into a drawer. When I turned back, his face had gone official, his eyes hard. "You had better get dressed and come along with me," he said. "I'm a cop."

His look, his words, his hard eyes paralyzed me. But at least he came together. He looked the part. I snatched on a dress, pulled on a coat, and went with him. Downstairs, Shorty came in as we were going out. "Hey, Miss Dorine, you need me today?"

"Yeah, I need you. Go get Sonny. Tell him he set me up with a hot one. I got pinched."

As nightmares go, I floated in a place where nothing seemed real among a bunch of loud-talking, loud-laughing folks rounded up in early morning raids of speakeasies. Driving down in a police wagon, women taking flasks hidden in inner pockets of coats, sipping, laughing, singing, enjoying. . . .

In court, I squeezed myself invisible, waiting for Sonny to come. I was invisible, no one looked at me, no one spoke, no one saw me caught up there in my nightmare. Everybody talking at the same time about the same thing, about how exciting, how excited, how fabulous to be rounded up in a raid.

Even the judge fitted the pattern of a nightmare, sitting gay instead of stern, talking to the partygoers, laughing, joking, giving advice. "I don't want to ever see you in my court again. Go home and behave yourself."

And they floated around me, over me, out of the court, still high, still laughing, still sneaking sips from flasks, still cracking wise.

Then there were but three of us. One man who had knifed a girl. One pickpocket—a woman. And one prostitute—me. And the voice said: "Prostitution! One hundred dollars bail."

How had I left home without money? "I—I don't have it. . . ." Someone said something about a bondsman. "What's it cost?"

"Got any money?" This man appeared at my side.

"Sure, loads—at home."

"Money at home ain't worth a dime." He looked at my dress, my plain coat. Compared to the nightbirds that had flown on home, I looked like I had just got out of bed. I had.

"Call home for somebody to bring it."

"Call?" Who? Tom, the only one I knew with a phone, was out of town. Where did Sonny stay? "Look, mister, get me out and you can name your price."

"Lady, I ain't out here for my health."

The judge held me over for trial. I cried. "Hey, don't do that," the shoplifter said as they led us out of court. "You won't get much time. Prostitution? First offense? One week the most."

Her face in that nightmare looked wise, knowing. I broke down.

And I kept crying. Sonny, Sonny, Sonny. Where the hell was he? Why didn't he show? Shorty had always been able to find him. . . . I dropped onto that cot in the cell that night and passed out from exhaustion. When I opened my eyes the next morning, a needlepoint of sunlight had poked its way into my cell from a window high up near the ceiling. One spot of light? Better to be hanged than stay in a pen for one week. I pulled the sheet from my cot, tried to tear it; the coarse cloth wouldn't give. I lay back down and fell on back to sleep.

The next time my eyes opened the needlepoint of light had become a big band across the wall. That felt better. I had wanted to hang myself, but I sure didn't want to die. I made up the cot and sat on it, waiting for the day to begin.

But the matron came to my cell before breakfast. "Dorine Davis? Come with me." And as we went down the steps to the guards' room, she said, "Your bail has been paid."

Thank God. Sonny had come through. But Goddamn, what had taken him so long? I might have hung myself in there and never gotten out again. Never set eyes on him again. Never seen my buck-eyed lover man no more. Never to be able to tell him what a simple mother he'd been in putting his trust in that son of a bitch of a foreign-born . . .

But Tom Rumley sat outside in his car, waiting. Big Red, seeing me, got to grinning, showing all of his golden teeth. "What the hell you doing here?" I asked. "Why ain't Sonny come for hisself?"

His grin got broader at my gratitude. "What you care why Sonny ain't here? I'm here, ain't I?"

"Since when Sonny's so tied up he needs you to take care of his business?"

Tom laughed. "Sonny's seeing to his business, all right, and I'm here seeing to mine."

Made no sense asking when I got to be his business, seeing I had no intentions of walking back into prison. So I got into the car next to him, not intending to say one mumbling word that he might mistake for gratitude. Tom started up the car, and after we drove a quiet mile I finally asked:

"How come you here? How you know where to find me?"

"Sonny tole me." I shut my mouth, not wanting to hear any more lies. In all likelihood, he had heard from Shorty.

"He knew I was in jail and he ain't come to get me?"

"Uh-huh."

"How come?"

"On account of he's sick and tired of you messing with him."

My heart twisted, cutting off my breath. "He the one set you up for the pinch, gal. Paid that cop good money to get you."

A lie! He had no business lying like that. Knifing his best friend? "How come you know so much?" I asked.

"The nigger tole me."

"If he tole you, how come you telling me? Ain't you supposed to be his friend?"

"Sure, I'm Sonny's friend—the best one he got. We was boys together. But being friends don't stop me from knowing when he's wrong. I ain't against the man, I'm for you—that's why I'm here."

Proof of his words was the daylight we were driving through. "Sonny is set for the big time, Dorine, lady. You got to know that. Ain't no way in the world you dumb as you act sometimes. Sonny ain't about to let you, or nobody else, slow him down."

"Guess he told you that?" But I didn't believe it.

"Sure he did. All I got to do is turn him on and turn the station to you and he gets to running out at the mouth. He ain't yet let up. You got any notion how hot that sucker is about the way you been squeezing him?"

"And so he got me pinched! Tom Rumley, hear me. Ain't one living man can do that to this lady and get away with it."

"Dorine Davis—pretty lady. Why you want to mess around with a stud like Sonny? You got class, lady. More class in one finger than all the broads in Sonny's stable put together. You even got more class than Tina. . . ."

Words hitting and hurting the way he intended they should. Words about to pull me under and drown me. "Who the hell is Tina?"

"That white broad you caught the slickster with at the Cotton Club." Lord, Lord, Lord, had Sonny told this red devil everything?

"Her name is Linda."

"That's what he tole you, gal. But that Tina makes more money for Sonny than all of his other fillies put together."

"What you trying to tell me, Red?"

"What? You ain't been listening? Everybody knows that Sonny's got hisself an outfit of stables with more fillies than he can bed. You the only one what don't. How you think he gets hisself in that Cotton Club? You think they loves him? Hell no. It's because he can do favors. . . . And where the hell you think he sleeps when he ain't with you? The streets?"

"How long's this been going on, Tom?"

"Hell, the sucker hit New York and went crazy. Tina's got a pad on Sugar Hill, baby. It takes up damn near a city block. Why you think he stuck you in that room? The only thing I ain't been able to figger is why he keep messing with you in the first place."

Because he loves me. Because I love him, I wanted to say, but didn't have the courage.

"What you wants to mess with a nigger like Sonny for, anyway? Both of you'd do better far from the other as space will allow."

Twisting, turning the wheel of the car, working it through the traffic as carefully as he worked the junk in his house. Talking offhanded, as though he didn't know he controlled the way of my heart, my mind, my feelings. "Sonny ain't nothing but a pimp. Sure he talks about getting into business—but the only way he can see doing it is through using pussy. And you ain't for turning no tricks to help him out. So—what's the use?

"Now you a right smart woman, Dorine. You got to know you can't change a man—not a nigger like Sonny—unless you stiffen him out for the grave. Now, who's that gonna help? Not one living soul. . . ."

Dull-eyed, I kept my head looking out the window, waiting for the one word to help me dispute it all. Knowing deep inside it was all true, and knowing I had always known. "Sonny ain't made for marriage, Miss Dorine. His mama ain't raised her son that way. If you keep trying to make a houseboy outa him, it's gonna land the both of you in a stinking dung heap."

"So what do I do? Sit back and shut up?"

"Why not? If there ain't nothing you can do to stop a feller that's doing what he wants to do, then just forget it and go ahead doing what you got to do."

"But Tom, I sent that man here. He used me. Used my money. Oh no, Tom, Sonny is a marked one. If it's the last thing I do, I'll get him."

"Why?"

"You ask that? The nigger put me in jail!"

"But I got you out, ain't I?" The careful driving got on my nerves. Sitting there, ready to bust, while he turned and twisted the

wheel as carefully as a fucking preacher at somebody's funeral—
mine! "And Dorine, lady, I can teach you how to make money—
more money than you ever seen in your life. And you don't have to
lay with nobody—excepting me. . . ." He flashed that gold grin.
"And that's only if you wants. You see, Dorine, I wants to marry
you. Now what you got to say about that?"

BOOK TWO

1

Seeing big, bulky, slow Tom grab a thick something, and with a few twists of his wrists reduce it to almost nothing, then make it disappear quicker than a thought between his legs and walk his big-gutted, flat-footed natural self, had to be seeing a magician at work. Boosting. He schooled me well. He showed me how to tell a good stone from fake, how to make a small thing disappear by passing it from gloves to sleeves—the hands being much quicker than I had ever imagined the eyes—holding it, feeling it with the pores of the skin, ready to ditch or stash, whichever might prove necessary. Tom impressed the hell out of me. I learned all he had to teach. And I declare, I went from hating him to liking him too much to marry.

"You see, Dorine"—he kept up his coaching even when we were on the road to Washington, D.C., to meet his gang—"white boosters can make themselves fade into the surroundings of them classy stores. The plainer they looks, the better. But a sales-somebody looks up and sees a black face, right away they say, 'Uh-oh, what we got here? Topsy?' See? Our risks is double, triple that of white boosters. That's why we don't try to fade into no background. We in the acting business. We calls attention to our black selves. We look rich, big-time. We walks with dough—plenty of it. Whatever them ofays believes when we walks in, by the time we walks out they got to know they dealt with class. There goes a gracious, well-bred, wealthy black lady. . . ."

The wind hitting the top of his Ford sedan, making it rock. And looking out at the naked, shivering branches determined to keep distinction between the white earth and the gray sky, I shivered too. Excited.

"What if I don't take to your gang?" I asked.

"They takes some getting used to," Tom said. "Even I got to admit that. But when you gets to know them, they some of the damndest, finest folks you wants to know."

"They might not take to me," I said.

"Well now, lady, you takes some getting used to, too, you know?"

"I might just be a bust. . . ."

"Naw . . . that you ain't," Tom said. He kept his eyes on the road, half smiling, slow-talking. "You first-rate—or will be—if you listens. Young blood—we been needing young blood. We been working together so long that we just about gone stale. And you—well, you the kind we needs—keeps the rest of us on our toes."

I liked that Tom had faith in me. What I had learned in a few minutes took some folks months, years to learn, he claimed. I believed him. That had always been my way. But it didn't make me any calmer going down to meet his folks. "They might hate me pushing myself in," I said. "They'll make things tough."

Tom reached over to pat my hand. "Leave them to me," he said. "After all, they's my gang."

But fear kept my teeth chattering, even when he sounded the bell of the stately D.C. house. And when the door opened, the sight of the tall, handsome woman looking down her nose at us had my feet itching to run. We followed her into the house and into the largest living room I had ever seen. Tom, standing in the doorway, spoke in a loud voice: "Look who I brought. The woman I'm 'bout to marry—Dorine Davis. No, she ain't crazy. She slick as greased lightning, sharp as a razor—that's who the future Madam Rumley is."

If Tom thought to impress those six—spread out over the back-to-back couches, looking like long-legged dolls propped there to decorate—he had another thought coming. They sat there staring at us, or through us, as though there wasn't much of anything standing in the doorway. If I had wanted to dispute Tom, there was not one soul interested. But then Tom threw back his big, freckled face, laughing, brightening the room with his solid-gold, big-belly laugh. And for a second I was sorry what he had said wasn't true. I made up my mind then that my next man had to be a big-belly laughing man.

The effect of his big laugh on this gang was for them to turn don't-give-a-damn eyes away. I took the measure of a vase standing in a far corner of the room, shouting out loud: "Expensive!" Wall-to-wall carpeting stretched out of eye's reach beneath closed doors leading to other places. Heavy satin draperies hung from sky-high ceilings, framing windows through which I caught a glimpse of leaves—hung over from the late, long-lasting fall—swirling around over a snow-covered lawn, around and around, in space that went far beyond the opening of the curtains.

". . . and what's more"—Tom kept talking—"Dorine here's our new partner."

My eyes would have had to be crossed to follow the workings of theirs. Some started from my head and worked down, while others started at my feet and worked the other way. I had to settle for reading them. I knew them all from Tom's describing.

Sally: She who belonged to the house, her tall handsomeness supported thirty-odd years. Light tan–skinned—a real Washington Negro—with a smile pulling down the corners of her mouth, leaving her hincty nose sniffing the air. Tom had said: "Sally and her husband goes for high-class. He won't own to knowing us. If he did he'd have to own up that his government chauffeur job don't come near paying his mortgage. Only he and the good Lord know what he tell hisself about Sally always out on the road." Coming into the house, I had heard the sound of kids. Sally had two—a boy, four, and a girl, eighteen months.

Grace: She lived in Philly. Schoolmarm type, right down to her midaged waistline. Coffee-colored, with a thin pointy nose holding a pair of silver-rimmed glasses at the tip. Grace's lips were pinched tight, making me wonder how the hell she softened them enough to manage her young man, Albert. Tom had said: "Grace got a nice, quiet husband who work for the post office. Don't quite know how she explains Albert always being around and on the road with her too. But she does just fine. Albert and her old man is tight buddies."

Albert: A never-get-old boyish look about him, slight build, wide grayish eyes that promised women he meant them no good, and a weak smile, from always-ready-to-be-kissed lips, that apologized for it. "Al's a con man from Birmingham more than a booster," Tom had said, "but a good cover man and an ace driver."

Ann: Baltimore. White, straight, bobbed black hair. Ann wanted to be an undertaker. She had gone into boosting to help her get a start. Both of Ann's parents were colored, Tom had said. I searched but didn't find a clue in her skin tone.

Bessie: Black—Mamie type—except that Bessie used red lipstick smeared over her thick lips, something that Mamie would drop dead before doing. Jewels flamed Bessie's neck beneath foxtails in that hot room. And the red hat hugging her head might have given Madam Vanderbilt cause for grief—if it hadn't gotten to fighting her purple dress. Tom had said: "Bessie decks herself out so she won't have to kick asses if folks mistake her for a maid." At the look of her, I got to wondering how the law hadn't first thrown her in jail, and then gone looking for a madam who had been robbed. Yet Tom had said that Bessie's feller, Bill, licked and loved every footstep she left behind.

Bill: Tom had said: "Bill can pass for white, except when he opens his mouth." Bill's hair was stocking-cap slick. Tall, trim, light unto whiteness, with hard lines seaming his face and a mouth broad with loving, until he smiled to show off his two front gold-capped teeth (we black folks and our gold).

Looking at them looking at me, I thought of Tom saying that of all boosters, black or white, operating from coast to coast, they were the best. They had earned Tom's respect. But if I didn't impress them, the feeling was likewise. Never before had I ever seen, all in one room, such a scramble of people.

Then white Ann said: "So, you think that you'll be ready to start with us tomorrow?" My back bristled at the nasal-sounding white-folks voice. Whatever Tom had said, I knew a white woman when I heard one. And Ann was white.

"I ain't here to convince you of nothing," I snapped. And she said: "My, you don't sound as though you're ready." Right off I hated her. I hated the cold smile, the black, searching eyes seeing through me.

"How you figger I'm supposed to sound?"

"Didn't Tom take that up with you?" She raised her eyebrows, all insulting. That forced me to think of Tom's coaching:

"When you walk into a store," he had said, "you got to act white, talk white."

"How you expect me to talk white, Tom Rumley?" I had asked.

"Hell, Dorine, that's the easiest. Don't *they* go 'round imitating *us*? Putting that black on their face, loosening up them lips: 'Yassa boss, howsa boss, Mammy how I loves you'—all that shit? They swear they sound like us. Well, we 'round them more than they be 'round us. So we imitate them. Go the other way. Thin your lips, tighten them to your teeth. Now say: 'How do you do, Mr. Rumley?' Slow. 'This-is-a-lovely-day-we-are-having.' "

So now I thinned my lips to say: "I-can-go-anywhere-and-do-anything-that-you-can, Miss Ann."

"Hot dog," Ann cracked. "She ain't backwards worth a damn, is she, Tom?" That second I searched her face for reasons I had thought she looked white.

The rest of them laughed too—loud laughing which brought Sally's husband, Buddy, into the room. He looked just as Tom had said: tall, light-skinned, with "good" hair and red lips that spoke of his heavy drinking. "Sally." He stared right into her face. "If you must take this trip tonight, I wish you'd come and explain to little Buddy before leaving."

"Why don't you have the maid . . ." she started, then, "Oh, never mind. Tell the dears I'll be right in." Buddy's slack red lips twisted. He seemed one second away from reading her. But lacking the courage, he walked out, never once looking at us. So whatever Tom had said, Buddy-boy did have respect for the hustle that kept those sky-high drapes swinging.

Sally, the rub-it-in kind, gave her husband time to deliver her message, butler-fashion, before following. And no sooner had the door closed behind her than Grace, twisting her face, imitating Sally, said:

"Tell the dears . . ." Her nostrils, near her cheeks, turned an angry red. "The bitch—just because she got those two brats, she thinks she's so goddamn hot."

"Grace"—Albert elbowed her, smiling—"you know you'd do anything this side of murder to have just one of 'em kids." Grace's eyes bucked out, like they wanted to even the tip of her nose, trying to quiet him. But Albert seemed to like teasing. He kept laughing, kept pushing her with his elbow.

"Honey," Bessie said, trying to prove to me that no matter how it sounded, they really were a team, "why don't you come sit by me? Let me give you some pointers." I looked away from her. Tell me? What? With those fur tails about to choke her? And those hands? Having work-roughened hands myself hadn't exactly built a respect in me for those of others. I hitched up my shoulders: no thanks. Bessie only laughed in her deep, smoky throat.

"Listen, baby doll, ain't nobody as slick as you coming in here thinking you is. I don't give a damn what Tom Rumley says." Why hadn't someone hipped her about thinning her lips? "In Philly tomorrow," she said, "I'm supposed to be your cover, see? I aim to look after you. But you best remember. From the first you walks in, I'm the one you got to look to, see? I'm the one what gives the signals, tells you what is what, and who is where. So don't you go in with your ass so high that that's all you can see when you looks over your shoulder."

I wanted to laugh. Who had told her that I had picked cotton and cotton seeds still knotted my hair? Hell, my nerves had been through the fires. Mamie had seen to that:

"Learn from them," she had told me. "Only a mongol idiot can't learn from them that's there to teach." She had kept after me. "Get yourself a madam. One like mine. Don't matter if she don't pay nothing. You keep her place spotless. Put yourself out for her. She know you can't live on what she pay. Ask her about getting you outside work and good-paying folks. If you keep her house top shape, she ain't gonna want to lose you. She'll get you work."

Mamie. Full of surprises. Schooling me on how to set up houses: "When you go to a new place, just take over. Make sure things shines. Go into every corner, cleaning, looking. Sure, the help ain't gonna like it. But you ain't in there to make friends."

We had to work with whites: "Black mens can't get to one hundred yards of them houses. But white mens? They can case a block like they was air, go into a mansion like a salesman or even a plumber and the mansions gets cleaned out all the while neighbors be tipping their hats."

Two rules never broken: "Never set up you main madam. Never keep nothing you lift. If you covet something, buy it in a store and keep the receipt. If you can't afford it, it just ain't for you."

Lord, I made money. Every fourth or fifth job I set up. I made more money than I had ever in my life. Working with whites was the thing. They cared nothing about me except information. I gave less than a damn about them—except an honest exchange.

But my luck didn't hold. Mamie had worked the game for years. At the end of my first year, my madam calls me. "Dorine," she says, "Mrs. Upton got robbed yesterday. It seems that everyone I ever send you to gets robbed."

"Everyone, ma'am?" I had to bite my tongue not to call her a liar that it was every fourth or fifth job. "I sure don't know what you mean, ma'am. Who all you done sent me to been robbed?"

Staring through my eyes like she can tell when niggers lie, and me staring right back, agreeing that she can.

"We-ll, maybe I'm wrong. I'm sorry. . . ."

"Me too, ma'am. 'Cause I sure liked working for you."

I quit. That day. Scared. If she really put her mind to it, she had to see the pattern. I left her house and left Cleveland. As far as nerve went, mine had been tested.

So when Tom dropped me off at this department store the next day, fifteen minutes after Albert had dropped off Bessie, I went tipping in. Eyes from all over the store gave me back this reflection of a fine, brown-skinned gal, in honey-colored velvet coat with silver fox skins draped down her back, spiked heels clicking, snug-fitting black hat with a little veil to add that touch of mystery.

I hitched my shoulders, pushed up my head, and made it across the room to the escalator. Getting on, posing, pride bursting through me like bubbles from champagne. I got off and remembered Bessie. I looked around and, not seeing her, decided to go on my own. I floated like on air until I found the suit department, then stood in the doorway waiting for this slim, blond, blue-eyed, impressed-look-ing sales-gent. "Is there something I can do for you?" he asked when he came over.

"Hello they-air. . . ." Ann had clued me in on the British ac-cent. "If you talk too near to your own accent, you might slip right back into it," she had said. "So go far out. English folks use a lot of air: he-air, they-air, whey-air. Americans hearing that accent coming from black lips never know where to put it."

"I'm looking for some de-air suits—blue, black, satin—don't you know? Can-you-help-me, de-air boy?" I throw him a brick of a smile meant to knock the eyes out of his head.

"What price do you have in mind?"

I shrug my shoulders "the world's the limit," open up my purse, worry over five hundred dollars in one-hundred-dollar bills, then snap the purse shut when I think he's seen enough. Right off, he leads me to this rack of precious and protected suits another salesman is showing to two white ladies. I hear prices like three, four hundred being thrown around. I go through the rack, looking bored. When I spot the suits I want—three of them—I walk over to a rack of cheaper, unattended suits.

Disappointed, Blondie follows. I take off my skins, my velvet coat, toss them careless-like down on a chair, then start putting on and taking off jackets, throwing them on the chair over my coat so quickly he can't keep up. All the while I keep my eyes on the other salesman and his ladies. When they move off, I pick up my coat and skins from the bottom of the heap. And as my man gets busy hanging up the mess, I glide over to the expensive rack. In one second (I declare Tom had to be proud), I have my suits well caught up between my legs and turn to smile into Blue-Eyes as he races toward me. Only before he gets to me, someone else has cut in. I look up into some dark brown eyes belonging to a big, burly-looking son of a bitch who acts right off like he owns me.

"Okay, okay, just drop them suits," he says. To hear that command is to obey. The muscles of my legs relax and the suits come tumbling down, damn ungraceful, to my feet. "Okay, come with me." He grabs my arm and half pushing, half pulling, he drags me through the store.

The money in my purse is to flash, to impress; it's also to grease bulls. I reach for my purse, but this sucker yanks my arm high, pulling my coat short, separating me from myself. I try to close my coat but he's hauling, half carrying me to the escalator. I try to get on. My ankle twists, a shoe heel snaps off. I reach down. But this simple joker yanks me up. My hat tilts over my eyes. I try to free my hand to push it back but he's got me in a lock. We go down the escalator. The reflection I get back from eyes all over the store is of this poor, beat-up black woman, coat open, hat twisted all sloppy around on her head. Tacky!

Downstairs I look around—no Bessie. Outside I search for our car, but this rough mother hustles me into one parked at the curb. In minutes I'm whizzed around corners of this strange city, then find myself getting out in front of a police station. Still trying to pull self together, to limp in in style, I get dragged up to the sergeant at the desk.

"What we got here, Tim?" this bulldog of an officer asks, not even looking up.

"Caught her red-handed," Tim answers. "Came into the store like a whore out of hell. Manager spotted her right off."

"Shoplifting, huh? What you got to say for yourself, Topsy?"

Right away ex-booster, ex-actress changes style. "Well, suh, my ma, suh. She down home sick, suh. . . ."

"Yeah, yeah, know all about it. Hey, Charlie," he calls to this redneck cop sitting with his feet on a desk. "Lock her up."

"Her name happens to be Miss Etta Lane." A tall, soft-spoken white man walks out of the corner shadows to stand beside me. Dark suit under dark overcoat, dark hat over gray hair, he looks like God. "And Miss Lane happens to be my client. I'll take care of her."

Buck-eyed sergeant and cops just look. The sergeant, scratching his head, says, "You don't say. . . ?"

"I do say." God's mouth stretches into a kindly smile. He leads me out, hand at my elbow. Not one penny has changed hands!

In his car hot tears, slipping and sliding, scald my cheeks (I cry at the stick of a pin). They hadn't let me down. I had messed up, made a fool of myself, and they still had bailed me out. Quiet, like its driver, the car weaved in and out of traffic, stopping, waiting, going on. Face in my hands to hide my simple tears, I took time noticing that the car had stopped stopping. Just kept on rolling. A push of cold clear air reaching in to me made me raise my head. Looking out of the window I saw a mess of crooked branches clawing the air, begging the sky. I wiped my eyes. "Where we going?"

In that distance he had put between us he didn't seem to hear. I blew my nose. "Where you taking me?"

A few seconds passed. The trees changed form, became skeletions, twisted, ugly, knocking together, demanding my life out there in the raw wind. I huddled in my corner. God stopped the car. "Right here," he said, reaching across me to push the door open. His hand went to his breast pocket. My heart stopped, then thundered against my chest. My eyes stretched out so far that cold air encircled them. They had decided to put me out of the way. I had messed up. I knew too much. . . .

I jumped out of the car, looked around for a place to run, hide. I found myself looking at this sprawling country house where I had spent the night—Grace's house. I looked back at the stud. He had taken out his watch and was looking at it. Putting it back into his breast pocket, he stretched his face out into its smile.

"Good-bye, Miss Davis," he said. "Try to be more careful the next time." Tipping his hat, he drove off, leaving me staring after the car.

Like someone had lit a match to it, the way my face burned. I hopped up the path to the house: big houses, big cars, big apartments to disappear into after jobs. Expensive-looking mouthpiece. Nothing small about the operation—excepting me.

Slow, not wanting to get there, I found myself at the foot of the steps. I stood, hating the thought of climbing them, wanting instead to run, to hide in the hedges, to whittle myself down to a shrub and stand invisible at the side of the path. But the door opened and Bill, his wide mouth open from one to the other of his ears, exposing all his big white teeth with the gleaming gold fangs, bowed to the waist. "Here she is," he called out. "Our big motion-picture star."

"Ain't she, though," Bessie said as I walked in. "Look at her. Miss It herself. Clara Bow ain't got a damn thing on our Miss Beauty. Hon-ey! You should've seen her. . . ."

Ann sat reading. So did Sally. Grace knitted. Tom, standing at the window, looked at me, scratching his head, while Albert and Bill kept nudging Bessie to keep up her clowning.

"How she do that, baby?" Bill kept his broad-mouthed grin going. Bessie hitched up her shoulders, stuck up her head, strutting up and down the room, shaking her narrow hips, her skinny knock-kneed legs looking like a matchstick cracked in the middle, both ends going off in different directions. But Bill liked the look of her. "Go on, Bessie, show us how she did that again."

"Bill, you ain't seen nothing until you seen our li'l ole Dorine strutting her stuff. Pre-tty! Lord, you couldn't miss her. Whooooeee! Big-time. What we gon' do about setting her up in pictures?"

"Where the hell were you?" I jumped on her to get her off me.

"Me? Baby, in the front row. Wouldn't have missed that show for the world."

Her not getting mad got me hot. "I kept looking for you."

"Baby, all you had to do was just bend that li'l ole neck. But that don't matter. You was the star."

"If anybody got to be star, ain't nobody more suited than our li'l brown gal," Albert said, grinning, his eyes sexed up. That made Grace look up from her knitting and squeeze her tight mouth tighter.

"I looked all over the store for you," I said to Bessie.

"Baby doll, I followed you up that escalator, saw you floating on air, got the message, and lit out to get help. Didn't want our star spending time in no lock-up, nosiree."

"Well now, Dorine," Tom said, and everybody got quiet. Grace put aside her knitting. Ann and Sally put down their reading. "You ain't been listening good as I thought," he said. His soft talking brought the tears flowing. "I guess I figured on that. That's why we started you in that store. Which, all things considered, ain't got the best of systems. And in a town where we got pull. But it don't happen like that always.

"We a team, Dorine," he said. "All of us. We works together. And we ain't a bad bunch." I hung my head, looked down at my feet half hidden in Grace's thick carpet. "Come," he said, and led the bunch of us upstairs into a bedroom.

He pointed to a scramble of things on a big rug-covered bed: coats, suits, dresses. "That's the business we did today. A couple of grand, give or take a little. If we had been caught with that, we could have been sent up—all of us—on grand larceny, same as if we worked all day and made ten times that.

"Now, we ain't the kind that mind taking risks, nor serving time—none of us. We in that kind of business; those are the chances. But none of us wants to do grand larceny for penny-ante stuff.

"Now, Dorine, I tole you: there's a heap of difference between being a penny-ante shoplifter and being a booster. We business. Big business. That's why we take so much time training a feller. There's only one way to do things if you work with us—and that's the right way.

"Now, the way you walked into that store. . . ."

"You said I had to act. . . ."

"Not that kind of acting. You ain't in vaudeville, Dorine. And no matter what you think, you ain't no motion-picture star. When you get in a classy store, you got to act so that in five seconds folks won't care if you black or white. You got to dress so."

"Bessie dresses—"

"Bessie got her lines; you got yours. Bessie knows hers. You think that maybe you can get around to learning yours?"

Embarrassed! Face flaming! Everybody held still, waiting for me to answer. I couldn't. I felt their waiting, their breath-holding. My head got heavy, heavier. Then Bessie spoke: "Hell, baby, what happened to you happens to anybody the first time around." Then Ann's dry, careless-sounding voice: "Anyway, that's good luck. First time caught, forever after careful." Grace's pinched lips softened, which softened her whole face. Snooty Sally got a pleasantness around her mouth (not her eyes—she always looked on as though she had no part of our circus). Bill showed all his white teeth with his sparkling fangs, and Albert's eyes promised he'd make me forget the whole thing.

Heat got to spreading through my body, warming me. They were big—all of them. Bigger than their houses, their cars. One great big family. My family. Bessie's scrawny arms encircled my waist, hugging me to her. "It won't happen again," I promised. "I swear to God and on the grave of my mother, it won't ever happen again." Bessie smiled. Her eyes, wide, black, deep, deep as all eternity looked through mine, and I got to wondering how in the world I had ever mistook this loveliest woman in the world for ugly.

Respect for Bessie brimmed my heart when I walked into that Chicago jewelry store and saw her in that silver fox jacket. Beneath it she sported a kelly-green suit. She wore red satin shoes, a purple hat with long black feathers curling halfway down her back (I declare I never knew where Bessie got her clothes).

That store, with its structured showcases set at different angles, its swirling browns as walls, and its rug sucking the feet into what seemed like a plush heaven, had nothing on Bessie. She stole the show. When I made my way to the diamond showcase I might have been a breeze blowing in a ninety-mile wind for all the interest I stirred.

"Hey, you!" Bessie's brassy voice cut through the room. "Show me this here bracelet you got in this here case."

In the quiet that her voice cuts through the room, customers move toward her to really see what they are looking at.

"If you don't mind, sir," I say to the open-mouthed showman over my case, "I would like to see that ring." I point to a decent-sized stone in a group of four rings surrounding one blue-white diamond in a raised oval setting.

Tom had said: "Never go for a chip; it ain't worth a second of your time." And: "Forget the big ones. They sets too heavy in a jeweler's head." But with all of Tom's coaching, I have a special way of telling a good stone: the tension my query sets off in the jeweler.

The ring I point to doesn't take the sucker's mind off Bessie. I try it on, look at it this way and that, and give it back. I point to another. To my eyes that stone looks good, but Bessie's floor show keeps claiming his attention. The third ring makes his eyes flick over me without seeming to, so I decide on that one.

All this time, Bessie's walking before her showcase, one hand on her hip, the other outstretched, admiring the bracelet, and while folks around admire her. My man keeps cutting his eyes over to her.

I wait for his eyes to flash to Bessie before I stash this ring. And when he looks back, I point to his prize. "But that's the one I really want," I say.

This time my man stiffens; he forgets about Bessie. Looking me up and down, he sees my rough hands. His face goes proper. "Madam," he says, "this happens to be a very expensive stone. It's worth thirty thousand dollars." Now that he has really seen me, if I had on a Russian sable instead of my quiet black wool coat I'd still look like a mop pusher to him.

"Oh, de-air, de-air; does that mean you shall not allow me to try. . . ?" I love the way I go British in my surprise. He stands all stiff, his mouth squeezed together, but something about my accent confuses him. He takes out the ring and puts it on my finger. But he hovers over it, keeps his eyes on it. He's come around to believing I'm a magician.

"My de-air mahn, this is just the ring I have beene looking for." I put out my rough hand to admire it.

His eyes flicker because nothing clicks. But before he can think it out Bessie yells:

"Take your goddamn hands offa me!"

Someone has actually touched her to see if she's real (white folks got all kinds of nerve). Hands on hips, foot patting the floor, Bessie throws her head around so that those feathers shake and tremble. "Yeah, I knows," she says. "I looks too good to y'all. I got this fine fur, my pretty satin shoes, and my suit ain't waitin'. I's hot stuff. Well, let me tell y'all one damn thing. I got a hell of a lot more where these comes from."

My man rolls his eyes heavenward, then, remembering me standing there, goes red in the face.

"De-air, de-air—these people," I say to put him at his ease.

"Oh, you're not from around here?" He's relieved.

"De-air me, no. Bri-tain, don't you know."

"I hope they don't have any of these overdressed baboons over there," he says, buddy to buddy. I shake my head, still smiling. Why get mad? I have what I came for.

But just to raise his pressure, I drop my hand with his prize ring to my side. That one act sweeps Bessie and everything else under the cobwebs of his simple brain, raises every pore on his body, strains every nerve. And to add to his misery I look him straight in the eyes and, keeping my frog-eyes from blinking, say in this real jinxed-up voice:

"Ye-es, ex-actly what I want. . . ." (Tom hates that I play with folks. Dangerous, he says; makes folks think of you in their sleep, remember you years later, spot you on the streets. But then I'm so young. . . .)

This joker has rubbed salt where I itch. I let him sweat. When I think he's about to shout for help I ease my hand back to the counter. I smile. "Ye-es, exactly the one. But for that money? I must ask my husband."

His relief to have the stone back in his hands travels with me to the door. And my back twitches when I feel his relief change to panic. I force myself to walk to the door. "Madam?" he calls. Confused. He's sure he hasn't taken his eyes off me.

Both the guard near the door and I turn.

"Yes?" I keep smiling. From the corner of my eye I see Bessie heading toward him.

"The ring. . . ."

"My de-air mahn. I told you, I just must talk to my husband first." One step takes me to the door. I hear Bessie:

"Hey, you, lemme see that there ring."

Two steps take me out to the curb. Albert drives up. The car door swings open. I jump in. We turn the corner into heavy traffic. Minutes later we're racing across town with this rock so hot it's about to burn the hidden compartment of the car. We park outside the Wardel Department Store. Waiting. . . .

Sitting there, nerve ends tearing apart, heart strumming, mouth ready to split into giggles, I act relaxed, look cool. But this excitement like a fire in me drives me day, night, day, night. . . .

In the mirror of the car I see Albert's eyes working me over. They tell me that what he wants most in life is to touch me, feel me, get into me. The only thing—I have to give the word.

Albert loves women. He hates the word no. The apology in his smile says: "I can wait. I'll never touch you unless you invite me." But Albert's too young—only about twenty-six.

Still, being nineteen, working with real go-for-broke folks with know-how, and knowing a stud like Albert was around, had to be the best of living. What did I need? A man with a belly laugh, a big man the age I liked—midaged—with a big-belly laugh.

Albert looks at his watch just as Sally walks out of the store—tall, handsome, snooty (I declare I learned all about uppity Washington Negroes through Sally)—and with the look of a peacock turns her head around before walking down the block. Seconds later Tom, with Bessie sitting beside him, drives by to pick up Sally. Seconds later Ann steps out of the store and stands at the curb. Folks stop and stare. Ann looks slick in black, a little black hat with a veil hugging her head. "Who is she?" people seem to say. "A motion-picture star? Lila Lee?"

A limousine drives up. Bill, trim in his chauffeur's uniform, jumps out, runs to open the door, tipping his hat as Ann steps in. Then he runs, jumps back into the car. They drive off. Albert and I wait; we look around. Everything is clear. We follow.

Bill and Bessie's house in the Woodlawn section of Chicago is not so grand as Sally's, not so country as Grace's. It looks like Bessie.

Bedrooms painted in bright colors. Bright curtains at the windows, bright printed spreads on the beds. Downstairs in her living room, her couch and stuffed chairs are a bright red mohair. A bright fire burns in her fireplace; the room is hot. On the walls little vases of artificial flowers, and on her baby grand piano, in the corner of the room, a giant vase of big bright silk flowers in every color that has been given a name. While we wait for Tom to fence the day's take, we crowd around the piano clapping and singing "Seems Like Old Times" while Bill, with his boater, bowtie, and cane, dances the soft shoe.

Bessie had the determination never to let winter in. She didn't. And the next day when we drove off, it was like leaving hot summer to take on the North Pole. . . .

Illinois, Wisconsin, Minnesota, the Dakotas, Washington, Oregon, California, then back to New York, to Harlem and spring. Crazy? The times. More than the money, the times. The gay times. The wild times. Getting-over-Sonny times. And for me, laughing, becoming the best of the best and being young.

2

The Mississippi River had washed over its banks that spring. We—Ann, Tom, Bill, Bessie along with me—went out to the concert that Duke Ellington was giving for the victims. But lines went around the corner. Instead we went to the Alhambra. A Bessie Smith–looking singer onstage trying to sound like her was singing "In the Dark."

Our Bessie joined in as we took our seats. Standing, snapping her fingers, grinding her hips. "Yeah-ah, sing that song, sister. You want to sing like Bessie—so go all the way.

"Yeah, sing it so I can swing it," she kept calling. "Get all the way down to the bottom, baby. . . ."

May in New York and the excitement from our long trip had that unsettling effect on us right through to our bones. No matter how slick we felt, how easy a time we thought we had had, getting back safe after all those months—a bit richer, wiser, we were all tight—needing to unwind.

"I'm with you, baby," Bessie yelled. "Sing it so I can shake it. Whoooooeeee, loose me so you can use me."

"Shut up, goddamit," a man shouted from behind.

"Who you?" Bessie turned and stuck her neck out partridge-like, peering into the dark.

"Never mind who I is," the voice came back. "Just set your butt down. It ain't made a glass."

"Damn right it ain't glass. It's earthy. My grandpa used his ass like a sandbag to hold back that Miss'ippi. Made history."

"I don't give a damn about your grandaddy's ass. Just fit yours in that seat, or I'm gon' come and shape it to size."

"Hey man." Bill jumped up, mad. "Who the hell you talking to? Show yourself, motherfucker, and I'll take your measure to fit the size of your grave."

"Will you set down," Tom hissed at Bill.

"But man, ain't you heard. That man was talking to my lady. Nobody talks to my lady—" Tom reached past Bessie to grab Bill. He yanked him down to his seat. "Show respect," he said. "That woman's singing. She's enough like Bessie Smith to warrant some respect."

We all sat quiet. But the singer had finished and was being upstaged by the announcer, a slick white cat with patent-leather hair.

"Ladies and gentlemen . . ." He held his hands up to quiet the applause. "Ladies and gentlemen . . ." The clapping died down. "This day will go down in history as one of the greatest days of all times."

"On this day—May twentieth, nineteen hundred and twenty-seven, Charles Augustus Lindbergh took off in his plane, *The Spirit of Saint Louis*, to fly across that mighty Atlantic in an attempt to reach Paris. We all wish him Godspeed. Let us bow our heads in one minute of prayer for his safe landing."

We bowed our heads, obedient as kids. "Who in the hell is Lindbergh?" I whispered.

"Damn if I know," Bill said.

"Me neither," Bessie said. "But if the fool's trying a stunt like that, I'm big enough to pray he makes it."

"But who is he?" I asked again.

"Ain't you heard the man?" Tom growled. He hated worse than anything not knowing what he was asked. "Some loony."

"What's he trying to prove?" I asked.

"That's a simple question, Dorine. That he can do it. Why else?"

Not satisfied, I nudged Ann, she being the educated one of the lot of us. But Bill answered:

"To spit in the face of the Lord. Why else white folks do such things?"

"Oh, Bill." Bessie crossed herself (something she stole from Catholics—"Only thing I ever stole in my life," she liked to say, "and the Lord give me his blessing for stealing it"). "I done give him my prayers. Now he got to make it."

"Who ever prayed for your grandpa when he tried to hold back the Mississippi?" Ann said in her dry-as-bone voice.

"I did," Bessie answered. "I figured if he was fool enough to think he was God, then I was fool enough to pray he made it—only he didn't."

"Look, if you all don't stop that noise and get to praying, I'm gonna come down there and *give* you my measure." The man behind us sounded evil, so we sat still, bowed our heads, and prayed.

But outside on the streets Harlem had gone crazy. Everyone had heard about the man crossing the Atlantic. Folks were out there shouting and cheering and blowing horns. One man called out to another: "Bet fifty dollars he makes it."

"No bet," the other said. "Goddamn right he makes it. We Americans do whatever we got the mind to."

"Lord, Lord, Lord," an old woman kept saying to those passing around her. "God gonna punish us. We ain't got no call to be acting like birds. If He wanted us to fly, He'd have give us wings."

104

"Woman," a man answered, "if we can sail the sea and we ain't fish, how come we got to be birds so we can fly?"

And out of the side streets young people and old came marching onto the avenue, blowing horns, shouting: "Lindbergh, Lindbergh, Lindbergh. . . ." Others picked it up. "Lindbergh, Lindbergh, Lindbergh . . ." shuffling in time. White folks, black folks, all out there. (When they heard he had landed, it was the same, with folks grabbing, hugging and kissing. I declare that was as close as I had ever seen blacks and whites together, but by the time Lindbergh's baby was stolen, some of the same folks were out there cheering Bruno Hauptmann, swearing that Lindbergh had more to do with his baby's death than would be told, and that he was trying to frame Hauptmann. But the Depression had set in by then—that goddamn Depression.)

We marched to the club where Fats Waller was playing. Marching, chanting: "Lindbergh, Lindbergh." We marched right into the club chanting. Fats picked up the beat. A young couple got up and started to dance. Folks got to clapping in time. The boy threw the girl out; she came flying back. He threw her out again, pulled her back, then ducked. She went hopping over his back. The crowd roared, went wild. They did it a second and then a third time (folks dispute me about time and place, but I declare that's the night the lindy-hop was born).

Later, as we sat at the table, I kept looking out into the night. I got to thinking of water—the Mississippi River rushing over its banks, the Atlantic which looked so much and so mighty, never ending. "Why did he do it?" I asked.

"Money and glory," Ann said. "They'd kill their mothers for money and glory."

"Or power," Tom said. "Most whites do things for glory or power."

"And dough," I said.

"Not necessarily. We do things for money," he said. "But white folks got that, so it follow naturally they got to do other things."

"What a shame," Bessie said, getting sentimental. "That poor man, up there risking his neck while we black sinners down here, boozing, robbing white folks. . . ."

"Damn, Bessie"—Tom's freckles flashed from being mad—"we

ain't robbing nobody. We only cutting a thin line out of profits. How the hell them kids you and Bill gonna have will make it to get power or glory if we ain't willing to cut a thin line off their profit to give them a li'l boost. . . ?"

"Yeah," Ann said, "I bet you ain't shed that many tears for your old grandpa that they gave to the Mississippi."

"Yes, I did, Ann. I declare I cried and I cried. . . ."

"Bessie," I said, "did your old gramps die in the Mississippi, sure 'nough?"

"Sure 'nough did," Bessie said. "Holding it back from flooding."

"Let me tell it," Bill said, his yeller face brightening with his flashy smile.

But before he could get started a shout went up in the front of the club. The real Bessie Smith had walked in. Fats switched to "Misbehavin'." Folks stood up calling to her. Our Bessie stood up snapping her fingers and shouting even as the singer moved toward our table. "Bessie Smith, Bessie Smith, Lordy, didn't I just bring the house down on the head of a broad trying to make like you."

"That's what I got friends for," Bessie Smith called back over the noise. "Bring down the goddamn ceilings on sons-of-bitch imitators." I hadn't seen Bessie Smith since Cleveland so I was set to jump up too. Then I saw the man whose arm she had hold of. I got quiet. The joy went out of the night.

They moved toward us, laughing, shouting out to friends through the smoke of the smoke-filled room. They stopped to chat, then moved toward us again. I sat.

Nothing had changed about him except that he looked better. More into himself. His smile said that. His well-cut suit said that. And he kept the hand with the diamond on the pinky moving, making sure it caught every eye. Lord, how happy he looked, laughing as though promised forever on this side of time.

They were almost to our table when a hand grabbed Bessie and pulled her over to another table. That left Sonny standing alone, near enough for me to touch.

"Hey, Sonny-Boy," Tom greeted him.

"Big Red," Sonny said, his eyes searching. Then he saw me. "Dorine baby," he smiled. "Sure am glad to see you."

I had expected to see his fat cheeks quiver with shame, fear. But his fleshy glad-to-see-me smile flashed. And seeing that, the Bibleful of cuss words that I had structured to slay him remained sealed behind my lips. I kept trying to push them through my mouth, my eyes. Understanding that, he turned to Tom. "Hey, Tom, whatcha been doing with my gal? Don't think I got over you stealing her from me."

Pretending to be deaf, Tom reached past him to grab Bessie, who had come up. "Hey, big mama, heard someone trying to sound off like you but she was no queen."

"Ain't but one of us, papa," Bessie said. "You got to remember that. I been at the Lincoln, seeing the Duke. Ain't had no time to offer prayers for the Lindbergh dude. But I wish him well."

Everyone got to talking. I sat. I had never passed for dull. Yet there I sat, letting Frog-Eyes flash a phony smile along with his diamond and get away with having put me in jail. Me—the one responsible for all his style. I tried, but not one thought turning in my brains made its way through to my mouth.

I saw them moving away, Bessie Smith and Sonny, knowing that I had planned for him never to walk away from me again—not alive. Never to walk again, to enjoy a joke again, to throw the bull at anyone ever again. And there I sat, actually looking at his back moving off. Eyes burning, I stared after them. I felt eyes on me and looked around. A few tables away, Big H sat with a group. He smiled that soft smile. His eyes said he had seen, knew the reason for my anger; he understood.

A change of mood wiped away my anger. I smiled. I thought of myself, the sophisticated lady, being handed into his Duesenberg. Somewhere in my mind I saw Sonny looking on from the sidelines—jealous fit to be tied. My smile widened.

"So that's Sonny." Ann whispered in my ear. Her voice had lost its dryness—sprung to life. I followed her gaze to where Sonny and Bessie Smith sat with a group of friends.

"Yeah," I snapped at her. "That's that no-good nigger." And just in case she didn't get the message, added: "When I get through with that two-faced, tit-sucking mother's child, his knees will be so bowed from bending, I'll use them for my bow. And that thing what hangs between his legs? I'll use that to string my arrows."

"My"—she raised her high-class eyebrows—"you don't lose easy, do you?"

"I ain't lost nothing," I snapped. "He has."

"He doesn't seem to know."

"That's for me to worry about."

Strange night—not the least of it my fast-changing moods. And why not? Looking back I see that the pieces of my life were laid out before me in that one place. Nineteen years old, gay, full of spunk and believing in my luck. What's more, I had a dozen roads to choose to get to the perfect life—I thought.

A big-gutted laugh shut off Ann's answer. I looked up. Big H stood at the table. "Hello, hello, hello, little lady," he said. But he spoke soft. I tried to see behind him to the one with the big laugh.

But Big H's eyes held mine. "I had expected to see you long before this," he said.

"Been out of town." I liked giving in to his liking-me look. "A lady's got to make a living, you know."

"True." He put deeper meaning to that word. "A *very* good living." He turned to the lady at his side. "Monica, I want you to meet Dorine Davis. Dorine—Monica Gaines." I had seen her that night at Small's. Although I didn't remember that she had black slanted eyes or velvet black eyebrows that contrasted to her ivory-colored face—the loveliest combination.

She twisted her lips into a half-smile at my "Pleased to meet you."

"And this"—Big H moved aside—"is Mr. and Mrs. Harry Brisbane."

Broad shoulders blotted out his tall, slender companion. Harry's light brown, almost yellow eyes glowing out of his black face. He took my hand and sent heat pushing through me, sticking my clothes to my body. Sensing my discomfort, he smiled. "Always happy to meet a lovely lady," he said. I pulled my hand from his.

"Hey, Big H, howya doin'," I heard Tom say. "Whatcha think of this boy Lindbergh?"

"Quite a feat," Big H answered, "if he makes it."

"How you mean, if?" Harry Brisbane reared back, throwing his jacket open, hooking his thumbs in his vest. "He makin' it, mahn. Excelsior!" He smiled to see heads turning. "Onward and upward! What can stop him?" I loved *his* West Indian accent.

"It's true that white men are still on their interminable road of conquest," Big H said. "The land, the sea, the skies. One wonders when or if they will ever stop."

"Ha!" Tom said. "Big H, you said a mouthful."

"Never!" Harry's loud booming voice and louder laughter filled me. "Mahn cannot stop! Never! And this thing white? What you talk? Is mahn! Mahn! Mahn shall go on and on. What is to stop him in this country? A mahn comes little and grows and grows. . . . Ain't it, lovely lady?" He smiled down at me. Whatever he said, I was willing to agree. "Mahn must conquer," he cried, "or be conquered—ain't it?" His voice to me was like music. "To stop," he said, "is to die."

"My friend has a profound respect for America, as you can see," Big H said. His eyes said he enjoyed being near me, wanted to stay to talk more. But his lady made an impatient move away from the table. Big H bowed. "He's been here only a few years, but he intends to make it big."

"Ah, well," Harry Brisbane said. "Money don't make me, you know. I make money." He laughed into my eyes again, then touching the tall, silent lady at his side—his wife—moved on.

"Let's hope to be seeing you all again," Big H said, following.

"Oh, my God," I said, watching that yellow-eyed, belly-laughing Harry walk away. "Who is that?"

"Who you talking about? Big H?"

"Who else?" Bessie said, cutting through my denial. "He's the one what ain't married."

"Big H ain't your kind of man, Dorine," Tom said. "Ain't no sense in having eyes for him. That man's intelligent."

"What you mean, Tom? That I'm dumb?"

"No. But there's smart and there's smart. Big H is an intellectual."

"And I ain't?"

"Dorine, you can't even read."

"That stops folks from being intellect—"

"Oh my God." Ann waved me quiet. I sat sulking, cutting my eyes at her.

"I ain't no intell—whatever you call it neither," Bessie said to comfort me, and Bill reached over to pat my hand.

"Don't you worry none, Dorine. Just remember that the stud is the *king*. He didn't get that way from being intellectual."

"Kings, queens, dukes, counts, earls. A damn court. Niggers of the world, here's your kingdom—Harlem," Ann said.

"What's wrong with that?" Bill looked blank-faced surprise. "What's wrong with us having our kingdom?"

"Have it," Ann said. "Whites will let you so long as Harlem stays poor with most colored folks scrounging, willing to scrub floors for a buck. If it really gets rich—treachery from the inside, greed from the outside. Kingdoms crumble." She snapped her fingers to show how fast.

"Ann," Tom growled. "With that kind of thinking what else could you be planning on being—'cepting an undertaker."

For me, that night—and days after—stayed a mess of confusion. How could yellow-brown eyes upset my thinking when I needed all my wits—and more—planning on how to go after Big H and tie him to me? But before I could unravel that puzzle a telegram came from home. Sister was sick. I had to go.

3

Missing Montgomery was like missing a toothache or a bad cold: soon forgotten, hated to be reminded of, never wanted to see or hear of again. "I sure ain't ready to face that town," I said to Tom when he drove me to the station. "Montgomery is my home. My family's there. There got to be something wrong with a feller what don't miss home." Much as I loved my family, only Sister and Son could get me back there.

"From the looks of it, you ain't gonna be missing New York none." Tom squinted, pretending to be trying to see over the boxes piled high in the back. "You got to be taking all of New York back with you."

Only the poorest of the poor went back home empty-handed. "Only thing short about me when it comes to my folks is time. And I keeps praying they never needs none of it."

"Just hope they meet you at the station." Tom comforted me with his loud gold laugh. "Else you'll look like a turd what missed its hole with all them bundles."

On the train as I waved good-bye, it came to me that Tom had become my home in the city. His big, country face, his big belly and liking-me eyes. New York and Tom had become my life. Settling back in my seat, I forced myself to think of the family. Janie—Son. Janie had to be pleased with the camel-hair coat with the beaver collar I had bought her. I'd have to sit on her to make her wear it. Or else she'd say, "Ain't it purty," then leave it hanging. That was Sister. Things never mattered to her—only people.

The kids, though—they'd go wild with their sleeping-eyed dolls with the long combing hair. And the bicycles. They'd run their friends ragged or till they dropped. Mildred, she'd just love the dolls I bought her—long-legged, with cigarettes stuck in the hole of their mouths, like dicty whores. For Son I had bought more clothes than needed, in all sizes—to help him remember me long after my visit.

"Don't it feel good to be going home?" The woman beside me had been wiggling in her seat for my attention, before deciding to speak. "New York ain't bad—for a spell," she said. "But nothing beats going home. Setting out on the porch in this fine weather, greeting neighbors."

"Going back to stay?" I asked to be polite.

"No, just looking in on the family. Got a couple of weeks off. Lord, the way we keeps going in that big city—'nough to weary the bones."

Smooth, brown face. Young, yet sounding old. My lashes went down to cover my eyes, to look her over. Plump, round, laced-up shoes supporting tired feet. Plain woman, plain ideas—even to the simple smile saying we had to agree because we were riding the same train, traveling the same way.

I looked over the coach: same people—almost—as on my trip into New York. Yankees with heads bent reading, discouraging talk; crackers, getting chummy with their black neighbors:

"Uh-huh," my chatty neighbor said. "I tell you, if it warn't for

111

this job, I'd never again set foot outside of Mississippi. But I got me this go-ood job."

"Do tell, what doing?"

"Housework," she said—bragging. "Housekeeping for some rich white folks." All that pride deserved some praise. So I said:

"Don't say."

"Uh-huh. Sleeps in. Makes every bit of thirty dollars a month. No bills. Saves every penny I makes. All I got to buy myself is shoes."

"Don't say. Feet gets tired? What you do to make all that money?"

"Cleans house—town house, you know? Pretty! Hardwood floors, honey. I keeps them shining. Does the laundry. Take care of two kids. Cooks for 'em. Cooks me up some greens, girl—hee-hee." She nudged me with her elbow. "Folks swear they can't eat pork. But girl, I drops a hamhock in them string beans and the folks say, 'Bertha, what makes them string beans taste so good?' I tells 'em, 'It's the hand, ma'am. Good ole country hands.' Hee-hee."

Big H jumped into my mind. He was the man I wanted to marry. Thank the Lord for his warm, serious, liking-me eyes. I could get him too—if I played him right. Talking to Bertha settled me on that score. I'd never have to scrub another floor for white folks. Not that I thought it possible to go backward. Still, how long could I keep working with the gang? Being poor and black went so natural together, it made the tightrope of having goddamn slippery. One wrong step—and there you go. . . .

Having decided that about my life, I wanted to rush home to my past so I could hop the first train back to New York and my future.

I stared out the window at the spurts of green that spring was trying to force into the junk-piled landscape, at the clotheslines crisscrossing backyards with faded, formless clothes flapping in the wind—flags of hardship. Children's faces pressed up to windows, children standing spindly-legged, lonely, trying to impress passing strangers with waving hands of friendship, but reminding them instead of echoes of poverty some had rushed away from. And me—hell, I never ever lived in the underbelly of any town or city. . . .

Yes, I had lived the good life in Cleveland. And I had left it for a better life in New York. Hot for Sonny. . . . I thought of Ann. I ought to have clinked glasses with that high yeller, smoochy-eyed bitch, wishing her better luck than I had. I hoped she didn't end up waiting at windows—nights searching for glimpses of a red car streaking by.

I kept having to force Big H back on my mind. But memories kept stirring up like grains of sand under surf. Memories of that buck-eyed bastard. How seconds before I went off to sleep, his hands moved over me, massaging my shoulders, my belly, drawing lines along my back, squeezing my breasts, teasing the nipples until my toes curled, so that I grabbed his big head in my hands, kissing his chin, his lips, his nose, those frog-eyes, until he pulled me under. His strong, knowing hands spreading out my legs. . . .

The nerve. Him walking into that club—and not a word of sorry! "Dorine baby. . . ." I ought to have Dorined his ass. Grabbed a bottle and brought it down on that hard head, splintering it. Hit him again, again. Watch that blood spurt. Spurting. Dark red, almost black—poisoned blood. Hit him with the top of that broken bottle. Expose the white bone of his head. God! Blood spurting, pouring down the sides of that big head. Down comes the bottle, cutting the ears—those little, mean, stingy ears. Hanging ears, bubbling blood. Thick, thick blood out of those little pig ears.

"Will you have a piece of chicken?"

"What!" I snapped my head around to stare into the oldish brown face of the woman who needed her rest. A greasy brown paper bag was stuck under my nose.

"Will you have a piece of chicken? That the way to say it, hee-hee. Don't say do you want some. No suh, that ain't polite. Will you have some?"

Goddamn. All them benefits and learning good manners too—all for thirty bucks a month. "No, I don't want no chicken." I jumped up to rid myself of thoughts of bloody pig ears. "I'm going to eat in the dining car."

Snatching my mink jacket—much too hot for outside, never mind for that stuffy train—I flung it over my suit and made my way past her rigid knees, up the aisle, feeling her eyes slide over me like slime. Fried chicken—indeed!

In the half-empty dining car three black waiters stood at attention, friendly smiles on their faces. They added more starch to the backs of their white jackets when they saw me at the door. Their smiles emptied along with their eyes as they looked through me. I hate black folks who put on airs to impress other blacks. I hate worse blacks that airs got to be put on to impress.

So number-one big-timer, mink and all, stared over their heads while strutting into the car. Standing dead center, I looked around and spotted this tall, fine, darker brother with quick eyes crinkling at the corners telling the world he was in on a big joke. "May I serve you, madam?" He met me moving toward him, his smile an I'm-with-you. And we were on.

"Madam Davis," I introduced myself, hipping him to the fact that he didn't have one worry with me when it came to etiquette.

"Ahhh, yes, Madam Daveees." He spoke loud enough to be heard all over the car. "How well I remember your last trip. Welcome aboard."

I slipped into the chair he pulled out, doing things with my hands to cover my brows and my surprise. "I am so happy you liked our country enough to pay us another visit. Are you enjoying this trip, madam?"

My tongue ties at the damndest times. "Cheerio, cheerio, cheerio, old boy," I answered, then heard the question. "Just grand. Just grand."

"I am so pleased." Educated boy—sharp eyes, bright. Knew how to arrange his smile—just right. "What will be your pleasure, madam?"

"I leave myself in your hands," I said, thanking God for Ann. That half-white chick had done well by me no matter what I thought of her.

The tall waiter leaned over me and winked. "Don't worry about a thing, baby," he said in a low voice. Then in his loud voice, said: "You do me the greatest honor, Madam Daveees."

On his way to the kitchen someone stopped him, and I heard him answer to her whisper, "Why, that's Madam Davees. Princess of Abyssinia. Daveees?" he said to another whisper. "Yes, that's an English name. I do believe Madam might have married an English count."

Smiles from all over the car turned on me. I returned them

with a slight nod (my greatest lesson of those days being that American whites, north or south, liked anybody better than they liked American Negroes). When my waiter came back with soup, I whispered, "Hey, what's your name, feller?"

"Eddie to you." Then to the room: "Master Edward Smith, the Third." Smiles and elbow-hunching spread at this waiter trying to make it with the princess, I guess.

He served me in style: roast duck with crispy skin and orange dressing, flowered mashed potatoes, peas and carrots, hot biscuits. For dessert, deep-dish apple cobbler—and the best coffee I have ever tasted. Folks got used to eating like this! Never again the brown bags of fried chicken.

The bill came. He took forever writing it up, then handed it to me with that half-wink. Two dollars! I tipped him ten—five for his pocket, and five for the show. "Baby," he whispered in shock, "you *is* class."

El-e-gant, to keep everybody guessing, I big-smiled around me, then sashayed to the door and out of the dining car, keeping my eyes over the heads of the other waiters. I knew they wanted more than anything to catch my eyes, to sneer me down, to have me talk to them so they could loud-talk me, expose me to that room full of whites. Niggers!

The old-young woman who needed her rest also had her problems. She took so long deciding whether to move her knees, I thought I might have to take another seat. When I did get by her, she twisted her head from me so hard that I had to think hard to remember if I had said something to insult her. I remembered I hadn't wanted chicken. I still didn't want no chicken.

Six P.M. in Washington, D.C. I raced to the ticket counter to be the first off that train on line—which might have been the reason I forgot about my being a princess, and why my eyes got to slipping off the sides of the redneck ticket seller's face when I said, "I want a sleeper ticket to Montgomery, please."

My words struck him dumb. He took a mighty long time to be able to speak, and when he did, he spoke slow so in case I lost his meaning, I'd be sure to pick it up along the way: "Ain't-got-no-sleeping-cars-to-Montgomery."

"Got to be. Ain't I the first one on line?"

"That so? Well, if there is, you ain't standing in the right place to buy 'em."

I stepped aside with my coach ticket and stood listening to the white guy behind me say: "One sleeper to Montgomery," and get it. I thought of going into my special brand of hell-raising. But dealing with a feller sloppy-eyed was not my style—especially when I knew, had known as deep as there was feeling in me, that there was no win. So I spent the rest of my three-hour wait trying to figure which one of the two black redcaps might be the one most likely to want to put one over on the whites. No reading them, except to tell that they never once glanced at the colored passengers grouped together waiting, but kept a lively chatter and grinning going with all the whites.

When the train came in, I took a chance. I went up to the darkest one. "Look, mister, why don't you try to get me on one of them front coaches? I'd sure be beholden to you." I flashed a twenty. It was worth more to me.

His eyes popped at the twenty, but he shook his head, kept shaking his head. "Be more than glad to carry your things, ma'am. But niggers ain't riding nowhere on this train but that Jim Crow car."

"Who says?"

"My job says."

I looked around for the other redcap, saw him burdened down with white folks' luggage, knew that there was no way in the world to get my things on the train alone, so I let ole Blackie take them. But right away I went down to five. And that was more than he'd make from any white.

"A fucking shame," I grumbled as he loaded my things. "Don't make no kinda sense, being treated like slaves. Ain't no more slaves."

"Serves her right." The young-old woman had been looking at me all the while. She waited for me to pass to say that. "Folks ain't got no calling going up north to get them big notions. Nothing I hates worse than one a them biggity niggers. Think she's something."

Seeing I didn't believe in folks talking to the air when they want to get to me, I turned on her. "Yeah, I swear I'm something. What you gonna do about it?" I waited to give her what I ought to have given the ticket seller, the simple-assed porter, the waiters in the dining car who wanted to jump all over me.

"But *you* got to ride in this Jim Crow car same as *we*."

No one ought to have been that happy about a law they had no hand in making. "That don't mean I got to like it." I pushed my face to almost touch hers.

"So? Do something about it—if you thinks you can."

Like she wanted me to slap her so she'd kick my ass. And I wanted more than anything to slap her so she'd try.

"What you gals carrying on so about?" A tall redneck stood looking down at us, ready to enjoy a good fight. "Some old nigra done y'all wrong?"

We stared at him, looked him up and down, then twisted our heads away and marched onto the train. Once inside, we broke our necks getting seats as far from the other as the car allowed. She sat up front, and I gave up the only window seat in the center to sit far in the back next to an old man.

Thankfully, the train plowed right into darkness, and I settled back ready to sleep. But there was no sleep in me.

In the dim light I watched the soot landing on my hand, kept brushing it, smudging it. In the next twenty-four hours folks would take me—and the rest of us—for Al goddamn Jolsons. Then I put my mind to thinking of my good fur jacket. Why had I worn it, warm as it was? Now the soot and grime eating into the skins would make it look like rat fur. Grime, eating into my poor coat, my soul, my mind.

Other folks were dropping off to sleep, and seeing them, like they didn't care, made my eyes open wider, made me evil, eviler. I kept peering down, seeing the thick neck of the young-old Bertha who needed her rest all the way in the front, and wished I had sat next to her, behind her. I'd knock the shit out of her. Every time the train rocked, I'd kick her ass. When she fell off to sleep, I'd slap her upside her head. If she yelled, I'd punch her in her mouth—bop! If she tried to hit back, I'd sock her—crack—on the jaw, knock her to the ground. She'd fall—splat. If she moved to get up, I'd knee her, stomp her. Simple bitch. One thing sure, the next time—if there was a next time—I'd drive. Made no difference if it took me one hundred years and if I drove every mile alone.

"Here, hold these plates." A feeble voice ticked at my ears,

117

exploding my evil thoughts like a bomb. I put out my hands, meek as a baby, to receive the two paper plates the old man put in them.

Everyone else in the coach seemed to be sleeping. The old man took down one big paper bag from which he took out smaller bags. From one bag he pulled fried chicken, put one leg on one of the plates and a backside on the other. Hard-boiled eggs—he shared two. From a third bag came potato salad. He spooned out two big spoonfuls. Then he packed everything back real careful, put them in the shopping bag, and put it up. "That'll last to where we going," he promised.

I hated that I was hungry. Hated that my weak bladder forced me to the toilet that cleaning folks made it their business to forget to clean.

"I know how it be," Pops said when I got back. "Gets used to being up north and forgets what it's like to be back home. Ain't easy. Ain't easy at all."

Forgotten? Hell, no. Folks don't forget what they run from. But it sure wasn't easy—and he was right there—to get away with being a princess up north, then get pushed back to the coalshed by crossing some damn invisible line. In the North I felt like a person and if, like some folks said, that was a lie, it was a lie I went for. That's what living meant to me. Feeling whole.

"Been riding these rails for many a year," Pops said. "Many a year." Thin face, might have once been light-skinned, but weather-browned now. "And every so often I runs into somebody who done forgot. So I brings me enough. When folks gets to sleeping, I gets to eating—them, the hungry ones, get a nose itching. I ain't never alone. Always got me some company. The ones what forgets. Ain't nothing else to do. Man my age don't sleep, no ma'am. So I brings food for me and my company. Heh, heh, heh."

Worn-down teeth, faded eyes. But not a thing wrong with old Pops's appetite or his voice. Matter of fact, he kept the night for his stage. During a spell when he fell quiet, I rushed to ask:

"Pops, you reckon things is ever gonna change down here?"

"Mmmm." He fiddled with his tongue. "Can't rightly say—rightly say. . . ." Then "Only way I sees it, is for all them crackers to die out. But them Yankees'll go long 'fore them crackers. . . .

"Them Yankees, now, they ain't got the what-with to fight off no dirt in they systems. Too clean—too clean. Yes, ma'am. Every man got to have his bit of grit. Bit of grit. Look. . . ." He held out a forkful of potato salad, waited for soot to settle, put it in his mouth, swirled it around, enjoying it before swallowing.

"Them's the things what keeps a man like me alive . . . alive. Makes me strong . . . strong. If I got to a place where warn't no soot, no grit to mix with my something-to-eat, I'd a been long gone . . . long gone. Now them crackers . . . they gets them they share of grit. Hear me, ma'am . . . they share of grit . . . so now they the ones to worry about . . . them crackers."

"What you reckon we better do about them crackers?" I asked, even though I figured he had lived past his good sense.

"Ain't much nobody can do about them," he admitted, " 'cept maybe have babies. Colored folks needs to have lots of babies. Lots of babies. Then we can just set on them . . . set on them real good. . . ."

"Pops, I'm talking about laws. Must be a way to get the laws changed so we don't have to sit in no Jim Crow cars. Don't have to be lynched."

"Oh hell, gal, when I was a li'l bit-a-thing, they had laws. Colored men made laws—we had colored folks in Congress—in *that* Congress. But things got so it didn't suit whites. One excuse after another. One excuse after another . . . got rid of every last one of 'em, they did. See, it ain't no law without power . . . no suh, no law without power. . . . We got to get so we can just set on 'em. Get loads and loads of babies . . . new folks . . . new young folks . . . long as they keep that voting—like colored folks do in the North. Then one day, they look around, and hot dog, there we'll be all around them in that Congress. They'll be took back—yes suh, we'll have us some power then."

"You reckon that they'll just sit there and let us get to the point where we can outvote them, Pops?"

Pops turned that around in his old gray head, then he shook it. Shook it like he was trying to get something loose. "Now that you ask—guess ain't no telling what them dern-fool crackers is likely to do. . . ."

I bit down into the chicken leg. What fool somebody had said I'd never eat fried chicken again? Goo-ood. And somebody had made the hell out of the potato salad, too. Seeing the soot building on that last mouthful, I swirled it around in my mouth. Sure didn't taste no different. It wasn't about to kill me. Might even stop me from dying hungry.

4

Even forever comes to an end. And none too soon. Brother and Mildred's husband, Morris, loaded my bundles in the back of Morris's old Ford. We squeezed in together in front. Tired, dirty, I had enough evil left to jump salty when they didn't make over me and all those presents the way I thought due.

Listening to the quiet in the car, looking out at the old town waiting for light to carve it into shape—the shape I had run from—I damned the ties that bound me to it. Ties that never broke or gave. No matter how far I traveled, they always pulled me back. Cold, sleepy in that dark, I suddenly felt old age touch me, frighten me. I shivered, shivered and sighed. "Oh, my God." Turning to see Brother's sidelong glance slip from my face. I glanced at Morris. His eyes stayed fixed on the road.

So I joked to break the ear-deafening quiet: "Damn, Brother, it's me who done traveled all this way to see you all. And neither one of you even looked at me good. I know I'm dipped in soot, my face looks grease-fried, my hair is nappy, and the fur I'm sporting done turned from mink to skunk. But it sure ain't saying much for y'all's imagination that you can't look past all that shit to me."

No sooner the words were said than I wanted them back. I wanted the quiet again. Wanted to shout: Don't say it. Don't say it. I don't want to hear. . . .

"Dorine . . . Sister's dead. Cancer." Brother's voice, gentle to ease the pain I had hardly begun to feel. "We knew she was doing poorly. Lost a heap of weight. Didn't eat."

Shock. That had to be why I didn't cry. I loved Janie. Loved her most. Soft Janie. Quiet Janie. Long-suffering, bearing the world's troubles—my troubles—never letting on about her own. Now she was gone? What about Son?

"She kept asking for you, Dorine. We sort of hoped you'd get here before."

Shopping had stopped me. What good was all the shopping—the camel-haired coat? I waited for tears to loosen my stricken heart. But only fear rose. Who'd care for Son?

"Who treated her, Brother?"

"Old Doc Mitchell."

"Doc Mitchell!" Old doctor, blind in one eye and had a hard time seeing out the other. Old white man, caring for folks—colored folks, poor white folks—since Mama was a girl. "Why ain't you all taken her to a hospital?" I said to whip up anger, to loosen the stillness of my heart. "Why ain't you all taken her to a decent place? How the fool know what was wrong with her?"

"Please, Dorine." Brother tried to calm me. But I wasn't opting for calmness. "She ain't suffered long."

"How he know she ain't suffered? By sticking that li'l ole light he sticks down people's throats? Folks up north suffer when they got cancer, Brother. Folks down here different?"

"Why you talking like that, Dorine?" Morris said, his tone accusing. "You know the way things is down here. You think we like it? What you suggest we do?"

"Sister's dead and that's all you got to say, Morris?" Schoolteacher Morris knowing all the answers. His resentment hit me hard. "How you know ain't nothing you can do if you ain't tried?" I said.

"You mean leave, Dorine? Like you did?" Of course his resentment came from discussing me with Mildred. She creamed at the sound of her voice condemning me for being in New York.

Getting out of the car in front of the old house, I forced my feet up the path, then up the steps. But they refused to step over the doorsill into the parlor. I stood at the threshold, staring into that room where I had spent my growing years. I wanted to turn and run, keep running.

But the house sprang out to me. Its smells rushed through me. Squeezing me, cutting through my flesh—bloodsucking.

No Sister Janie to act as a shield between me and it. No Sister to be a buffer between me and my family—that family waiting to grieve with me, shorn of speech, wide, dark eyes drinking me into them, cutting off my last chance to escape.

Dry-eyed, I struggled against that final step, hating them, pulling away from them, from their grief. Then Mildred ran out of the kitchen.

"Dorine, Dorine." She threw herself at me, pushed herself into my arms, crying on my shoulder. Straightened hair, long, stringy, hanging to her back, face half mad with grief. "We buried her yesterday. We tried to wait."

I looked over her shoulder to the kids heaped together on the old couch: Lil and Ruthie—Mildred's two, six and five years old; Sister Janie's two, Jennie Mae and Jane, named after Mama, around the same age. I looked around, saw a neighbor standing with a bundle in her arms. I looked beyond her and saw Son. Fat, black, eighteen months old and walking. He leaned against Joseph's one good leg, pulling on him for attention. But his Papa Joseph sat, back to the room, head bowed, grieving for his wife. I kept looking at Son, wanting him to feel me in him, to look at me with love—the kind he was showing his uncle. But Son kept pulling at the crippled man, pulling on the one he knew as Papa.

The girls, though, looked at me. Supported me with their eyes. Those eyes said it was hard for me, for me who had not expected it. Harder for me than for them, who had lived knowing of its coming. Nor did they look away when Brother and Morris got to hauling their boxes in. They had to know they were filled with prizes for them. But they kept looking at me, wanting to comfort me. Suddenly I loved them—loved them all—my family. I walked toward them. But the neighbor with the bundle stopped me. "This is Janie's youngest," she said. I stopped to look at the bundle—a baby. Janie had had another baby when there was Son?

I looked from her to the walls, and saw finger marks where I had spent all of my young life scrubbing. On the floor were bits of paper and hairpins, a safety pin. A wet diaper hung on the back of a chair. The disorder loosened my tongue. "Oh no," I said shaking my head. "This will never do. No matter what the sorrow, ain't nothing worse than living in a slovenly house."

The next morning, as sunlight washed my eyes, I jumped out of bed and opened the bedroom door, calling: "Okay, okay, you all, it's cleaning-up time."

Jennie Mae came out of her room sleepy-eyed to stand in the doorway. "It's Sunday. Folks don't do housework on Sundays."

Mama's sacred scripture jumped to my mouth: "Cleanliness is next to Godliness." Then added, "Ain't no way in the world for Him to fault you for working to get next to Him."

In the shortest time the rhythm of the house took over—and it was a good rhythm. We washed down walls, changed bed linens, aired mattresses, scrubbed floors—brought them back almost to their natural whiteness. Then we got to taking that old stove apart. We scrubbed it, burned it, and put it back together. "Sister must have took her vengeance out on Mama, allowing this much grease to accumulate on this old stove," I complained. When we had finished, I took a white handkerchief and wiped it, then showed them the spotless handkerchief. They only smiled.

Son had been looking at us through it all. "See," I said to him. "This is what's waiting for you the next time I come around." He ran from me to stand in the doorway of Joseph's room. "Ain't no sense in you running," I joked. "You can run, but you ain't going nowhere—not from me, anyway."

He ran into the room, where he stood rubbing his back on Joseph's chair and looking out of his big, Dorine-looking buck-eyes. A twinge in my heart almost made me say I was fooling. Instead I turned my attention to looking over the parlor and the kitchen. The sparkle cheered me. "Now that wasn't hard, was it?" I said to the girls. "And this is how I want to see this place the next time I come."

"What you mean, the next time?" Mildred said, coming out of the bedroom. "Dorine, I hope you ain't thinking of running all over the country now that Janie's dead. Not with all these kids here to care for."

That squeezing took hold of me again, cutting my breath. Somehow, somewhere, something had set me up for the moment. Even before I woke with my mouth spouting words of soap and lye, those words were waiting to be said.

"What I been doing if not caring for them, Mildred?" Even to my own ears my voice sounded thin. "After all, Janie ain't worked a lick in her life. Joseph neither since he done lost his leg. Ain't that caring?"

"Money ain't everything, Dorine. These kids needs a woman's hand."

"That's what your hands are for, Mildred." I spoke, hoping to remind her that some of that money I sent every month went to her and her schoolteacher husband.

"I got my family, Dorine." Mildred had been living to tell me those words. "After all, Brother's been with us since we got married. That ain't fair to Morris. I been here tending Janie since she got sick. That ain't fair to me."

"She your sister. You live here. Who else should be tending her?"

Seeing the trapped look in my eyes, hearing my words getting thinner and weaker, gave her strength. She stood, her lean, never-to-be-fat self solid before me, her eyes wild, as though daring me to make it by her to the door. That squeezed me into being nasty:

"And their father? Ain't nothing wrong with him. Nothing wrong with Joseph except he got one leg. What's wrong with his mouth? His hands? Sure ain't nothing wrong with his thing. He ain't had but one child until he lost his leg. Now he got three. How come he had to go on and have another baby after . . ."

"Son?" Son being brought up as Sister's own forced her to talk soft so the others didn't hear. But she added: "You old enough to share in the family responsibilities now, Dorine. I ain't gonna take care of my kids and all of Janie's, too."

The clean smell of the house hit my nostrils. I looked around the kitchen and the white walls, lanced by the light of the sun, smiled. A wind rustled through the house, shaking a loose branch outside the kitchen window, and the branch hitting against the windowpane sounded like applause. Goose bumps crisscrossed my body, itched my palms, and to show her there was more than a little strength left in me, I pushed past her, grabbed my purse from the bedroom, and left the house.

Montgomery had not changed. Walking from the dirt road where the colored folks lived to the paved streets where the white houses were built, I had no special direction. All I knew was that some way, I had to leave. I had not come to Montgomery to stay. Nor did I have any intention of bringing any kin, not even Son, back to New York with me. Montgomery was for kids. New York for me. Yet here I was, trapped. The kids had me. The town. . .

I kept noticing how black folks still stepped out of the way for whites, smiling, friendly, "How do." At the old grocery store I stood where I could see the back entrance where black boys wrestled, played marbles, or just stood waiting for the whites coming and going through the front door to be served.

"Lindbergh . . ." Hearing the name made me stop automatically to listen to the crackers leaning against a picket fence talking. ". . . made it. Ought to have dropped in the sea. . . ." "Yeah, make good picking for them sharks. . . ."

Noticing me listening, their red faces, faded eyes hardened: Yankees, foreigners, big-city niggers ought to have been born just to die. Not my world—not my world.

Over at the black Baptist church, men and women, moving slow, smiling quiet, nodding heads together in spiritual accord, their hearts soothed, souls healed by the fiery sermon of a hell-raising preacher. Spring straws, white gloves to lighten dark clothes. Respectable. Lord knows, black folks sure were the most humble, the most respectable folks living. No, Montgomery hadn't changed, that was for sure. And I was even more sure when some respectful sisters stopped talking to look me up and down, their eyes staying a long time on my hatless head that early Sunday afternoon.

Walking, walking, walking. Walking, walking, walking. I had never before walked to Miss Elizabeth's—long gone along with her gentle ways. The flowers that pushed out yearly had gone to hell at the back of the house. The shade trees—under which the Mama-cooked lunches had been served and eaten, along with soft talk, polite laughter—had all been cut down. Now the well-tended lawn, purposeless, spread out only for its looks. A new breed of laughter roared from the open windows.

The old man I flagged down for his two worn mares and buggy earned the five dollars promised with his good nature and love of gossip, more than for the strength of his mares' legs. During the long ride leading out of the town, he filled me in with news, past and present, of folks I knew—most I didn't—as we clickety-clacked along the lonely road that had more memories of my raped youth than he had stories to tell.

Master Norton's country house, as dead as its owner, still looked grand through the tall grass that had grown way above my head. Grass had replaced the paths that led from the main road to the gate, and from the gate to the house.

Vines and brambles struggled against me as I fought my way to the back of the house. Wild birds shrieked at my strange appearance. Insects scurried out of reach of my feet or grabbed hold of my ankles and bit. Big, buxom yellow-and-black bees kept forcing me in one direction until I came to the bordering fence leading to an open field. Judging from the distance from the house, it must have been the back lawn where the first car I had ever ridden in had been kept. The road the car had taken to rejoin the main road was also overgrown with grass, grass that joined the woods beyond.

With my back to the fence, I looked through the tall weeds, through the hundreds of winging butterflies, hopping birds, recalling to mind the distance between land at the back of the house and the road. Then I saw the crosses—two—side by side. Working my way toward them despite the biting insects, my fear of bees, the tricky ropelike undergrowth that snared my ankles, I finally came to stand before them. I stood beside the highest mound, looking down at the grave—Master Charles Norton's grave.

Perhaps there was an answer to my coming here. I didn't know. I waited—waited for a sign. I hadn't walked all day and traveled this far just to look down on the grave of a soulless man. And given the fact that he was soulless, how could he give me a sign? Yet I stood. The warmth of the sun pressed on my shoulders; the air around buzzed with life; small nameless insects swarming over the tall grass hit against my face, got in my eyes, and were pulled in with the breath I breathed in. Yet I stood. And as I stood I thought of Mildred, heard her voice from before:

"What makes you think you can just pick up and leave Montgomery? You got responsibilities. Janie needs you." I heard myself answer: "You here, ain't you? How come you can't help Janie?"

"I got to go to school" had been her excuse then. Mildred had been the only one of us girls who cared about school. She had gone to the eighth grade. "I can't look after the house, help Janie, and keep up in school."

"Well, that's what you gonna have to do," I had answered. " 'Cause I'm leaving. I hate Montgomery."

"Hate Montgomery? Where else you know?"

"No place. But if the train takes me to hell by mistake, that's all right, too."

"You blaspheme!" Shocked. "Do you know what happens to young girls up north?" I thought of telling her what happens to young girls in Montgomery. Instead I said:

"If I was old enough to work in white folks' kitchens when I turned eight, I'm old enough to cut out of Montgomery now I'm thirteen."

"That's the truth." Janie had spoken up for me. "Dorine been working same as any grown woman. So she got the right to leave if that's what she want."

"You holding Dorine to her selfish ways, Sister."

"Enough, Mildred." Janie, the oldest, the sweetest, the quietest, let us get away with most things, but when she spoke, we listened. "No one got a right calling Dorine selfish. She always shared with us and you know it."

Remembering how I had always given them pennies while stashing away dollars, her words shamed me. "Anyway, Dorine ain't like the rest of us," she added, talking good sense. "I reckon she rightly belongs north." That had settled matters. Then Master Norton came.

We had not seen him for a long time. Miss Fanny had died before Mama, and had been sick long before that. He had had no excuse for needing me. When Mama died, he had sent food and money. So when he walked into the house Sister greeted him, apologizing:

"We ain't had the time to come over to thank you, Master Norton. But we do appreciate what you done."

"I know it ain't easy for y'all now that Jane is gone. No one working and all," he had said. "So I come to offer Dorine work. She can come stay with me."

Big man. Kindly man. Standing tall in that room, his good intentions gleaming like a halo around him. "That's mighty kind of you, Master Norton." Mildred spoke before the spit had dried on his mouth.

"I can't come with you, Master Norton," I said.

"Dorine got plans of her own," Sister explained.

"Plans? What kind of plans can make her turn away from ten dollars a week?"

If a fly had pissed on cotton we'd have thought it a clap of thunder. Ten dollars! Mama had never made more than two dollars a week in her entire life.

"Every week!" Mildred's voice thinned, making me think we'd have to pick her up off the floor.

"I ain't giving up my plans."

"Don't decide now, li'l Dorine." He smiled, sad, understanding. "I'll be by tomorrow for your answer."

He knew us! God, he knew us! No sooner had the door shut when Mildred turned on Sister. "Janie, you ain't gonna let Dorine do no fool thing like going off and leaving all that money."

My first real knowledge in this world was of how money goes around changing folks and them not knowing it. Yet it hurt when Sister turned to me: "Dorine," she said, "Master Norton's been mighty good to us. Now that he ain't got no missus. . . ."

Trapped, feeling every hope I had slipping away, I shouted: "What I care what Master Norton ain't got? Ain't nothing changed. I'm leaving."

"All that money . . ." Mildred's eyes looked glazed.

"I got money!" I snapped at her. "I got all the money I'll ever need."

"All you needs, sure 'nough?" Sister's quiet eyes puzzled into mine. "All, Dorine? 'Nough to keep you till you gets your first job. . . ?"

Years of hoarding seemed almost to spill out onto that floor, hoarding and deceiving. I hated her knowing I had ever deceived her. So I wiped my mouth dry and bowed my head. When Master Norton came the next day, there I waited, packed bag and baggage, with my happy sisters waving me on.

But the second the car got under way, I got to crying. I cried and cried all the way out of town and down that lonesome country road that had been our fucking station. "What's the matter, Dorine?" he wanted to know. "You mean you ain't happy coming to stay in my big house?"

"No, suh, I ain't."

"Seems to me you'd be right glad to look after me—Miss Fanny being gone and all—I ain't got me nobody."

I kept the tears coming; my nose got to running. "I don't want to stay."

"We can get a li'l piece anytime we wants, if you stay. Ain't you gonna like that?"

"No. I don't want that."

"You liked it."

"No! I ain't never liked it."

Quiet. Quiet. Quiet except for my sniffing. Not looking, but wanting to look, to see surprise touch those quiet, gentle eyes. Did hurt pull his thin lips down, or did they stay pulled together, the way Miss Fanny's had when she looked after us going off together? I wanted to see, but didn't want to be caught looking.

"You mean you ain't *never* liked it?"

"No! I never liked it. I don't like nobody touching me! I don't like nobody to go in me."

Quiet. Then, "I didn't know that. If I had, I swear I never would have . . ."

Mother wit made me let that lie circle the car, knowing that he had made himself believe that all the finagling, the force he had used to get my maidenhead, the strength he had pitted against my young girl's strength, had been *my* doing. To dispute him meant giving him a chance to take me right there, exchange his feeling for mine, pretend that my shouts of pain, my struggling, were proof of my liking it. I kept crying, letting the quiet do its work.

"No matter what I say, you aim to go?"

"Yes, suh."

"Where to?"

"Cleveland."

"Where you getting the money?"

"I got the first five dollars you ever give to me, Master Norton."

"How much you got in all?"

" 'Most five hundred dollars."

"That's mighty fine. Mighty fine saving for a li'l gal. Ain't no wonder I always known you'd make a real fine woman. 'Most likely a right rich woman, one day."

He drove to the house, left me in the car, and went inside. He came back with a stack of bills. One hundred dollars. "To help you on the way." Not wanting him to confuse gratitude with a change of heart, I took it without thanks. He drove me to the station, waited for the train, and put me on it. Only when the train started did I wipe my eyes and blow my nose. I stared at him as he waved good-bye. I had made it. I'll never see you again, master. Never see you again, master childfucker, pussysucker, never see you again. Spinning around my head, spinning to the turn of the wheels: master, master childfucker, pussysucker, childfucker, pussysucker, childfucker, pussysucker.

Yet here I was, my feet rooted in the ground, next to what was left of him in this world. This world rimmed by the dark tones of a setting sun, where soft winds rippled the high grass so that grass hitting on grass released sighs, deep sighs that spread and spread and spread out of hearing, where winging butterflies and pinpoint gnats joined in a silence that forced a loneliness within a loneliness, a deep calmness that I joined—for why leave? This calm came as close to freedom as I had ever known. Rooted to that spot, thinking of Tom, of Ann, of Sonny, of Big H. What did I want from them? What did I need, here in the center of peace? I stood a long time—so long that the day lost the last of its glow. A coolness fell.

Then a strong wind blew, rustling the grass. Whispers sounded in my ears. Fingers touched the back of my neck, trailed a line to the tip of my spine. The hairs at the back of my neck stirred. My feet tore themselves out of the ground. I found myself flying, my feet treading the grass like Christ must have treaded water.

I fell into the buggy, out of breath. "Hey, what's happening?" the old man asked. "Something bother you out there?"

"Ain't nothing bothered me," I said, panting. "But what say we put some life in these old mothers, feller? Let's get some distance between us and here."

Dawn the next morning, a knocking at the door woke me. I heard Jennie Mae talking at the front door, and a second later Brother walked into my room. "Dorine, you up?"

"Yeah, I'm up." He came to sit at the foot of my bed.

"Got to talk to you, Dorine."

"What about, Brother?" I tried to read the expression on his face in the dimness of the room, but he kept his head turned from me.

"Mildred and me—we been fussing."

"What about?"

"She wants me to give up school and come over here to look after Joseph and the kids."

I bolted upright in bed. Brother was seventeen, and there was nothing to say a seventeen-year-old wasn't accountable just because he was a boy.

"I ain't quitting school, Dorine." He put the burden right back on my shoulders. "I got plans."

"What plans you got, Brother?"

"I aim to be a doctor, Dorine."

"A who?" I knew light-skinned doctors here and there. But I only knew two dark-skinned doctors. They were in New York and they were West Indians. "Here? In Montgomery? Where you going to school?"

"Right here. In Montgomery. Until my sophomore year. Then I'll go to Fisk—or maybe north."

There were none too many dark-skinned boys going to college.

"That ain't easy as you think, Brother."

"I ain't planning an easy life, Dorine. I know what's out there for me. But I'm not about to be a preacher; and the way I hate to pick cotton—I can't be a sharecropper, not if I tried. Settling for a railroad job don't excite me none, and I'd die before I'd be a porter."

I studied Brother's face in the shadowy light of the room. And it came to me that he was so much a stranger that if I'd seen him on the streets of New York, I might pass him by. Darker than the rest of us, his face had a sweetness, with teeth curling out so that he had to work to keep his upper lip down around them. His eyes were soft, but dead-center of them reminded me of me. To buck him was to lose him. Why lose him if I could use him?

Just like that I knew what had to be done. "Brother, I know it's hard for folks who wants to study to hang around—cotton picking and all that. Look, you go on back to Mildred's and get your things.

You and me, we'll work something out. And don't you worry, Brother. Long as I live you'll get your schooling—until there ain't no schooling left to get."

In less time than it takes to tell it, I had dressed and was hurrying to the trolley to take me across town to Miss Jessica. I knew I'd never be able to ask Mildred to look after Son, but now I felt free, released from doing time. On the trolley, I walked to the back right along with the rest of the black folks, as though sitting in the front seat of anything was stranger to my knowledge.

I gazed out the window at the trees fleshing out of darkness, at cats stretching out of sleep, heard dogs bark, roosters crow. I hummed. Dawn had that effect on me, whether hitting the road with Tom or just walking out into a new day. The lifting of the burden of darkness, the stripping of sleep from my mind, made everything new, different. I hummed. Problems didn't exist, after all, except in the mind. Then I thought of Sister.

It struck me hard. Dear Sister, dead six days, buried only three, and I had yet to shed a tear. I closed my eyes, trying to force tears. None came. But I'd just as soon leave off grieving for New York—if I ever got away from Montgomery to get back to New York.

Miss Jessica lived in a shack next door to the tar-paper shack of Big Willie Hopkins, with her brood of children nobody knew who had fathered. She washed clothes—and had since I remembered—to make a living. She also kept an eye on tetched Big Will, keeping his clothes clean for the game he shared with her when he went hunting.

Making my way through the woods that ran along the side of the trolley tracks, then up an alley where pigs lay scratching their backs in mud, I turned a bend around a clump of trees, and just like that Miss Jessica sprang to life, like I had thought her up that morning. She stood in her yard, bending over her washtub, scrubbing clothes. Roosters, pigs, dogs raising hell as I walked toward her, and she kept scrubbing, not hearing. I walked right up to her and said, "Howdy, Miss Jessica." She jumped, looked at me, narrowed her eyes to study me, then said:

"Seems I know you."

"I'm Miss Janie's grandchild."

"Bless my soul." Sparingly built, wiry, she had looked the same since I was born. Wiping her hands on her faded cotton dress: "You must be the one they call Dorine? Big-city girl?"

"Yes'm."

"Heared of your sister's passing. Sure am sorry. Janie was a mighty fine gal. Come home for the burial?"

"Got here a bit late."

"Oh? Too bad. Know you grievin' 'bout that."

"Something awful."

"There's another sister, too—Mildred?"

"Yes'm."

"Must be hard on her."

"Mighty hard."

"And Brother—a fine young man. . . ."

"Yes'm." Hard cutting through southern manners. "He's the one I come to see you about, ma'am. Brother's needing some help. He'll be staying on with Joseph."

"Tut, tut, tut, poor Joseph. Must be hard—him with only one leg and all."

"Yes'm."

"You think I can help?"

"Yes'm. That's why I'm here, ma'am."

"Do tell."

"Miss Jessica, there's the baby, you know. Bubba. He's in the arms. Then there's Son who ain't but eighteen months. The girls—they ain't no trouble. They right smart. But the babies—they be needing a woman's hand. Washing, cooking, keeping things clean. . . ." Miss Jessica had kids that were not much younger than I was. "Brother will be looking after things. The way I see it, Miss Jessica, I'll be sending money home every month. And in gratitude, I'm sure Joseph will see to it that you gets—maybe as much as ten dollars. . . ?"

"That much?"

I had figured I could get her for five. But I had to make it hard for her to refuse. "Worth it to me, ma'am. I'd stay myself—only I got this important business? I'm good at my word. . . ." The faded edges of her eyes—which had stuck to my thinking through the years—brightened. Ten dollars could go far. . . . That left but one more worry; I tackled that back at the house.

Going into Joseph's room, I sat on the bed and looked at him where he sat in a chair, facing the wall. Son stood at his side, still trying to get his attention. I hardened myself not to look at him. "Joseph," I said, "I know that Janie's done spoiled you right along with the rest of them. That was Janie's way. But don't you be sitting there trying to follow her to the grave. Hell, these kids belong to you as much as they did to her, and she did her bit by them—and by you—while she was here. Now it's up to you. I'm going back to New York. If you wants, I'll send you one of them chairs for you to get around in. But I ain't staying here to look after your kids. They yours; if you don't want to look after them, no one else will."

If he told me to take Son and go, I'd have lost. I held my breath, waiting. At first he sat, not moving. I waited. He looked down at the fat head leaning against his leg, which had been cut off at the knee. A tear rolled down his cheek. He laid a hand on Son's head, and I breathed again.

Lord, if anyone had told me that I'd ever have been glad to get on a Jim Crow train, I'd have called them all kinds of liars. But get on I did. Happy: I welcomed grime and soot, getting back to New York, to Tom Rumley—and my future.

5

"Ain't she sweet? Give her space on this old street." "Looka here, looka here, looka here. Look what you gettin' when the chippies get to steppin'."

Black studs sporting their best, holding up the corners of Harlem, spends half their lives calling after hincty chicks. If the chicks got nice, the studs would haul ass, and if the studs stopped calling, the chicks would start bawling—standoff all the way.

"Bay-bee, you the reason I done give up ca-ream-y coffee for cho-co-let." "I'll let you keep me blue, baby, if you let me have some of you."

High heels clicking, hips slightly switching, hincty all the way. Head high, eyes on the bright lights, the reds, the greens, the ever-moving lights that dazzle. Strutting toward my future. Yet actually, so much time had passed between the first thought and the act that the excitement had fizzled. Pure need had driven me out of the house. Need to be with a man. Need to be out on the streets of Harlem again.

Shimmering in white, man-catching white, strutting down the avenue on my way to The Club, to my promised future, I turned down a block—the wrong block. I knew it from the feel: the dark, the crowd—that certain kind of heat. Heat of folks crowded to-gether—sitting on stoops, looking toward the bright lights, the ave-nue lights. Kids playing from the stoops out onto the streets. Men sipping from bottles wrapped in brown paper. Folks staring (jeal-ous), nudging each other as I walked by.

"Hey, girl," a man shouted. "Where you goin'? A house rent party?" A mistake. "Hey, take me with you. . . ." I heard his fast running feet, and although I knew he was standing in one spot, pretending, nonetheless I quickened my steps, making it to the next avenue.

I hated walking on side streets. Sporting folks seldom do. We hated to think of folks not making it. One slip, and there we'd be. Why remind ourselves? We hustled to get out. Hustled to stay out. So we walked avenues and the broad main streets.

On the next block the low music of The Club, sounding through the door, welcomed me. I climbed the steps of the brown-stone, rang the bell, and when the door opened, walked by the for-mal-looking gent who had opened it and through the foyer as though I was a constant visitor. Standing in the doorway, I looked around for one familiar face. I saw a few. A couple of baseball players, friends of Tom's. In one corner I spotted the numbers banker Casper Holstein, sitting with another "king" of policy, a man someone had pointed out to me as Wilfred Brunder. Most of the diners, though, I had never seen. They looked classy, well dressed, and spoke low. But I knew that downstairs in the gaming room fast action was going on. And upstairs in Big H's office, he had a direct line to the Wall Street Boys where they called in the number of the day. And a line to the racetracks where his horses ran.

Standing in the doorway, shimmering, I waited until even the murmur of voices quieted, until heads turned and jaws dropped open, before I walked into the room—cool, proud, glad of being a hit after my sweaty moments on the next block. Then my eyes strayed to the far corner of the room where a woman sitting alone kept turning the pages of a newspaper. My pride stumbled, begged me to pay heed to the door at my back inviting me out.

I half turned just as his soft voice said at my shoulder:

"Dorine? Dorine Davis. This is a most delightful surprise." The familiar round, brown face, the wanting-me look in the honest, warm, serious eyes, put me at my ease.

"I was just passing and I thought—"

"And you remembered my invitation. Good. You have no idea the pleasure. . . ."

His hand under my elbow, Big H guided me to the corner table and the lady. "Monica, you do remember Dorine—Dorine Davis?"

The lady looked up, saw me, looked through me. "Oh?" she said. "Yes—isn't this the young lady we met the night of Lindbergh?" (For years we remembered times as Lindbergh, before and after.)

"Exactly."

"So happy to meet you again," she said.

"Pleased, I'm sure." It didn't take much guessing to know that she was no happier than I was pleased.

"Sit down. Sit down." Big H pulled out a chair. "I'll be back in a few minutes. I am in the midst of a short discussion." He pointed to a group of men at a table.

Mama's lifelong preachment jumped to mind: "You ain't got to have learning to use mother wit." My mother wit told me to get the hell out. I sat. Seeing Big H walking away to join his friends, I bit back shouting: Is this the table you keep for your women? I smiled at Monica. "Hope he doesn't hurry on my account."

She looked up pleasantly, then went right on reading. The thought jumped to mind: Are they married? No. But are they friends too tight to loosen?

The men with Big H were of another world. It stuck out on their faces—a certain self-confidence. It also showed in the respect of other customers who looked from time to time over to their table, and in the faces of the men who stood over them, listening to but never interrupting their conversation. Five of them sat at the table. But aside from Big H, only two stood out to me. One a light-skinned, thin-faced, dapper gent in gray, with a twirling mustache and goatee. He had fiery eyes that he kept flashing over Monica. The other was tall and brown-skinned. He had long legs, unable to fit under the table, which he crossed as he reared back in his chair, relaxing. A waiter stood at attention a short distance from them, awaiting their whim.

"Strange joint," I said.

Monica's head came up. "Strange? How so?" Hearing the displeasure in her very British, very West Indian accent, I shrugged and tried to change the subject.

"Sort of busy . . ." What else? The room itself was so low-keyed, it tended to be a bore. But everybody and their brothers knew that The Club had the fastest action in town.

"Yes. Quite," Monica said and bent her head again. I gave the goateed gent competition studying her thick black hair so carefully set thickness on thickness, right down to the V of her stylish bob.

Sitting, she still looked tall. Fleshed out so that one line showed to the bend of her neck. Ivory shone across her broad cheekbones under tight skin, which she never wrinkled even to smile. The lids of her slanting Chinese eyes were unlined as she moved her eyes from place to place. Her black, black eyelashes, sooty black, fascinated me, made it hard to tear my eyes away to examine her face. When I did and noticed the thick, full lips, the flat nose-bridge, I wanted to pull my stomach up from where it had fallen, wanted to shout: Your features ain't good. But with all that beauty, what the hell were "good" features?

Someone had loved this chick from birth. Somebody had cared. Beauty had been branded so deep into her skin, it had burned through her flesh right to her soul. Just looking at her forced my mind to take account of the black women I had known, heard about, had seen with their high-yeller daughters. I remembered the combing of those heads of long, black, curly hair, the ironing of those pretty eyelet or stick-out organdy dresses, the pulling on of long white stockings with the care to make them fit—no wrinkles, no creases. High-buttoned shoes polished to outshine the brightness of the sun as they went to school, to parties, to competition with other light-skinned youngsters with their stick-out dresses. On their mother's black faces that look—a mixture of pride and fear—fear that their precious possession might by some oversight of the Lord, or some simple act of nature, attract a speck of dust, dirt, or— God forbid—the coveting eye of a poor dark-skinned stranger. No woman—black, white, or in between—unless born of royal blood, had ever come through such care.

The well-cared-for, well-bred look of Monica kept my attention, until a voice from the other table spoke so I heard it above the music. I looked over to where the tall, handsome man sat frowning. "Du Bois," he said. "Whatever you might think of Garvey, we are here to see how best to go about preventing his deportation."

"Whatever I think is hardly at issue here, Frazier." The light-skinned, goateed man spoke, his eyes still on Monica. "I'm the first to admit that Garvey is a man of extraordinary ability. It's he who shows animosity toward me. Mention my name and he starts foaming at the mouth."

"Can you blame him?" the man Frazier asked. "Especially since the government keeps using your articles about him as proof that black people are against him."

"That happens to be the government's problem, not mine. My articles may be critical, but they surely can't blind honest men to the facts. Garvey's followers number in the millions."

"But we must be together on this," Frazier said. "Defrauding by mail! My God, what a trumped-up charge! If they'd charge those who really use the mail to defraud, the jails would be overflowing. What I'm suggesting is that you ought to temper your criticism— right now at any rate."

"I'm a critical man, Frazier. I write critical articles. I've been saying for years that Garvey is misguided. He's an honest man—I believe a very sincere one. But a fool. Why should I change?"

"You feel no responsibility in this?"

"I do. But if I were to openly support him, I fear Garvey will choose to remain in jail. He thinks I'm worse than the devil because my skin is light."

"Come on, Du Bois," Frazier said. "Perhaps your trip to Liberia might have a little something to do with that."

Du Bois's head snapped away from Monica. His mustache quivered. A silence settled over the table. "I have nothing to apologize for," he said, his voice clear, sharp, determined to fill the space left by the sudden silence in the room. "I went to Liberia with the most honorable of intentions, and came back with the most honorable of intentions. My report can vouch for that."

But another man looked up smiling slyly. "Du Bois, you have to admit that having gone as Coolidge's representative—"

"I admit nothing." Du Bois cut him short. "I am more convinced than ever that Liberia will achieve greater independence if aided by this country."

"Unhappily," Big H put in, "the Negro people will always be suspicious of those of us who work with this government. They feel we are betrayers of their cause. Going to Africa as minister plenipotentiary was bound to raise questions. It's a heavy mantle. I face the same problem when I have to deal with men in the capital. But what are we to do? How can we refuse to work with men we believe are sincere? What we are here for tonight and what we must try to come to—is some kind of consensus on the best approach of trying to prevent Garvey's being deported."

"Exactly," Frazier said. "Nothing can be gained by being overcritical of Garvey, except to give his enemies fuel against the black people."

"Frazier," Du Bois said. "Believe me, I'm concerned as you that Garvey's movement not be stopped. Garvey's case is pure and simple—a violation of the First Amendment. Garvey's right to free speech."

"My God, what oversimplification!" Frazier uncrossed long legs to lean over the table. "Man, the government is sparing no effort in trying to muzzle black folks by beheading them—and you talk of it being a simple matter of free speech?"

Big H put a hand on Frazier's. "It's true, there are those who use our articles to divide us. But does that mean we must deny ourselves our right of honest debate? Must we always look over our shoulders before we write, speak? Or can we demand our difference—and still retain the right to condemn this, or anything we oppose?"

"Okay," Frazier said. "Supposing that the First Amendment is Garvey's best case. How do we go about convincing him that it's in his best interest to let our lawyers defend him?"

"Ah-ha." The goateed man pointed his finger. "To convince him!" He twisted the ends of his mustache. "Will that pompous ass allow men qualified in the workings of the law to replace him as his defender? That, gentlemen, is the crucial question that will determine the fate of your Marcus Mosiah Garvey, President of the Provisional Republic of Africa. His nonsensical belief in his divine powers. Not any article that I shall write now—or ever."

Heads in the room turned as his voice rose. Men standing around the table got to whispering.

Bored, not getting anything from even the music, I yawned. I looked around at the pictures on the walls—scenery mostly, some houses, a picture of a king and queen—all in heavy polished wood frames. The heavy drapes at the window were dark blue. Not interesting. I looked down at my fingers tapping the table, noticed the bright red polish showing up the big-knuckled dry-from-lye-and-brown-soap skin, lying close to Monica's long smooth-fingered stranger-to-work hands with their well-shaped unpolished nails. I eased mine off the table, sneaked my silk gloves from my purse, slipped them on, then threw back my hand on the table and went to tapping again.

Monica never noticed. Her head bowed over the newspaper showed her trying to follow the conversation at the other table without appearing to. Tired of the quiet, I said: "Sure is taking them a long time to finish their business."

The beautiful, nonsmiling face looked up. "Big H is an exceedingly busy man." She spoke slowly, taking each word apart. "A man with such a complexity of interests and enterprises must by the very nature of his involvement have little time for inconsequential matters."

I passed that through my mind—once, twice—then looked over my shoulder. No one stood there. I looked back into her slanting eyes. No laughter. She had to be talking to me!

"Oh de-air." I got my best British accent going. "When Big H *invited me* he-air, I had no idea of the configeration and derigumation that I'd find."

Her eyebrows shot up. "Beg pardon?" No wrinkles on her brow.

Hell, the woman had to be way older than me—at least twenty-six! Yet no way to stick a pin to get even.

"Yes, indeed." I waved my silk-gloved hand. "I satuate and insituate that of course Mr. Big H had to be a man of means. So I stultified when I decided to arrive. I certainly didn't expect all the convecation and stuff."

That's right, bitch. Sit there and stare. I might never have read a book in my life, but one damn thing, you ain't read every one ever written. And you damn sure don't know every word in the diction-ary. "And it's all so aggravating, don't you think?" Like she had turned to stone, the way she sat. I asked a question, fool, answer it. I kept smiling.

She raised her eyes to look over my head. I turned to see Big H standing over me, looking at her. An understanding of laughter passed quietly between them and it burned right through me. I jumped to my feet.

"I had no idea that you were this individual with all these interectives." I kept on. If I was wrong, then dammit, I was wrong. Go ahead and laugh, simple motherfucker. But laugh loud so that everyone can hear. Go and laugh and leave me the hell on alone. "If I had known, I'd never have devored to come."

"Dorine," Big H said, smiling. "Look, I want you to meet—"

"Sorry, but interesting things have been rendered onto me. Don't have time now—I must trilly on. Toodle-oo."

Burning, smile ground into my face, I switched by the lot of them and out of The Club. All that goddamn talking, talking, all the world-changing.

I walked home in a sweat, hating them, and looking at myself in the mirror, I said to my pretty brown face: "So—that's the end of *that* future. If that isn't the shortest, goddamndest romance ever dreamed up." Then I really got mad, thinking that the fools never did get to know that they had been in the presence of the greatest big-time booster ever.

Still, I expected him to call. And when he didn't show that day, and the next and the next, a madness started growing in me. It was one thing for me to walk out on him, another for him to ignore it. I knew I hadn't misread the slime beneath the warm, honest interest in those eyes.

I was still mad the day the messenger brought the flowers. Long-stemmed roses. I stopped the boy before he got to the elevator. "Hey feller, come back here and read this for me."

"What? I got to read it too?"

"Yeah, because depending on who it's from, you might have to take it back."

He took out the card from the box, and read: "Tonight at eight. Must see you—Big H."

I had expected him to beg. He hadn't. I kept the flowers. But I had news for him. Being a woman didn't keep me home waiting. And a dozen roses was no payback for a burning face. By eight o'clock I'd be so far from home, he'd need a bloodhound to find me. And at eight sharp, I began to dress—stitch by stitch: one sheer black negligee, one pair of mules, two sprays of perfume.

It would be a ninety-degree day in the north pole before a no-account sucker chased me from my house. He wanted to play. I'd put him through some changes then send him back to his Monica. Laugh, Monica baby, just keep on laughing.

At nine o'clock, after I had combed my hair for the tenth time, oiled my body and wiped it to a dull shine for the sixth, perfumed myself so that I got to smelling like a sixth-rate whore, I thought of throwing my coat over my negligee, floating on down to The Club, walking in and going up to their table, saying real loud: "Baby, those beautiful flowers you sent." All the while letting my coat slip off slow, easing it down to the floor. . . .

The bell rang. I went to the door to find him standing there, a bottle of champagne pushed out to me.

"Dorine, I'm sorry to be late." His voice, so soft, after my long wait, brought the tears. "Come, come, what's the matter?" he said. "What's worth all those tears?"

"My sister." I kept crying. "She died. Seems I never get a chance to grieve." That was no lie. Not since leaving Montgomery had I shed the tears I had planned to.

"Dorine, you're too young and too adorable to ever grieve," he said, following me into the bedroom, where I'd gone for a handkerchief. I blew my nose. "You think so?" I had waited. I had known he'd come. And here he was. Where were those cusswords I had been planning?

"I do. I've never met anyone so adorable. I haven't been able to keep you off my mind."

"You just here to make fun of me?"

"Fun?" His soft round face lit up with a smile. "Why fun? You're great. I don't know anyone else who could have thought to do what you did that evening."

"What did I do?"

"Make up an entirely new language to deal with a situation which annoyed you—to prove a point."

New language? Situation? Point? What point? My face burned from thinking. Determined to throw all thoughts of that night as far from my mind as memory allowed, I asked, "What will you drink?"

"I don't drink."

"Me neither."

I left him to put the champagne in the icebox and went into the living room to put on the Victrola. Then back in the bedroom, I arranged myself on the chaise longue. Lying back, I let my negligee fall from one knee. He wanted a vamp? That was me. Sitting next to me, he put one hand on my exposed knee.

"She's pretty," I said, then bit my tongue for letting on that she was right there in my thinking.

"Monica?" he asked. "No, Monica is not pretty . . ." That pleased me. I looked down at my dry-skinned hands. Folks naturally saw things different. I saw Monica as pretty; he probably was so used to her, he saw her another way. ". . . Monica is beautiful. One of the most beautiful women I know."

"Oh?" A sickening feeling hollowed a space from my head

through to my stomach. How could a man who had come to lay one woman be complimenting another? "You . . . gonna marry her?"

"Oh . . . I don't know. I think I might have waited too long. . . . A man gets busy, you know? Plans get put off."

I hadn't expected him to be honest—not that honest. "She expecting you to?" I asked, wanting to push his hand away, cover up my leg.

"I . . . really don't know. Monica and I . . . we are such good friends."

"Only friends?" I tried to stop talking about her. After all, the man was here. Deal with him or get him out.

"As a matter of fact, no." Warm, friendly, honest eyes gave the message: See, I don't lie. I don't intend to lie. Take me as I am. "Monica is important—very important to me."

Then why are you here, mister? What part do you want to play in my young life? I don't use seconds. I don't have to. So let the doorknob make a space where you think you hid your ace.

His hand reached up to my neck, massaging. "Monica is a very intelligent woman," he said. "She did her schooling in London. We have been friends for . . . so many years. . . ." Massage, massage. "A man can get so involved"—a sigh, regretting—"in so many different ventures—that what had been a certainty loses its urgency."

All that beauty that someone had spent all that time on wasted? All that high-yeller care—and Monica, you got to go through the same shit as me? Over a man! Can't happen to me no more, now I see where it's at. No, sir.

Big H, his honest, serious eyes looking into mine. Did it matter that they weren't shifty and slimy like Sonny's? Did it matter that he spoke only the truth? Did that hurt less? No. I know, Monica baby. The same pain. Same old pain.

"How old are you, Dorine?"

"Just turned twenty."

"That young? How is it that you got mixed up with a man like Sonny?"

This man knew my business! He had made it his business to know! "I *was* that young."

Squeezing and massaging my shoulders. "It's strange about men," he said. "The more a man has, the less excites him. The less

144

he is excited, the more he craves. The greater his cravings, the less able to achieve true fulfilment." He kept looking deep into my eyes. "Do you understand anything I'm saying, Dorine?"

So. All that gentleness—that honesty—hell, money had taken away his need to lie! Sure, I understood—had kept up with him all the way. All he had said was that he had been busy; now he was too goddamn tired for an ordinary fuck. He had to have a trick—and I had been with Sonny.

I had met guys like him before—thanks to Sonny. White guys, though. Guys so caught up in moneymaking they needed an electric charge to give them a rise. With them, an ordinary fuck magnified their lost manhood, made them carry loaded guns around to blow out their screwed-up brains.

Big H's hand worked at my titties. The scooped-out feeling spread to my feet. I lowered my eyes. Did I really want this? No. I had sort of wanted a big black stud with laughing yellow-brown eyes. How did lying here near-naked get me to him? I kept turning that around as Big H kept working away at my titties. But then I looked up, and seeing his longing-for-me eyes, I shrugged. Monica baby, intelligent lady, move on over. Those who don't make it got to take it. I'm picking up these chips.

Slipping off the chaise and going to change the stalled record, I danced back into the room shaking my hips, rolling my belly, winking. Then turning my back I wiggled my ass.

Yeah, I knew how to make it rise. I had done it for strangers to please Sonny. Why not please him? Hell, he had a million bucks. Sonny hadn't had a dime.

Big H eased himself back on the chaise. He folded his hands beneath his head, his anxious eyes waiting. I stretched my arms to the ceiling, giving him a good look at my body beneath the flimsy gown. I danced. He had seen me dance before—but never like this. I twisted my ass up to his face, moved out of reach. I danced across the room to the window. I slipped the robe off one shoulder, letting the gleam of young skin hit his eyes. I turned—slowly, to expose one tit. Keeping my belly rolling, I danced up to him. I leaned over to let the nipple brush his nose. Danced back. He waited.

Kept working my belly, moving close, close, close, almost to his face. Threw one leg up. Opened up for him to get a quick glimpse between my thighs. I pulled the robe around, turned my back, kept working my ass. I moved away.

He loosened his tie.

The gown fell to my waist. With both titties bared, I snake-hipped, did a mess-around so that they shook as I worked down to the floor. Legs open toward him, I lay on my back and did a fucking movement. Turned. Did a fucking movement on my stomach. Working myself to my knees with backside and titties shaking.

He took off his jacket. Damn! A hard number.

On my hands and knees, keeping my back to him, I kept up that screwing movement. I pulled the robe up over my ass and wiggled. Working up to my hands and feet, still wiggling, I posed a wicked second, looking at him from between my ankles—looked at him looking up me as far as eyes could see. He sat at the edge of the seat and tore off his shirt.

When I saw sweat wetting his top lip, I stood and ran to him, stopped before him, throwing my leg up again. I kept my breathing hard, my belly working.

He unbuttoned his trousers.

My gown wide open, I stood open-legged, hand between my thighs, spreading the lips of my pussy apart. Then worked my belly and ass as I walked backward. Halfway across the room, the lips still pulled apart, I did a backbend as far as I could bend. I stayed that way seconds, then danced over to him.

He took off his pants.

Naked, he lay, eyes staring, sweat streaming. I snake-hipped, opening my knees wide, put one leg up to the side of him. He grabbed me. Held me. I snatched away, danced to the far side of the room, looked to make sure he had a big hard-on, then belly-danced back to him. Turned to work my butt, then just stood before him, my butt working.

He grabbed me. Pulled me down. I slid to the floor. He slid on top. I kept my hips moving, moving. He pushed into me. Too late. I had done my work too goddamn well. He spent over my legs.

"You are good," he whispered in my ear. "Good for me." The stamp of approval. "A man needs a woman like you, Dorine. To make him relax. Dorine—Dorine . . ." Like a prayer. "You have no idea what this means. It's not easy, you know. . . .

"So much to do. So much work all the time. It's not only my—

little empire." He said that with a smile in his voice. "It's not only the Garvey business—just think of the role the United States Navy plays on the islands—my island, the Virgin Islands, Haiti. The amount of suffering they're inflicting. Do you know they actually believe that because we have black skin, they can push us back into slavery reminiscent of our slave past?"

The stud had to be kidding! What the hell did I care about those goddamn islands? Baby, I'm here—right here! All that action has left me with a need—a big need. I need one more second—not a goddamn speech! But feeling his joint, cold and shriveled against my thigh, I thought of having to get up, to put the stalled phonograph to playing again, to go through that routine! No, God, no—nothing in the world I hated worse than goddamn acrobatics. So I snuggled close, close—and let him talk me to sleep.

All that work! I lost more than twenty pounds during the first six months. Still, beneath all that loving and laughing, the feeling kept slipping and sliding through me that things were not exactly what I wanted. Not being able to read Big H kept me off-balance. But I played the game around *his* New York.

We went to horse races. We sat in grandstand seats. I shouted, waved, and yelled myself hoarse trying to bring his horses home. "You do enjoy living—don't you?"

Knowing he meant including lovemaking, I batted my eyes. "Sure do," I said. Game-playing.

We went to a Sugar Hill spot. Stepping out of the Duesenberg and pushing through a bunch of staring open-mouthed white and black folks, then walking up the steps of the white-stoned town house, togged to kill, and having Big H fumble in his vest pocket for the golden key to open the door impressed the hell out of me.

Then we stepped inside. Clara Bow–dyed redheads, bleached-blond mulattoes took hold. "Big H daar-ling, where have you beene? Why didn't I see you at my soiree?"

"You do know Miss Davis, don't you?" Big H forced eyes to look at the space by his side they must have thought empty. "Miss Dorine Davis. . . ?"

"Oh?"

"Charmed, I'm sure." I used charm and my big-teethed wide-mouthed grin to hide my anger. After all I *had* the man. . . .

Sitting at the table with Big H's men friends—a group who called themselves the Wall Street Boys (brown-skinned, curly-haired, and high-yeller guys who worked for some of the big Wall Street firms—as messengers), I kept seeing how they exchanged glances whenever I talked to them. I knew they were embarrassed to be seen talking to someone so brown—charm or no. They spoke because of Big H being there, but then they twisted their necks (almost snapping off their heads) turning back to their half-white chicks. That forced me to forsake game-playing. I called to the waiter: "Hey honey, let the champagne flow for these Wall Street suckers. Ain't no cure better than champagne for tired feet."

At The Club I spent so much time smiling over Monica's head—bent over her newspapers—and trying to charm a roomful of Big H's old, tired friends that I got tired. The evening I passed my tongue over my exposed teeth and found them cold, I had enough. I missed not working with my gang; I felt guilty not sending more money home. That made me question whether being a kept woman was the woman I had in mind being. I hated having limits on my spending when it was somebody else's limits—especially since Big H hadn't made it plain in words where our thing was heading.

The next morning I opened my eyes when Big H got to tipping around, searching for his clothes—scattered every whichaway from our wild night session. He found his trousers and slipped them on.

"Daddy," I called, holding out my arms. He came, leaned over me. I put my arms around his neck. "One minute, sugar," I pleaded. "That's all I needs." He let me hang. I wiggled my hips. He pulled away.

"I have to be in Washington early this afternoon," he said, buttoning his fly as though hiding something precious.

Limp-dick-quick-on-the-trick bastard, what's so damn precious about that thing? "Important meeting with a senator," he said, slipping into his shirt.

I kept on moving under the covers, staring at his hands in the mirror as they buttoned the shirt. If he buttons to the last button, I'm finished. It didn't seem right. It wasn't right—no way I looked at it—for the man to leave me in the same predicament every goddamn time. He had to know. Just played too busy to care. Giving me money seemed to be his answer. It wasn't my answer. He buttoned the last button, reached for his tie.

148

"Baby." I got to begging. "One minute ain't gonna make you miss no train." His honest eyes got sad. I got mad.

"This is a very important meeting, Dorine dear." He tied the tie. "Just to be able to discuss my island's problems with a legislator who has sympathy. It doesn't happen very often."

I heaved my titties from beneath the covers. He straightened his tie. "Come back to bed, man," I said. "You don't need to undress. Just unbutton that fly." His eyes smiled, appreciating my acting vulgar. He reached for his jacket.

"Look, feller," I said. "I loves you. You got to know that."

I did. That had to be my reason. I didn't need his money. Couldn't stand being used as a cum-box. And I hated the hell out of doing acrobatics. It had to be love. . . .

"And I am very fond of you," he said, moving his shoulders to make his jacket fall smooth. "But I must go. I have to impress on the senator that we on the islands will never allow them to treat us the way they treat blacks here in America."

That purged my need. Sweat jumped to my nose, cusswords got to battling one another to be the first one spoken. Big H came to stand over me. "Will you miss me?"

My mouth twitched to say: You goddamn simple monkey chaser, what makes you think I'll miss that goddamn monkey talk? Instead I said: "When you getting back?"

Mistaking my anger for need, he pecked me on the forehead. "In a few days. I'll miss you too, Dorine."

The minute he closed the door, I jumped out of bed. I looked out the window at his chauffeur, already at the door of his car. I waited until they pulled off, then put on my robe and went down to Tom Rumley's.

"Whoooeee," Tom said opening the door. "Look who we got this morning. Dorine Davis, in person. You come to give us a fashion show, or you doing us an honor by your presence?"

"Don't talk that shit to me," I snapped. "I come to ask a favor."

"Can't help out," Tom said. "Ain't made my first million yet."

"It ain't gonna cost you one cent to set me up for a crack at the Brooklyn Bridge," I said. "If it costs, I pay."

"No, you ain't," he said. "Because I ain't gonna do no such fool thing."

"You said—"

"No such a thing."

Selling the Brooklyn Bridge had become daily news in the daily newspapers. Tom and I had talked about it. It had stuck in my mind as something I wanted to do. Now it seemed the one thing to keep me from going crazy.

"What's wrong between you and your old man?" Tom asked.

"Who said? I just need something to do—something new and mind-rocking."

Ann lay on the couch in the living room when we walked in (she had taken to staying in New York more than in Baltimore), her face looking pinched as though ready to receive old age. "Look who's here," Tom said, sitting in his stuffed chair and leering up at me. "Dorine Davis, come to give us a show."

"What about it, Tom?" I asked.

"What about what?" He kept turning his head to look at me, walking around, restless, scared that I might bump into one of his precious pieces. He had added to his junk collection a baby grand piano, which took up too much room. Its stool had to sit on top. And a bear head—pushed in between family pictures—because, he said, "I shot it." Nobody believed him. Nobody believed Tom knew how to shoot.

"Set down, set down," he said when his head got tired of turning. He looked me up and down; his smile got slimy. "I do declare you act worse than a pussycat in heat." He ducked my dirty look. "Dorine girl, I know how these things is. You wouldn't even be down here if things was working out between you and your old man."

"Tell me one time things work out right between a woman and the man she wants." Ann's drier-than-whiskey voice turned me on her.

"Things is working out just fine between me and my man." Not wanting them to think it was because Ann was seeing Sonny, I added: "Big H is gone to D.C. to see a man about some islands. After all, we can't just let white folks think they can push them West Indians into slavery emmencent of their past." Then getting mad, I said, "They deported Garvey's black butt—what the hell do they do about them islands—sink 'em?"

Tom laughed. "Dorine, you known Big H was a big shot when you decided to snag him."

"Ain't done no such a thing. He come after me. Anyway I ain't here to talk about my affairs. I come to talk about work."

"After you played dead while Grace got busted?"

"Don't put that on me," I said.

"Makes no difference," Tom said. "We sure ain't gonna do no work this soon after a bust." He shook his head, then laughed. After a few seconds, Ann sat up laughing too. Then I laughed. And there we were the three of us cracking our sides laughing at poor Grace's bust—at least the way Albert had explained it:

"That Grace," Albert had said. "She knows she got stuff—maybe three four-hundred-dollar suits—stashed between them fat legs. She's on her way out when I cut out. But I get to waiting in the car. Five minutes, Grace ain't come. Ten minutes, and Grace ain't come.

"I get scared thinking that maybe the bulls done got her. Now Grace is my lady. I got to go back even when I don't want. And what do I see? The woman's still up on the same floor. Only now she got this li'l white brat, dragging him around by his hand. The kid's lost.

"Now I'm thinking that she's turning the kid over to a sales-somebody. But no, Grace got this kid, taking him around looking for his ma. I stand in the doorway making signs. She won't even look. I keep moving my head to catch her eyes. She won't look. I get to making signs like a clown. Drop the kid, I'm saying. Let's get the hell out. . . .

"If I was a clear pane of glass, Grace would have seen me better. And there she is—my Grace—those simple glasses on the tip of her nose, making her look intelligent while she acts like a damn fool.

"I tell you the woman's raising hell. She's talking about folks having kids what ain't responsible. Raising so much hell, a bull comes over—then she gets to raising hell with him.

"And me—I'm making my eyes pop, I get on one foot, then the next—acting the fool, to draw her attention. Drop the kid. The words are busting out of my sweaty head. Drop the damn kid. . . .

"Then I take to noticing how Grace is twisting up her legs. Now you know how weak Grace's bladder is. But the damn fool woman don't seem to know it! She's standing, legs all twisting, talking up into this bull's face. Next I see him pointing, leading her! From the way she's walking folks got to be taking bets on whether she makes it to the john. She does—almost. When she sees the door, she takes one leap. Just as Grace goes through the door, plop—suits fall right down—at the bull's feet . . . .

"Sucker looks down, keeps looking, don't know what the hell he's looking at. Well, you know who wasn't waiting till he found out?"

We laughed (at what would be our lifelong joke, called Grace's Long Piss). But when I could talk again, I said, "It's okay for you guys to lie low. But I declare I'm about to go out of my mind."

"Let the kid have a try, Tom," Ann said. "Can't you see how charged up she is?"

"Why?" I asked, mad that she understood what was happening inside me. "You just want me out of the way so you can get your hands on Sonny."

"See?" Ann said. "The kid's crying for a pinch. We can't afford to lose her too. Do something, Tom."

"I don't mix hustles, Ann," Tom said. "Dorine don't know one damn thing about the con game."

"If she don't do that she'll end up doing something else," Ann said.

"Like what?" I lit into her. "Like making things tough for you and Sonny?"

"The only thing keeping me from Sonny, baby, is Sonny."

"Jesus Christ!" Tom threw up both hands. "Don't you two get to raising hell in here. My best two gals and both got studs what don't mean them no good."

"Whatcha mean, Tom Rumley?" I said. "If I want Big H to marry me, I can get him just like that." I snapped my fingers. I believed it. Rich and intelligent as Big H was, like most men, he loved his prick. Not getting it up scared him shitless. He'd marry me to keep it rising.

"You pretty and all, Dorine," Tom said. "Just my type. But I seen a-many raving beauty what tried and ain't made it with Big H." Knowing he was talking about Monica near drove me out of my mind. It showed me how much I really wanted Big H. But I had him. What to do to keep him—even with his one-second action?

"Bet me. Go on and bet me," I cried.

"We had better do something, Tom, or Dorine might try hard enough to win that bet—and end up married."

"Ann, that's white folks' game," Tom said. "Them con artists go after them immigrants fresh off the boat—most ain't seen a black face before. They'd look up and see Dorine, and go to yelling for the police."

"Makes it tough," Ann agreed. "But Dorine's known to be good in bad corners."

"It just ain't her speed," Tom said, but I could feel him giving in.

Tom finally set me up. He hired two white guys who worked with a Jewish mobster in the Bronx called Dutch Schultz. I had heard that he was tough and hated blacks. But Tom, like Sonny, believed in dealing with whites. A question of money, he liked to say. He rented an office on Park Row, near the Brooklyn Bridge, and got papers fixed up for me to resemble worn documents. Then I was in business. But before he let me loose Tom warned: "Dorine, I got lots of faith in you. But be careful. Don't go shooting off at the mouth—even about things what don't seem important—get it?"

Seeing that our gang were all so closed-mouthed about things folks swore we suffered from lockjaw, I had to ask: "What the hell would I be talking about to white boys?"

"Well, you know what they say about a word to the wise, Dorine?"

"What they say about a word to the wise, Tom?"

"Helps them over mountains—and from slipping in puddles—and drowning."

7

Pure excitement wiped away my evil spirits when I stepped onto that bridge and walked along the pedestrian walk looking down into the water on that cool-for-August day. Dressed in a faded cotton dress, shapeless black coat, my hair tied with a black kerchief like the immigrant women walking to and from Brooklyn and Manhattan, I looked like one—a black one. Hearing the noise of the bridge traffic: cars honking and braking, horses clippity-clopping, the bells over their heads jingling. I hugged myself, feeling good.

The first day I walked, got the feel of the bridge, read faces: those most likely to be an easy hit; the hoarders who kept their loot stashed under mattresses and walked to work, worked hard, and walked back to save a penny. I guessed at humble workers who needed to scuffle to make a dime—their eyes showed the suffering of it; those with fearful eyes, hugging possessions, with mouths ready to call the law; and those willing and ready, just waiting to take on the hustlers of the world.

Riding the subway mornings, then back home at night, I studied faces, too. Hardworking men and women, the dinginess of their lives worked into the pores of their faces, their clothes—the older ones, that is. The younger ones always had a promise in their eyes, some their future hopes painted in bright colors on their faces. Hardworking black women, shopping bags brought to work, filled out evenings with stuff from their madams' houses. Pain.

The noise of the subways burrowing through dark tunnels was a head-buster. I promised myself on those mornings that in this life I'd sooner flirt with death, go to prison a hundred times over, before I'd sit in that train day by day letting the ear-splitting noise be a must for me to break bread.

On the third day, summer came back and with it, memories. Already used to my daily walk, I allowed my mind to drift. I let it drift around Big H, how important he was to me; and what a laugh to have him caring for me. I thought of Sonny—of all I had done for him—and wondered about him and Ann. What would she do to him? be to him? Would he sit still for her? And then I thought of Master Norton. Master Norton stayed on my mind like a knot that blood washed over and never washed away. I thought of our long drives from his house to mine, of his big car and my pride in riding in it. I remembered his hand on my leg, him playing with me while he drove, and I thought of the day when his hand came away with my first blood.

"What you been doing, Dorine?" he had asked.

154

"Nothing, Master Norton," I said.

"Why ain't you told you had your menses?"

"I ain't never had nothing like that, Master Norton. I swear I ain't."

He rushed me home that night, went into the house and said to Mama: "Janie, Dorine here's getting to be a woman. Sure hopes you careful with them nigras around here."

And Mama had answered: "You ain't got to worry none, Master Norton. I got troubles enough without any of my gals bringing shame down on this old head."

I reckon it was from that night that I had no more use for Mama. No feelings. Not even when she changed, overnight, from this strong giant of a woman to that shriveled old thing on her deathbed. Deep down inside I believe I was glad she had gone, released me from bondage. Lord, there had to be a sin in that, rejoicing over Mama's being dead when I knew she'd done her best. Thinking of it brought out my tears.

"Hey there, auntie. What they done to you?"

My heart flipped at the cracker voice. It was him! It was him! I couldn't see him for my tears, yet I knew. I cried harder. "Hold on there, auntie. What these folks done to you?"

That "auntie" bit got to me. I had put on a little weight, but not near enough to be taken for nobody's auntie. "They robbing me, suh. That's what they doing. Lord knows I don't know what I'm doing up here trying to talk business with them Yankees."

I turned for him to get a better look at my face, and he said: "Why, you ain't nothing but a li'l bit a thing. Tell me what they done."

"Well, suh, I come north, suh, because of this here property. You see, it belonged to my grandpappy. . . ."

Little by little I allowed him to pull out my story about how my grandfather, this rich white from the North, had gone down south directly after the Civil War and had put my slave great-grandmother in sin. " 'Deed he was sorry, suh. 'Cause when he died, he sure deeded his property up north to her. Well, suh, my grandmammy had ten kids, one my ma, another my Cousin Edwin's pa. So when they passed, it was natural the property come to us chillun."

I had gone over the story with my partners, but as I kept talking to this big, soft-looking, gentle gentleman from the South, it kept building. I told him how Cousin Edwin had come north to find that part of the Brooklyn Bridge had been built on our property. " . . . Now the deed says that anything built on that property without due consent of the owner—due consent, suh"—I made a point to prove my knowledge of the law—"rightly belong to the owner, suh." Then I added pridefully: "This bridge we standing on, suh, rightly belong to me."

Sure sounded good. I liked the feel of it, and of the telling to this well-bred cracker who ought to tell me to go to hell but wasn't about to. Sure, his eyes kept getting wary; doubts drifted in and out along with the fog of the deepening day; but he was mine all the way.

Soft hands, soft face, soft bulging belly, clothes that spoke of him being around the world and back, and a familiar way of knowing black folks. Yet, as Tom said, there's one always around who ain't had time to read the papers.

Hunched like two old buddies on that bridge, I kept feeding him information about how Cousin Edwin came north but had been killed in an automobile accident. Only he had sent the deed back before he died. "And that's why I'm here, suh. Only them real-estate folks—the ones got claim to handle the property—they wants to give me five hundred dollars for the deed. But suh, they promised Cousin Edwin fifty thousand dollars! I told them, 'No, suh. I knows my property is worth fifty thousand and that's what I wants.' Yes, suh, Master Hiram"—his name was Hiram Jackson—"I stood right in their faces and told 'em. Then Lord, did they get nasty! Tried to take the deed from me. That's what they did. I run. Lord, I got away from there."

"You sure you ain't pulling my leg, gal?"

"No, suh. See for yourself, suh." I took out my papers and handed them to him. "That deed says that Grandpappy bought this here property in 1800. Deeds don't lie, do they, Master Hiram?"

Hiram Jackson took the deed, squinted at it, and I took it from him, put it back in my bag, and hugged my bag to my chest. "Why ain't you been to the police?" he asked.

"What! No, suh. These here Yankee polices is worster than them crooks."

He nodded, agreeing. "What about these here real-estate folks?" I gave him the Park Row address. "You think maybe you want me to look into this for you?"

"Oh, suh, I'd be much obliged, suh. I know I can trust a gent'man from the South."

"Now I ain't promising . . ."

"Yes, suh, you just let them know they can't go around making a fool of Bertha Lee, even if she be's a nigger."

"I best hold that deed."

"Take my deed? No, suh. This here is all I got; least I got that for fare home." He looked at me, wanting to change his mind, but I know when a cracker's sworn to come to the help of simple home niggers. "The Lord done sent you to me, Master Hiram. I known He'd send someone like you. Ain't nothing beats a southern gent'man."

I took him around to the office but it had already closed. "I'll come back first thing in the morning, Bertha Lee. I promise."

"Bless you. Bless you, Master Hiram."

Everything depends on two things: the first is that Master Hiram shows that next morning. I know he will. As deep as he can be, he's mine. And he does:

"I'm here to inquire about property belonging to a nigra gal name Bertha Lee, heir to one Master Elias Anderson," he said to my two partners from the way they tell it.

Marty and Bo exchange looks. Nervous. But Marty, the slick one, takes over. "You a friend of hers, sir?"

"Just let us say I know her. I'm making it my business to see she ain't cheated."

"Are you accusing us of something, sir?"

"Just let us say I know how you Yankees operate. Bertha Lee ain't none too smart. But she knows what rightly belongs to her. Now she happens to be holding on to a deed to some mighty valuable property. I'm here to see she don't get cheated."

"I don't think I like your attitude, sir." Marty acts insulted. "We are not in business to cheat anybody. We have a legitimate business here." He points to a wall full of licenses and awards. "Your girl Bertha Lee came in here with this so-called deed. And I must say we were very kind to her. Why, we even offered her five hundred dollars for that worthless piece of paper. Then what does she do? Runs out on us. You know how excitable niggers are? I—I might have gone up, offered her, say, five thousand for that lousy piece of swampland."

"Suh"—Master Hiram pulls himself tall—"that land is not swamp. I happen to know that. I saw that deed myself."

"He seen the deed. He seen the deed." Bo jumps up and down, excited.

"Oh?" Marty puts on the cagey show. "You know. What else do you know?"

"I happen to know that the Brooklyn Bridge is built on that property, suh. That makes that swampland, as you call it, worth more—a lot more—than a few thousand dollars."

"Marty, he knows. We can't lie to this man," Bo pleads. "He'll bring the law. He'll get us in a jam."

"I see it's no good lying to you." Marty turns smooth. "That land is worth a pretty penny to us."

"If we can get our hands on it," Bo says, "we'll control the bridge—gateway to Manhattan." Bo, not being the smartest, is ready to blow the whole deal. Marty puts up his hand to shut him up.

"My partner is excitable," he says. "We will, however, have a small claim on the bridge—a million-dollar claim?"

Marty waits for that to sink in before he says: "But we must have that deed!" He shuffles through some papers, giving Master Hiram time to sound out our second need: that he is not as honest as he really thinks he is. They wait for signs: a movement, a blink of an eye, a foot shifting, a change of breath. Of course, he can walk out; then we have to try another. But Mr. Hiram doesn't move. He just stands there real quiet. That's it.

Annoyed, impatient, Marty pushes him: "Look at that cousin of hers. Boy comes in, we promise him fifty grand. We actually give him five, for starters. What does he do? Gets drunk. Wraps himself around a lamppost. Kills himself. We are out of five grand—and the deed.

"Mr. Jackson. Niggers just don't know what to do with money. The same thing will happen to your little Bertha Lee. Give her a little money and see. You are her friend—and a good one, I can see. Get that deed from her. Bring it to us. We'll split fifty-fifty—a million fifty-fifty—and you'll be doing her a favor."

That afternoon Master Hiram Jackson has ceased to be my protector. "Bertha Lee," he says when we meet near the bridge, "I declare I did all I could. But like you say, them Yankees are a thieving lot. Now I don't want you to go back home with nothing to show but a hard time. And I happened to find out that every deed that predates 1860 is null and void. Null and void. Still, I might be able to do something with it. So I'll just give you ten thousand dollars for that paper and see if maybe I can do something . . ."

Ten thousand! The suggested price was five—an extra five for his conscience. He was my man all the way.

"Ten thousand, Master Hiram? Well, that ain't nothing like the fifty they done promise Cousin . . . but if you say . . ."

That night I met Marty and Bo at an Irish grill on Eighth Avenue. I gave them their cut—five thousand split three ways. We sat talking, with them giving me a word-by-word description. When I was ready to go, Bo said, "What you gonna do with all that money, Dorine?"

"What's it to you?"

"Nothin'," he answered. "Except niggers ain't used to holding that kind of loot. Whatcha gonna do with it? Buy grease for your hair?"

Knowing that I'm holding on to five grand that he was ignorant of ought to have been satisfaction enough. But I got hot. "Feller," I said. "That what you just stuffed in your pocket? That ain't nothing but pigeon shit. The millions that pass through hands in Harlem would make that plaster you call hair stand on end. And I ain't talking about Madam Walker's beauty products, neither." I stalked out. But the instant air hit me, I knew I had made a slip.

Whispering money in a room where there's one racketeer is like passing well-wrapped fish under the nose of a cat. It made no difference if it was play money, they were duty-bound to check it out. So my slip kept me jumpy. In a few days all of the high that my hit had pumped had been brought down by sandpaper nerves. I kept praying that Bo had taken my bragging as nothing but bull. Whites were known to believe that colored folks were dumb about real dough. Looking at Tom's reflection in the window and hearing him talk about hating to mix hustles, I wanted to spill all. But what had I really said? Nothing.

I brooded as I stared at the empty space beneath the lamppost, wishing the Duesenberg would appear. It seemed to me that cars parked under that streetlight controlled my heart's blood. All the while Tom, sitting on the couch behind me, kept talking:

"To me, it's a matter of principle. Sticking to the hustle I know. That's how I keeps check on myself."

"Quit groaning because you got a bet to pay, Tom."

"I ain't jiving. That's how I know when I'm slipping, when I'm getting old."

"You ain't about to admit to neither. So why all them principles?"

Keeping him there acted as cushion for my worn-down nerves. Forcing him to talk, to laugh loud, fill the room with his big-gutted, rambunctious, good-natured self, let the flow of his words wash down my unease.

"You ain't understood what I said, Dorine."

Yet that didn't make Tom one whit less special, with his big laugh, his sun-spotted face, his golden grin.

"That's what I'm talking about, old Red. What slowed you down so you like the bed better than a good hustle?"

"Now that ain't nice, Dorine." Then he chuckled. "Matter of fact, a pair of shoes slowed me down."

"On some flat feet?"

"Naw—my own feet." Tom eased his big feet onto the coffee table to look at them while he talked. "One time me and some of my boys were let in on this hijacking deal—before my boosting time. Unloaded this truck of shoes being shipped to a department store. Good shoes—couple a hundred pairs in the lot.

"Had nothing better to do than go through the load to find this one pair. Pre-tty. Expen-sive. Only ones like them in the whole shabangle. Like they were put there just for me. Only one thing, though. They did not fit. Still had to have them. Forced them size elevens on these size thirteens. But they looked so goo-ood. I wore them. Kept wearing them. Honey, dressed in my tight pants, derby, sporting a pipe, and them shoes—I was in there. Sharpest thing walking—or limping. Yeah, them suckers had me limping so bad, you'd have sworn I done had infan-tile paralysis. Had to go every-where I went by car. Limp to the car—limp out. And when I got somewhere, had to set like a hen on a nest full of eggs.

"Remember going back home to visit. Brought them shoes

along—showing off, you know how young boys is? One night me and the boys took some chicks to a roadhouse way on the other side of Maryland. I had to set all night looking at other folks jig. We gets to riding back, and wouldn't you know it? Fool car breaks down. Ten miles out of nowhere and the mother breaks down. There I go limping up this country road. . . ."

The Duesenberg pulled up under the lamp, taking my mind away from Tom.

"A couple of miles . . . let go of . . . pride, pulled them suckers off. You hear me? Pulled them suckers *off*. Why did I do that? Pebbles cut through my city-bred feet like butter. Feet jump out like balloons . . . hitched my arms around my buddies so they could carry me . . . them simple broads . . . laughing like they on some goddamn picnic. . . ."

Big H's chauffeur got out of the car, went to open the back door. Just then two other cars—black—drove up. One pulled up in front, the other alongside. Two men jumped out of each car. They had surrounded Big H.

". . . laid up for weeks"—Tom's voice hitting my ears—"feet ain't never been right. . . ."

"Cops," I said.

"Lord . . . them mothers . . . throwed them. . . ."

A brief tussle out on the sidewalk. Running back to the cars. The sidewalk empty except for Big H's chauffeur. He lay stretched out on the sidewalk. "Them ain't no bulls. . . ."

"Way I figgered . . . devil had a hand in putting them shoes in my hand's way. And the way I thrown them suckers—got to have landed right at his goddamn feet. . . ."

"Tom," I said. "Them ain't no bulls."

"Whatcha talking . . ."

"Grays. They done snatched Big H. But I swear they ain't no cops." Tom came to stand at the window just as the chauffeur got to his feet. We both headed for the door and took the stairs instead of waiting for the elevator. The chauffeur had just come into the lobby when we got down.

"What's with Big H?" Tom asked when he saw the bleeding over the chauffeur's face. His head had been hurt, his nose was bleeding. "Big H hauled in?"

"No, suh, them ain't no cops"—the chauffeur spoke my fears.

The corners of his mouth foamed and he was shaking. "They said they was, at first. Said they was hauling him in for questioning. But when Big H asked to see their badges, they just roughed him up. Socked me—then they put him in their car and headed uptown. Naw, they didn't go down, they turned. I seen them heading up."

"Bronx boys?" Tom said, and my heart got to shaking like it wanted to expire.

Minutes later we walked into The Club. Tom went to the bar to talk to the manager, a college student Big H had trained. "What's the word from Big H?" Tom asked.

"He just left—not more than a half-hour—to see you, I thought, Miss Dorine," the kid said.

"He been snatched," Tom said. "Call his lawyer. Ask him to check the precincts."

An hour later Big H's lawyer, Barnes, came in to tell us: "Cops ain't got Big H. Nobody seems to know what happened. Got any leads?"

"Maybe. Maybe punks from the Bronx?"

"Schultz!" Lawyer Barnes's eyebrows shot up. Fear needled his eyes. White, medium, well dressed, well fed, he had earned his place on Big H's list of friends.

"Ain't calling no names," Tom said, studying his shoes. "I guess we just got to wait."

"Wait!" The manager, his young face torn by fear and loyalty, looked from Tom to Barnes. Outclassed, he knew that whatever he said had to be downgraded. Still he tried. "What if they kill him?"

"Kill him? What for?" Tom kept looking at his shoes. "Folks don't go around killing to watch other folks die. They got to want something. So we got to wait."

"Can't we call Sergeant Battle?"

"Don't need no stars."

Being the first black cop on the New York City force hadn't been easy for Sergeant Battle. White folks had made it tough. From all over the country they used to visit his beat to shout: "Nigger, nigger on the beat, big black and ugly got two left feet." But Battle had stuck it out. Tom hated him. Said he had gained his promotions from practicing on niggers' heads, seeing it was forbidden for him to beat on white folks. Whatever his notoriety, he had earned Big H's friendship.

"We ought to call him, Tom," Barnes said. "Knowing he's interested might put respect into whoever."

The kid reached for the phone but just then it rang. "The Club," he said, when he picked it up. He listened, handed the phone to Barnes.

"Barnes here," the lawyer said, then: "You guys must be kidding. Where do you think we can raise that kind of—"

The voice at the other end rose, cutting him off. Then Barnes said: "Tom Rumley's here. Hear of him? You know of him. Well here he is." Barnes handed the phone to Tom, who in turn listened. He whistled, then hung up.

"They ain't playing. Seventy-five grand. That's what they want—or his life, they said."

"God," Barnes said. "Who and how? How did they know to pick on Big H?"

"That ain't the hardest," Tom said, not looking at me. "If mobsters get interested and wants to know who's the big black in Harlem—all they got to do is ask. Big H's name slides off the top."

"Somebody trying to cut themselves in. . . ?"

"At seventy-five grand—they have."

"Do we pay?" Barnes asked. A silence waited for the brave to judge. Who was to decide to take a chance on Big H dying?

"A lot a loot," Tom said, shaking his head. Then repeated. "But they ain't playing. And if they are—it ain't in my nature to find out. . . . They wants that I should act the drop-off man. Anybody got objections? They'll be calling back with instructions."

"Where will you all get that kind of cash?" I asked.

"We'll get it," Tom said. "Big H is good—ain't he?"

"Yeah—we'll get it up." Barnes nodded.

The night grew old, older, and we waited. We sat in the office while the young manager lived up to Big H's trust in him by keeping business going as usual. The laughter of customers drinking and dining on the main floor, the shouting of gamblers from the basement level, reached up to us in the upstairs office. The sounds of glass against glass, of music, hit at us, keeping the face of The Club's owner before us. That gentle face, the smooth, brown, shiny face, those honest, warm, dark brown eyes. With every sound: a high laugh, a sudden quiet, the rumble of arguments on the lower floor, we who were waiting looked at each other and saw him.

At midnight Sergeant Battle—real big, dark, and far from ugly—walked in. "Hey, Barnes," he called as he came in. "What's this with you? Been checking up on Big H at the precincts. The young punk here says talk to you. Where's Big H? What's happening?"

Tom and Barnes exchanged looks. "I think we got to keep this muffed, Battle," Barnes said. "Looks serious to me."

"From me? Come on. What's happening? If it's happening to Big H, it's happening to me."

"That's what we're scared of," Tom said, sounding sarcastic.

"Oh, come, Tom. You know I ain't gonna do nothing to hurt my buddy." Tom didn't answer, so Battle appealed to Barnes. "Hey, I'm his friend. His number-one man. . . ." He looked at the young manager. But both Barnes and the kid were waiting for Tom.

"They snatched Big H this evening in front of my house," he said. We think that maybe it's the guys from the Bronx." Battle waited. "That's all we know. We here waiting for word."

"From the Bronx, huh?" Battle nodded. "We'll see. We'll see." He walked to the door just as two other flatfeet, grays, walked in. Big men. One had a scar across his face that had healed raised, the way black folks' scars healed. It made him look the match for Battle in toughness.

"Look who's here," he said when he saw Battle. "You dinges sure get around." (In those days white cops didn't need to hide their hate from us.)

"Yeah, I gets around," Battle answered, his bigness warning how far to go. Scarface tried to stare him down. Couldn't. He turned to Barnes. "Mr. Barnes, I hear you been asking around for Big H. Something happen to him?"

The lawyer shook his head. "Not that I know of."

"Can you tell me where he is?"

"I have no idea."

"What about you, nigger?" Scarface looked at Tom.

"What about me?" Tom slid his eyes over him.

"Where is Big H?"

"Here—if you see him," Tom answered.

"You coons always got to act wise." Scarface reddened. "Like this one here." He poked his thumb in the direction of Battle. "He been around since I was a boy and finally made them stripes."

"And when I finish with you, you'll still be a boy and I'll be wearing bars," Battle sneered.

"Make sure they don't weigh you down, get in your way," Scarface laughed. "Walk soft, nigger. Walk soft."

"I'm too heavy, man," Battle whispered. "I'm just too god-damn heavy to ever walk soft."

They circled the room. The two whites looking over the office, the files, the machines, their hands in their pockets to keep from tearing the place apart. They knew better. Battle kept his eyes on them. When they left, he said, "I'll stay on top of this—don't worry."

We breathed easy when they had gone. Being in the presence of real hate is like standing in the gateway of hell—it scares you shitless thinking you might be sucked into the fiery furnace.

Hours stretched. Night gave way to dawn before the phone rang. Tom answered. "Yeah—this is me." He kept his eyes moving from one to the other of us, making us pay attention. "Yeah. Gotcha. We got to wait till the banks open, man. Then we got to go around to raise what we can. Yeah, Barnes's still here. Gotcha, gotcha. But listen, friend, you ain't got us. We happen to know you punks. But you don't know how many we be, or what we subject to do. You got our man, right? But if so much as a prick shows on his pinky—watch out. You won't know which way we be coming from."

Neither did I. With all Tom's big-mouthing, black gangs didn't work like white gangs. Most blacks didn't work in gangs. Our big guys—Big H, Casper Holstein, Wilfred Brunder, Pompey, Miro—blacks and Puerto Ricans who had built up the numbers racket on the penny bets of poor folks—were cream-of-the-crop gentlemen. They walked around with creased pants, with spats, top hats, canes. They didn't carry guns. Their runners worked days and went home to sleep nights. The only ones who caused them trouble were cops. They had to have their take. And who went around shooting cops?

Folks like us—our gang—didn't carry guns. Who wanted to kill? All we wanted to do was make money to live in style. We did. We left the killings to the ofays.

The black cats who carried guns were for the most part loners who went for bad. We let them be what they wanted. The world, to us, was a wide-open place where we floated in our kind of freedom.

So as I listened to Tom saying: "That is right. Don't even let a rosebush touch him," I got to wondering how to shoot if someone stuck a gun in my hand. What did a feller do before pulling the trigger? It's a cinch that if Big H's life depended on it, I would. . . . "Naw," Tom said, "you don't have to worry—nobody at this end is doing any talking."

But the word was out. By ten that morning, newspapermen and some of Big H's friends burst into the office. "What's this about Big H being kidnapped?" folks were asking. "How much they want?" "Who is it?" "Got any ideas. . . ?"

They crowded into the office, so that to breathe we had to push our way out. And as we walked down the stairs, we met Scarface coming up. "Look," he said. "You had better work with us on this if you don't want your friend to get back in a box. You spooks don't know how these big boys operate."

We pushed on by him on our way downstairs. And as we neared the landing, we heard a clear voice rising over all other voices: "Gentlemen, we have absolutely no information to impart at this moment. It so happens that Mr. H. is momentarily out of town. He and he alone can refute these ridiculous allegations. If you will return—perhaps tomorrow—I am sure he will be only too pleased to respond to all of your inquiries in person. Good-day, gentlemen. . . ."

Monica Gaines had come in, and as cool as you please, taken over.

Twenty-four hours after Big H had been kidnapped, Tom, with two of Big H's boys, got ready to make the drop. They brought down the leather satchel that they had filled with money they had drawn from the Chelsea bank that day. Entering the dining room where we sat, Tom went right over to Monica at her corner table, and putting his hand on her shoulder, said: "Don't worry, Monica, everything will be okay. Take my word." She looked up, unsmiling but grateful. Then he came over to my table. "Dorine baby, pray for me. I just might be needing it."

If he had put a knife to my gut, he couldn't have hurt more. Tom, *my* friend, comforting that other woman when he knew I loved, had been in love with, Big H, had been seeing Big H for such a long time. I bent my head, not to look at him but to hiding my will to murder. My hands held on tight to one another in my lap, stopping their urge to pick up a chair and go to work upside his big, red head. From the corner of my eye I looked at his big, bad feet, shuffling toward the door. A damn shame gangrene hadn't set in that night in Maryland. Ought to have got them cut off right up to his waist. Lord God, may he never in life talk to me of working with him. Never again. Especially if I held a weapon in my hand.

Twenty-four hours and more without sleep, and my mood had soured. I sipped Coca-Cola, trying to keep awake, while Barnes took turns sitting first with me and then with Monica. The chauffeur stayed loyal to me. He sat with me steady. The manager played it smart. He kept upstairs in the office. Other friends of Big H sat at different tables talking. Battle kept coming and going. He spoke mostly to Monica, she being the high-yeller one. Eviler than I had ever been, I kept fighting sleep, not wanting Big H to walk in and find me asleep and Monica awake. But my head kept going down, down, down. . . .

Another dawn, another day. The natural funk of my body pushed my head up. I looked over at Monica. Sleep had gotten to her, too. Only a few others had stayed—all asleep. The chauffeur, across from me, kept starting up because of his own snoring and talking to himself. I put my head down and closed my eyes. But they kept opening, kept getting wide, wider. Worry, about Big H, but more about Tom. He could have gone around New York twice and over.

What if those guys had taken him at his word and had decided to shoot it out? Tom didn't know a thing about guns. If he tried to shoot one, more than likely he'd end up shooting his own self— danger from two directions.

A sudden banging of garbage pails outside made me jump. Made me think of bodies being brought and dumped in front of The Club: one—two—three. . . . I tried to stand, to push myself up. But like a nightmare, weights kept my butt heavy to the chair. God help me. I closed my eyes. Prayed. What if Tom was out there? He still might have life in him. I might help—if only I could move. The vision of Tom lying on the sidewalk filled my mind. The way he lay—on his back, his big belly a mountain, eyes closed, mouth open. . . . Those motherfuckers shooting out all those pretty teeth. Nothing but empty space where Tom's gold had been. I put my hands up to cover my face, hide the sight.

"What? What? Whatsa matter?" The chauffeur woke. "Oh, it's you," he said. "Hey, man, sure am glad. . . . What take you so long?"

I spread my fingers apart to peep through. Sure enough, Tom and the two other men were walking in. "Tom!" I jumped up and ran to hug him, tears brimming my eyes.

"Well, looka here," he said. "Look who's glad to see this old red nigger." He smiled—all those pretty shining teeth.

"I ain't never been gladder."

" 'Course I known all along. But you ain't never told me you cared before." He went around, giving the message: he had dropped the money. We just had to wait. Then he came to sit with me. We waited together. . . .

All through the day folks kept coming and going, coming and going. No Big H. In late afternoon this woman, wearing a long black dress under a long black cape, came to stand in the doorway, looking around the dining room. Tall, wiry, the whites of her eyes so bright they shone like flames out of her black face. They rested on us, and she came toward us, saying: "Tom Rumley, don't gi' we money away to dem white sons a bitches!" Harsh, quarrelsome, threatening, her West Indian accent cut a sharp difference to Monica's refined one. "Dey pokin', lookin', tryin' to learn we business. Gi' dem a cent and dey comin' . . . De plague!"

Looking over to Monica, she raised her voice. "Dey does kill and shoot one anodder. Dey does kill and shoot dey own mudder, dey own fadder for money—de plague! Dey does go through de world smellin' for gold . . . killin' de people . . . thiefin' dey land. . . . Like ants dey does go! Like disease! De plague!

"Tom Rumley, gi' dem one cent and dey comin' back! De plague! To wipe we out. . . . You does hear me, Tom? Barnes, you too, you white son of a bitch! Don't you go bring de plague down on we heads."

"Madam Queen," Tom said, bowing his head, humble. "We done made the drop."

"You done what!" The whites of her eyes flashed, and I held

my breath for the explosion that, when it came, sounded louder than thunder: "Pancakes!" Her loud voice rolled, then cracked over the room. "Sons a bitches!" She stretched her arms out, pointed bony fingers to include all of us. "Dey kick all-you ass outa Greenwich Village. You take it! Dey kick all-you ass outa de Tenderloin! All-you take it! And your blood did flow, like fire, in de streets a San Juan Hill! You take it! Now dey wipin' up de streets a Harlem wit all-you ass! You does bring de plague down on we little kingdom. . . .

"Pancakes! Sons a bitches! Pancakes! Sons a bitches!" She whirled, her cape flapping out behind her like wings. I declare she seemed to fly out of The Club. And long after she had gone, her words lingered, echoing and reechoing throughout the silent room.

On the fourth day after his kidnapping, Big H walked into The Club. His eyes were red; bruises around his neck and wrists, his face swollen, spoke of some bad times. His clothes, rumpled from being slept in; the pretty white shirt, gray, torn, buttons missing down the front—yet he came in smiling. The minute he walked in, friends surrounded him. Reporters, policemen, and most of those who had made The Club home for the few days, milled around.

Hell of a time to be proving a point, but I sat. Monica had not moved, so I had not moved. If she stood, I intended to jump up and stand shoulder-to-shoulder with her. She only sat looking on. So I sat looking on, keeping her in dead-eye's view. I hated that she looked calm as though dirt and funk hadn't touched her. That she looked cool, in charge of herself. I knew I wasn't.

We waited as, little by little, the crowd drifted away, leaving only a few friends. I waited for them to leave. Monica waited for more. She waited for something I didn't have. Time.

Big H kept smiling, kept talking to everyone. His warm, honest eyes, reassuring everyone he was home and well. Then over the heads of his friends, his eyes turned automatically to the corner table and for an instant rested there.

In that instant they had looked into each other's eyes, unsmiling, hardly greeting. Yet a feeling so deep, so pure, passed between them, it had no need to reflect on their faces. In my mind I saw a picture of my work-hardened hand stretched out on the table next to Monica's. I stood up. The next instant, he had seen me. He came toward me, arms outstretched. "Dorine, Dorine. I'm so glad. . . ."

I let him take my hands. Let him kiss me. I was happy to see him, relieved that he had come back to Harlem safe and sound where he belonged. But as glad as I felt, as happy to see me as he seemed, I knew that if I took him home with me that night, every night, if I married him and Monica never saw the inside of his bedroom, I'd still be a trick to him—second best. And Dorine Davis never intended to settle for being nobody's trick, and never the hell in life intended to settle for second best.

We walked out of The Club—Tom with me. Smiling. My head in the air. That love affair was no more. I had given it up. I had decided it was not for me. Still, for the life of me I had to keep swallowing and swallowing that thick lump in my throat. And when Tom handed me into his car, the tears just gushed. (I declare I cry at the prick of a pin any old goddamn how.)

BOOK THREE

1

The Depression that followed the Wall Street crash of '29 messed with the lives of lots of folks. It changed my status. I got myself a chauffeur—James.

Straight-backed in his uniform, like a motion-picture chauffeur, young, light tan, with sad brown eyes that had caught my fancy from the first, James had been formed in the flesh to suit my purposes. "I declare, James," I liked to tease, "you work for me because you like to show off as much as showing me off." James smiled, bashful, as he dragged his top lip down to hide rotten front teeth, wrinkling the skin about his eyes.

Showing off on that warm-for-March afternoon that had pushed folks out in numbers, we drove where mostly white folks lived, to give them a treat. Seeing eyes pop out of heads, necks from collars, jaws hanging slack, while James stretched up proud, and I, draped in skins, sat back pretending to be enjoying the view, while all the time we were digging ofays digging us.

"Well now, Dorine, don't know about that." James's slow drawl spoke of West touching South: Arkansas. "A guy hates to be hanging just to be hanging. . . ."

The Depression had lots of out-of-work guys hanging around the streets. I had picked the cream off the top, picking James. Actually, we had picked each other. For the best part of one year we had been looking at one another before he decided to speak.

"A guy hates to be hanging just to be hanging" were the first words he had said. "What say I keep this beauty shining for a couple of bucks a week?"

"Do you better than that," I answered. "A room with meals if you can drive."

"Lady, that's my name, Truck-Driving James." We had stuck. James took care of me while I was in town, and the apartment and car when I wasn't. The best thing about him: he appreciated my style.

To keep our show going, we drove south along Morningside Park. At 110th Street we drove east along Central Park, turning north on Madison Avenue, through the Spanish and Italian neighborhoods, to Mount Morris Park, where our white audience got mixed in with the West Indians buying into the brownstones. Then on to 125th Street, turning up Seventh Avenue, where shouts and whistles greeted us and cats called out to us. To James: "What you putting down, brother hound?" "Don't sit there too stable. The lady'll think you ain't able. You'll miss out, my man." To me: "Lady, don't think I ain't a lover 'cause I ain't on rubber; skin's the toughest ride in town." "Madam, give me something to remember you by—them furs. . . ."

Depression, and black studs still turning a fact into a crack. Young studs on the corners, well pressed, grinning and bowing to us. Old gents were out, too, sporting derbys, three-piece suits, walking sticks; and on that warm March day, rushing spring with straw hats, boaters for Americans, panamas for West Indians. They strolled, or stood in little clusters, chatting, holding on to or posing with their canes, among the parade of people rushing by: women, starched white showing under coats, dashing off to church or some other place, their kids following; girls, cotton stockings on skinny legs, bows tied to braids sticking out from under tams; boys in knickers, Vaseline-greased faces grinning under too-big caps. Seeing us, they all stopped, big-eyeing as we cruised by.

And on that afternoon I saw him again: a face staring out of a window like a picture on a wall, flashing by—too familiar to miss, too precious to be real. "Let's do that block again, James."

James, always with me, turned the car around at the next corner, drove down a few blocks, then turned uptown again. But we went by too quickly to be sure. "Let's do it again, James."

This time, in turning, cars stopped us, a red light stopped us, forcing me to the edge of my seat in a sweat, knowing that by the time we reached him, he'd be gone. But no. There he stood, one foot propped on a stool, elbow on knee, staring out into the space outside of the restaurant window.

When James stopped the car, I sat staring at him, waiting, hoping that he might look over and, seeing me, invite me in. But his thoughts were on other things, far away. So I got out and went up to the window to stand before him. He moved his eyes, trying to see past the obstruction, but I kept moving with his eyes, and finally he looked, and seeing me, he smiled.

"Hey, feller." I went in joking. "Don't you be flirting with these broads passing by. That messes the hell outa business."

"Who, me? Flirt? Nomahn. It just me friendly look."

I kept looking at him, expecting him to say more in greeting me. When he didn't, I asked: "Don't you remember me?"

"It ain't likely I forget someone so lovely," he said. But his eyes showed no recall.

"You're a friend of Big H," I said, not really wanting to mention Big H. "We met at a club the night of Lindbergh."

"Lindbergh! That's going far back . . . four years."

"Four years! Already!" The time had gone by fast. Without seeming to, I looked the place over. It was a well-set-up room. The counter in front; tables with white tablecloths in the rear; two waiters standing around in white jackets, waiting for the late-evening customers. Clean. No "fast action."

"Your name's Harry—something or other," I said.

"Brisbane. Oh, God, but your mind good."

"Better than yours, anyway," I said.

"Don't mind me," he apologized. "It the business—you know?"

"Not doing so hot?"

"How you mean?" He took his foot off the stool to stretch his pride tall. "Business is good. It early yet—wait till later."

"It's a lovely room," I said and watched his handsome face light up in appreciation.

"Ahh, yes—me little paradise. . . ." But then a flash of pain. Deep. I almost felt it, saw it in his blinking eyes, the spread of his nostrils. But only for an instant, and a smile spread out his face. "I call it The Rising Sun. . . . But tell me, how you does remember me?"

Tall, big, broad-shouldered—and those eyes. . . . I sure hadn't forgotten. He had been hanging not four inches from the front of my head, waiting to be thought out. "You're not easy to forget."

I looked into his eyes, flirting.

"Thanks." He laughed the big-bellied laugh I declare I had been praying to hear. "Likewise, I'm sure." Crummy—sweet. "But I ain't got a mind good as you," he said. "The name . . . ?"

"Dorine—Dorine Davis."

"Dorine, Dorine, Dorine . . . It like music, yes?"

Gay, gay unto madness those yellow-lit eyes. No bookishness there. Thank the Lord. No rich man too busy for a natural hard. Fine meat—all the way down to his strong-looking legs. The look of him got me weak-kneed embarrassed.

"By the way, what's with Big H?" I asked because I could think of nothing else to say. I hadn't seen Big H since his kidnapping. Hadn't wanted to. Hadn't wanted to deal with the letdown feeling of being easily done without.

"Big H, back home you know. This Seabury Committee thing. It got all the big boys taking cover. But Big H coming back—soon."

"Damn shame. . . ." I said, thinking of how one thing led to another: the notoriety over Big H's kidnapping had sent Judge Samuel Seabury digging into the Harlem numbers racket, folks said. And so a lot of folks were cutting out—going back to the islands, to wait it out.

"What about The Club?" I asked. "Closed?"

"Nuh. The manager, Odel? He holding it down for now. . . ."

"I see the Seabury Committee didn't start investigating you yet," I said, looking around.

"Who me?" His eyes widened, shocked. "How you mean? Madam, The Rising Sun is a business that ain't never been in nothing shady. Nomahn. Not me—never!"

The place looked prosperous—too prosperous to be making it just as an eating-place. Reading my mind, he laughed. "You see, little lady, I a mahn money don't make. Is me the moneymaker." I remembered that song. He seemed to like to sing it. But honesty didn't give room for much conversation. I waited for him to keep bragging. But a couple came in and he moved toward them. I made for the door.

"Hey." Harry came rushing back, stopping me before I opened it. "Don't make this the last time." He flirted so far down into my eyes, I thought he might be looking at the soles of my feet.

Feeling small, helpless, tingly, I winked. "That's a promise. It's hardly the first."

Then strutting, heels clicking, fur tails draping careless-like down my back, I trillied to where James stood bowing me into my big, black Buick. The stud might be a monkey chaser, but he had to have lived damn near all his life in trees not to be impressed by that number. I settled myself comfortable in the car, posing, before turning to wave. But Harry had gone. "Home, James," I said in a small voice. The car pulled off. Harry still hadn't come back.

Love runs its course like a river. Put an obstruction in its path and it's bound to change directions. The words came to me in a dream. I sat up in bed, repeated them over and over. Satisfied that I knew them well enough to tell Tom, if he talked about me being fickle, I snuggled back to sleep. I kept repeating them while taking my shower the next morning. Then ready to go down to tell Tom about Harry, I opened the door and came face-to-face with a Western Union man. I jumped back wanting to slam the door shut, to shout: Dorine Davis don't live here.

"The elevator man says this is Dorine Davis' apartment. You her?" Right then, I knew that someone, somewhere—God, or the devil, one or the other—had conspired to keep me away from Harry Brisbane—the man I wanted more than I wanted most things.

I took the telegram down to Tom and handed it to him. "Open this on my life, Tom. If it's calling me home I declare I'll sit right here and die." I followed him to the living room, where I found Ann sitting on the couch. I sat next to her waiting for him to open the message.

"Ain't no use you dying right off, Dorine," Tom said. "Not when you think of the sport we can have when you get back. But you got to go. Your brother-in-law done had a stroke." I groaned. Ann, mistaking disappointment for grief, put an arm around my shoulders. "I'll go along, Dorine—just for the ride."

"All the way to Montgomery?"

"Why not? Beats staying around town, seeing all our kings scattering. Who knows where the arm of the law will fall next."

"What you got to worry about?" Tom asked. "They ain't thinking about boosters—yet. Anyway you got your money in a vault. I tried to tell that simple Miro that's what he should do. Or invest some—like me. Put money in bars—in our black baseball teams. But no, he got it in the bank where all they had to do was look. He got to have known he ain't paid taxes."

"But who pays taxes on gamblings? Anyway, the way I see it, this kingdom is mighty shaky. Investigations has a way of growing. I'd just as soon go along for the ride—if it's okay with you, Dorine."

"Suit yourself."

Harry wasn't in when I stopped by The Rising Sun to tell him I was leaving. "Where's your boss?" I asked the counterman.

"He'll be in late," the man said.

"Got an address where I can reach him?" The stud looked me over from beneath his eyelids and hunched his shoulders. He wasn't saying. At the back of the room, two men were cleaning up, clearing the tables, mopping the floor. No use asking them. An empty feeling of having missed out, of having been set up against time, touched my heart. But the next morning, driving out of the city with Ann— at the feel of the car rocking in the wind, the smell of early spring, the excitement of the early morning air—I told myself: If you and Harry have waited four years, Dorine Davis, it can't hurt to wait a couple of weeks.

And in that big black Buick, we two women alone gave in to that feeling of specialness that doing what few women do gave. Ann and I had never been close, yet we shared a closeness. We had driven the length and breadth of the United States; we had bedded down in cars during snowstorms; we had driven miles along the Painted Desert, felt our smallness looking over the Grand Canyon, known our ignorance floating on the salty waters of the Great Salt Lake; had driven miles on plains where no eyes saw us—and had enjoyed every minute of it. But we had never been south together. . . .

And so we talked, laughed, told and retold our tales, enjoying them as much in the telling as we had in the doing, until we hit Virginia. Then the faces of folks staring in on us—two women alone,

one white, one black, chatting easily, friendly—with unfriendly eyes, inquisitive eyes, downright hateful eyes, forced us to slow down.

We had packed enough food to last us the two days we had given ourselves to get to Montgomery, for we had no intention of stopping at restaurants where I had to go to the back or Ann had to "pass" through the front to eat. Nor did we intend on going into toilets marked "colored" or "niggers"—me from necessity, Ann from choice. Instead we fought our bladders, making them hold out for empty stretches of road where we squatted behind bushes, in the woods, or at the side of the road by the car.

"Motherfuckers stayed awake nights planning the ways most impossible for folks to get along," Ann said. "And they damn sure succeeded."

"That they did. But I'd take this over them Jim Crow trains any day," I said. "At least I can pick the bush I wants to squat behind."

I was glad Ann had come with me instead of James. Not only could we squat together without hiding, but we were used to this long cross-country driving without sleep. We knew what it meant to be tired and to keep on going.

And we were that kind of tired leaving Georgia and heading into Alabama, having taken turns through the night on our non-stop—except for gas and squatting—trip.

"Won't be long now," I said as we drove through the last stretch where the tall pine trees on both sides of the road spun out of the darkness as the early morning sun touched them, and as though that bit of light was all they awaited, birds commenced to singing in the mist from the dew that had forced the trees to give out that heavy-clean smell peculiar to green things but sharpest with pine. It gave a pleasant feeling of drowsiness. Most of the night we had been the only car along the way. The strain we had felt from the eyes of folks looking in on us had given way to the content of having the world to ourselves. Ann leaned back, her eyes closed.

"That's the prettiest smell . . . sure is pretty out here. Makes me wonder what the world would be without folks. Wouldn't it be a great place?"

No sooner had she said that than I looked into the mirror and saw a car driving up behind.

"That would mean without you and me too, wouldn't it, Ann?"

"What would be wrong with that?"

I laughed. "Tom says you got the makings of a good undertaker, Ann. If we all go, you won't have nothing to undertake."

The car behind kept coming closer, closer. A Tin Lizzie. I thought for a moment of driving faster and losing it. Instead I slowed down, letting him pass so we could have the place to ourselves again.

"That would be all right too," Ann said.

"Well I just can't see this world being a better place unless I'm in it," I said. "Not even half so good."

The Tin Lizzie had driven up alongside. The driver, a tall, thin-faced redneck, looked in, squinting at us from some (to my way of seeing) evil-looking eyes. I slowed down. He slowed down too. Ann, feeling our speed slacken and hearing the car beside us, sat up. He stared at her. She stared at him.

I slowed even more. He drove on but slowed in front of us, forcing me to trail behind.

"If I go any slower, I might as well stop," I said.

"Then stop," Ann said. "Let's see what he's got to do."

I stopped. So did he. "Let's find out," Ann said, opening the car door.

"I'm not going out there," I answered. "This car is protection. That buzzard can do what he wants. But all he got is that Tin Lizzie. I swear out I'll knock the shit out of him if he gets out of the car and starts something. I'll flatten the son of a bitch so he'll have to be scraped off this damn road."

"We can always do that," Ann said. "I'm for letting the sucker tell us what he's after." She got out of the car and went to stand by his, resting her elbows on the window. I kept my eyes on her serious face. That's all I could see in the dim light of dawn. I wanted to see her expression, or tell if she was reading him from the way she stood, but she just stood there talking. Finally she stepped back and he drove off.

"What you tell him?" I asked when she came back. She shrugged, took the Thermos of water, poured some on a handkerchief, and, as I drove on, scrubbed her face and put fresh makeup on before putting her head back on the seat.

I was about to turn off the highway when another car—a sheriff's car—pulled alongside. He waved us down. I waited as he walked over to us then around the car, taking a good look at our license plates.

"What you doing in this here car, gal?" he said, squinting.

"I'm driving it, Master Sheriff, suh?" I said, smiling. My nerves were tissue-paper thin from being tired and from the redneck stopping us, as well as not knowing what Ann had said to that critter. Nonetheless I knew my place. If I owned up too quickly to having that car, he'd declare I was one of them uppity niggers who had gone north and picked up airs.

"Where you git it?" he asked.

Ann sat up, pulled herself around to look at him, and I knew why she had done the makeup bit. "Something wrong, sheriff?" Miss South herself couldn't have sounded softer, sweeter, more the coquette.

"Oh, ma'am"—he tipped his hat. "I ain't seen you. This here your gal?" Big, portly, hard gray eyes staring out between folds of flesh. What in the hell did he want?

"Ye-es, she is." Ann got to smiling, slow. "Something wrong?"

"Mighty queer, seeing a nigra gal drive. . . ."

"That's why I brought her with me, sheriff—on account of she can."

My spine got right stiff at them talking about me. But for whatever reason he had stopped us, I knew it the better part of reason to act dull. I took to playing with my fingers.

"Y'all from around these parts?" he asked.

"We sure 'nough are, sheriff—right from Montgomery."

"What y'all doing with them New York plates?"

"I do declare, sheriff—ain't you the smartest? So happens this car belongs to ma friend . . . Dorine Davis? You must have heard of Miss Davis? She bought this car in New York, and wouldn't you know?—them Yankees made her buy these New York plates."

My heart got to thumping. That lie sounded like first one thing and then another. Damn fool playing around, about to land us both in jail. Yet my lips spread out to show all of my pretty white teeth; my eyes went dull.

"You see, Miss Davis come on ahead," Ann said. "The governor—Governor Miller?—he was expecting her for lunch. She come on the train and. . . ."

"This gal drive all the way down?" Suspicion seeped through his every pore.

"We take turns."

"Don't sound likely. . . ."

"Well, I do declare. . . ." Ann pulled herself tall, insulted.

"Where's your gal from?"

"Right here—Montgomery. But sheriff, if something's wrong—'pon my word, you best call the governor. Miss Davis is waiting."

He kept looking from Ann to my white teeth, the dumb-but-devoted look spread out on my face. And when he tipped his hat and stepped back, I stopped myself from grabbing him and spitting in his face.

"Been having a mess of trouble with them Yankees driving through these parts lately," he apologized.

"You don't say. Sure am sorry to hear. . . ."

Looking at the fool getting back into his car, after listening to that simple-ass tale, made the hot sweat burn. Hatred that he had believed her, but worse, hatred of Ann, playing the lead and getting away with it. Not that I wanted to be hauled in—nothing like that. I kept my simple grin going and drove slow—slower when I saw him behind, forcing him to trail me until he turned off.

"Goddamn son of a bitch!" Ann exploded. "Tired as I am? If he had followed us another mile, I'd have taken my gun and blown the shit out of him."

"What! You got a gun?" I had never knowingly been near to folks who carried guns—surely not one likely to use one. I thought of Ann and the redneck. What had she said to make him drive off? I tried to study her tired face under the thick bobbed hair. Going home, most folks around us hearing her talk had to know she was black. And folks in Montgomery, black or white, didn't cotton to black folks talking tough to whites.

"I—I ain't never carried no heat," I said.

"Ain't no sense in carrying one unless you planning on using it." My scalp crawled at the matter-of-fact way she said this.

"Would you have shot him sure 'nough, Ann?"

"Sure—same as you'd have run down that redneck if he had stepped out of his car." I drove on real quiet, thinking about that. And not knowing what I might have done if I thought he meant us harm, I laughed. Ann laughed. We laughed together. Then as we rode on I felt relaxed to ask: "How's things between you and Sonny?"

"Like always," she said.

"Y'all still seeing each other?"

"From time to time."

I never talked about Sonny with Ann. Sonny happened to be a hunk of my life that I still claimed certain rights over. "You still think a heap of him, don't you?" I asked.

"I love the nigger."

"And Sonny?"

"Sonny loves Sonny."

"And—what do you intend to do about it?"

Our eyes met in the mirror. She looked into my mind and laughed. "No, I'm not going to shoot him. Folks don't shoot the Sonnys of the world—not to change them. They wait for them to do themselves in."

"Sonny ever proposition you?" I asked.

"Would he be Sonny if he hadn't?"

"I ought to have warned you," I said. "Told you he was a no-good pimp."

"Sonny? A pimp? No, a fucking dreamer. He don't really hate women. He just worships money—or what he thinks money can bring. He'll use anybody and anything to get it."

She fumbled in the glove compartment, where she had stashed her flask, and took a swallow. I marked that well. All along the way, she had taken a nip here, a nip there. But talking about Sonny, she took a mighty big swallow.

"I'm glad you were able to say no," I said.

"Baby, I'm a future undertaker, not a whore," Ann said. "I decided on that long before I met Sonny."

"An undertaker. . . . Such an awful thing to be, especially for a woman."

"Awful? No more than anything else. So many more awful things, Dorine. Things folks do to folks without thinking. . . . Let me tell you about this little black girl, born of a light-brown-skinned mother and a light-brown-skinned father. Only she came out look-ing white. This made her parents very happy. They knew that if she wanted, she could go on to great things—even a wealthy marriage to a rich white. They kept pushing and pushing, and then they sent her off to an aunt who was passing. This aunt sent her to a girls' finishing school.

"The things this girl had to listen to! Some ugly shit about black folks: 'Look at old black Sambo,' girls would say about black men working in the school as porters, or out on the street. 'Look at that lazy coon. Why are niggers like that?' 'Sure, they must have come from the apes.' 'Ann, why do you suppose they ever brought those baboons from Africa and brought them here to dress them up like men?'

"Can you imagine, Dorine? Having to listen to shit like that and laugh. Keep laughing, knowing all the time you're laughing at yourself—at your mother, your father?

"God, do you know how much hate there is in white folks? How deep it goes even in the best of them? Hate! They had to nurture it deep in their culture to go around the world killing off people. Hate in them, baby, is so natural they mistake it for intelligence.

"I remember teasing my roommates for the hell of it. 'Bet you didn't know that I am a Negro,' I'd say. 'Both my mother and father are Negroes.' They'd look at me as though I had gone clean out of my mind. 'Ann,' they'd say, 'don't you dare say such things about yourself! Are you crazy?'

"If I had said I was a thief, a whore, a murderer, they might have laughed, joked about it. But to say I was black. . . .

"That's why I decided on undertaking. Being an undertaker in a white undertaking parlor, so I could do them up the way they are. I'd make up their faces all pious, and beneath their clothes I'd fuck up their bodies. Cratered souls. I'd have such a ball doing it. Because that's where they are, baby. Why do you think they created religion? Superstition? Why do you think they spread the gospel, pretending to believe in Lucifer and every word written in the Bible? To give a reason for their fucked-up souls. They believe in power—and when they go after it, they want Lucifer there as a fucking excuse. . . .

"Anyway, going to New York turned out to be my undoing. Being in Harlem, meeting Sonny, changed my life—drove me to drink"—she laughed. "You wouldn't have believed that Sonny was

184

good for anything. But now I give less than a damn about white folks' souls and the crazy undertaker who fucked over their bodies. I can't live a whiter-than-thou life in Baltimore anymore. I love feeling free of it, and of being around black folks in Harlem, being my own black self."

"But Ann, as fine as you look, why bother with somebody like Sonny? They got some fine studs around Harlem."

"It be's that way, Dorine, baby. . . ."

Who was I to say? I had hung on to Sonny for a damn long time. And Big H? I had clung to him as though life depended on it. And now Harry Brisbane? With all that flirting in his eyes, and the weakness that brought over me? "You know what I say, Ann? I say that love runs like a river. Put an obstruction in its path and it's bound to change directions." The great-sounding words out at last. And Ann said:

"Hey, that's pretty good. Where did you pick up that one?"

"I thought it up."

"Well go on with your smart self. I didn't know you had it in you." And that was the first I learned that Ann had always thought me a dumb broad.

Evilness rose out of the earth like vapor as we drove through town. It leaped out of eyes, seeped through the pores of crackers along the roadways. They looked like eagles ready to spring in at us. I kept my eyes on the road, giving Ann directions as she drove, cussing myself for not having had good sense—especially after that sheriff—to stop and pull off the New York plates.

I expected that any minute we would be stopped, and barring that, for a simple joker to jump out in front of the car, to be hit, giving them the excuse to haul us in. The feeling of evil is a scary thing. Whatever Ann had said, I believed in God. He had His way of warning—go slow, take care. Ann, without one word from me, paid heed. I kept looking around for black faces, for familiar faces—witnesses, just in case. I spotted a few—in this town usually bustling with blacks. My eyes caught theirs in passing, and theirs shifted. Looking back to make sure of their fear, I found them gone. . . . What the hell was going on in the old town? A feeling, but my mind went racing back to days of being shuttered in to dark houses, of listening to whispers. . . . Then I remembered Old Man Witlow. Sweat popped out on my brow. Thank the Lord for Ann. Drive careful now, baby—drive slow.

Pulling up in front of that old house—dirty, tired, whipped—I had never been so glad to get to any one place in my life. And remembering how happy I had been on leaving, I said: "Well, Ann, we made it. Now we got but one worry—getting out."

Joseph, his left side paralyzed, his cheek twisted so that saliva escaped from his loose lips to flow back to his pillow, looked mighty pitiful. And making it too hard to bear, his right pajama leg, under its stump, had gotten twisted up in the bed sheet.

I stood looking down at him as quiet as in the presence of death. He stared back, his eyes begging. God, why hadn't he just gone on and died? I looked over at Ann on the other side of the bed, her face serious. I got to wondering if she was thinking how best to set him up in his casket to resemble a man. Thinking that forced me to smile to show Joseph that the way he lay there, hanging on to life with his eyes, had to be the best way. But the thought jumped to mind, unbidden, if he had to die at least let him die while I was there and save me a trip. Begging eyes. Begging for what? What the hell did he want from me?

The strong smell of coffee boiling, of sausage cooking, of hot bread baking forced me out of the room. Pushing past Brother, who had come to stand in the doorway, I went into the kitchen.

"Lord, Miss Dorine, sure am glad you come home." Miss Jessica wiped bony hands on her apron, nodding toward the corner where Jennie Mae sat eating breakfast with Son and another little boy. I had longed to see Son. But I refused to look at him. My unreasoning anger against Joseph had carried over to him. I looked instead at the other little boy beside him. "This sure's a terrible time," Miss Jessica moaned.

"Ain't nothing that bad, Miss Jessica, not when you got this house smelling so good," I joked.

"You know me." She laughed a high, cracked laugh. "Am here at the crack of the morn. Ain't got no more babies. My gals—the big ones—helps out, unties my hands." Wiry, gray, fading eyes, faded smile, strong hands—Miss Jessica was still my best-thought-out idea.

"Things all right at home?" I asked.

"Well, this depression, you know? No more cotton to pick—mills done shut down. . . . But getting by—thanks to you, and the Lord."

I went to the table, still keeping my eyes from Son. "Whose little boy?" I asked, pointing to the pretty curly-haired boy, with long eyelashes fanning his face.

"But Dorine," Jennie Mae said. "That's Bud."

"Bud?"

"Yes—Mama's last. Our baby brother."

The shock of having forgotten Sister's last went through me. He was no baby. Four years—at least. Son too, I noticed when I had worked up the nerve to look at him, had stretched. Still round with baby fat, nevertheless he had a serious, manly expression on his big, round, black face, and him not yet six. Jennie Mae, when she stood next to me, reached up to my shoulder!

Kids are the measure of time—or I could convince myself that it had been only the day before when I had run from the old place vowing never to return.

Yet I had come back. And although the kids had stretched up to another time, from the look on Brother's face, where he stood in the doorway staring at me, I judged some of the same old problems were left over.

"Where's Jane?" I asked for the niece named after Mama.

"She's off to her piano lesson," Jennie Mae said.

"Piano lesson!" My eyebrows went up. I looked around at the dingy looking room. "Piano lessons when this house is in such a mess?"

"What's wrong with the house, Dorine?" Jennie Mae asked. "We cleaned it good—knowing you'd be here."

"I hate to think of what it looks like when I'm not expected." I spoke to include Miss Jessica, who had stopped on her way to take our breakfast into the dining room. "Well, I hope that Jane's not too tired from all that playing to help out come morning."

"But Dorine, tomorrow's Sunday."

"And the Lord saith cleanliness is next to Godliness."

But the next morning, Brother got up right along with me. And while drinking coffee, he said: "Dorine, what we gonna do now?"

"About what, Brother?"

"About Joseph. These kids. You can see for yourself, I ain't able to handle it. I got my studies. I want to be leaving soon."

That's all I had thought about since getting the telegram. "I reckon Mildred's got to give a hand," I said. That had been my one plan. Ever since her husband had run off, I had had to send her extra money. "She ain't got but two kids, and this house is big and it's strong."

"We ain't the same family, Dorine," Brother said. The quiet in his voice spoke of his fear that at twenty-one he might be getting beyond the age to collect on my promise. "Mildred ain't the same— not since Morris left."

"Don't matter, Brother. We got to stick together. Or how else we gonna accomplish what we want?"

Brother sighed. He looked at me from those eyes that seemed deep from learning behind eyeglasses. "You best go see her, Dorine."

"Don't worry, I will. Mildred's ass ain't gold, Brother. She's always doing the accusing, and she's the one who always acts selfish."

I had a whole basket of things ready to say to Mildred. For every question she asked, I had an answer. Mildred never got tired of trying to make me feel guilty. But I had paid the price to get her loyalty.

Putting off the cleaning until the next day, I set off with Ann. We walked the two miles to Mildred's instead of driving and calling attention to our New York plates. Even walking we got our share of attention: whites standing still, gave us slow, hateful head-to-toe stares. Most were curious about Ann. Black folks too. Their eyes slid away as they dragged their kids from us. A cold sweat broke out at the back of my neck. I had the urge to grab hold of Ann's hand and run like hell—back to the old house, or nonstop to Mildred's.

But being city slicksters carries its own rules. Whatever the reasons for the strange acting, we had to deal with them. So we blank-faced-cold-stared at staring eyes, strolling easy, even swaggering. Bad city folks promising a real hurt to any sucker simple enough to think of tangling with us.

Everything about Montgomery was gloomy. The trees, tall, sober, dark, enduring, had the same quality as the people. The magnolia with their heavy scent put me in the mind of death. I heard birds singing and thought of mourning. Mourning who? Joseph? It sure wasn't about to be me.

Lil, Mildred's oldest, had grown like a reed, thin, long. Her octopus arms wrapping around me pulled me into the house. "Girl," I said. "If you ever grow to them arms you'll be damn near a giant."

"Oh Dorine . . ." Lil giggled. "But I do declare I'm glad you're here. Now everything will be settled." How? Miracles?

"Where's your mother?" I had no intention of being pleasant until I had settled what I had come for.

We went into the parlor, hearing as we went a voice from the radio: ". . . the nine nigras and two white girls from the railroad at Paint Rock to Scottsboro . . ." Ann and I went toward the radio I had sent Mildred to keep her company. But Mildred, standing at the window, switched it off when she saw us.

"Dorine." She came toward me. "You brought us company."

"What was all that about?" Ann asked her.

Lil answered. "We don't know what to make of it. Seems some white girls and black boys got caught traveling together on the railroad. You know these whites. . . ." She stood staring through the curtains, out into the road, worried.

"Sit on down." Mildred offered Ann a chair, then sat facing her. "You're Dorine's friend?"

"Yes, I am," Ann answered.

"That's nice. I don't have any, you know—friends. . . ."

Something amiss. I looked at Lil. But Ruth, Mildred's youngest, came in with a tray holding a pot of tea and a dish of cookies. "Dorine—how long will you be staying this time?"

"I'm here a damn sight longer than I want to be already." I thought of our walk over and waited for Mildred's usual comeback. Instead of answering, Mildred got up and walked back to the window. "It's the railroad, you know," she said. Pulling the white lace curtains back and looking out. "The railroad took him off—and the railroad will bring him back." I blinked.

"She's talking about Daddy," Lil whispered.

"Morris," Mildred said. "The railroad took him off. . . ." Then I knew what I had missed about her. Her jealousy. Even when she had been glad to see me, resentment had always hovered right near the surface. Without it her face had lost its meaning. Standing in the sunlight, her thin body in that starched cotton dress looked scooped out—a shell.

"Why didn't you write to tell me about this?" I asked.

"Made no sense writing, Dorine," Lil said. "You been doing so much already. We know you doing the best you can."

Tears filled my eyes. Love has that effect on me. And looking into Lil's serious, dark brown, narrow little face, I fell in love with her right then.

"How long. . . ?"

"Pa's been gone a year," Ruthie said. "Since then . . ."

"You two take care of her—and the house?"

"Yes, ma'am, me and Ruth," Lil said.

"But that's too much for just two little girls."

Nine and ten years old, with all they had to make do on the little money I sent. But Mama's teaching had come through to them: the house sparkled. The curtains at the windows were standing out with starch. The floors had been scrubbed and polished. And Mildred was so well cared for in her spotless cotton dress, her hair parted in the middle and braided. The long-legged dolls I had brought her from New York sat in their careless hussy poses around the living room.

"What happened with Morris?" I asked.

"He lost his job at the school," Ruthie said. "Then he just went off . . . folks say to get work on the railroad. But he ain't ever said—just took off."

"I come here thinking that maybe y'all should move together into the old house. That's all paid for—and with the kids—and Joseph . . ."

Even as I spoke, I heard Brother's words. No, they sure were a different family. Yet I kept on. "That way you kids can be together, and Miss Jessica . . ."

"Sounds great, Dorine," Lil said, her narrow face, her bright, smart-looking eyes looking into mine. "Nothing I'd like better than to be with Jennie Mae and help her with the boys. But Ma ain't leaving that window. That's where she wants to be. I'd be scared to force her. If something happened, I'd blame myself—and I declare I'd hate that. . . ."

The South made women of little girls.

"You know I can't just leave you two here alone. . . ."

"But it's all right, Dorine." Lil took my hand and laid it on her lap, rubbing the back of it. "I declare it is. We got to be with Ma—and neighbors helps out—and we got you."

Whatever they said, they knew and I knew, once having seen them, that I had to do something about them.

On our way back home I said to Ann, "I thought this Depression hadn't touched me, and here it is about to drive a crate over me."

"How so?" Ann asked in her matter-of-fact voice. "I don't see it that way. Something tries to use you, turn it about and use the hell out of it."

"The Depression, Ann?"

"Why not? From where I stand, the Depression ran over this town. Nobody's working. But Dorine, you work regular—what's more, you can't complain that you're not making money."

Ann got prettier with time. She was always a good-looking woman. But when you got to talking and looking into her intelligent eyes, she got downright beautiful. So back at the house I said to Miss Jessica:

"Who do you know around who is strong, clean, and needs work?"

"Mother Rivers." I knew Mother Rivers. A big, strong woman who had been a midwife around our part of town as long as I remembered. The next day I sent for her.

"Mother Rivers, see that man?" I said, taking her into Joseph's room. "That's my brother-in-law. He's been a man to my sister and a good father to the kids. I got to have someone to look after him. I don't want him lying around in piss day or night. And I'm willing to pay."

"How much?"

"Five dollars a month."

"Well, now, Miss Dorine. There's some others will work for that. Not me. I'm used to handling money."

"Name it."

"Twenty dollars."

"You'll be getting room and board."

"That's where I was when you sent for me. In my house. Eating." She looked at me hard—hefty, evil, but with a look about her. . . . At any rate, poor Joseph would hardly last out the month.

"Fifteen," I said.

"Okay, I'll go with that."

To Brother I said: "Now, all you got to do is hang in and see to it that things work out. When and if they do, you can take off."

"Dorine, I'm twenty-one. I don't have that many more years."

"All the more reason you see things work out. I promised I'd pay your way. My promise is good. What does it gain either of us if I stay here?" What was there for him to say?

Then I got one of Mildred's neighbors and asked her to cook and sit with Mildred while the kids were in school. I offered her five dollars. She took it. She had been helping out for nothing.

Darkness came quicker than I remembered. No sooner had the sun come up before it had set again. I had been planning on meeting up with Ann, but when I finished with Brother I looked through the window and saw Ann coming back from her walk. The day had already faded.

"If this isn't the damndest, scariest town I ever did see," Ann said, coming into the house. "Dorine, if you're finished with all your business down here, what say we get the hell out—right now?"

"I'm finished with the troublesome part," I said. "But come morning I got to get these kids on the ball and give the house a good scrub-down."

Ann's usually calm eyes showed the strain of the long drive we hadn't rested enough from, and the heavy atmosphere. "What the hell for?" she snapped at me. "You don't live here."

Seeing that explaining wouldn't tell the full story, I took down the old family album. There were not many pictures. One of the old house when it was newer, with a young Master Samuel standing out front, blond mustache reaching down to his chin, posing with his hat to his chest. One of Mama in the backyard, a dress as black as her face and as severe. The collar of the dress stood up to frame a head of thick hair, parted in the middle and pulled back, making her look the queen of evil. The picture of my mother had faded as much as her likeness had faded out of mind. But the one of Sister, Mildred, and me, with Brother when he had just started to walk, was sharp and clear. It spoke of the family closeness. That was all—

except for the loose photo of Janie I slipped out to take with me. I had just closed the album when I looked up to see Brother closing and locking the shutters.

Even on cool nights I hated closed shutters. And that had been a hot, troublesome day. "Brother, I got to have air tonight, even evil Montgomery air," I said.

"Not tonight, Dorine," Brother said. "Something mighty queer's happening around this town, and I ain't aiming to find out."

"Seems to me if something's about to happen, you should make it your business to find out," I said.

Brother stood before me, blocking my way to the door. "Don't be no fool, Dorine. That door stays closed."

"Brother, you got to be fooling," I said, upset because this brother whom I had sworn to stick by was bucking me.

"No, I'm not, Dorine," he said, his serious eyes looking dead into mine. "The trouble with you is that you been up north too long."

God, how I hated folks saying that to me. It made me feel like nothing—like the sheriff had made me feel—grinning when I wanted to be serious, simple when I wanted to be smart—like a spirit floating around without meaning.

We kept staring at each other, and I got to thinking of Joseph, dying in bed, not able to go to a hospital. Of Morris, running off and leaving his near-senile wife—and I looked at this tall, black brother who wanted to learn everything, yet was too scared to find out anything. . . .

"Learning don't all come from books, Brother."

"You looking at me and saying that, Dorine?"

I doubted we understood each other. But while we stood trying to figure that one out, a loud pounding at the door made us jump, and a shouting—"Big Brother, Big Brother"—forced Brother to open the door.

Miss Jessica rushed into the room, out of breath, her gray hair standing out over her head, eyes wild, mouth shaking—the soul of fear. "Oh, Big Brother, they done gone after Big Willie! They gone after Big Willie!"

Big Will Hopkins had been tetched as far back as I had thoughts to think. Big, black, walking as though he owned the space he walked through, never looking to the right, never looking to the left. Big Willie, the one man known to walk the streets of the town never stepping out of the way of folks—neither whites nor blacks—never going in through the back doors of stores. He walked from home to town and town to home, rifle slung over his shoulder, pistols strapped to his waist, talking to no one—neither white folks nor black folks. Black folks called him a "bad nigger." White folks called him a "crazy nigger." They all let him be. We kids scrambled out of his way, scared to death, when we saw him coming. The only ones known to befriend him were Miss Jessica and her kin.

The talk built around Big Willie and his craziness told of eight men—whites—who had raped his daughter, killed her, and left her in the woods naked. And Big Willie had taken his daughter, with neither clothes nor coffin, and had buried her way back of his house, down the slope where the creek crossed.

Years later, Big Willie's wife had died—no one knew from what or why. And Big Willie had taken his wife—with neither clothes nor coffin—and had buried her way back of his shack, down the slope where the creek crossed. Years went by and Big Willie lived on alone, never talking, never looking at one living soul save Miss Jessica and her kin. So why, after all the years, had white folks gone after Big Willie—on this night?

The quiet in which we waited in the dark old house had been cut out of my childhood. A deep quiet, a listening quiet, except for Miss Jessica, sitting or kneeling on the floor, moaning or praying. The sound coming from her throat added to the quietness. And in the bedroom, right off the parlor, a man lay dismantled, listening, too, to that quiet, while hanging on to life with his eyes. And the children, bunched up on the couch, listened to the quiet outside of the locked doors, outside of the shuttered windows, a quiet that squeezed the darkness, wrung the meaning out of our lives.

Sitting there listening to the stillness, the awful stillness, listening to the grief, the moaning coming out of Miss Jessica's throat, and thinking of poor Joseph, hanging on to life with his eyes, thinking of the kids, of Brother, of me—sitting there waiting for the dark to break—just waiting, waiting, waiting, stretched my nerves, stretched my nerves, stretched my nerves. . . .

I came to myself walking. Walking down the long dirt road, walking in the dark, dark night, walking past shrouded houses, waiting, noiseless houses, laughter-stilled houses, whisper-filled houses, houses where folks huddled, wrung out of meaning . . . silent . . . silent. . . .

But brave dogs barked. Brave crickets cricked; brave grasshoppers rubbing noise into the night gave it a fit about their right to life . . . and then a cloud slipped from the face of the moon—a big, heavy, moody moon, hanging through the trees, making sense out of darkness. Moonlight grouped trees, stretched their shadows into giants, a crazy quiltwork of shadows to which I ran from moonlit paths, threatened by the silent town, the sightless houses.

How long had I been going when I knew I had been seen? Was being followed? Eyes had pulled my form from the form of the trees I hugged. Peering through the darkness, I tried to find out the viewer. And I saw a figure moving across a moonlit path, losing itself in the darkness of trees. A spirit? Flesh person? I waited, not breathing, not knowing, not able to see where it had gone.

A touch. I jumped. Flesh—a thin hand. It held mine. An arm, a body, soft beneath the feel of cloth. My hand kept searching—a neck, hair, straight, bobbed. Ann!

The spirit of adventure overcame us as we ran from shadow to shadow. And it was right that she had come with me. That she had come out in the dark with me—we southern-northerners, who played at the game of life together, risked our freedom together, loved, flirted in the same self-denying quest for love, or death, or happiness—whatever that meant. And this need, drawing us against our wills to the other side of town, pulling at us through curiosity born of shared experience, despite our fears. Fears which nourished our womanhood, making us two of a kind.

The unshaded stretch of streetcar tracks we had to cross to get over to Miss Jessica's side of town lay exposed in the bright moonlight. And we made for it, fearless—we had left terror in the heaviness of the dark, silent, shuttered house. Alive with the meeting of body and spirit, lightened by the sense of adventure—of our adventure, of our having dared what others had no thought of daring—we skipped along. Ann's softness, her legs brushing mine, the deceiving smallness of her arm hooking mine, the feel of her hard muscles under the soft thinness of her arm, the hardness of the little pistol she carried in the pocket of her cotton jacket. We had a purpose.

If our thoughts ran together, she, like me, had to be thinking of our gang: of Tom, his big, golden grin, his bad feet; of Grace, her pointy nose and pinched mouth; of Albert's sly grin; of Bessie and Bill, their crazy clowning, their love. . . .

I thought of Big H, too, and how much he had taught me. Of Harry, his big-bellied laugh, the laugh I had waited so long to hear, the promise in his eyes. I sighed. I supposed Ann to be thinking of Sonny, never mind his being no good. On a night filled with no promise at all, the thought of love is better than no thought at all. I hugged Ann's arm tight to me, regretting for one moment that I might be leaving my youth on this side of the grave.

Then we heard it . . . the sounds: Shrup—shrup—shrup. . . . Stopping, starting, stopping, starting—shrup—shrup—shrup . . . following us! A dog? A man? Someone who had spotted us? A frightened or an evil something—taking aim, wanting to maim, intending to kill?

The distance between us and the shading trees on the opposite side of the tracks seemed like forever. The moon shone brighter. My back grew broad, broader. We walked on, our eyes peeled, our hooked arms loosened. Ann's hand slipped out of her pocket. Lord, hadn't I known it? It was sure we had come to Alabama to stay! To die! That high-yeller woman wasn't about to ask questions—and I sure wasn't about to hear her ask none. We slowed down. Ann shoved me. I dropped to one side. Ann spun around. In that second we heard:

"Miss Dorine . . . Miss Dorine. . . ." Miss Jessica came trotting up.

"Wheee," Ann whistled, weighing the .22 in her hand. "Don't you never do that. Don't you never sneak up on a living soul like that again."

"I ain't sneaked," Miss Jessica said. "I run all the way. When I seen y'all leave, I ask maself: What is I doin' here? Is me the one got kids over there. Is me who got to be going on home. I would have been home, 'cept I seen them mens, heared what they was about. I plum lost my head—I run back, thinking I reckon somebody ought to do something." She trotted to keep up. "Lordy, if somethin' done happen to my younguns. . . ."

"Ain't nothing happened to them that ain't happening to the rest of them out there," Ann snapped. "You say the oldest is grown. Then they got sense enough to be scared like everybody else."

Miss Jessica's coming had messed with our closeness, had killed the hell out of the adventure, the game. Now that someone who really had reason to be was out there, it put a big question mark over our fool reasoning. What in the hell were we doing out there?

We heard the guns cracking in the distance, and that forced us on. A brightness of fire lit the sky, giving the moon competition, and that forced us on. Smoke darkened the paths of the woods, and as we walked toward a jumble of noises—roosters crowing, donkeys braying, pigs squealing, dogs barking, trumpeting our coming—the sun shot pink sprays overhead. The brightness of fire died down; the moon, still big through the trees, tried to keep its soft light working. But its time had come.

Daylight made us visible and we slipped into lingering shadows as we went, trying to separate sound from sound, voices from animal noises. My throat burned from the smoke settling at the back of my tongue. And then we were there.

Sidestepping pigs scratching their backs in the mud, the chickens running loose as we rounded the bend, we flattened ourselves against the clump of trees and stared across the space separating us from Miss Jessica's shack.

The yard was bare, the shacks silent. Yet we knew that eyes stared at us from the slats of doors in every one of those miserable shacks bunched together on the other side. We raced across the road, the yard, up the rickety steps ready to break down from our weight. The door opened up to us.

"They done kill him, Ma." The voice reached us before we spilled into the kerosene-smelling darkness. And as we stood grouped, the youngsters around us shivering, I shivered too. Tall, skinny, children of poverty and fear, holding on to one another for courage, and still afraid. "He run down to the creek, Ma," the biggest of the boys explained. "They followed him. Burnt down his shack and took off after him. They been shooting, Ma. He dead—I know he dead. . . ."

We walked on—Ann with me—into the bitter aftertaste of smoke spun thin by the morning breeze. We walked up to the space where there once had been a shack—Big Willie's shack. We stopped for a moment to look at the smoldering remains, then we walked on, heading up the slope, then down to the creek, the silent creek. And as we walked, a shuffle of footsteps: naked feet, slippered feet, sneakered feet, feet pushing through pebbles, feet slapping on mud, feet dampened by the dew on fallen leaves. We kept on walking: *Communion*. Down to the creek, the silent creek where a little girl lay buried with neither clothes nor coffin. Walking, walking, footsteps growing in numbers. Naked feet, slippered feet, sneakered feet. Feet pushing through pebbles, feet slapping on mud, feet dampened by the dew on fallen leaves. We kept on walking: *Communion*. Down to the silent creek where a lady lay buried with neither clothes nor coffin. Kept on walking. Naked feet, slippered feet, sneakered feet. Feet pushing through pebbles, feet slapping on mud, feet dampened by the dew on fallen leaves. Kept on walking: *Communion*. Going down to the creek where Big Willie had gone to die.

We saw him. Ann with me. A hulking shadow on the bank of the creek. We reached him first. Ann with me. And we stood looking down at this big man, bigger in death than I had remembered him as a child. Kneeling, his head toward the water, but he had turned to stare over his shoulder, his eyes reflecting, even in death, madness—or laughter one. Bullet holes had opened spaces through his head. Bullet holes through his face, bullet holes up and down his back. But his eyes stared over his shoulder, reflecting laughter—or madness one.

Blood had flowed and was fast drying, flowed thick and remained sticky; blood had bubbled out of bullet holes, stopped up bullet holes, remained black and sticky. Bubbles of blood spun out of sticky bubbles, dried into transparent hardness. . . .

Hands turned Big Willie over, hands stretched him out on the bank of the silent creek where he lay, hands crossed over his chest, fingers around the barrel ends of the two guns. And no man attempted to close his eyes, staring out, reflecting laughter—or madness one. But men got to scurrying, counting spent shells beneath him and around him. And men got to scurrying around, looking for blood—other folks' blood. They found some a few feet away; they found some a few yards away; and they found some a good fifty yards from where Big Willie lay. And near to Big Willie's body, down near the creek, they found the print of a body that had been dragged in its own blood. Turned onto his back, Big Willie stared out at us from those wide-open eyes, reflecting the madness he had lived with—or laughter one.

"Them guns cocked and they empty," one somebody said. Eyes looked into eyes and looked away. Looked into eyes and looked away. "Poor Big Willie," one man said, bent on grieving. "Sure won't never go a-hunting no mo'. Never forgit the time I seen him hit a li'l ole partridge—more than five hundred yards in the air—same time he was movin' a speck out his eye."

"Which eye?"

"Bof of 'em."

The air slackened around us. Yeah, the white folks had had their night; the black folks had to have their day.

We walked on, leaving for those who chose the job of burying Big Willie down by the creek, with his empty pistols—near to his girl and his wife, near the creek—without coffin. . . .

And as we walked a boy behind lamented: "I known it would happen. I heard on Master Brown's radio, 'bout them black boys and them white gals—and I known something was bound to happen—then I look up and seen Big Willie coming down the street and into the store—I said inside myself—it him. He the one. They got to get somebody—now they got they body."

"And you know what, boy?" The old man walking alongside him grumbled. "So did Big Willie."

The farther from the creek we walked, the brighter the day, the lighter folks got in spirit. The whites had to have a body. It wasn't their body. Relief—but something more. . . .

Coming to the clearing near the woods, two crackers stopped us. "Hear they got crazy Willie," one said.

"Yeah, sho did," the old man grumbled.

"Goddamn shame," the cracker said. "Hear tell they shot ole Willie while he was praying down by the creek."

Old-Timer scratched his head. "Prayin' suh? Now, I don't rightly know 'bout that, suh. His hands, they were mighty full—but warn't no Bible he had in 'em."

"Praying or pissing," the other cracker said.

Old-Timer thought a bit. "Don't know about that neither, suh. His thing warn't out, and his pants warn't wet."

We walked on, and another man said: "Reckon we'll ever get to know how many of 'em Big Willie took?"

"Not if they got it to tell," Old-Timer said. "But I'll tell y'all one thing—the next cracker what asks me about how Big Willie died, ah'm gonna tell 'im: 'No, suh,' ah'm gonna say. 'Big Willie warn't down by that creek praying. Pissing neither. He was saying to them mens just like he been saying to y'alls mamas—I got it cocked—come and git it.' " The men got to laughing. Ann and I kept walking, staring straight ahead: seeing Big Willie, his blood pushing through those big holes, had our knees to buckling. We walked on, too scared to think, too scared to talk. When we got to running distance of the old house, I breathed regular. Only then did I think about cracking.

"Ann," I said, "what the hell did you think you was about with that li'l ole twenty-two?"

Ann kept her eyes dead on the house, her face pinched, her black eyes staring. I read her: while those who had seen Big Willie and had to live with the truth of him needed jokes to help them through, there was but one thing we needed—to get the hell on away.

And at two the next morning we sneaked from the house, got in the car, and drove through that old town without lights. Only when Montgomery was far behind us did we chance to put them on. And only then did I remember the old stove, and damned the time I hadn't had to get the kids to working on it.

Eyes red and ringed with shadows, two days of dirt worked into our pores from our long nonstop drive to New York, Ann and I had but one thought when we hit my apartment—bed. One minute later James and Tom followed us in. "I hope you gals known that the reason y'all got home safe is on account of I wore out these knees praying." Tom's worry showed through his laugh. Even his brown freckles shone with sweat of worry. "Yes, Lord wore these old joints right down to the bone. . . ."

Ann sat up from the couch where she had stretched to discourage Tom from staying. "Old Red, you talk like you know the times we been through. You going in for star reading?"

"Ain't I, though?" Tom said. "No sooner y'all rode outa here than those black boys got snatched off the train."

"What black boys?"

"Them hoboes they taken to Scottsboro." Looking from one to the other and seeing our faces gone blank, he said, "Happened right down where you gals were—Alabama. Nine of 'em—swear out they raped two white broads. Hon-ey . . . them crackers been kicking niggers' asses—ain't even bothered to take names—all up and down them highways. But ought to have known you two had sense enough to stay put until them simple mothers got cooled down."

Ann and my eyes locked, then pulled away. I tried to remember what thought had pushed me out of that old house into the Alabama night. What? Never to see my swank apartment again? Never to see Harry? The Lord sure had moved in His mysterious way.

2

So ten minutes later, too tired to think, and too anxious to sleep, I was in the backseat of the car on my way to Harry's, James at the wheel. And looking out on the Harlem scene it came to me on that gray, chilly March day, that when a black feller got cut in Alabama, folks in Harlem bled. Folks out there had caught fever—Scottsboro fever. Men and women stood at corners talking quiet, mad as hell. They were not eyeing big cars so much as looking in at their own feelings. Hands in pockets, mouths pinched tight, eyes staring at sidewalks or out into space, looking deep into what they were about.

Too early for the Garvey folks, nonetheless a crowd of his followers had gathered on his corner. And on the corner a block away an overflow crowd spilling into the street were marching, carrying signs. We had already driven past when I noticed that the woman on the podium was white.

"You see that?" I asked James.

"Yeah," James said. "Folks done gone crazy out here. White woman standing there raising hell—talking about stop lynching."

"That what she talking about sure 'nough?"

"Yeah—that Scottsboro mess. They ain't nothin' but damn Communists."

"How's that?"

"That's what folks say," James said. "Out there wanting to change things."

"You don't believe things needs changing, James?"

"Sure, but they ought to be raising hell about something decent—not about simple niggers messing with white trash."

Sweat rose up out of my pores to mix up my dirt and grit. I stared hard at the back of James's clean, proper-looking neck. Did my being so tired make me suspect he wasn't as bright as I had thought? "You believe that, James?"

"That what they say."

"What who say, James?"

"Them two broads—the newspapers . . ."

"What them black boys say, James?"

" 'Course they say they ain't done it."

"How come you don't believe them?"

"What else they gonna say?"

"Guess it's a matter of lenses," I said.

"How's that?"

"How a goddamn fool adjusts his mind to what's being told to him," I said.

"I don't get it. . . ." Of course he didn't, with that clean, proper-looking neck.

"Let me tell it to you my way, James. Don't you ever in life believe that a cracker gal's gonna admit being fucked by no black boy—unless she's been put up to it. If you do—never tell me about it, not again in this life—you get me? Oh sure, they gets fucked. Them low-down hussies pulls down their pants in a minute to a black man. That's because black men can't tell. And when they pull down them drawers, brother, it's a hell of a lot safer for the men to go on and do it—so long as nobody sees."

"You believe that, Dorine?"

"I knows it, fool! I seen many a black boy who run from that li'l patch of rusty hair—but for them that run, ain't no place to hide, no room to holler, and no goddamn where to go."

James pulled up in front of the restaurant. I slammed out of the car before he showed me more of his ignorance. But my sweat had boiled up. So I took a few minutes wiping the grime it had pushed out of my pores.

The restaurant had but a few customers. Harry sat with a couple. When he saw me he got up. "Hello, hello." He walked toward me, a hand outstretched. "Don't tell me—Dorine Davis—ain't it?"

A handshake? But I had rushed, dirty and tired, to make sure he still had that hot look for me in his eyes. "How you take so long to come back?" he asked.

"Been out of town," I said, my eyes roving over him—seeing his thin lips, the strong chin, the smile that softened both. "Been visiting my family—in Alabama."

"Alabama? But all-you does have trouble down there—no?"

"Montgomery," I rushed to say. Then added: "Same difference."

Goddamn man, what next? How did an American girl move from hello to the bedroom with a West Indian—with this West Indian, who pretended to be having trouble remembering my name?

That little trick kept pushing the relationship almost back to the starting line. Why had he come on like that? Hell, in the thick of shit I had been thinking—no, praying—to get back to him. The trick unnerved me, had me waiting for him to make the next move. While I waited, my eyes traveled over him, moving from his chin back to his eyes, his mouth, his wide chest, his broad shoulders, his arm—and then I saw the armband.

"Somebody dead?" I asked.

"Yes—me wife."

My eyelids peeled back so that cold air hit my eyeballs from all sides. Wife? Harry married! But the stud had stood right in that very room flirting. He had promised all sorts of things with those eyes. And it had been an act!

Pain caught me in my rib cage. Tiredness fell heavy on my shoulders, added weights to my feet. I looked to the door, tried to move toward it. Weights held me down. I put out my hand to touch the counter. I held on to it. Then I remembered her—tall, thin, light-skinned, with curly hair in a bun. But her face remained in a shadow—Harry's shadow. Tom had said "an aristocrat"; Bessie had said . . . But I had blocked her out!

"I-I-I'm sorry to hear," I said.

Muscles twitched in his cheeks; his eyes got red, his nose shiny. "Thanks for your sympathy."

"It-it must be hard. . . ." I had to swallow from dry mouth.

"Cancer. . . ." His voice cracked hoarse from tears too near the surface. Cry, son of a bitch, and I'll cry too.

"So sorry," I said.

Harry blew his nose—loud, honking snot—in a well-used handkerchief. "It's nice that you come," he said. "Don't make it so long again." He turned away. Dismissing me!

"We'll see about that." I spoke loud enough to pull the attention of customers. Then letting anger fuel my tired feet, stalked out. Ignoring James, who sat surprised at my quick appearance, I headed up the block fast.

I had expected—expected . . . Whatever, it hadn't been that he was married. Worse—the man loved his wife! I heard James's footsteps behind. Hating for him to be giving me his rotten-tooth grin at my being put down, I quickened my steps until reaching a corner where sign-carrying marchers chanted: "Free the Scottsboro Boys! Free the Scottsboro Boys!"

Blocked from crossing, I took out my handkerchief to catch my overflowing tears. Harry Brisbane had been playing with me. God, how I hated being played with.

Tiredness, the dirt, sweat, my need for sleep pushed me over the edge of depression. I wanted the car to hide in. But when James walked up behind me, I kept my head turned, pretending to be listening to the woman on the platform across the street.

The white woman had just finished. As she went to her place on the platform, a heavyset black woman stepped up to the podium. She waited for the chanting to quiet down and when it did, shouted: "We Negroes are sick and tired of being raped without redress, of being lynched without reason, of being treated like second-class citizens." Her voice rising like that of a Baptist singer.

"I am standing here before you this afternoon to join my voice with those of my comrades who say: Stop lynching in America! Free the Scottsboro Boys!" Shouts, cheers, deafened me.

The cheers died down and she said: "We Negroes upon whose backs this nation was built; we who helped make this nation great; we who have shed our blood in its defense; we who uphold the principles for which this nation claims to stand, say: Enough! No more! No more shall we shed our blood at the hands of bloodthirsty bigots! No more shall we tolerate the actions of those whose constant thought is to turn back the tide of democracy!

"This is our land! We have shed our blood to build it and if we must, we shall shed our blood to free it. But it shall be shed in the name of Liberty! Equality! For true human dignity!"

I waited for the shouts to quiet while someone behind me whispered: "It's a shame, those boys being used in such a way." I had thought it was James who'd come up behind me, but this was the voice of a well-spoken stranger.

"Sure is," I agreed without turning.

"It creates dissension in our ranks," he said.

"Does it now?" What a good feeling, hearing that woman speak, and seeing the marchers—white folks and black folks, old folks and young folks, all together. I had never seen such a thing in all my life!

"Those poor boys will surely be put to death," he said.

"You said a mouthful, mister. No way in the world they can escape."

"Why must they use those boys' suffering as their propaganda?"

"That what they doing sure 'nough?" I asked.

"We know what happens in the South," he said.

"Don't we though."

"It's not new to us. But it's *our* problem. Why should they bare our problems to the world?"

It came to me then that we might be talking about two different things. I turned to see this midaged, light-skinned, curly-haired, educated-looking man—one of those whose dissension from the darker brothers was a way of life. "Still talking about them crackers, mister?"

"No—these Communists . . . Why must they—these reds—expose our dirty linen to the world? This is an American problem. It must be solved in an American way."

I cut my eyes over his tweed hat and suit, the cane on his arm. "Still talking about them boys, mister?"

"Yes."

"They *our* dirty linen?"

"Wouldn't you say?" He raised his brows, daring me to disagree. "Must we show the world how the whites treat—"

"That got to be hid?"

"This kind of meeting only serves—"

"Hid from the world? Like what happened to Big Willie is hid? Nobody must know?"

"Big Willie. . . ?" He frowned trying to recollect.

"Yeah," I said. "Big Willie Hopkins."

"May I ask, who is Big Willie Hopkins?"

"Mister, you ain't standing there telling me you ain't never heard of Big Willie?"

"Should I have? I haven't read anything . . ."

"It ain't in no newspapers, mister."

"Then how do you expect me. . . ?"

"I don't," I said. "Because you a goddamn fool!"

Snatching a sign from a passing marcher, I hit him on his head. His hat fell off, exposing a head full of mixed gray curls. I hit him on his curly head, and when he bent to pick up his hat I brought the stick down on his back. The sign had come off the stick by then, so I hit him with the stick. Kept hitting him. He walked away. I followed. He ran. I ran behind him, using his back to rid myself of all my tiredness, my anger.

"What's going on here?" I looked up into the face of a policeman at the corner.

"Officer, this woman's attacking me," my educated friend said.

"Ain't got a thing to do with you, officer," I explained. "This here's black folks' business, and got to be dealt with in black folks' ways."

The cop looked from the stranger to me. Chances are, as sweaty and evil as I looked, he thought of running me in. But James came up just then. "Miss Davis, is this man bothering you?" James really knew how to put on the dog.

"Yes, James," I said, pulling myself tall. "This bum's bothering the hell outa me."

Seeing my uniformed chauffeur and supposing me to be a swell, the cop asked: "You want me to run this man in, miss?"

"No, let the fool go," I said. "Just warn him about going around insulting ladies."

Driving me home, James waited for me to tell him what had happened. He kept looking at me in the mirror, trying to read my expression. When he couldn't, he asked: "What happened back there, Dorine? I saw you talking to the stud. The next thing I knew, you had hauled off. . . ."

206

I let my eyes rest on the back of James's clean, proper-looking neck. "The goddamn fool. Out there talking against them Communists and them Scottsboro Boys, and he don't know a damn thing about Big Willie Hopkins."

James sat tall. Still. His shoulders twitched once, twice. Uncomfortable. But he held still. I waited. James might have been curious, but he was no fool. He kept getting taller and stiller, and didn't split his lips to ask who was Big Willie. That's what I liked about James. He might not have been all that bright, but he sure had a way of sensing danger—and knew how to stay the hell on away from it.

When I got home I went to bed and slept for two days. Then I woke up to lie in bed looking at the ceiling. In the clear light of that early morn I knew exactly what I had to do. I had heard the voice of that woman all through my sleep. She had reached me as those Garvey folks never had been able to. But then, they had been talking about Africa. She was talking about me.

I heard Tom and Ann in the next room. But what they said held no interest for me. They were my friends—had been. But sometime in sleep, I had broken with them.

Tom came into the room and stood at the foot of the bed. "Hey, little lady, it's time you was getting up. We hitting the road this morning."

"You got to count me out from now on, Tom," I said. "There's only one thing I'm interested in, one place I got to go—and that's to join up with them Communists."

"Not today, you ain't." Tom shook his head. "You and Ann been gone long enough. And the way you been sleeping, like you intended to spend the rest of your life in bed. But it's time to get up and start to rolling."

"As God is my witness, I'm through, Tom. I'm tired. I'm mad. I hate the way things been happening to me—to us. And I'm ready to fight with anybody who's ready to fight them crackers."

"Sure sounds pretty," Tom said, smiling and rubbing his clean-shaven chin and cocking his eyes at me. "But what you gonna do about money?"

"I got money," I said.

"No you ain't, Dorine," Tom said. "Them Communists out

there got money—the white ones. If they don't now, they will. Some of them got folks what died and left them money. Some works in offices—stuff like that. The young ones—they getting trained to get a decent-paying job. Now, when your li'l bit of money runs out, what you gonna do? Go on back to scrubbing white folks' floors?"

One thing I liked about Tom: his way of reasoning things out. I lay in bed, turning what he had said over in my mind. By the time my feet hit the floor, I had already thanked the Lord one hundred times that He had saved me the trouble of unpacking.

3

Forgetting about Harry Brisbane had become my main occupation in life, until coming back from our coast-to-coast trip. Lying in the backseat trying to sleep, I heard Tom say: "Ann, I do declare, I'll never understand women. Here you are, pretty, high yeller, you go for bright—so why you wants to make your life miserable? What you want with Sonny—a wedding ring?"

They thought I was asleep, but my mind had been running pretty much along the same lines: Here you are Dorine Davis. You go for pretty. You got a fabulous layout, you drives around in a chauffeured car—then how is it you're going home to an empty bed?

"Wedding band?" Ann laughed. "Heavens no, Tom. If a stud like Sonny ain't married at his age—that automatically makes him the nonmarrying kind. I want Sonny. I saw him, want him, and I'm willing to pay the dues."

"Oh, and here I was feeling sorry for you," Tom said. "But you got what you want—heaps of misery. . . ."

I sat up, and looking over Tom's shoulder, tried to push the car home. But Tom, not able to see into my head, kept up his careful driving. Why had I been going around the country trying to decide whether I ought to join the Communists to stop lynchings, when the

208

man I wanted was the marrying kind? More—he had just become single and in need of a woman's sympathy.

Lord, why ain't I had the faith to see Your hand in this?

We drove into New York at eight that evening. At home I jumped in and out of the shower in less than five minutes, then toning myself down to the marrying kind, in an outfit of dark blue with a snug-fitting hat and pumps, I found James, and we were on our way to The Rising Sun.

Six months I had been on the road! A hell of a long time for a man looking as good as Harry to be alone and needing a woman. Chances were a smarter woman than I had been had already made a line to him. As the car slowed down in front of the restaurant, I jumped out. And before James had finished parking I stood at the door. Just stood there. My mind a blank. When it got to registering again, I looked up, then down, the avenue, making sure James had stopped at the right place, looked back at the padlocked door. Putting my nose up to the glass, I tried to imagine tables and chairs in the darkened room. But even in the dark, a restaurant without fixtures, without a counter or the tables with the white tablecloths, was just a square, naked, ugly room.

James, coming up behind me, peered in over my head. "Looks empty," he said. His simple words forced me to move away. I went to the nearby stoop, where a drunk sat examining the tips of his shoes. "Hey, feller," I said. "What happened to the guy who owned this place?"

The drunk kept looking at the tips of his shoes. "What place?"

"The Rising Sun—the restaurant that used to be here."

"Dunno."

"You taking up too goddamn much space to be not knowing something," I snapped.

"Lady"—the drunk pretended to be cowering against the stoop—"I ain't taking up much of that—I swear."

"You out here," I said. "You got to know some of what's happening."

"Place is closed," he said brightly, giving out precious information.

"I ain't blind. How come it's closed?" I asked.

He hunched thin shoulders, rubbed the stubble on his chin, put a clown smile to twist his lips. "Depression," he said. "Them's that got, lose. Them what ain't got, got nothin' to lose."

"How long's it been closed?"

"Lady, I don't be counting time—not even hard times."

Seeing the way I looked at the drunk, James led me back to the car. I wanted to stomp the man. "Hey lady," he called after me. "Ain't what I tole worth a dime? Better give it while you got it." I slammed the door hard, then turned to James.

"How come you didn't know that Harry had closed down?" I asked.

"I ain't been keeping tabs on Harry," he said.

"Why not? What good are you to me if you don't take care of business?"

"Way you lit outa here the last time, Dorine, I'd swear out you didn't want the stud to be your business."

"James, your vision ain't worth a cent of your pay. So start looking. And you better find him. Or from the hole in the ground where you'll be viewing, an outhouse will look like a fucking mansion."

"Dorine, Harry ain't no street stud; where you expect me to look?"

"James"—I tried showing patience because of the stricken look in his eyes—"lizards, snakes, even hard-to-find studs comes out for air sometimes. When Harry comes out, you just be there. . . ."

We started right in looking. I made him drive me to The Club. Big H was the one person I knew who knew Harry. Odel was going in when we pulled up. I called out to him and he came over. "Where's Big H?" I asked.

"Back home on his island," he said.

"Thought he was due back long before this."

"He comes and goes, comes and goes—here lately, he mostly goes," Odel said.

"Well—he was always one for helping his people," I said.

"Good thing, too." Odel laughed. "With Dutch Schultz moving in and taking over, he'd do well to stay with his people. Better that nest than no nest at all. . . ."

The look of the boy-turned-man turned me off. Slyness had grown on Odel like moss. Years had no business changing such trusting eyes to deceit. Greed oozed out of him like body odor. I looked up at the entrance to The Club, remembering the time when he had snapped to with respect. I imagined I heard music, the clatter of machines upstairs, the clink of glasses in the dining room, chips hitting chips downstairs. I thought of Big H, his round, brown face, his honest-looking eyes, the way he made me welcome. . . .

"I guess you must own the joint by now," I said. But Odel heard the bring-down as praise. "Not yet." He leaned toward me, buddy-buddy. Since when had he decided that I deserved his confidence?

"What about his friend Harry Brisbane . . . know him?"

"Yeah."

"Where do I find him?"

Odel hunched his shoulders. "Who knows? Another monkey chaser what folded up his tent and sneaked off like a A-rab . . . yukyukyuk."

"That's enough funk for one day," I said. "Come on, James."

But Odel had upset me. Schultz taking over the rackets in Harlem naturally kept me upset. And Big H—I felt responsible (I never completely let go of my men). And Harry? I tried to picture him back on a little island. I closed my eyes and remembered his loud bragging on that first night. The way he talked about being in America. I shook my head. No, Harry had New York in him—branded deep.

In the next few days we looked up one street and down the next. Harlem wasn't that big. If we didn't find him one day, we had to another. Looking was tough on the heart. Harry looked special. But lots of studs around Harlem had wide chests, broad shoulders, and were damn good-looking. A pair of broad shoulders got my heart to lifting and pumping one minute; the next, it stopped and dropped to my stomach in disappointment—and it did the same with the next pair of broad shoulders.

That going on day after day forced me to question my health. That's what I was about the day we stopped for a light and a car pulled alongside. "Dorine, Dorine. . . ." I looked out and into a face so familiar that although I hadn't seen it in years, it might have been the day before. "How you doing, girl?" Sonny's fleshy face with its blinking frog-eyes smiled over at me. My heart pounded up to normal (like I say, I never completely let go).

"How you think I been doing, old nigger? Except doing time."

So this black Cadillac with its red leather upholstery had been the reason I hadn't seen the flashes of red zipping past my window.

"Oh, Dorine." Sonny laughed and waved his hand. "You still bringing up that old stuff? Just look at you—big car, chauffeur—you ought to thank me for putting you next to Tom." I waited for him to blink. When he didn't, I knew he meant it. "Girl," he said, "I been looking for you."

"I ain't moved."

"I been to your place. But guess you was out of town."

The light changed. Folks got to honking from behind. "Look, Dorine," Sonny said. "Have your man follow me. I got some big talk for you." He drove off, and because I didn't say different, James followed.

We drove down a street of brownstone houses. Sonny pulled up before one with a marquee stretching out across the sidewalk, with big letters—S-O-N-N-Y—printed on it. I followed him through the door of a street-level entrance and into a room that had been set up as a dining room. A black-tied maître d' stood near a bar, and a red-coated waiter stood waiting for customers. Sonny led me through the back door of the room into another larger room where a slick-haired man sat pumping a piano. The roll played: "I'd rather be alone. . . ."

Heavy drapes cut off all light from the window. Only a red light in a corner outlined people sitting around the room, drinking. From a room beyond, the smell of frying chicken came through to mix with the smoky smell of the smoke-filled room.

"Well," Sonny said. "What do you think?"

In the dim light I imagined I saw Sonny smiling. I looked around the room. "What you want me to say? A joint's a joint's a joint. . . ."

"Oh, come off it, Dorine. You can see this ain't just any old joint. It got class—at least possibilities. All I need is a little loot. We can make a mint here."

"We?" I squinted through the smoke to get a good look at his tricky face. "Start again, Sonny. You? expect me? to put money. . . ?"

"You got the money, Dorine."

"If I do, or if I don't, I ain't accountable to you. This is your joint. How come you running it if you broke?"

"Who said I was broke? I just want you and me to be partners."
A lie. Sonny was broke. Sonny stayed broke.

"Me? That's what you were looking for me for? To be partners?"

"Sure."

"You got friends," I said.

"None as good as you, Dorine."

"What about Ann?"

"Ann? Are you for real? That chick would drink up my profits. What she didn't drink, she'd give away. Ann goes for generous. No, Dorine, you the one somebody I know I can trust."

The man kept pumping at the piano. Someone in the far corner sang: "You will always be my necessity; I'll be lost without you."

I bit my lips to keep from laughing loud. Sonny had nothing but friends—none he could trust. No one trusted him. Women, like me, like Ann—he went through our friendships like epsom salts, draining us, no apologies, no regrets. In a flash I knew why: Sonny didn't take the blame for things he did because Sonny didn't know when he had done wrong! No, he wasn't out-and-out crazy. Something in his head just needed adjusting.

Seeing into Sonny's twisted mind gave me a wheel in his life. I knew it! So instead of laughing and calling him the names that rushed to mind, I said: "You know you can count on me, Sonny. Just give me time. I'll get back to you. . . ."

That revelation lit my mind. And days later, while waiting for a light to change on my way home—and eyeing a pair of broad shoulders swinging down the avenue toward me—I saw myself as a snake coiled around Sonny's brain, watching him think. Scary. What I wanted most from Sonny was distance. But seeing into his murky mind tied me to him—gave me a stake in him.

Suddenly I turned the wheel to park the car at the curb. I had spotted a black armband on the gray suit that draped the broad shoulders I had been eyeing. A street sign hid the face, but my heart went into its leaps and lurches. So even when his face cleared the sign, I kept my eyes on the arms, the clenched fists, the strong-legged stride. He came abreast and I stole a look at the grim jaw, the black skin that rippled over it, the tight, thin lips, the high nose with its wide, flaring nostrils. "Hey, feller, where you been hiding?"

Brown eyes turned to me. Then Harry Brisbane tipped his hat, nodded his head, and kept on walking. By the time my mouth had closed, he had gone halfway down the block. Putting the car in reverse, I backed down to meet him. "Hey, mister, ain't you heard? I said hello. Least you can say likewise. . . ." Crummy? Sweet? The man kept right on walking. I kept backing down and might have backed across the street, but the light changed, the cross-traffic stopped me.

Making a U-turn, I drove far enough down to meet him on my way up. "Look, mister, my name ain't Hoover, so I ain't responsible for your place closing. Cross my heart. So what do you want from me?"

He tipped his hat again. "Miss Davis, ain't it?"

"You goddamn right it is. Dorine Davis, the same one what's been combing these streets looking for you."

"For me?" Skimpy eyebrows shot up, surprised, giving me a see through the yellow-browns. "Why me?"

"I got some talk for you."

"Talk? What we got to say? I ain't know you. You ain't know me. Still, I glad to see you doing so good." He nodded his meaning at the car, then crossed over to the other side of the avenue.

Cars prevented me from making another U-turn. I waited, watching him as he walked away down the avenue, praying he wasn't ornery enough to turn down a one-way going-the-wrong-way street. And as the traffic thinned, I raced around to catch him mid-block, then turned the wheel so that the car jumped the curb, mounting the sidewalk. I drove across it, blocking his way. Two men talking near him jumped three feet into the air. Harry just froze. I pushed open the car door.

"Look, feller, I wore up a lot of rubber, used up a lot of gas, and spent a hell of a time looking for you. Now that I found you, you ain't going nowhere—so get on in this damn car."

"Don't you do that, man," one of the men warned. "That woman's crazy. Go in, you subject never to get out."

"Hush your mouf." His friend grabbed his shaking friend with shaking hands. "That fool woman's likely to kill somebody out here. And it might be you. Go on, get in, mister, and take her the hell on away from here."

The liking-me look had jumped into Harry's eyes. "I give up," he said, getting in. And as I drove off down the avenue: "Now that you got me, what you plan doing with me?"

The question gave birth to the plan. "One guess," I said, gassing the car down to Central Park. His wonders to perform. . . .

I had found my special spot in the park one summer when the fleet had been in. Walking through the park, looking for a place to sit and forced to move on because every bench, tree, stone, and blade of grass had been covered by a white sailor suit with a skirt beneath it, I had stumbled onto a path leading to a wooded area. A tree had fallen, had taken root and sprung up again. The fallen trunk made a natural love seat. Tall trees on all sides gave the spot a feeling of a private room. And the sailors had missed it!

Harry appreciated it. He stood looking around at the screening trees, listening for and hearing no voices. Looking at the sparrows hopping around, the squirrels hanging on to trees upside down, looking at us. "But you got yourself a private parlor here," he said. "This where you take the men you kidnap?" He turned to me. "Hey, girl—girl, what you doin'. . . !'"

I had already taken off my skirt and blouse and was rushing to get off my brassiere. I intended to shock him. It seemed the way to hold him.

"Look, girl," he said, talking fast. "What you want with me? I ain't got nothing. Me bank close tight, tight. All me money gone. . . ."

"I wasn't looking for you to support me, Harry," I said. "Only to make love to me."

"But you bold, yes?"

"I bold, yes." I kept my eyes teasing to put his mind at ease, and sitting on that seat made for loving, I pulled off my stockings.

"You too fast for me," he said.

"I'm trying. . . ."

"Wicked—you a wicked woman. . . ." All that accusing might have embarrassed me into thinking again—if his eyes hadn't been wading through my nakedness, ready to take the plunge. I kept on undressing.

"Harry, I ain't had a man in a long time—and if I don't have you. . . ? Why don't we just go on and be wicked?"

His eyes got deep and brown. Yet he made no move to take me. I went to him, unbuttoned his jacket. "What you doing?" he protested. But he helped me take it off. I worked on his tie.

"What if the police. . . ?" he said.

"They'll only shoot us." He laughed then and took off his hat. God, what a relief to see him take off that hat! My hands were already busy unbuttoning his pants.

And on that Indian summer day, a cloud moved to cover the sun. A chill wind hit my butt, driving me into Harry's arms. He held me. Kissed me. Surrounded me, forcing me into him. He pulled me into him, tried to pull me through him. Another gust rustled the drying leaves of the trees. Then there we were, his weight over me, his hands opening up my legs. "What make you think I a sailor boy?" he groaned.

"You ain't nobody's boy, baby. You're a man—my man."

"But I got family," he said. "What you want with a man with family?" Too late.

He pushed into me, pulled me into him, worked me, held me, protected me from the pain of dried leaves, stones, wind. "Oh, God, Dorine, but you sweet, sweet, sweet. . . ."

Wild. Like the Son of God. Sweeter than sweet. No hard work, no trickiness, no goddamn acrobatics. Loving, loving, sweet, sweet man. How far did a woman go to find her man? How long did she have to wait? How did she know when he was for her? I knew. I knew. I knew.

Back in the car, I headed as straight as a well-aimed bullet for Sonny's. That's the kind of mind I have. Keeps working at the damndest times. "Hey, girl—where you going? I tell you, I got me children. I got to go home."

"What you need more than going home, feller, is a job. You got one."

I turned the car down Harry's street, then asked myself, What the fuck are you doing in Dispossess Alley? We sporting folks had sworn off streets like this for life—pretended it wasn't happening: furniture piled high on the sidewalks, kids playing follow-the-leader over them, dogs frisky, tails wagging, tearing into cushions, spilling feathers, cotton stuffing every whichaway—while grown-ups looked on, taking sips from pints of bathtub gin. Why in the hell was I here? Because Harry hadn't asked me? The man was nothing but a bunch of secrets. We hadn't slept a full night together. Six months and I hadn't met his girls. Hell, I had paid for the privilege when I put money up to save Sonny's joint so Harry could have a place to work.

He had been doing great. Women dug Harry. Sonny had been doing a big woman's business since Harry went to work for him, never mind that Harry didn't like after-hours—hated joints. When things got better and he was on his own again, I still would be the reason he had made it.

To keep from hitting some simple jokers standing in the street who thought their asses were made of iron, I thought of turning back. But my deed didn't go with my thinking because I found myself pulling up in front of Harry's building. Then I sat in the car wondering if the better part of curiosity wouldn't be to flip a coin, letting heads invite me to drive on, or to spit in my hand, hit the spit with my fingers, and follow the direction of the biggest splatter.

The front door and everything I sensed about Harry warned me that my coming was forbidden—it might even mean the end for us. Drive on, sister, even after all the time you spent tracking the stud down. A little piece is better than no piece. But sound reasoning spoke out: Dorine Davis, ain't you tired of lighting on sugar with no substance? Go on and see what you got yourself into, so that you can get the hell out while you have time. . . .

I left the car and headed for the stoop—Mama's old saying echoing loud in my ears: If a filly hadn't messed with an ass, Dorine, she'd have never give birth to a mule.

The strong smell of stale foods—a mixture of all that had ever been cooked in that building—hung like an invisible curtain, which I pushed into but never quite pushed through. But the building had seen some good days: hand-painted glass panels, set alongside plain glass replacements, framing the door. Beneath the worn linoleum good tile gleamed. The banisters were of hardwood, though long worn through its varnish.

Two floor-length apartments took up each landing of the five-story walk-up. Harry lived on the fifth floor. I looked up at the steep climb and fear thrilled through me. I wanted to turn back but continued—slowly, climbing stairs being a stranger to my style. At each landing I rested, and listened to babies crying, women singing, radios playing. On the fourth floor I looked up the flight leading to Harry's door. I knew his door from the feel it gave me. My heart, beating fast from my climb, beat even faster. I had to push myself on. And when I finally made it to the top, I fell against the door, and leaned waiting for the return of my breath.

The silence on the other side felt accumulated, stretched over a period of time. It rested heavy against the door, giving birth to the thought that those inside might have long died and were waiting for someone to bury them—or they might have moved and the house had long been empty—and waiting.

The loud brassy ring of the doorbell that broke the silence brought my eyes to the finger that had pushed it. I waited again, listening, an uneasiness rising. Then I heard footsteps—heavy, pounding toward me. As they came I conjured up the picture of a giant, eyes blazing, towering over me, ready to do me in.

The door opened. Just as I had imagined, Harry stood looking down, all the way down. Then finally seeing me, he shot up his skimpy eyebrows, the yellow glowed bright, brighter, until his eyes seemed two blazing torches in his black head. The skin around his mouth turned an ash white. Seconds passed. He kept staring. I felt myself shrinking, shrinking. To prevent myself from melting through the floor, I put my hands on my hips.

"What you doing here?" He whispered loud, and this warned me. Common sense warned me: Dorine, go, get the hell out. I held myself there. I really wanted to go now. Was even willing to leap down the flight of steps to the next landing and take off.

"That the way you treat a lady?" Now that I had my breath I forced a laugh. "Your lady?" I waited for an answer and when he didn't, I kept on. "Them's a lot of steps to climb, feller—and this sweetness ain't climbed them to hang on this side of the door." He stared at me as though thinking he could will me away. Only when he realized that I wasn't about to break my neck running did he step aside.

The long hallway I entered faced an empty walk-through dining room at the other end. As he closed and locked the door, I looked over his shoulder to an empty living room: "So," he said. "You had to come. I hope you satisfied." Pride, then, had been the reason for all that rage? My skin crawled. Still I joked.

"Hell no, why you think I walked up all them steps? I ain't had near enough."

The joke seemed to stick a pin in his rage. It emptied like a balloon. His eyes smiled. I breathed easy. But the suddenness with which it went had an unsettling effect. It kept my heart hammering.

He led me down the hall, stopping at the first door we came to. He pushed the door and I followed him into a room, bare except for a bed, with a sheet carelessly drawn over it, a chest of drawers, and at the window, a shade pulled down to hide an air shaft.

"This ain't the fairy-tale bedroom you done bring me to," Harry said, mocking me. I hadn't come to mock him. Nor had I come to lie. The apartment was like nothing I had ever lived in or would have allowed myself to live in. I bit down on my lips, hiding my displeasure.

Farther down the hall he pushed open a second door. A child lay across the bed reading. She looked up, annoyed that we had disturbed her. I shifted my eyes from hers to look around the room— as bare as the first had been—but her staring pulled mine back and I found myself looking into her flat, Chinese-looking eyes. What did we want, hers seemed to demand. Why had we walked in on her? She couldn't have been more than eight!

Never one to encourage sass from kids, scolding words jumped to my mouth. I bit them back and followed Harry out. We walked down to the empty dining room then through it into the kitchen. There we found the second girl, this one about eleven-twelve. She stood at the kitchen sink, cleaning fish, the blood from the fish smearing her hands to her elbows. She looked up smiling when we came in.

"What a lovely girl." The words fell unbidden from my mouth. She had to be the prettiest child I had ever seen. Tall and delicate as a young tree, with a wide-mouthed, even-teethed smile, velvet-brown skin, and her father's yellow-brown eyes made even lovelier by long black eyelashes and heavy black eyebrows.

"You're Daddy's friend?" she asked. "We didn't know that Daddy had a lady friend." A quick look from her father forced her to change to: "My name is Linda, and that's"—she nodded with her chin toward the door—"my sister, Gloria. We call her Gogi for short."

The younger one had followed us. She stood in the doorway, her bony arms and legs sticking out of a middy blouse and outgrown dark skirt—grinning. And I found myself wondering which annoyed me most, her sassy look or that grin that put her up as the twin sister of an imp.

"Me daughters," Harry said. My intentions had been to greet them, tell them how grand to meet them and that I thought we ought to be friends. But looking around the kitchen, seeing the cracked ceiling, the broken windowpane with newspapers stuck through to keep out air, the broken-down sink where Linda was scaling fish, the worn-out linoleum, I decided to say: Good-bye, I hope we meet again in the *distant* future—real distant.

Damn, it was one thing to meet a handsome stud in a night-club, with rich friends. He sure had impressed me in his swank restaurant. But this slum! God no. Definitely not the style I had been working hard to keep—and not the style I intended to get used to. So I opened my mouth and heard myself saying:

"My God, Harry, how in the hell can you live like this!"

"Like this!" he shouted. "You a fool? We ain't live like this. The children's mother dead. Me business close down. I sell everything—house, car, furniture. I-I-I—me good friend, Charles, he let me stay here. It he house. But only till The Rising Sun rise again. It ain't for long—thanks to you." This note of hope he spoke in a whisper to reach my ears only. And even knowing this, knowing he wanted to spare his girls, keep a special picture of himself for them, my mouth kept on: "Not for long? Damn Harry, if it's only for one minute that's one minute too goddamn long."

My words hit them in the place they all shared—their pride. Their faces closed against me. The young one, sass spread over her face, narrowed her flat eyes. She looked from my head to my feet and back, then turned to walk out. "No honey," I stopped her. "Don't you go nowhere. Not when I'm doing the talking. If this is the first time you hearing me, it sure ain't gonna be the last. One thing I do best in this world is talk."

And just like that I took over—and ended in a mess that any

titsucking baby would have the sense to crawl, scamper, or just stand up and run like hell away from.

Feelings. That's what moves me—more than any laugh laughed, or word spoken, the feeling slipping and sliding beneath—in my chest, my stomach. A feeling of permanence, finally. Why not? With Harry moving bag and baggage into my apartment? With his kids sleeping a bedroom away?

Great kids. Linda started right in looking after the apartment. I might even have brought Gogi around with all the new clothes and with them driving around in a chauffeur-driven car. But she chanced to hear Tom saying:

"Dorine, what's this all about? You in family?"

"I'm in love, Tom."

"With all of 'em?" he asked.

"They go with the deal, Tom."

"That's a big deal, Dorine," he said.

"You don't have to worry none," I answered. "They'll be earning their keep." I looked around and saw Gogi in the doorway, her flat eyes accusing. I hated that she had heard a meaning not intended. But what to do?

I dug the New York Harry opened up for me. Foreign. Not upper, not lower—just plain West Indians. And they dug brown-skin American women. "Bring me an American girl, nuh," Sandy, Harry's round, fat friend said, blinking from behind gold-rimmed glasses. "A young, brown-skin one just like you."

"So what if she ain't so young," Charles, the tall, ugly friend who had given Harry the slum apartment, said. "Just so she American and brown, with a spirit free like Dorine." I loved it!

Harry took me to Van Cortlandt Park to see cricket matches. And while the players hit the ball with the flat bat, Harry, his chest poked out, strutted peacock fashion among the men. "Look at that big shot," I heard one say.

"Oh, you ain't know?" Charles explained to me. "Harry's a big man. A big-shot cricketer back home—a big-time wicket keeper." From the tone, that had to be the nearest thing to God.

They were Catholics. Harry took me to visit my first Catholic church. The holiness, the quiet, the smell of incense, the kneeling and praying before lighted candles impressed me. The next day, I went back with a bottle and stole some Holy Water: "I love me wife," he had said. I knew that. "She was me life," he had said. So I hung her picture on the wall, and beneath it I put an altar, with candles and my stolen Holy Water. Later I put Sister's picture up too—that way we were all family—tied in a lasting knot.

Happiness—something I had never taken too much notice of before—was coming back home after months on the road, knowing I had *my* man waiting. Happiness was lying in bed and listening to Harry helping his kids with their homework. Linda mostly. Gogi always knew more than anybody. I even got used to Gogi's strange ways. Her reading in her room while everyone was enjoying each other in the living room. Happiness was picnicking in the summer in the parks, giving a big Thanksgiving dinner and giveaway early on Christmas morning—something I never in life cared about or even knew I missed. Happiness was keeping the bed warm for Harry when he came home on cold mornings, and loving, loving, loving till he fell out, by late afternoons, to rest and go back to work late evenings.

Happiness had become my way of life the day I came down into the lobby after a long trip, to find our doorman gone. The elevator man told me the doorman had been let go. I went up to Tom Rumley to see if he had heard. "Tom, what's with the doorman?" I said when he opened the door.

"Fired."

"When they getting a new one?"

"I called up. The landlord says he can't afford one."

"Can't afford! With all the money we paying?"

"Just telling you what the man said, Dorine."

"What did you say, Tom Rumley?"

"What's there to say, Dorine?"

"What I'm saying. I'm moving—cutting out."

"What good that's gonna do?" Tom asked. "He'll only cut up your apartment and get twice the money." (But old landlord had already begun to cut up apartments when we *had* a doorman.)

"Tom Rumley, I ain't about to let no goddamn ofay son-of-a-bitch landlord mess with my style."

I turned in a huff and bumped right into Sonny, who was walking toward me. "Dorine," Sonny said. "You the one I'm coming to see."

There's this sixth sense of hustling folks. They know when danger's about. Whether it told in Sonny's face, or just the tone of his voice, I had this sudden quickening of my insides. My feeling of permanence, my happiness was on the line. "About Harry. . . ?" I asked.

"Harry! Hell no. About me."

"What about you, old nigger?" I asked, relieved, expecting him to hit me for more money.

"Dorine, you know I been trying to hold onto this joint. But I can't. Since they repealed Prohibition, them legal bars selling good whiskey cheap been screwing up business. I can't keep up. I got to shut down."

"Shut down? What about Harry?"

"Harry! What about me? Shit, Dorine, Harry's just losing a job. I'm losing my goddamn drawers."

4

But it was more than just a job. It hit me when we were two years in our new apartment and I heard Harry say, "This is the house. Is bound to bring me luck." Playacting! The words jumped to my mind as I lay looking at him smiling at me through the mirror. Harry's good bed-action must have stopped up my ears to the fact he kept repeating the same words every day. Surprised at this sudden knowledge I shifted my eyes to the flowers on the dresser. Irises. In the living room we kept fresh roses. We had daisies in the kitchen, chrysanthemums in the dining room—I made James fetch them at least twice a week. How long did it take those suckers to bring the luck they were supposed to?

Two years in our new apartment, a block from Central Park (as close as we could get, the houses on park side not being open to blacks). Sunlight flooded the windows of the apartment, lighting up the hardwood floors that Linda and James kept a hard shine on. Everything clean, everything lovely, the way it ought to be to bring luck. And Harry still out of work.

"And this is me day," he said. That had to be the jinx! This playacting and knowing it. This pretending to believe what he said. He adjusted his hat, turned to look at the back of his brown suit (he wore gray some mornings too. Nights, when he went to Sandy's or Charles's to gamble with his West Indian friends, he wore dark blue or black), he smoothed down the black armband—destined to be worn for life—then stood back to see the fine figure he cut. "Mahn got to look he best to get the best, ain't it?"

I bit down on my bottom lip to keep from saying: Feller, if you really wants work, don't be going out there trying to outdo Rockefeller. This is overhall times. These is WPA times. "Why don't you stay home today, Harry," I said instead, stretching and letting my titties shake to see if that charm would work. "You know I got to go on the road tomorrow."

He kept admiring himself in the mirror, giving himself one last look. Seeing my charm didn't work, I said, "Baby, if you don't get that job early, what say you come on back and let's knock off a li'l piece—before the kids get home?" Harry's West Indian thing kept him from making love when the kids were home, except if they were sleeping.

"Oh God," he laughed. "But that all the woman think about."

He had to be kidding, seeing the rent got paid, the 'fridge stayed stocked with food, his kids went to school looking good. He always had money in his pocket and went out nights in a chauffeur-driven car. Even a fool had to know the little money he won gambling didn't pay for that.

"Tell me something better to think about?" I teased.

"But the woman fast, yes?" He laughed. Kissing me, he ran to the door, afraid I might grab and rape him—some such thing.

I waited until I knew he had gone from the building before going to the window to look out at him taking those long strides up the avenue—rushing. To where? Did the stud really think that dressing like a big shot and walking the streets would luck up a big-time job? No baby, my mind screamed out at him. The only thing you got working for you is right here in your bed.

Tom and I had the unspoken rule never to discuss Harry. But

that day, sitting on his bed and watching him pack for our next-day trip, I wanted to talk. So did he. I knew he did by the way his eyes kept avoiding mine, and I thanked the Lord that I wouldn't have to be the one to break the rule.

"What time we getting under way in the morning?" I asked, pretending not to notice he had something to say.

"Reckon about five."

"When is Bessie and Bill getting here?" I asked.

"Directly—ought to be here about now."

"Expect we'll be getting to Boston in enough time?"

"Uh-huh." He stuffed his shaving things into the kit and laid the kit on the bed, then stood scratching his chin, real serious. Finally he blurted out: "Dorine, why don't you do something for Harry?"

"Like what?" I asked, relieved that we could talk finally.

"Like setting him up in something. . . ." But Tom had always thought I was doing too much for Harry—and for his kids. He had stayed on my back, until we had finally stopped even mentioning them.

"You don't think I been doing anything, Tom?"

"Oh, you keep him pretty. But I ain't talking about stuff like rent, food, clothes."

"Stuff like that cost too, Tom."

"Come off it, Dorine. Folks can always eat. I didn't think you ought to have messed with the stud, seeing he was West Indian and all like that. But you did. So you should go all the way." He stuck his fingers in his back pockets, swaying over me schoolteacher-fashion. "Dorine, I seen Harry yesterday—in that One Hundred and Twenty-fifth Street cafeteria. Just sitting there, over a cup of coffee."

"Must have been waiting for a big shot with a big deal," I said, hating that I sounded sarcastic. Tom stopped his sway to catch my eyes.

"Like who?"

"Who knows?"

There weren't many big shots we knew hanging around these days. The Seabury Committee, with their gang-buster attorney, Thomas E. Dewey, had done their job well. They had cleared up the rackets of our friends, leaving Harlem wide open for Dutch Schultz

225

and his boys. When our black royalty hadn't bowed out quietly, the Dutch had handled them personally. Alex Pompey had told Tom and me what had happened to him:

"In my pajamas. Can you tie that? Them hoods dragged me out of bed in the middle of the night and down to this apartment. You'll never guess who it belonged to. Dixie Davis's old lady. Can you tie that? We made that turkey. Now he's the Dutch's mouthpiece, giving him the goods on us.

" 'Pompey,' Dutch says to me. 'You gonna be the first nigger in Harlem I'm gonna make an example of, because you told me a lie. You promised to turn over your business to me and you has not done so. We want your business, Cubano.'

"Man pulls back his jacket and I look at this forty-five he got in his belt," Pompey said. "So I don't tell him I ain't never made no such a promise. 'On the head of my mother, Pompey, you cooperate or else.' Jesus Christ! On the head of his mother! What to do?"

Now the signs swinging over Alex Pompey's handmade cigar shops bore the name DUTCH SCHULTZ CIGARS. That beer baron of Prohibition had replaced *all* the kingpins of the Harlem numbers game. Instead of our black gentlemen numbers banker and their royal-acting selves, hoods with .45s were running the show. No, there weren't many big shots left for Harry to wait around to see. So I said to Tom:

"What you want from me?"

"You'll think of something—if you try real hard."

The ringing bell took him from the room before I had the chance to answer. I heard him greeting Bill and Bessie in the hall-way. "Dorine's in here. Been trying to convince her she ought to set up her old man. But you know Dorine. Chintzy! Just hates to get up off that loot. Guess she figures if she throws dirt in them vaults, her money'll spring roots."

Bessie and Bill came in laughing. Bessie looking calm in a dark-colored dress. Before I could comment on it she shouted, as though I was across the street, "Hey there, sister, tell this man it ain't spending what's bothering you. It's thinking of ways to keep that man where you wants him—in bed."

"Tom can say many a thing about me, Bessie," I said, getting mad. "Being chintzy ain't one of 'em."

I had thought of setting Harry up in some kind of business. But what kind? A rooming house would have tied me to it. I wanted to be on the road. A joint? Harry was too honest. He hadn't really dug working for Sonny, because the joint wasn't legal. The way I saw it, The Rising Sun should have been rising still. Harry just had too many don'ts.

"You ought to have seen Harry yesterday," Tom said. "Sitting there pretending he didn't see me until I made him. Looked so lost."

"I do what I can," I said. "I got lots of folks to think about. I ain't no millionaire."

"But baby," Bessie said. "Ain't Harry the man you tied your life to?"

"And he lives a damn good life! His kids too! He ain't got no complaints coming." Bessie and Bill exchanged glances. They looked at Tom. Tom shrugged. They had been talking about me! Behind my back! What the shit was that all about? "Look," I said. "Whatever you guys think—a woman's entitled to her limits."

After the Boston trip, Tom dropped me off at two in the morning. Running through the heavy rain, I rushed upstairs to bed and cuddled against Harry's back to sleep. I awoke the next morning reaching for him. He had already gone. Snuggling beneath the covers I kept listening to rain hitting against the windows, hearing cars splashing water against water.

Half awake, half asleep beneath the sounds of the rain, I kept hearing footsteps—walking, walking, outside my door. Harry. Knowing he hadn't gone out perked up a need for him. On a lazy rainy day when there's nothing to do, there's no use doing. Except in bed. Too lazy to move, I lay counting the times Harry walked up and back, up and back the long hallway, from the bedroom to the dining room. Once, twice. With each count, I felt my need rising. On his third time down, I turned on my back waiting, ready to call him when he walked to the door.

Instead of footsteps I heard shouts coming from the back. "What! You ain't take me for a man! But I am a man! The man of this house!"

Jumping out of bed, I made it down the hall and through the dining room. In the back room James sat at the edge of his bed, looking frailer than nature ever intended him to be, with Harry looking down at him. Breathing hard. James kept fumbling with the buttons of his shirt, looking downright pitiful.

Seeing me in the doorway, he jumped up and ran into the dining room, making me the barrier between himself and Harry. "What's happening here?" I asked, standing solid between them, looking from one to the other.

"This—boy—" Harry sputtered, his eyes still on James. "I tell he to go to the store for me newspaper and Camels. He ain't want. What he think? I his playmate?"

Gogi usually got Harry's newspaper and cigarettes before she went to school every morning. Why hadn't he sent her? I turned to James. Over his shoulder I noticed the chrysanthemums drooping in the vase. And their dying—like the gloom in the house—fell like weights on my shoulders.

"Why didn't you go, James?" I asked.

"Dorine, I was going. I swear. Harry woke me. I got right up. I told him I wanted to see if you needed something too. He blew up."

Harry kept his eye on James. I kept my eyes on his balled-up fists. Fear formed a hard knot in my stomach. Was he actually going to hit James? For not going to the store!

Fear that he still might forced me to wait in the dining room while James finished dressing and went out. Back in the bedroom I stared out at the rain, hearing Harry's footsteps along the hall. We had to have it out. I searched through my mind for the right words. The playacting had ended. His restlessness was bound to grow. I walked to the door and called:

"Harry, I want to talk."

He didn't want to. The quiet filling the hallway between us said that. The quiet kept on for a long time, until finally he walked up to me, then by me into the room. He went to the window, where he stood looking out. Even with his back to me I saw his jaw working, his hands clinching, unclinching. I sat on the bed.

"Harry," I said. "I—I know how unsettling it's been—not being able to find work. It's been a long time. You know you don't have to work. But if you feel you must—what's wrong with WPA?"

Harry spun. The skin around his mouth had turned an ash white. Flames lit his eyes and grew, searing through me. My mind scuttled around its darkest corners searching for words to unsay those I had just spoken. Paralyzed, I knew I was about to be shoved into the darkest, deepest of pits. Insects scurried over my body, opened up passages in my brain. Once again I stood outside myself, at the door of Harry's slum apartment looking up at him, waiting for a tragedy—a goddamn tragedy to happen.

"Dorine." James had come back from the corner store. I jumped up, flung the door open, shouted: "Come in. Come in. Come the hell on in."

"I can't, Dorine," James answered, trying to hand me Harry's newspaper and cigarettes through the door. "I'm wet."

My eyes popped. Only a few minutes before he had used me as a barrier; now he stood talking like a fool! So what if he dripped over the floor—flooded us all the hell out into the street? That's where we needed to be—safe in the goddamn storm. "Here," James said, handing me a letter. "This here's from Montgomery."

"Man, come on in here and put that shit on the dresser. I'll get Linda to read it when she gets home."

"Linda?" Harry asked. "Why you must wait for Linda? Cahn't you read?"

And like that first time, his anger vanished in one instant! But the man had scared me shitless! I turned on him, ready to tear into him.

"No goddamit. I cahn't read and I cahn't write either."

"But you make joke?" Putting his fingertips in his back pockets, he rocked, staring down at me, smiling. Smiling! "You mean to stand there, in this big United States of America, and tell me, you cahn't read?"

"No, I ain't 'make joke.'" I kept mocking. "I went in one door of the school and out the other. Since then nobody's been fast enough to catch up with me." I had never tried to hide that I couldn't read from Harry. Neither did I offer the information. Harry had never seemed interested. When my mail came, James or Linda had always been around to read it for me.

"But how you does get along?" Harry asked. I stared hard, letting his words settle and fill the room, wanting for him to hear what he had had the nerve to ask. But after a long silence, he still hadn't.

"Harry—I 'does get along' just fine."

"But you will learn," he said. "What's more, you starting right now!"

Taking my hand, Harry pulled me into the living room, where

he sat me down. Pulling a chair next to mine, he guided my hand, teaching me the ABCs. And on that day, with rain falling outside, and Harry and me inside, we went to schooling instead of screwing. And I learned the alphabet, vowel sounds, and some three-letter words. And for months—whenever I was home—Harry sat down with me to teach me how to read and how to write. I learned. Not so good as I might have if I had been younger. But enough to write letters home. If that was all Harry had ever done for me—that was more than most folks had. So one day after my lessons, I stopped him on his way out.

"Harry, I'm gonna let James go."

"James?" Harry said. "But why? True, the boy does vex me sometimes, but he's a good boy."

"But I don't need a boy, Harry. I need a man. Someone to help me out—with my business. You see yourself how hard it is for me—not able to read. And you and me—we work so good together, Harry. . . ."

I had decided the day when James had looked so shaken, when my fright had told me I had to do something if I wanted Harry with me. I was only waiting to find the words not to mess with his pride. And the words, when they were ready, had shaped themselves.

"I need someone who knows more than James. Someone to look after the bills when I'm gone—my banking. It ain't easy, Harry. It ain't been easy for me. . . ."

"But why you ain't tell me before?" He searched through my eyes wanting to believe, and seeing how much he wanted to believe tears jumped to my eyes (I cry at the prick of a pin). Seeing my tears he accepted guilt:

"Oh God, Dorine, if I did know you need me—I'd have ask you long time. . . ."

That night I broke the news of James's leaving at dinner. Harry had gone out. "How can you do this to us?" Linda said, throwing her head back Garbo-fashion. "We love him so." Gogi looked from James to me. I waited for her to object. But she only looked back to her plate. Gogi tried never to speak directly to me. It had become habit. This once she wanted to. She was unhappy. We all were, James being a part of our family. Sitting there, he looked young enough to be their brother. But James was damn near my age.

"I hope you see this is for your own good, James," I said. "You're young. You can't go through life working for room and board and the li'l money I throw your way."

"Yep." He agreed. He probably resented that I was letting him go for Harry's sake. But it was also true that James had always been a feller who needed to be pushed. I had just pushed him. . . .

5

We didn't miss James as much as I had expected. In a few months we had stopped talking about him. And by the time a year had passed, he never entered my mind, except on occasion. Maybe because the house grew so much livelier with Harry driving for me, and doing my banking, and the bill-paying and everything else I could think up to show him he was needed. I had never known how much my happiness or the life of the house depended on Harry until he was no longer unhappy.

"Yeah." His loud bragging voice and belly-laughing held us to the table. "A wicket keeper. That's me." He looked us over, Bessie, Ann, Tom, Bill, and me. "You ain't know—but that's the biggest man on a cricket team," he said. "And it God truth when the Prince of Wales come home to play—it was he and me. And is me who win." He pushed back his chair getting up and stood a moment looking around for praise.

Bessie gave it. "Go on with your bad self. I ain't known Dorine been hooked up with such a important gent'man."

"How you mean?" Harry's chest expanded at Bessie's admiration. "Royalty ain't mean a thing to me. I beat the ass outa royalty." He left to go to the bathroom and Bessie winked.

"I do declare, Dorine, that man gets purtier and purtier."

"Sure do," Tom said, rearing back in his chair. "He's looking and sounding right good. Seems a shame you couldn't do no better by him than to make him a messenger boy. But I guess that beats nothing."

Bessie nudged Bill, thinking I didn't see. Ann stared trying to shut Tom up. I turned on him. "Don't you be no damn clown, Tom Rumley. Harry ain't no messenger. He's my husband—don't matter if we ain't tied by law." He knew that Harry and I passed for husband and wife.

I looked up. Gogi stood in the doorway. How long had she been there? What had she heard? "What you want, girl?" I snapped.

"This dress is too small," she said.

"Lordy," Bessie said, pulling Gogi in from the doorway. "This child sure has grown. How old is you, baby?"

"Twelve," Gogi said.

"Twelve! I do declare time flies. Dorine, look at these titties on her. I do declare these kids about to push us into old age."

"Hey girl," Bill said, holding Gogi's hand. "What you wants to be when you gets big?"

"I don't know," Gogi answered.

"What about being a hairdresser?" Ann asked. I had told Ann I wanted to put the girls in a beauty school.

"Hairdresser!" Gogi looked down at her, hurt, disappointed. "I'm going to be rich—like Dorine."

"Do tell," Bill laughed. "How rich is that?"

"I'm going to have big cars—and live in big apartments. And I'm going to dress in peach satin around the house."

"Why peach?" Ann asked, encouraging the usually quiet Gogi.

"Because"—she glanced at me, shy—"brown skin goes so well with peach. It makes the prettiest combination." It was as near as she had come to saying she noticed me entertaining Harry in the bedroom.

"What you gonna do to make all that money?" Tom asked. Gogi stared at him for a long time before deciding to say: "One thing I'm not going to be—is a messenger."

Embarrassed eyes looked at her, then away, looked at her then away, until I said: "Girl, take that dress off and come and clear off this table."

"Well," Bessie said, as Harry came to the doorway. "I—sure don't know what we gonna do about that dress."

"Why make a thing about it?" Harry answered. "If the dress too small, take it back."

"How can she?" Gogi asked.

"If she can't, I will," Harry said.

Once again eyes got to shifting into eyes and away, shifting away from Harry. Gogi stared at him. Stared at him, her eyes fixed as though staring into his soul. A know-it-all kid and a know-nothing daddy. My dress got to sticking to me. My scalp crawled.

True, I never discussed work with Harry, no more than I did with Gogi. Neither had I lied. Harry's being honest made me respect his not wanting to be talked to. But shit, he was the closest somebody to me. He had to know!

When the gang came to me, they always sat around, as we were doing now. We joked about our close calls on the road, stretching out near brushes with the law into our lifetime jokes. How many times had we sat around this table, recounting Grace's long piss—and Harry laughed. So how could Harry Brisbane, husband-manager, stand pretending innocence? The way he strutted around, peacock-proud, since doing my business, so pleased to have the bank president bowing, almost—calling him Mr. Brisbane with that respectful tone used for important folks. Now there he stood acting above it all.

A finger of pure meanness pushed into me. And it stayed with me all the next day. We went to the bank, and on our way home I made him stop at my favorite German butcher. I had no plan of what I intended to do. I only knew I had to do something.

"Hello, Mrs. Brisbane," Mr. Meyer greeted me. "Where have you been hiding?"

I showed my mouthful of teeth, walking up to the counter. "Been out of town," I said, letting my eyes roam over the place careless-like. Then I saw this sack of frankfurters—about twenty-five pounds—lying on the corner of the counter in a gauze bag.

"What can I do for you, Mrs. Brisbane?" Mr. Meyer, a big man with purple splotches on his wide face, had gained my respect. He was the best butcher around Harlem. Unlike most butchers who sold ready-to-stick-into-the-bag cuts of meat, he cut his meats to order.

"I think I'll have some beef liver, Mr. Meyer," I said. "You know how I like it."

He left us to go into the refrigerator. The minute the door closed after him, I winked at Harry, to make sure he looked, then slipped the sack of frankfurters from the counter and made them disappear between my legs. "Hey girl. . . ." Harry's mouth dropped open, not understanding what he had seen. "What you doin'?"

I grinned, winked, pleased almost to laughing that his face had gone three shades of gray. "But—you cahn't do that. . . ."

Mr. Meyer came out with the slab of liver. He showed it to me over the counter. "How does that look to you, Mrs. Brisbane?"

"Just fine, Mr. Meyer. Will you cut me about seven slices?"

"How do you want them?" Mr. Meyer asked.

"In a bag!" Harry said, almost shouting.

"Don't you think we ought to let him cut it first, Harry? Slice it thin, will you, Mr. Meyer? You know just how I like it."

"We ain't want it a-tall," Harry said.

"But of course we want it, Harry dear." I smiled, gentle, teasing. "Why do you think we came in?"

Harry's eyes had gone to slipping and sliding around as though their sockets had been greased. The butcher started to slice the liver and Harry started twitching at my side. I keep smiling, but slowly it's coming to me: I've made a mistake. The way Harry is shaking, I decide to get the franks back onto the counter.

But Mr. Meyer comes over with the liver. "Will this do, Mrs. Brisbane?" And when I nod, he puts it on the scale. "Having company?" he asked, making small talk and looking at me. I'm stuck with the frankfurters. And to my nod, "Will that be all?"

"Yes, that will be all," I answer. But a thin line of sweat has broken out over my top lip. No sack of franks in the world is worth losing the best butcher I ever had.

Putting the liver in a bag, Mr. Meyer hands the bag over the counter, his purple-red face stretching out, smiling. I put my hand out for the bag. But grabbing my arm, Harry pulls me. "Come, come"—his voice is hoarse—"let's get the ass out. . . ."

"For God's sake, Harry." I shake his hands off. "I got to pay the man."

"Ha-ha," Mr. Meyer laughs. "That husband of yours is an impatient man. Some men can't stand to shop."

"Ha-ha," I laugh. "Everything takes a little getting used to." I put a warning in my voice, trying to calm Harry. But he's shaking and can't stop. I hand Mr. Meyer ten bucks. Before he can get my change, Harry is pulling me by the arm again. Pulling me off-balance.

Now, I have a twenty-five-pound sack of bulky franks between my legs. Under the best of circumstances I have to use a little skill just to walk normally. But there is Harry, pulling. The grease from the franks is melting against my hot legs. The bag starts to slipping. I'm trying to appear cool. My smile is straining to get off my face. With an effort I hold on to it.

"Ha-ha," I laugh again. "The way my husband acts, you'd think money just spouts out of concrete—places like that. . . ."

Every word I use is to open up Harry's ears, force him to listen, to hear me. If he can't stay with me, then go. Give me a chance. But Harry is so scared he can't think. Can't hear. My big eyes sticking out of my head have no effect. Mr. Meyer hands me my change. Harry, frantic, gets behind me to push me out.

By this time even Mr. Meyer gets puzzled. Curious. When Harry finally gets me out on the sidewalk, Mr. Meyer comes to the door. I get desperate. I tighten the muscles of my legs around the slippery franks. Harry keeps pushing. It can't hold.

"Goddamit, leave me be!" I shout. "Go on and open up the goddamn car door!"

Harry rushes to the car, opens the door. And while I'm praying that he's seen enough gangster movies to know that the getaway guy stays behind the wheel, he rushes back, gets behind me, and pushes.

By this time I'm reduced to taking teensy-weensy steps. My one hope now is that the show is so great Mr. Meyer's not able to leave to go back and find this bag of franks gone.

Two feet of sidewalk standing between me and the open car door. I have to make it or give up all—my butcher and the respect he's always shown me. But my legs are all sweaty and greasy. The franks have slipped down to my knees. I walk knock-kneed, pigeon-toed, to hold them. And this simple joker behind keeps pushing.

I make myself as stiff as a board and lean back, trying to pick my toes up so I can slide along the sidewalk on my heels. We start off, Harry pushing. But it doesn't work. I gauge the distance to the car. I must take my chances one way or the other. I make a flying leap. I land at the car door; the franks land in the gutter. Thankful now to have Harry behind me, I snatch up the sack, flip it into the car, and jump in. Harry slams the door and rushes over to get in on his side. In a sweat, I glance over. Mr. Meyer is still at the door. I wave. Mr. Meyer lifts his hand.

Swoosh . . . down the avenue, I find myself racing through city traffic, going this way and that. We live on the next avenue, around the corner from the butcher. But Harry *has* seen gangster movies. Instead of going around the block, he's got to make this getaway. I find myself in this car, doing eighty—like a bat that's missed hell—flying through Central Park.

Harry sits at the wheel, hunched over, his head pushed out of his collar, ready to go through the windshield. Tires screech as we take curves on two wheels. Funny as hell. I want to laugh, but shout instead: "Hey, feller, slow down. Where the hell you taking me?"

My shouting only makes him feed more gas. I try to read his mind. But that's stopped somewhere back there. And even I got sense enough to be scared of a scared nigger sitting behind the wheel of a racing car.

"Feller"—I lower my voice, trying to get through to him, to force his mind back to what we're about—"this ain't the way home."

But he's making this getaway. I sit there thinking: Here I am, a big-time hustler—a real artist in my trade. I have taken all kinds of chances. I have boosted furs, diamonds, the best in clothes. I have money in my vault, so much jewelry that chances are if it had been drawing interest, I might damn near be a millionaire. And here I am, about to lose my life over a lousy sack of franks.

I prayed for the police, then changed my mind. Poor Harry would kill us both for sure if he thought he heard a siren. Then, driving out of the park, the car hit a bump. Harry lost control of the wheel. The car skidded into the opposite lane toward an oncoming coal truck. I grabbed the wheel and turned. The car hit the curb, mounting the sidewalk before Harry hit the brakes.

"You black sons of bitches!" the driver of the truck yelled. "Who the hell give you niggers license to drive!"

The rough voice pulled Harry back to himself. The miracle of having survived had us both weak, worn, and looking at each other. Seeing Harry's still-gray face, I shook my head, thinking of the chances we take when we mistake cowardice for honesty, then changed my mind: Harry had to have a special kind of courage. As scared as the sucker had been, it needed a special kind of courage to have stayed instead of running out on me—no reason to thank him or the Good Lord.

Finding my voice, I said: "Damn, Harry, if a bag of franks is gonna be the death of both of us, I best take them the hell on back. . . ."

"But you cahn't do that."

"No? Just move on over, mister, and watch."

I took the wheel, turned the car around, heading back uptown. As I drove, sensing him cooling down, I said: "Damn, Harry, I hate to think of what might have happened to the lot of us if you had accepted the fact that half of the things at the house is hot."

"Hot. . . ?"

"Stolen, feller, stolen . . ." And as we drove back through the park, with the bright oranges and reds and browns brightening the early dark of the afternoon, his quietness grew deep, deep, deeper. Finally he said:

"Is true. . . ?"

"You goddamn right it's true," I said. The meanness that had touched me, starting it all, didn't let up, so I added, "Every bit of it that can be moved—including the clothes on your kids' backs. . . ."

Holding on to the steering wheel, I waited for his rage, wanting it, anxious to take him on. But he laughed. "What the hell you laughing at, feller?" I asked. "You know you come damn near killing the both of us—all on account of a lousy bag of frankfurters?" Harry kept on laughing, bending over, holding his stomach. I looked at him from the side of my eye, getting mad, madder. Then I got to thinking of the scene in the shop, and how gray he had turned when he was scared. I saw him hunched over the wheel of the car, his head sticking out of his collar like a turtle while he tried to drive us, straight as you please, to our death. Then I laughed. And there we were, both laughing, tears running down our faces. Every time we tried to stop, the sight of us—two heisters making our getaway through Central Park—made us double over again.

We laughed all the way home. Yet behind the laughter there was that note of pain. Harry would never drive for me again. He would never want to. I wouldn't want him to. From here on in, we had to get on the best we could—with his pride, his rage—and his idleness.

The spring when I went down to Tennessee, to laugh and cry and be proud that some of the money I had been putting out for years had begun to bear fruit, had to be the happiest one of my life. Brother was graduating from Fisk. Up to that time I had suspected Brother wanted to stay in school forever, to get back at me for having trapped him at home for so long. Then there he walked—tall, lean, older than most, with a locked-deep quietness—stepping up to get his papers.

Being happy made me decide to drive Brother on to Montgomery. I had promised the girls I'd hurry back home. They wanted me around—protection against Harry: He kept the house in a state of fear, rushing in and out, so wild that if the job he wanted exploded beneath him, he still wouldn't see it. The wilder he got the stricter he became with the girls. He expected them to clean the house, then go into their room and stay behind the closed door. It was as though he thought they might be killed, kidnapped, or raped if they even sat in the living room.

The strain of living in that apartment was so tight I hated the thought of going back. Being free from it made me want to stay that way as long as time and space allowed.

"Dr. Davis," I joked with Brother, as we left Nashville. "Suh, when do we be setting up our offices in Montgomery?"

"Offices?" Brother said.

"Doctor's offices," I said and Brother laughed.

"I guess we'll have to wait a bit for that, Dorine."

"Wait? What for? You don't have to worry none about money."

"It's not money this time, Dorine," he said. "I can't practice medicine in Montgomery. You must know that."

"I know no such a thing," I said. "That's what I been paying for—I thought." He hadn't told me different.

I kept looking at him, where he sat next to me. Brother had begun to bald in front. His buck teeth, unlike the hard teeth of us girls, showed spots of decay. Years of pushing had left him looking years older—although he was almost two years younger—than me.

All that responsibility. Yet he had done what he had set out to do. So had I.

"They won't license me to practice, Dorine."

"What *they* you talking about, Brother?"

"What *they* would I be talking about, Dorine?" He had a kind voice, soft with a no-playing-around quality. But after all that planning?

"Ain't that why you went to Fisk, Brother? Ain't that why we had to get you all this education?"

"You know that's why."

"Then when you reckon you'll be starting?"

"You must know I looked into this. You must know it means a lot to me, Dorine."

"Why in the hell didn't you look into it before, instead of after?"

"Dorine, it ain't no sense in *us* arguing."

There was strength in his quietness, in his eyes, small behind his silver-rimmed eyeglasses, in his long, thin fingers, tapping on his knees. I looked from him to the giant trees stretching along the sides of the highway.

"They ought to be glad to have you," I said.

"I know."

"They need you."

"I know."

Black folks needed doctors. Old Doc Mitchell, who had taken care of black folks and poor whites around our part of town, had been old long before I was born. He had to be feeling his way to kids' tonsils with his cane.

"We got to fight them, Brother."

"Fight who, Dorine?"

"Them crackers—that's who."

"How do we do that, Dorine?"

"Blow their goddamn brains out."

Brother laughed. "You have been up north too long, Dorine. Things will change in Montgomery. It takes time. But one day blacks and whites will be able to sit down together and work out their differences."

"How you figure, Brother? If they can keep your black butt

from doing what you want, why they got to sit and talk?"

"There are some good white men, Dorine."

"Which ones?"

Brother laughed. "They're around. How do you think we get along? How do you think that we have schools like Fisk, like Montgomery State, if they didn't support them. . . ?"

The green of the countryside spun off in my eyes at Brother's reasoning. Sure I was proud he was educated. I believed in education, but not at the risk of having crackers run the schools and then set themselves up as judges on what my hard-earned money was supposed to accomplish.

"You don't have to stay down here," I said. "Come on up north. They got black doctors in New York, in Philly. . . ."

"I'm not leaving Montgomery, Dorine." Brother's calm voice got my blood to racing. I kept trying to hold my temper. I had planned on having one member of my family a doctor. "What you figure you owe this place?"

"This is home, Dorine."

"Even when they stop you from making a living?"

"I'll make a living, Dorine. I'm going to teach."

"Doctoring?"

"No—history." But he didn't have to go away for that. Hell, they had teachers' training schools in Montgomery. "Of course, I'll have to go back to school—take a few courses. . . ."

Damn if I hadn't known. Brother intended to keep on in school as long as I was around to help out. There had been no time limit set on our agreement, but I hadn't expected to support him for life.

I got real quiet, feeling the car beneath me—smooth, with its new slanting windshield—a windbreaker. Such a small thing—a slanted windshield, and a car just rode so smooth.

"Ain't no real money in teaching, is it, Brother?" I asked.

"I don't aim to get rich," Brother said. That got me quiet again. I did the hustling, other folks did the dreaming.

"What you got against money?" I couldn't help asking.

"Nothing. . . . But, Dorine, Montgomery needs good teachers same as it needs doctors."

"A damn lie!" That's all educated folks did in Montgomery. Teach or preach. "What you got against leaving? It ain't as though you'll be leaving the country." Another damn lie. The South was down south; the rest of the country was the USA.

"We can't all leave, Dorine." Brother knew those words generally shut me up. "Somebody got to be here to try to change things."

I looked hard at Brother. All that time. All that good money. And I ended up with an educated fool for a brother. "So—you're gonna change Montgomery! You're God?"

"Montgomery's got to change—sometime. . . ."

"That's what Methuselah tried to hang around for but he ain't made it."

"And young black folks are most likely to change when they learn more about themselves."

"Like what, Brother?"

"Well—about ourselves in relation to the world around us, Dorine. Our relation to the whites—to the Indians—Dorine, do you know that our family most likely has Indian ancestors?"

"Indians!"

"Yes—Muskogee Indians."

I looked at this brother, on whom I had spent so much for so long to see that he went through school. "Oh, Brother. Shee-it!"

Montgomery had not changed. Nor was it about to, from where I sat looking out. Folks standing around that country town looked the same as I remembered them. Crackers, lounging at roadsides, squinting at my New York license plates, spitting. Streetcars, the front seats near empty, black folks packed like wieners in the back. Around the old black Baptist church, folks in their go-to-meeting clothes—men wearing their felt hats, women their straws and white gloves, laughing sweet, talking gentle—like a worn page torn from times gone by.

But the old school, where Sister and I had hit the front door only to leave through the back, had fallen in on itself. A new school—Brother said it had separate rooms with a teacher for every room—stood in its place. At the old house, the girls were studying as though study had become a disease they had caught.

Janie and Jennie Mae were at it when we went in, their worktable cluttered with stacks of books and papers. "Dorine!" They looked up in surprise when I walked in with Brother. Jennie Mae stood up stretching. "I declare this is a shock. It took near a miracle getting you here."

"Near is the word," I said. "Seeing Brother ain't finished school yet. We got to wait for the real miracle."

She laughed, embarrassed, coming to kiss me. "There's nothing wrong with teaching—is there?" Then she already knew. It had all been discussed and settled. They had just waited to fill me in.

"Depends on whether it's done from street corners or if you spends your life waiting to get in a classroom to do it, I reckon."

"How are our cousins?" Janie changed the subject. "What are Linda and Gogi studying?"

"I don't rightly know. . . ."

I doubted whether they did. Girls in the South settled for what they wanted sooner than those in the North. All the girls were about the same age. Yet it surprised me that Janie and Jennie Mae had not kept the little-girl quality. Their teen-aged faces had the settled look of gentleness intended to move with them through life—southern life. Their voices had slowed down to a drawl. I could almost see them in go-to-meeting clothes, walking to and from the old Baptist church—laughing sweet, talking gentle.

". . . But Linda is as pretty as a doll. And Gogi"—I started to say fresh, then sassy, then I thought of her curled on her bed around her book, forever reading, her face fresh with sass when interrupted, and said—"as bright as ever."

The old place reeked from lack of care: all that studying when the chairs they were sitting on needed polishing! The cushions on the couch had been jumped on, stomped, and were coming apart at the seams. And the floors! I held back from running into the kitchen to inspect the old stove.

"And Harry?" Brother asked. "You haven't said a word about him all the way home. What is happening to you folks up there in New York?"

"You know New York—things always changing. . . ."

Only the more things changed into what I had wanted, the less sure I was that I wanted change. Harry, with his wild dashing in and out of the house, anxious now to get me in bed. I didn't know if I wanted him—or even cared. All that brooding. Brooding over the kids. Brooding over me. Resentful of me going on the road. And always that feel of a fucking tragedy about to happen. . . .

Brother waited for an answer. But then this thickset kid with big bedroom eyes came bounding into the house and into my arms, his body smelling like a yard dog on a rainy day. Sweat made him almost too slippery to hold on to. But I held on, squeezing as though my life depended on it. In New York my fondness for my family usually centered around Lil—her smartness, the way she looked after Mildred. But seeing Son—a real live ten-year-old boy, stinking with energy—I felt a catching in my throat. I blinked and turned to the other boy who had come in with him.

"Whose little boy is this?" I asked.

"Dorine," Jennie Mae said, her voice reproachful, "that's Bud—little brother."

"Oh—Bud. . . . Come here and give your aunt some sugar." Tall for his age, and the prettiest of all, yet for the life of me, I never remembered Sister's last child.

Joseph sat propped up in his wheelchair in the back, catching the sun. Mother Rivers—big, strong, stern-looking—sat beside him crocheting. I ran my hand over his head. "Glad to see you making it, old thing," I said, not meaning it. Paying Mother Rivers to keep him alive added a strain on me I sure didn't need. And what for? "Mother Rivers sure did you the world of good," I said.

Good care leaked out of his pores. Sitting in the sun, he looked healthy despite his twisted face and unblinking left eye. Mother Rivers had spruced him up in a bright, well-pressed cotton plaid shirt and a cotton blanket around his lap, shouting he had held out longer than he had any right to, and useless as he was, might just hold out forever.

I stood a few minutes letting him squeeze my fingers—once, twice, three times—then patting him on his head again, I headed for the kitchen.

Sure enough, the kitchen floor needed a scrubbing; fingerprints decorated the cupboards—and that old stove. My hair raised from my scalp at the sight of the grease burdening it.

The two families shared Miss Jessica. I found her at Mildred's, ironing. Wiry, face lined and toughened instead of wrinkled; shrinking instead of aging, her body had become like that of an underdeveloped girl. "How's it by you, Miss Jessica?" I said, being polite before getting to what I had come for.

"Fair to middlin'," she said, laughing at some joke. "Since last ah seen you, got maself two grandchillun."

"Do tell. . . ."

"Grandsons—my eldest girl. . . ."

"She still live over town?"

"Same house . . . all girls. . . . The boys, they done gone off—no more cotton. Mills done closed down. Seems this Depression is lasting. . . ." A fucking lifetime. "Reckon we'll ever see the end of it?"

I shook my head I didn't know. The world had changed, when Miss Jessica and I had the same set of worries. "Reckon things will ever be back to where they was?"

"I reckon," I said, but I hardly remembered how things had been, or if I wanted to go back there. "Even in Montgomery, things got to change," I said.

"I pray the Lord . . . men folks gone to Mobile, Michigan, St. Louis. . . . Something got to bring 'em back."

"Dorine," Lil said when I came into the parlor. Tall. Taller than me—almost grown to her arms. She looked down at me from her pointed, bright, Mildred-looking face. "Why didn't you tell us you were coming?"

"I didn't know it myself," I said. Ruth stood beside her. She had her father's square build, his reddish skin and hair, didn't look anything like our family. "What are you girls doing with yourselves?"

"Studying," Lil said. "I'm thinking of going to teachers' college."

"A family full of teachers," I said.

"No, ma'am, not me," Ruth said. "I'm aiming to be a doctor."

"Girls don't go in for doctoring," I said.

"Nothing like trying," Ruth said.

"Brother tried and he ain't made it."

"But things will have changed so much in Montgomery by the time I finish my schooling."

I looked at her, nodding. She had taken something from the family after all—from her simpleminded mother. "What? Y'all planning on having an earthquake down here?"

"Oh, Dorine." She laughed.

Simplemindedness had preserved Mildred in time—except that her hair had turned white. "Planning on staying with us for some time, Dorine?" Mildred asked, and I searched her face—but none of her old meaning had come back.

"Only as long as it takes to clean up the old house and to put my foot down on the gas."

That wasn't as true as it sounded. For the first time since leaving Montgomery, I wanted to stay. I tried to examine that immigrant feeling in me. I told myself that the kids had stopped being weights, and that they were people, a joy to talk to.

". . . Which brings me to the reason I come. I want all of you to come over and help put that old house in order."

"Dorine. . . ." Lil screamed out laughing. She pulled me into her with her long octopus arms. "I declare, you will never, never change."

They came early, bringing Mildred with them. And while Mildred sat in Joseph's room, the rest of us took the house apart to get it together.

Lil and Jane took beds apart and put them out in the sun. Brother started washing down walls. Ruth and Jennie Mae got to scrubbing floors (using rubber gloves!). Miss Jessica collected the dirty things around the house and got the washing board and tub working out in the back.

Son kept peeping out at me from Joseph's room as I gave out chores. "Come on, Son," I said. "I want you to—"

Son backed away. "I ain't gonna clean no greasy old stove!" he shouted.

Surprised. I hadn't even mentioned the stove, intending that we all tackle it last. "You will if I say, or get your butt whipped." But Son kept shaking his big head.

Pretending to be going for a switch, I ran out into the yard. When I ran back into the house, Son had gone. "Where'd that li'l ole devil go?" I asked.

The others bent over laughing. Brother pointed out the window, down the road, at Son running, dust kicking up at his heels. "Y'all sure spoiled that boy," I complained. "He's plain rotten."

"Papa spoiled him," Jennie Mae said.

"That legless hunk of flesh ain't got the wherewithal to spoil a living soul," I said.

"Son's got a hard head." Brother looked at me. "He was born that way."

My face flushed. I looked away quick, scared I might give away secrets to the kids. "You got to take some of the blame for that, Brother," I said.

"Dorine," Lil said, "don't blame anybody for Son. Son's just Son."

And then we got busy cleaning. Got so busy that when I looked in on Joseph and saw Mother Rivers crocheting and talking to Mildred, I interrupted: "Mother Rivers, I want you to—"

"Ain't no cleaning needs doing in this room," she snapped at me. "It's clean as I wants—and seeing I'm the one in here taking care of this hunk of flesh, I'll do the deciding."

Joseph's good eye smiled at me, so I settled for being grateful that he, at least, hadn't taken me too serious.

The next day, as bright and shining as the old house, the family lined up in the front yard to bid me good-bye. "I want you all to keep this house the way I'm leaving it today," I said before getting into the car. "You can never tell the day I'll be coming back."

Son pushed his head from behind Brother and Janie and grinned at me, waving me away.

"That's okay," I teased him. "Wave me away. But the next time, it will be between the two of us—and see who you'll have to stand behind then." Son laughed and squeezed to the front of the family to wave me on. I drove off, but as I looked back at them standing in front of that lovely old house, panic near overcame me. What if something happened to me? What if I never saw them—or him—again?

That was the first time since leaving Son with Sister that I had felt any special concern. When Sister and Joseph had insisted that Son be raised as their own, I had been relieved. Happy. That had solved my problems. And now? I shrugged. He was home with his sisters, his papa, and his uncle. Nonetheless a sadness—akin to grief—gripped me as I pulled up in front of my building.

246

The doorman opened the door. I stepped into the lobby and heard Harry's loud voice. For a moment I thought of backing out and running. But the doorman was pretending not to be looking at me. So I forced my feet past the elevator and climbed the stairs to our second-floor apartment—and into what seemed to be a storm.

Gogi. Of course Gogi. What had she done? Looked at him with that sassy look. That was worse than telling him off. I had seen him trying to look away from it—as though that disrespectful look was a weapon.

The door opened even before I reached it. Linda stepped out into the hall to pull me in. "Thank God you're back, Dorine," she whispered. "Things are awful here."

I looked around, my knees going weak from relief: no one had yet been hurt. The house looked the same. Linda took my bag from me and brought it to the bedroom, leaving me to walk down the hall alone. I walked slowly, hearing Harry shout: "I'll bust your ass! So help me God, I'll bust your ass."

I walked into the dining room and looked around for flowers. No flowers. Even the vase had been moved. A sigh shook my body, a pain, a missing of something I never truly had, losing something my woman's soul had longed to nourish.

Harry's broad back filled the kitchen doorway. From beneath his arms, I saw Gogi, on hands and knees on the kitchen floor, scrubbing. Neither had heard me come in. Neither looked up as I stood in the dining room a short distance from Harry.

"Hey, feller," I called out, trying to soften up his anger with the happy sound of my voice. "I'm home. . . ."

Neither heard. Harry's anger made him deaf. Tears blinded Gogi. And because of her blindness, she kept dipping the brush into the bucket of soapy water and scrubbing the same spot on the floor over and over.

"That ain't the way to scrub floors," Harry said. Rushing to her and picking up the bucket, he emptied the soapy water over the floor, shouting: "That the way to scrub floor!"

Gogi jumped to her feet, screaming: "That's not the way I wash floors! That's the way you wash them! So wash it, wash it, wash it!"

Harry's hand struck out. Gogi slid through the water on her back. Scrambling to her feet, she grabbed the leg of a chair and came up swinging. Harry caught the chair by another leg, turning, twisting; they wrestled, quiet, angry.

Slipping and sliding through the soapy water, I rushed in to grab still another leg of the chair. I shouted: "Stop it! Stop it!" Gogi's strength surprised me. I had always thought her weak, completely at her father's mercy. "Goddamit, stop this shit and listen to me!"

They stopped. But still holding on to the chair, they stared hard at each other, breathing hard. "Girl," I said, "what's wrong with you? You got to be out of your mind, lifting a chair at your father."

"Blame me!" she shrieked. "Go on. Blame me. You didn't see what he did!"

"Makes no difference," I said. "That man's your father! The Lord saith: Children, obey thy father and thy mother so thy life may be longer on this earth that the Lord thy God gaveth thee."

Never in my life! A child raising her hand to her father? Nothing could have changed that much! I had grumbled, even cussed at Mama. But always under my breath and even then a long way from her hearing. And the Lord knows Mama was often wrong. That chair raised against Harry shook the foundation of my world. I declare I heard Gabriel's horn blow.

But all I gained, speaking the good Lord's name to that child, was to have her face close up, her mouth clamp shut, and a stare through narrowed slits of her Chinese-looking eyes. She walked out of the kitchen, through the dining room. Linda met her in the hall, put a protective arm around her, and together the sisters walked to their room and closed the door.

Harry too. He brushed past me going out of the room. He might not have even seen me. Or maybe he just couldn't forgive me for not having been there as the buffer he wanted between him and his kids. I stood in the dining room alone. Lonely. Guilty. I had been acting as a buffer—not a wife. A protector. Who was I protecting?

That night I tried to bridge the distance that had grown between us. I closed the space between us in bed by moving up to Harry where he lay hugging his side of the bed. Pushing against him, I played with his chest:

"Sweet, sweet, sweet. What they done to my sweet man?" It had to be painful for a man's child to raise its hand to him. Harry was a hard man—but a good man with his kids. He cared for them. So what if his temper sometimes got out of hand? That was no cause to be disrespectful. So damn disrespectful.

"Harry." I pushed my softness against him, kissed his shoulders. The heat of his body felt as though he had a fever. Because of his hurt? What to do? What to do?

"What you want with me?" he said. His voice sounded muffled. My hand played with his chest, his stomach, his prick. His prick was hard, hot. Yet he lay stiff, tense. "Dorine, you a big woman—a somebody. You ain't need me—me problems."

"Our problems, Harry," I said. "That's what being together's about, ain't it? That's what love's supposed to be about?"

But I was thinking of Son then. And I thought about Mildred and about Joseph, sitting half dead in a wheelchair, refusing to die. Harry's problems were all here under this one roof. Shee-it. My problems took up the whole of the goddamn United States.

"Love?" Harry said. "Ain't love to be between people moving the same way? You moving. I stop still."

Because his prick was throbbing stiff, I kept rubbing up against him. But the difference in our problems had pushed a puzzle in my mind. I couldn't think it out. "Does that mean you don't love me, Harry?" I asked, still rubbing up against him, feeling how soft I was against his hard, muscled back. I massaged the muscles on his back, his arm, his chest, massaged his prick—fondled it. Kept fondling, knowing he had this big need for me, and wanting to answer to his need, I said, "We been through some hard times. It ain't been easy. But life's been hard for lots of folks."

He had to know that. He had to be aware that most folks, even in hard times, didn't have a Dorine Davis in their corner. "And we ain't done bad, Harry. We live good. We share. That's love, ain't it— seeing kids grow?" And as I talked the years we had lived together passed before my eyes. Years that had seemed damn long, because they hadn't been easy. But we had given to each other. So what more—what more?

"And now you're saying you don't love me, Harry? Then what's love? God, the times we been through, don't they count? I couldn't stand for you to even think that, Harry."

He turned then, pulled me to him, beneath him, pushed into

me with a suddenness that had nothing to do with me—or with love. His dry heat entered me, dried me up. I pushed against him, fought him. But like an unfeeling rod he rammed into me—in-out-in-out-in-out, bruising me, tearing my insides. I wanted to holler rape. I screamed.

6

Depression. A plague over us—the crumbling of our kingdom and more. More than the white gangs taking over policy in Harlem, more than the riots from Harlem to Detroit where black folks were getting their heads beat in begging to be able to work. More than the warped and twisted soul of the southland being exposed to the world. More than the invasion of Ethiopia by Italy, and the riots taking place between Italians and black Americans on the streets of Harlem. It was that—and more.

Max Schmeling, the German, beat Joe Louis, and the hearts of black folks bled. Joe Louis beat Max Baer, and the groundswell of black voices rejoicing seemed to admit that the salvation of black folks rested in the hands of a black boxer's gloves and not in the hands of God, after all.

No one escaped! Hitler came down on the Jews in Germany. Germany invaded Europe, and that was Depression. Lord, I looked up in the sky one morning, saw the *Hindenburg* flying low, and said: "That ship's got to blow." And it did. And that was Depression. The despair of our souls. The tragedy of poverty, and poverty and tragedy so thick in the air, in our nostrils, our mouths, that even all those who swore they had escaped had in some way been trapped. A hell of a time for a marriage to be played out. But that was the time ours had to be played out—to the sorry end.

Depression squeezing our souls. And on that winter morning, dressed to go on the road, with Harry shouting: "Going, going, all

250

the time gone. You think I ain't see what you doing—you and your mahn. . . ."

The girls, trapped in their room listening behind their closed door to the rage, the pain, the jealousy. "You better stay gone this time."

"You ought to be damn glad someone's working so you and your kids can eat."

"Oho, so you feeding us now."

"Now? Nigger, that's what I been doing since I known you."

Tied together. No vows. No ceremony. Yet he didn't leave. And I couldn't. Hard times, the things we had been through, driving us apart—holding us together—and the bed.

"Feed us? Feed us. You mean you go out of town with your mahn, acting like a queen, while my children stay here and act like your maids."

"I don't ask your kids to do nothing I ain't done before they came and that I can't do when they leave."

"Go then. Go and watch—see if you ain't come to a empty house. See if we ain't gone."

"Go on, goddamit. Only for God's sake stop jinxing the hell outa me. . . ."

Depression stalked us out on the road. We were all infected— touchy, jumpy, like being caught in a net we didn't see, yet knew about and had to keep fighting.

"Hey, baby." Bessie in one of her outrageous hats, long, lime-colored feathers bringing early spring to a cloudy winter day. "Show them pretty white teeth, roll them bedroom eyes. Life is for you, Dorine baby, you young thing. . . ."

"That's right," Albert said. "You're young—and I'm still around." And as Tom drove through the cold Chicago streets, I looked at the back of Albert's forever-young neck and wondered what a fool thing that he and I hadn't made it. We were out there— had been for so long. Single, young—he was nearer my age than Harry. Free, no burdens, no goddamn burdens.

"I tole Dorine about shacking up in family," Tom said. "But no. M'lady always thinks she knows more than her ever-loving teacher."

All those years gone by, and to Tom it had been like standing still. My trials with Harry, my family—girls pushing from children to teen-age—and to hear Tom talk, it had all been just bad judgment.

But far from feeling that my situation was mine alone, I felt trapped in that net along with lots of others—flung in the middle of somewhere, forced to watch as a big, thick-wheeled truck bore down. Helpless, yet fascinated, the feeling of being crushed beneath its wheels and not able to move. Forced to listen to the sounds of crumbling bones, of flesh spattered against flesh, the fresh smell of blood gushing into blood, of bone pressed into bone—all of us reduced to one mass of unthinking pulse and pain. And not able to do anything against the giant mangler.

What a strange feeling—doom opening a curtain around my mind, exposing a knowledge, long known and long hidden: Harry wasn't well.

Despite my heavy fur coat I shivered, kept shivering, in the cold car parked across the street from the jewelry store in which Ann had gone to boost a diamond.

Albert and Tom in the front seats also seemed to be sunk in gloom. Only Bessie, sitting in the back beside me, acted her old gay self. Looking across to where Bill kept walking in front of the jewelry store, Bessie kept purring:

"Ain't he purty? Can anyone wonder why I loves the ground which holds his yeller feet?"

Even in his heavy chauffeur's overcoat, Bill's trimness gave him an edge against time. Walking up and down in front of the jewelry store, stomping to keep blood circulating, Bill still pulled the eyes of women passersby, hunched down from the cold, in his direction. For my part, I thought the play with Bill and slim aristocratic Ann elegant.

Sally walked out of the jewelry store. Bill looked at his watch. Flicking her eyes to where we were parked, Sally walked—tall, stately, the Washington peacock—down the block. We turned our attention again to the door of the store.

One minute, two. Bill studied his watch again, walking, blowing into his gloved hands. Ann had never before made a joke of Tom's split-second timing. Three minutes, four. . . .

"What the hell. . . ?" Tom drummed on the wheel of the car

and looked around. "Uh-oh—what's that car. . . ?"

A big black Dodge was parked a few yards behind Bill's limousine. And we hadn't seen it! "God, how come Bill ain't spotted them boys?"

The two men must have been slouched down out of sight when we drove up. One sat behind the wheel, the other in the seat behind. We all turned our attention to Bill, trying to force him to feel our minds, to turn, and seeing the guys in the Dodge, decide his next move.

Bill looked at his watch again, then at the door of the store. Then our minds aiming at him forced him to examine the block. He turned, saw the car, the men. He froze. But only for an instant. Then he moved toward the limousine.

In that instant, two men ran from the jewelry store. One cut in front of Bill, blocking his way to the car. A guard came out after them, gun in hand. One of the running men turned, fired. Bill hit the sidewalk. The guard fired back. The gunmen jumped into the car. The car sped off. Bill still lay on the sidewalk. The guard went to him, turned him over.

"Eeeeeeee." Screeching tore at my eardrums. "My man. . . ."

Confused, I looked across the street, saw Bessie kneeling beside Bill, still screaming. What had happened?

"My man, my man. . . . What you all done to my man?" Blood spurted from Bill's chest. Bessie lowered her head, the long feathers from her hat sopping up the blood. "Lord, Lord, Lord, what they done done to you—Bill?"

A crowd cut her off and I turned to Tom. But he had gone. I sat. Albert sat. We looked at each other, not moving. Something had happened, something terrible had happened, something had in one instant changed our lives. . . .

Tom came back dragging Ann with him. He pushed her into the seat next to me and said to Albert: "Go on, pick up Sally. See you all back at Bessie's."

We drove across town. "The guys came in," Ann kept repeating. " 'It's a stickup,' they said. One pointed a gun. Dorine—it was so big—so goddamn big."

She begged me to see, told me without telling that it was as big as the guns that had opened up holes in Big Willie years before. "I was set to go," she said. "I wanted to cut out. But I looked into the barrel—I couldn't move! Do you hear?" And usually cool, calm, dry-talking Ann screamed, hysterical. "I couldn't move!"

And Albert: "But it wasn't our thing. Not our kind of thing. God, that had nothing to do with us."

Only it had. Guns had been used to take over Harlem. Guns were being used for killing and for stickups. Just as our gentlemen numbers runners had to deal with it, so we hincty boosters would have to decide what to do about it.

The Depression—that fucking jinx, hovering over us all. The poverty, the shadow over our souls—Harry's, and Bill's, and mine.

And sitting in Bessie's living room, surrounded by her bright, beautiful never-to-die flowers, seeing her colorful print curtains dancing in the firelight as we shivered in our coats from cold and fear of things not known, we expected Bill to appear suddenly in his bow tie and boater, to dance the soft shoe the way he had done so often in this room. He had to appear. Bessie had to appear to play the piano and sing "Seems Like Old Times" as Bill danced. They had to do their routine in all of their usual loudness, or the fireplace would never again give heat, and the house would be forever cold—nothing in our lives would have meaning again. . . .

And as we sat waiting, each deep in thought, Sally jumped to her feet. "I—I—I have to go—that's all!" She must have been having a hell of a time struggling inside. "The police might come. You know . . . I can't get mixed up in this. . . . The children, you understand?"

We didn't. I didn't. Her husband? Her kids? How did she think she could protect them? Why did she think she could? Why did she feel that what touched all of us had no bearing on them?

She left us sitting in the living room. We heard her footsteps on the stairs. We heard her in the bedroom over our heads. Then we heard her coming back—Miss Aristocrat. "Buddy—the children—you understand. . . ." I still didn't. Seeing her so guilty, so unsure, I wanted to hold her there. Don't go, I wanted to say. You can run, but from where—to where? Drive as fast as the wind, but you ain't going nowhere. A turned-up nose ain't the kind of protection you can use against our kind of jinx. We sat listening as the motor of her car started, then stopped, started and stopped, then caught. We heard her pull out of the driveway and we sat listening as she drove off—and were still listening long after the sound of the motor had died away.

"I ought to cut out too," Ann said. Her face was still pale, haggard, but she had calmed down. "After all, I was in the store. The police. . . ." Yes, with our kind of jinx, who needed to be questioned by police? Get away. Get as far away as possible from any possible involvement. But Ann sat. And we sat. Ann was different people from Sally. Our kind of people—the kind doomed to wait with friends come what may.

And we were glad we waited. Tom came in with Bessie, and she needed us. We had not failed her. Friends. Buddies. Did it matter about police and questions, as long as we stuck together? What could police do about the shroud hovering over us—over everyone? What answers did they have? What could they, with their guns and billies and loud voices, say that had meaning—against what had happened, was happening everywhere?

Bare-headed, face crusted with blood, blood matting her hair, Bessie sat hugging herself, rocking herself, moaning, in mourning. She held all of the things I had been thinking, feeling, all that had been locked in my innermost thoughts.

I tried to wash her face. "Leave it be," she said, turning her head. "That's my blood. I wants to keep it on my face, over me—you hear?" I rocked her in my arms the way I had seen her rock Bill's dead body. And rocking her I kept saying to myself, in a sort of surprise, a confusion: My God, her life is changed. My life is changed. All of our lives will forever be changed. Bill . . . is . . . dead. . . .

Tom handled the police. He made all the arrangements for the funeral of his longtime friend. We stood by Bessie's side while Bill's coffin was lowered into the ground. And until the last shovel of dirt was thrown over the mound. Then we all had this urgent need to leave.

Bessie still needing us had the pull of death now. We had to get away. Home—New York, Harlem—drew us. Anxious, guilty, nonetheless we packed. Albert comforted us. "Don't worry none. I'll stay on here with Bessie. I'll be around as long as needs be."

Hearing what we wanted made us look away from each other. Relieved. We had to go, but we were leaving her in good hands. After all, wasn't Albert one of us?

Rich city slickers
all dressed up to kill
but when they gets 'em hamhocks
they sure God eats their fill.
City folks, city folks,
slick as they can be,
but when it comes to chitlins,
they country just like me. . . .

Or maybe it was just to get away from the feel of death. Because when I suggested that we detour all the way to Maryland, to Tom Rumley's favorite roadhouse, no one was against it. For me, the nearer we came to New York the less I wanted to get there. As we sat shivering near the wood-burning stove, I didn't know if I was shivering from fear of Harry—what he might do, what he might have done since I left—or the natural fact that the open barn of a place was damn cold and needed a dozen more wood-burning stoves to give just a little heat.

Summers, the roadhouse (a damn sight different from roadhouses white folks talked about) had been a ball. Bright fires lit the air and colored the trees as pigs were roasted on the open barbecue pits. Women and children, laughing, talking, moved from laden table to laden table in the big yard. In summer, the band about fifty or more strong strummed guitars, shucked washboards, beat on bottles, shook tambourines, and blew horns, making our kind of country music. Kids slow-dragged around the floor, moving into each other, raising a funk with their sweaty, sexy bodies.

But smells couldn't survive the cold in that big room, not even the smell of chitterlings cooking. Small clusters of women at the stove kept the food warm, while big-eyed toddlers stood around us watching us eat. Teen-agers in front of the three-piece band stomped their feet to keep warm. Tom, tearing meat off the sparerib with his teeth, barbecue sauce dripping from mouth to chin, brown freckles glistening from the joy of eating, seemed the one person in the place not cold.

"What the hell you hanging on for, Dorine?" Tom asked, eyeing me pick at the plateful of chitterlings my mouth had been watering for. "If you and Harry ain't made it all these years, you ain't likely to start at this late date."

256

"We been making it," I said.

"When was that? I ain't known the time. And just look at you now—act like you scared to go home."

"Who? Me?" The fact of Tom noticing fear in me conjured the image of Harry's face, his yellow-brown eyes lit, staring.

"Yes you," Tom said.

"Whatever you think, Tom"—I tried to still my heartbeat—"I happen to love the guy. . . ." I had. I had very much. Might still.

"Hear that, Ann?" Tom spoke with his mouth filled with food. "The lady says she's in love. Dorine don't even know what love is."

"She sure had a lot of experience trying to find out," Ann said.

"Tole her to leave them West Indians alone." Tom wiped his mouth. "But that's a lady what don't listen."

"Listen to what?" I asked. "I needed Harry and Harry needed me. It's important having someone with you who thinks you're special."

"Don't know about that," Tom said. "I goes home to a empty bed most nights. I might not like it. But I don't take to habits what hurts this red nigger."

"Men like you," Ann scoffed, "gets in the habit of living empty lives so that they don't miss anything."

"Sure we do." Tom grinned and wiped his mouth with his bread. "When I think of how Dorine and me missed them times we might have had, I know my life ain't been full. My heart hurts. But I'd sooner be alone in my empty bed than be miserable with her."

"So you don't know, Tom. You can't know what being with somebody you can trust means," Ann said. "I know. I never had one."

"Trust to do what?" Tom said, his mouth full, his eyes cutting Ann. He waited to swallow before going on. "To keep my bed warm? To get a hard-on? Trust to mess with all my good stuff in the house? No thanks. I can do all that by my lonesome, and don't make no-body miserable doing it."

"Trouble is, you been in the rackets too long, Tom," Ann said. "You forgot what it means to have faith in honest folks."

"Honest folks?" Tom threw down his paper napkin onto his empty plate. "I'm with the only folks I know what's honest, Ann. I believe in folks honest enough to make money. In these United States that's what counts. I got faith in Dorine always making herself a buck. And I might even trust her if she'd admit that what's got her tied to Harry ain't got nothing to do with love—but that thing he got between his legs—hah.''

"What a low-down thing to say, Tom Rumley.'' Ann shivered, looking over at Tom, then downed the rest of her corn liquor.

"Then why else would she hold fast to the tail of a nigger what slid downhill fast as Harry?''

"I told you. Love,'' I said. I looked from him to the small band beating out on the washboard, sticks, and flute. The group of teen-agers around, clapping their hands, stomping:

> City folks, city folks,
> slick as they can be,
> but when it comes to chitlins,
> they country just like me. . . .

"Bullshit,'' Tom snorted. "Why not just say it's hard on you women who got to be out there working hard? I understand if you say you got to afford a li'l trim. And at y'all's age? Calling it love's as good an excuse as any.''

"I'm a damn sight younger than you, Tom Rumley,'' I said. "What's more, I look better. And the day I got to buy cum is the day I start doing without.''

"Uh-huh.'' Tom wiped his chin. "Now them's honest words. As cheap as you is, Dorine, and as hard as you loves to squeeze a penny? When you talk like that, I got to trust you.''

We laughed and that eased my tension. I fell to eating my chitterlings. The band had switched to:

> Gi' me some hogmaws—boy,
> gi' me some a dem hogmaws.
> You scarce see me wit a nickel,
> am a rich man wit a dime.
> But a plateful a hogmaws
> will get me every time. . . .

Tom's jokes on me had paid off in relief. By the time we drove into New York, we had squeezed them for all they were worth. A heaviness had laid over us since leaving the city. We—all of us—had in our way known something had to happen. It had happened. And there we were—the New York bunch—pulling in safe. Our lives had changed. We were in mourning. We had to deal with it. But god-damn—we were back.

Tom pulled up in front of my door and went to open up the trunk for my bag. I got out, and leaning over to say good-bye to Ann, felt myself yanked backward, spun around—slam! On my back on the sidewalk I stared up into a mouth shouting: "All-you think you can make a damn fool outa me! Try it! Try it! I ain't no jackass like you think. No goddamn jackass!"

Harry, his fist drawn back, leaned down. "I'll show you—you and your mahn. . . ."

Tom grabbed Harry's arms from behind. Harry turned. For one minute they were locked together. Then I saw Tom in the air. I squinted up: What the hell was that two-hundred-and-fifty-pound man doing floating around on air? Then I scrambled to my feet. I ran to Harry, held his arms to keep them upstretched, whispering: "Put him down, easy now. Please put him down." Harry's wild-staring face showed no understanding. I screeched: "You crazy son of a bitch, put that man down, you hear? I'll have your ass thrown in a motherfucking nuthouse!"

My screeching went through his brain like a shaft. He stared at the blood spurting from my mouth down my chin and into my coat. The yellow glow died, slowly. He lowered Tom to the sidewalk.

Tom tested the ground careful, making sure he stood on solid sidewalk before coming to me. Then he bundled me into the car and we drove to Harlem Hospital.

Late that night, six stitches closing my split lip, Tom drove me to his place. "No, Tom, I got to get home," I said.

"Back to that crazy fool? No suh, I'm not letting you."

"You talking about my man, Tom. That's my house. I got to get there."

"Talk to the girl, Ann," Tom pleaded. "Tell her she's about to get herself killed."

"She has to do what she must, Tom," Ann said. "Dorine is okay."

It was long past two o'clock in the morning when Tom brought me home and took me upstairs. Harry had been waiting. When I put my key in the lock, the door opened. "Tom. . . ." His scanty eyebrows shook. His eyes begged. "I ain't mean it. . . ." And it came to me that in the years I had known Harry, his eyes had gone through as many changes as he. They had been playful once, flirtatious. Then they had turned angry, condemning, resentful, and then shifty. But now they begged. "I ain't know what happen to me," he said.

"I come up to tell you, Harry." Tom stood with his back to the door, looking at Harry, not wanting him to misunderstand. "If anything was going to happen between me and Dorine, it would have happened a long time before she ever knew you. And if it had started since, your hands ain't big enough to give me a beating to stop it. . . ."

"I know," Harry whispered, his voice hoarse, the tip of his nose shiny. "God, but I know."

The smell of coffee woke me the next morning. I lay in bed, stiff, sore. My lips were heavy, dry. I was thirsty. I looked over to the dresser and saw a vase of chrysanthemums. Chrysanthemums— Linda had brought them from the dining room. I needed that special kind of lift. The sun shining through the curtains brightened them, and they brightened me. Reminded me I had been happy in the house, in the room. Miserable, frightened, sad—but happy.

Linda came into the room, her eyes swollen from crying. She saw my face and rushed to kneel at my bedside. Putting her head against my stomach, she moaned: "Dorine, Dorine, this isn't living. It's merely existing."

One thing I didn't need was all that damn playacting. But what to do? How to turn a sweet, unselfish girl away because she liked to act like Greta Garbo?

I lifted my head and looked into Gogi's tight, set face. She stood in the doorway. "I hate his guts," she said, her flat eyes showing she meant every word. "No one will ever know how much I hate that man."

"Stop that talk, Gogi." Funny how much easier to deal with sass. "Don't you ever let me hear you talk against your father. Do you hear me, girl?" I sat up to look her in the face. "The Lord saith: Children, obey thy parents—"

"Do you hear me?" She cut me short. "I never cared what he did to me. I can take care of myself. But I hate him for what he did to you."

Hardly able to move my stitched lips, I pleaded with her, "Gogi, your father is more to be pitied than scorned. Harry isn't well."

And so I said what I had been thinking, feeling, for a long time. The love I had for Harry had changed. He was sick—a man in need of pity. I pitied him.

After the girls had gone off to school, I lay in bed looking at the flowers—just looking, not thinking. Harry came in with my breakfast—bacon, eggs, juice, coffee. On the tray he had put a rose. "Harry"—I touched my mouth—"I can't eat." I smiled, apologizing, not wanting him hurt any more than he had been hurt. "Where's the car?"

"Outside—the garage man just bring it. . . ."

"I have to go out," I said.

"You want me to drive you?"

"No, I need to be alone. . . ." He held me against his broad chest with all of his old gentleness—trying to turn the clock back to once upon a time.

In the car, I headed for the George Washington Bridge, and then the Palisades. I drove around Palisades Park for a time, that almost empty park where a person here, and one there, picked at twigs and shrubs laid bare by winter. Parking the car, I climbed onto a boulder overlooking the Hudson River and, in the harsh breeze that rivers bring, stared over at Manhattan. Strong gusts of wind blew against me, tried to unseat me. But I held on to the stone with bare hands—I had forgotten my gloves. But to me, that wind, the cold, nothing threatened me any more than the things of life had. And as the ice floated downriver, and ships sailed up with working men on board stamping around and swinging their arms for warmth, I forced myself to remember Harry from that first night—the night of Lindbergh. Tall, handsome, loud-laughing, the madness in his eyes. . . .

Yes, even back then it had been madness. Madness had attracted me to him. But then had been the time for madness. Harry had had the dream, the drive, the energy to use up his madness. We all had, coming as we all were from nothing with nothing to serve us but our spirit. We had had to live bordering madness even to decide on the kind of life we wanted. But madness isn't courage!

The loss of Harry's wife. . . . "Dorine, she was me life." An anguish bowed my head, just as a gust of wind forced me to hold on to the boulder with stiff, aching fingers; forced me to see, clearly: I had never been able to do anything for Harry. "The Rising Sun will rise again!" The tail-end of his dream had been washed away by something called Depression. And there wasn't enough money, not in the city, not in the country, not in the world, to save Harry Brisbane. The stuff of his dreams had already gone when I had walked into his restaurant. Who could stop his wife's cancer from spreading? Who could hold back the Depression? The time of Harry Brisbane—honest hard-worker—had passed, or maybe as Tom Rumley had said, there was no place for honest men in the United States. Maybe the time for honest men hadn't yet come. . . .

He was standing on the corner waiting when I drove up. Dressed in his gray suit under a black overcoat, his shoes reflecting the sun, he did indeed look the man of substance, beyond doubt.

He got in the car to drive the few steps home. "I been worried," he said. "I think that maybe something happen."

"Something did," I said.

Upstairs I slipped into my peach satin dressing gown, sprayed myself with perfume, and got into bed. He came to me, held me, cradled my head against his chest, caressed my face, kissing my cheeks, my head, my chest, the stitches on my lip. "I'm sorry, so, so sorry. It hurts, hurts, hurts. I must be mad, Dorine, mad. . . ."

Tenderness had always been his way. Gentleness in bed had been his greatness. His way of entering into the deepest part of me had made me thirst like hell for him even while far away from him. I scraped all those places of my body and my mind, trying to find that need again, that thirst which made for joy every time, the feeling which opened up a world of funky words. . . .

But I had thought him out. I lay in the arms of a corpse, a dead man caught in the trap of a dream—stinking. How to empty the trap? What words to use? It demanded more than honesty, needed more than courage. Something deeper, deeper than words ever thought of. It went to the gut of feelings—a something already missed, missed, missed. . . .

It's hell making love to the dead. A corpse gets desperate. It holds on to you for its life. The lips of the dead bruise, trying to pull life from you. . . . And so what had taken up so much time in planning, so much energy finding, so many years trying to hold on to, had become the tool of my own punishment.

Still I tried. But no one can breathe life back into a corpse. And he knew. "You think you going to leave me?" he said. "But you lie. I'll kill you first." I believed him.

But I had no intention of dying. As soon as the swelling left my face and the stitches were removed from my lip, I went looking for apartments—two of them. I found one—a small walk-up for my-self—on Sugar Hill. And two blocks from where we lived, I found another for them. That building, once elegant, still had a blue-eyed, white elevator man—a hangover from bygone days. He doubled as a super and did both jobs badly.

The apartment had been lovely. It had a long hallway. A pan-try—big enough to hide the ghosts of butlers—adjoined a large kitchen. A back apartment, its two bedrooms overlooking a back-yard with trees spread out to join the trees of the brownstones on the next block.

I brought Harry to see it. He walked from room to room looking it over. Strange. Silent. God, I pitied him his silence. But what to say? He who has the money does the choosing. It had been such a long time since he had had any. Tears stung my eyes. He had only me. He no longer gambled with Sandy and Charles or his other West Indian friends. Custom had always kept him from closeness to his kids. I had been all. . . .

I went to a movers, hired two moving vans, and explained to the men just how I expected them to go about moving my things. Then for the next few days, the girls and I spent our free time packing. Harry walked the streets. I drove by him often—without him seeing me. Standing at some corner, tall, good-looking, still looking good, if a little drawn, he still sported his black armband, mourning his dearly departed. And once I drove by as he stood looking on at WPA workers digging a ditch to enlarge an avenue. On a stoop nearby, kids bunched together were shouting and teasing the men with the usual WPA jibes: "Hey you, stop leaning on that shovel." "Man, don't you know this ain't playtime?" "Naw, it's get-to-work time." "Be damn if you gets paid and I ain't fooling you, Mr. WPA man. . . ."

I felt his need as he stood listening. I knew his confusion, his pain. Tears stung my eyes. God—tears stayed right near the surface and tight in my throat, day and night, night and day. And those days, those nights got fewer, fewer.

Saturday—moving day. The first van came at eight. I took charge, telling the movers where I wanted what furnishings put. When that van was almost filled I said to Harry: "Go on over to the other apartment and wait so you can tell the men where you want things put."

Gogi and Linda were packing in the back. The first van left and the second van came. When the men had partially filled the second van I went to them in the dining room. They had taken the curtains down, and the sunlight flooding into the room lit the polished floors, the white walls, almost to blinding. The room shone like a palace. We had kept it so well. We had, after all, not been too bad a family.

"Girls, go over to the other apartment to give your father a hand. I'll finish up here," I said.

And from the window I watched them—Gogi and Linda—their arms locked, their heads touching, as they walked up the block, never dreaming that this was the end of a time—my time in their lives. And seeing them on the threshold of being hurt, so close, so pure, I broke down and cried.

7

No one was happier than Sonny when I moved back to the uptown scene. I hadn't finished unpacking when he rang my bell. I opened the door to see him—dark blue cashmere overcoat, skin boasting good soap and smelling of better cologne, slick smile lifting heavy cheeks, frog-eyes blinking—sharp on my doorstep. I had come home.

"Bay-bee, sure am glad you done quit serving time. We needs you."

"For how much, and for what you wants it, Sonny?"

"Dorine, don't smile at me in that tone of voice. Just wait until you see this new layout. Girl, what a setup. We can net a million."

"Nigger, I put you down for having gone way past your first million."

I knew about Sonny's swank after-hours spread on Sugar Hill. And word had gone out about his "blond Cadillac," with the blond society chick he showed off driving up and down Seventh Avenue.

"Oh, but I'm on my way," he smiled. "Only Dorine, I needs me a partner. What say if I cut you in fifty-fifty?"

"What will it cost me?" I asked.

"It ain't only the money, I swear. I got folks working what goes through my profits like wind going through sand. I needs somebody to look after the joint."

I thought of telling Sonny no. I wanted to say what he really needed was to clean up his act. Look after his own business and quit playing the avenue. But the gun that had brought Bill down had done more than mess with our hearts. The way I felt, if the hoods wanted the world they had to have it. I had lost my feel for the road. So instead of refusing I said to Sonny: "I'll give it a look-see."

Sonny's new layout—a nine-room apartment that took up an entire floor of a swank Sugar Hill building—impressed me. It had a barroom, bigger than my entire apartment, separated from the rest of the joint by a padded door. Behind the door were six "private" rooms, with their own toilets—and a back exit. The floors and walls were covered with thick rugs to keep out sounds. Right away I wanted to be cut in, as partner. Then this chick walked in.

Sonny's face broke into a simple smile. "Dorine, I wants you to meet Sugar—my Sugar."

Sugar was brown-skinned, looking like I must have when I first hit New York. Small, with big eyes and a big pretty-teeth smile. She was dressed to kill. Sonny looked at her, digging her. Sugar smiled at me—a smile that had nothing to do with her eyes: That chick had not been softened by cotton fields. She had been nurtured by the city and its hard places. She wasn't about to understand Sonny's need to

265

mess with blondes. And knowing Sonny, nature-bound to mess up, I backed out. But needing to work I said:

"Sonny, I ain't for no partnership deal. I'll lend you the money if I can stick around until the joint starts paying off."

I hadn't worked a joint since Mamie's back in Cleveland. But not being one to forget what I once learned, I set to work schooling Sugar on how to run an after-hours place.

I worked long hours. I never left Sonny's until the last customer had slipped off heading downtown where he belonged. Then going home, too tired to think, I fell into bed and to sleep.

But being tired didn't keep me from seeing Harry's face—a tiny snapshot on a far-off wall, getting closer, closer, bigger, bigger. By the time I fell into my deepest sleep I had to jerk myself awake. Nightmares every night! Every night! The sucker haunted me!

I had brought my little altar with me. And the picture of his wife, seeing we were good friends by now (anyhow, I was the only member of that family who prayed). I knelt before the altar. "Madam," I prayed. "I done what I could for as long as I could, so please make that son of a bitch leave me be!" Her smile, which went all the way back to the sadness in her eyes, promised. But no sooner I fell off to sleep, the same goddamn nightmare.

Months of hard work without sleep took its toll. Tom, worried about how haggard and thin I was getting, said: "Don't tell me you fool enough to let Sonny mess with you again?"

"Sonny? You kidding? I'm still about Harry. I keep thinking and thinking. . . ."

"Takes time," Tom said. "You lived lots of years with him. But you'll live past this time too."

Leaving Tom's I drove up to Sonny's and parked, not wanting to go up. Five o'clock. Sugar, with her big smile and suspicious eyes, would be up there, going over the books. I suddenly felt the need to go on the road. I thought of the deserts, the mountain trails we had traveled. I thought of driving out to the other coast. Working on the road was what I needed to get me together.

I was about to drive back to Tom's to try talking him into a trip when I saw the white Cadillac parking a few cars down.

I had no intention of spying on Sonny. But being there, I saw no reason in turning my head. Sonny got out of his car and helped this blond chick out, then led her into the lobby. Thinking of Sugar, I honked my horn. Sonny looked around, saw me, and came over.

"Papa," I said, "you don't want to do that." Sonny blinked.

"Do what, Dorine?"

I jerked my head in the direction of the blonde. "That."

Sonny made his eyes bulge into mine. "What time you say you was starting this evening," he said, putting me in my place.

"I ain't said. But now that you mention it, I ain't. I stopped by to remind you—you owe me, papa." And driving off, I headed downtown to my old Central Park neighborhood.

I walked into the elevator of the once elegant building I had rented for Harry and the girls. I waited for Blue-eyes. One minute . . . two. He didn't show. I took the stairs. The building had to be the last one I wanted to be in. But since leaving my apartment earlier— maybe even longer than that—I had known that I'd end up here.

On the third floor I walked back toward the apartment, slowly, wondering what might possibly happen to prevent my reaching it. I stopped to listen at the doors of neighbors' apartments, stilling the temptation to ring bells, ask questions, and, hearing in answers reason to, get the hell out. Then I'd go to Tom's and beg him to let's get out of town.

At one door, the overblown voice of Kate Smith sang about Coming over the Mountains. At another, shooting, the clopping of horses' hooves.

I pressed my ear to the door, listening. No one home? Then I remembered the other time—that silence that accumulated around Harry. My heart beat, beat, beat. . . . I put my finger to the bell and heard again the other bell of long ago, shattering the silence. So instead of ringing, I unlocked the door with my key.

The door opened into darkness. I stepped inside, listening. The silence held. I closed the door and leaned against it. My heart leaped. A thin strip of light at the other end of the hall cut across the wall.

I tiptoed toward the light, knowing it had to be shining through the pantry from the kitchen. But such quiet? I forced myself to think back to that other time. Then, they had all been in their special parts of the house, doing whatever they saw fit. And now?

What if I slipped in, looked around without being seen? I might leave without anyone knowing I had been there. I came to the pantry, looked in. As I had expected, the light came from the kitchen. I walked into the pantry and stood in the darkness, my mouth dry from fear, my need to run. I waited, straining for something called courage. Whatever reason I had come, I had to have an answer. And because I refused to run, I fought myself to inch forward, inch to the threshold of the kitchen.

And there he was—Harry, or somebody—over the stove, stirring something in a bucket from which steam passing like mist over his face rose to the ceiling. Water ran down the wall like tears. Through the layers of steam his face had a strange, spiritual quality. Harry? A stranger? Harry had never been so thin. This person's waist was so slender it didn't hold up his pants, which fell to the narrow hips. My eyes moved upward to the chest covered only by a merino, then to the shoulders—Harry's shoulders.

I waited for him to turn and, seeing me, do his worst. I had been gone for months without one word. The sight of me had to drive him into one of his rages. Harry kept looking into his bucket, stirring, stirring. His lips moved. He whispered. The whisper grew loud, louder:

"Goddamnsonofabitch!" The explosion made my pores rise. I held myself in the doorway.

"Harry?" I spoke softly, and his whispers faded back into his mouth. He kept stirring. "Harry!"

He looked up through the rising vapor, saw me, pushed his head through the mist to see better. My heart bled. Harry—but what a change the months had brought! His face had lost all its fullness, had sunk beneath his cheekbones. His eyes had gone into his head. They stared out from beneath a jutting forehead.

"Dorine. . . ?" he said. "Dorine? Where you been?"

"What are you boiling in that bucket, Harry?"

"Paint." He smiled a little-boy smile. "Am mixing paint. You ain't know it but I a good painter—the best painter in the world. . . ."

I collapsed against the door. Relief. But what had I expected? A roomful of corpses? Blood? A bucket of hearts and brains boiling away? My bladder loosened itself in relief. I twisted my legs, trying to hold back pee.

"Yes," Harry said, "the best damn painter in the world—nobody can stop me. Nobody!"

"Who's trying to stop you, Harry?"

"They . . . They ain't know, though—I the kind of man what make money. . . ."

"Where are the girls, Harry?" He went back to his stirring.

"Harry!"

"Goddamnsonofabitch! I'll kill they . . . kill they. . . ."

Cold sweat ran from my pores, sticking my clothes to my body. Twisting and turning my legs, I made my way out of the pantry, into the hall, and then to the bathroom. Searching and not finding the light, I moved around until I bumped into the toilet bowl. Sat, then finding the lid down, jumped up, wetting myself as I pushed up the lid. Then I sat in the dark, wondering about the girls.

Leaving the bathroom, I walked on up the hall, past the pantry, going into the back of the house. I went first into Harry's room. Against the lights shining through the trees from the buildings of the next street, the furniture stood like zombies in the curtainless room. Leaving his room, I went to the room I had chosen for the girls. Then I breathed again. A thread of light seeped from under the door. My ear to the door, I listened, heard the rustle of paper. I tried the doorknob. The door was locked.

"Linda? Gogi?" I pushed against the door. "Linda? Gogi?"

A squeak of bedsprings. Something heavy being moved from the door. The door cracked open. Eyes peered out. Then Gogi stood in the doorway, grinning her impish grin.

"Dorine! I thought you had gone for good."

"What are you doing?" I pushed past her into the room. A mess—clothes and papers scattered all over and a book lying facedown on her pillow.

"Reading."

"Reading!" A man in the kitchen, sick—mad, sick, and there she was, dressed only in a slip, lying in a dirty room, unconcerned—reading. And as I looked around at that upheaval that had to smother her if it ever fell down on her, she pushed the heavy chest of drawers to block the door.

"What's that for?"

"To keep him out," she said, the imp smile still lighting her plain face. Her attitude seemed to put me on her side.

"To keep your father out? Girl, do you know that your father is a very sick man. . . ?"

"Not so sick that he doesn't want me dead." She hunched up her shoulders, laughing.

"What do you mean?"

"He tries to kill me—all the time."

It was sure those simple books she read had touched her head. "Kill you—how?"

"He chokes me," she said. "He beats me. Yesterday he was choking me when the super came in and stopped him. He—Daddy— had left the door open—by accident."

My eyelids peeled back looking. The girl stood at death's door. I believed her. But there she stood, as calm as you please, as though saying there's a wind blowing outside.

"Where's your sister?"

"Linda? She ran away."

"Ran away!" In my mind, my heart, when I left I had thought that Linda, loving Harry as she did, loving Gogi, would look after them both. "Where to?"

"Linda couldn't stand him anymore. She got herself a sleep-in job in Far Rockaway. Taking care of a baby."

"How did she get it?"

"Through the *Journal-American*."

"What about school?"

"She quit. You don't know how bad it's been around here, Dorine."

"So—you're alone with him. . . ."

"Yes." The flat, Chinese-looking eyes stared into mine—accusing. Blaming me! "Everybody's gone—and I'm here alone with him. . . ." Her impish grin replaced her sass.

I looked away from her not to strike her. "Do you hear from Linda?"

"Sure. I call her. She comes on her days off. I let her in through the fire-escape window. If Daddy knew she was here, he'd kill her for sure."

I hated her. The calm, easy way she took things. "Aren't you scared?"

"Who, me? No. I'm not scared of anybody." I declare if she had put her hands to her hips and patted her foot, so help me God, I'd have slapped the shit out of her.

"Then you're a damn fool," I said. Without any proof I knew that only a breath separated Harry from coming through that door and killing her. And as though I needed proof, I heard him calling from the other side of the door.

"Dorine—you in there?"

"Yes, Harry, I'm here."

"Come out!" he shouted. "Come out and leave that wicked thing by sheself. I gon' kill-kill-kill!"

The chest flew to the other side of the room as the door opened to Harry's kick. He charged in, trying to get past me to Gogi. "Goddamn rude . . . I kill she—kill she!"

And the fool girl shouting from behind me: "Let him come! Let him come! Who's afraid of him?"

Keeping that girl, begging for her death, from her death, I performed a miracle. Harry had the feel of iron in his thin, muscular arms; the feel of a man who had gone beyond strength. And that little slip of a girl behind me, screeching like a chick gone wild: "Let him come—let him come!"

Trying to get by me to Gogi, Harry almost picked me up. I shouted. "Harry, you hurting. Stop it!"

My loud voice confused him. He backed out of the room, then rushed down the hall and, like something wild, slammed out of the front door.

"My God, where's he going?" I asked. He had gone out in his undershirt and drooping pants.

"Don't mind him." Gogi shrugged. "He'll be back. He always runs out like that when he gets mad."

"Then you ought to get down on your knees and thank the Lord he does," I said. She shrugged again. "Why didn't you run away?" I asked.

"And go where?"

"Get a housework job—like Linda."

"And quit school," she said, as though the thought was a stranger to her. So she'd stay in the house with him, if he killed her? Just so she wouldn't quit school? Exasperated, I looked around the

271

room. "Gogi, put that goddamn book away before I throw it out the window, and get to cleaning this damn dirty room."

I left the house and went to the corner store to call Tom. "You better get here," I said to him. "Harry's in a bad way."

When I got back upstairs, Harry was in the kitchen again, stirring his bucket. I stood in the doorway, studying him. "Why do you need all that paint, Harry?" I asked.

The little-boy smile jumped back to his face. "Oh, you ain't know? I working for Charles. I painting for he."

So his West Indian friend had come to his aid. "But must you work so hard, Harry? Come on and get some rest." And as he kept on stirring: "You can always finish tomorrow," I pleaded.

He stood a moment, looked at me; then a cry of pain rushed out. "Where you been?" Rasping sounds came from his chest—the sound of water rushing over rocks—of the tide racing toward shore and being pulled back into the sea. "Where you been?" He came toward me. I thought of running, getting out of his way; instead I opened up my arms. He rushed in. "Oh, God, Dorine—yes, yes, I tired. I tired. . . ."

I led him to bed. The moment his head touched the pillow, he fell asleep. But a light sleep. He kept pulling out of it. Looking around and seeing me, he drifted off to sleep again.

I lay next to him, massaging his head, his shoulders, his neck. I worked at the tight neck and shoulder muscles that refused to loosen even in sleep. I kept massaging, and feeling my hands, he slept. The doorbell rang. I went to open it. "Tom, go down and call an ambulance. Harry can't stay here."

When I got back Harry's eyes were open. "Who was that?"

"Tom," I said. "He's gone to call an ambulance. We have to get you to the hospital."

"Yes." Tears flooded back to his pillow; tears stuck in his throat. His words were hoarse, blurred. "Yes, I sick, Dorine. I sick, sick, sick. . . ."

Tom came back and the three of us waited for the ambulance. Harry kept sleeping and waking, holding on to me. I rode to Harlem Hospital with him in the ambulance. Tom followed in his car. And while Harry was being admitted, Tom and I sat—Tom, his hands clasped over his spreading belly, looking out over the tips of his shoes. I held on to him. We rode up on the elevator and waited for Harry to be moved from the stretcher to his bed. I stood beside his bed until he fell off to sleep. Then Tom and I walked down the long corridor and stood waiting for the elevator. We were still waiting when we heard a shout. Looking up, we saw Harry racing toward us. His white hospital robe was loose, flapping around his naked body. His face was twisted. Saliva foamed at the corners of his mouth. And from his mouth came snorts like those of an over-worked animal. We stood paralyzed as he came. Then more shouts. Men came running from all directions. They grabbed Harry. He fought, throwing them around. Finally two attendants jumped him from behind, bringing him down to the floor. In seconds, the rest had fallen over him. When they stood up, Harry was in a strait-jacket. They led him back to the ward. Only then did Tom and I have the strength to move again.

Back in the house, I woke up Gogi. "You have to call Linda and tell her to come right home," I said.

"So he's gone?" she said.

"Out of his mind," I told her. "And you can consider yourself lucky." And, not caring what she believed, I said: "The Lord moves in mysterious ways, His wonders to perform."

I had no doubt that Harry had held on to what small bit of sanity he had until knowing that Gogi was safe. Seeing me and being able to touch me, he had simply let go.

Tom and Ann went that first weekend to visit Harry in Central Islip with us. The doctor refused to let us see him. "I'm sorry, Mrs. Brisbane," he said. "But Mr. Brisbane has been so violent. I don't know what effect seeing you and the children might have on him."

On the second weekend, Tom went with us. Harry wheeled himself out of his room. We took him out onto a balcony where we looked down over the gardens to see other patients walking around with their visitors. Tom, looking over the balcony, joked with Harry. "The next time we come, you'll be showing us around down there." He pointed below. But Harry's attention was all for Gogi. "You ain't know what a strong man you got for a father," he said. "You would be so proud. I take these little men around here and throw them around like matchsticks."

Not having been close to her, he was saying in his way, I hurt you, I'm sorry. Gogi stared at him, a tight smile on her face. Then she looked away. But he's dying, I wanted to say. You must forgive. You must forgive. And Linda, sitting next to Harry, holding his hand, rubbed it to soften the hurt her sister's attitude caused.

"You are the biggest and strongest Daddy in the world. We're proud of you."

"Yes, Gogi," Harry said. "Your father can give Joe Louis a run for the money. . . ." As a silence grew thick around her, waiting for her, she turned, stared at him. "I know," she said.

The third weekend, Gogi was in bed when I went to pick them up. She looked up from the book she was reading. "Dorine, I have this awful headache. I won't be able to go with you."

"Get up from that damn bed," I said. "We don't know how long your father has. You got to go."

"Really, Dorine—I can't."

I stilled my hand from yanking her out of bed, throwing her book out of the window, and going after her head with a broomstick. "Your father loves you, Gogi," I pleaded. "Don't do this to him."

She looked at me quickly, then looked away. But she had given me the message: I could not change her mind.

"Please, Gogi," Linda pleaded, tears in her eyes. "You can't disappoint him so." Closing her eyes, Gogi lay still, her hand to her forehead.

That child. Where had she developed her willfulness? Locked in her room over those goddamn books?

We found Harry in bed, his strength used up. He had had a bad time. His head was bandaged, his face swollen, his lips chewed raw. We stood around his bed. He looked from one to the other of us, then looked at the empty space around us. Linda went to sit at the side of his bed. She took his hand, to rub. Standing at the other side of him, I kept touching him, praying that we were enough.

He looked at her, moved his eyes to me; then, with a surge, one word came from deep in his throat: "Go-gi. . . ."

"Gogi's home—she's sick with grieving," I said. "She wanted to come. . . . She was sick."

On our way home, Linda exploded. "I hate her! Oh, God, how I

274

hate her!" What to say? I had never met someone so young as Gogi without forgiveness in her heart.

Harry died two days later.

I held the funeral service at the Catholic church where he had first taken me. The church was packed with friends—most I had never met—and family who had crawled out of the woodwork, none I even knew they had. They all come out to mourn. My friends were Tom and Ann—and of Harry's friends, Charles sat with us.

"These poor, poor children. . . ." Family and friends clucked their tongues and shook their heads. "First the poor mother. Now the father. Sad, sad, sad indeed. . . ." Of Harry's friends, only Charles comforted me. "What to do? What to do?" He opened up his hands in a helpless gesture. "None of them know what you been through. . '

Linda broke down in a fit of screaming and had to be taken into a room at the side of the church. Poor Linda, loving Linda—how much of that was actual pain? How much acting? She did hurt, I had no doubt. Gogi?

All through the service, I sat dry-eyed, looking at her dry expressionless eyes, staring at Harry's face. All those whom I had never met cried. Some with heartfelt tears. Miss Gogi sat dry-eyed, looking at her father's raised face.

"It is so they does grieve," I heard one woman telling Charles. "They does feel it worse, you know. Those what suffer inside. . . ."

I knew better. No suffering hid behind those eyes. I hadn't surprised one trace. Strange girl. I had known her all these years and I had never been able to look inside her head. Sure, Harry had abused her. He had abused us all. But to sit there. . . ?

Trying to figure her out kept me from crying, kept me from hearing the high mass that I had paid all that money for. That girl rested on my mind like lead. We sat in the same pew. When Linda was taken away, only Tom sat between us. I kept looking at Gogi, sitting between Ann and Tom, her eyes on the casket. No expression. The congregation got up to sing. Gogi sat, trying to make up her mind whether to keep sitting or join the rest and stand. When with a hunch of her shoulders she decided to stand, she looked over to me, caught my eyes—and winked!

I got her number then: Gogi was glad—more, relieved—that

Harry had died! She thought she was free now. After all, she must have reasoned, I had gone, Linda had gone—and now with Harry gone and only poor Linda to look after her. . . . The nerve! Standing at that poor man's funeral rejoicing!

"Well, little monster," I swore under my breath. "If you think any fourteen-year-old that I have something to do with will be running around this New York, you sure got another think coming." But fate must have decided that Gogi be free. By making her come and live with me, I bucked fate. The very next time I went on the road, I got nabbed.

BOOK FOUR

1

Piss reached out to hit me full-face as I stepped into the once swanky building. I turned, thinking to go back out. But the stoopful of men I had had to wade through coming in (wisecracking men who had never cracked my way) changed my mind. Them not even seeing me added to the knowledge of how beat-up I really looked. I kept on to the elevator and, getting on (the first self-service elevator I ever attempted to ride), pushed the button for the fifth floor. The door closed and I waited. So did the elevator. I pushed another button, then another. Then I pushed the one saying "open." The door stayed shut. Trapped. Prison hadn't been like this. Shut in— yes. But with breathing space.

I banged on the door and was about to shout murder when the door opened. I jumped out. Holding my breath, ducking to get under the suffocation of the stale pee, I made the stairs. Nothing in my life had prepared me for such a change. When the landlord had kicked out the doorman and had started cutting up the lovely apartments to rent as rooms, I had warned Tom: move. Five families squeezed into one apartment the size of the one I had lived in alone. Five families using the same kitchen, five families using the same toilet, had to cause friction—ready-made cause for riots. It had done more. It had turned the whole building into a fucking outhouse.

On Tom's floor the paint had peeled off the walls. Plaster on the ceiling curled down, giving guessing games to those laying odds on when it would fall. The thick carpets—our mark of high living—were gone. The tiles they had covered were in need of a good scrubbing. The structure of the building, made to last forever, had saved the damn thing from crumbling.

The Harlem I had just ridden through had changed too. Apartments facing Central Park were now open to "us." Riding up Seventh Avenue, I had seen kids playing on stoops where uniformed doormen had once stood. The taxi had stopped for a light at Garvey's corner, and the man shouting from the podium in front of a bookstore bragging one million books had been small, light-skinned. He had been holding a Bible to his chest, shouting: "Save this country for democracy, they say. But whose democracy? I'll tell you whose—the white man's democracy, that's whose. . . .

"And this NAACP . . . you know what that means, don't you? The National Association of Asses and Cretins—that's what! They go begging: Massa white man, they say, we lo-oves you. We wants to fi-ight for you. So ple-ease, let our boys in them back lines, where they only half safe, go up in the front where they ain't no way safe. Let them go in the mouths of the cannons, suh, to prove our love. . . ."

Folks laughed; the little man stomped his feet. The taxi rolled on.

The crowd was not as large as I had remembered. Nor did it feel as mad. Sweat, the almost bursting-at-the-seams agitated feel, was gone. But then five years, no matter which way you held it, was a long time. The change might have been in me, my way of feeling and seeing from the distance—like living in two places at the same time, one in the mind, the other in the flesh. But the stink of this once fabulous building had nothing to do with imagination.

Clicking high-heeled shoes coming up the long hallway inside the apartment perked up my ears. Tom had moved? I had thought him forever there—a prisoner of his junk, the permanent fixture in the building. But why not? Who did I know in life could allow themselves to live in this shithouse?

"Who is it?" a woman's high voice called through the locked door.

"Dorine," I answered.

"Dorine? Who Dorine?"

"Excuse me," I said, "but I had a friend who used to live in this here apartment. Wonder if you can help me."

"What your friend name?"

"Tom. Tom Rumley. . . ."

The door opened. Eyes peeped out over a chain. Seeing me, the chain came off, the door opened. She stood eyeing me, suspicious, and I did likewise. Wearing a bathrobe—probably dressing to go out, from the look of her face thick with the best Woolworth had to offer—which didn't hide the fact that her black, smooth skin was damn young. I put her at about twenty-two. The perfume stinking out through the door had nothing to do with her being a maid, either. She invited me in with a jerk of her head, supposed to show me I was nothing to worry about.

Prison clothes were not fashioned to bring out the best in folks: cotton dress under a black shapeless coat, a felt hat pulled down over broken-off hair kept nappy and dried out from years of washing in hard soap and harder water, with no pomade to soften those braids pushed up beneath an old lady's felt hat. Skin shiny and tight from lack of cream—no makeup. And weight—I must have put on twenty pounds—resting on flat laced-up oxfords.

Nonetheless I bit my tongue from telling her: Hussy, if I looked one-tenth as good as I intend to—given a little time—I'd give you one hundred reasons to slam that door in my face.

She let me walk up the dimly lit hallway alone—proof that she knew I had belonged once. I expected Tom to pop out of the living room, arms outstretched, to greet me with his big, expanding self, his gold grin. God, I had been aching to hear his big-belly laugh. I had been missing it. Tom Rumley, my friend. Knowing he lived in New York had made New York the one place to come to.

I stood in the doorway of the living room, looking around the room, wanting the familiar to rush at me, overwhelm me. I expected to be hit by new additions. But no—even here, changes. No additions—subtractions: the bear head; the pictures of moving-picture stars; the corners of the room empty of old newspapers and magazines. I gave the chick high marks for trying. Poor Tom had to have gone through hell.

But he had won some points: the family pictures, looking blank, facing into a world they didn't know and cared less about knowing, still hung on the walls. The piano stood in its space, the old Victrola still in its corner. And there was a stack of magazines right next to Tom's favorite stuffed chair, within easy reach, where Tom sat reading.

He looked comfortable in old clothes—a sweater, pants unbuttoned at the crotch, giving him belly space, his tender-looking feet propped up on the old hassock. The freckles on Tom's face had spread, so that his skin looked brown in the front, with his red coloring forming a border going back to his ears.

Tom squinted at me from over gold-rimmed eyeglasses set low on his nose bridge. "Who in the hell is it?"

"If you don't know by this time, old nigger, then you got the wrong lenses, or your brain's in need of a good dusting."

"Dorine! For God's sake, girl—when you get out?"

He fumbled to get up, and seeing the effort it cost, I went to him, put my arm around his shoulders, and eased him back into his chair. "This morning," I said.

"Well, sure am glad you finally come out. A bad time, Dorine. We did everything we could."

"I know that. But what to do. Jinx time. Thank the Lord, the jinx had time to wear out."

It had been a bad deal, all around. An investigation of officials in Philly had those we had depended on doing more time than I had. My lawyer, even the judge we had fixed.

"But five years . . . damn." Tom shook his big head. "Was it hard, Dorine?"

"Hard. . . ?" I sat on the couch facing him. "Naw . . . You know me, Tom. Way I figured, ain't nothing hard to do unless it's hard in the head. Jail like anything else is a state of mind. I had to do time, I knew it, I did it—tried to make things as easy as I could. . . ."

I had. Knowing that there was always a cause a feller got in trouble, I had gone in looking—and had found two. One a white six-footer we called Saint Mary, the other a black girl, Beulah—looked as though her face had been through a meat tenderizer from colliding too many times with razors.

The first day Saint Mary sounded me: "I hear all niggers got tails," she said. Knowing she hadn't waited for me to check that out, seeing there were three black faces already there, I made my frog-eyes go fearless:

"Sure 'nough?" I said. "And I hear white folks up north all went to school and supposed to be intelligent. Now I see that's a damn lie."

"I ain't never been inside a school," she said. "And I ain't never seen inside a nigger's drawers."

"I ain't never seen inside no white woman's drawers neither." And because all her friends were grinning and nudging one another, I put in: "I hear tell they got asses like baboons, red and nasty, skinned inside out from fist-fucking. You pull your pants down and show me yours, and I'll show you mine."

"Okay," she said. "But if you're lying, you gonna kiss my ass, right here and now."

"Two things I do best," I said. "Kissing asses and kicking them."

She turned, pulled her pants down. I looked at that broad, hard-muscled behind and swallowed hard. The bitch was strong, and could make me kiss that ass; worse, she knew I knew.

"Go on and kiss," she said.

"But I ain't tole no lie," I answered. "If that ain't the ass of a baboon, you got to tell what is. . . ."

The women got quiet. Saint Mary turned, and thank the Lord, the matron, hearing the quiet, came in. We went back to work and I worried the rest of that morning.

But later, in the yard, Razor-face came for her play. I had been waiting. "You sounded right hipped this morning," she said. "Let's see what you really can do. These peckerwoods in here is prejudice. We needs your help to settle with them—this evening."

I had to be born the day before to think that four blacks could take on a prison full of white inmates. And I had to have been born that very morning to think they had been waiting just for me to commence to do battle. "If I had wanted to fight prejudice, I'd have joined the Communists," I said.

"Bitch." She raised her voice and I reached out, grabbing her by her collar. Then I kneed her in her stomach—once, twice. Her knees buckled, and I pushed her back and went right down with her, straddling her.

Grabbing the two inches of her hair, I slapped her head to the concrete flooring, and holding it down, I raised my other hand heavenward: "The Lord saith, 'Bear thy punishment as He bore His on the cross and only good shall come to thee.' And He hath saith unto me"—I bassed—" 'Dorine Davis, go thee among thy sisters in prison and bring the Word. . . . Say unto them—He who wants to gain the Gates of the Kingdom—heed!'

"Heed thy sister. Be humble and follow her preachings. . . ."

"Got the woman to believe I was Prophet Davis," I said.

"How you pull that one?" Tom laughed.

"Pure instinct," I said. "I looked down praying one day. When I looked up, I had them. Never knew I had the power before."

"Power? What power?"

"To keep a prison full of women in touch with the souls of their dearly departed."

"Oh my God, Dorine. . . ." Wide-eyed, he showed the front of his pretty gold smile. I looked around, missing the old bear head. It had been one of our life-time jokes on Tom. "Well, at least you got through. You happy?"

"What's happy?" I asked. "A big hunk is out of my life, Tom. Whatever I say, there's a hole going through me that has nothing to do with me. I had to serve time. I did. I'm back. I got to pull my pieces together."

"Where you fixing on staying, now that you're out?" he asked.

"I thought to stay here—until I got myself a place."

"Here? Oh. Sure—you can stay. Gladys ain't gonna mind."

My scalp crawled. Sweat jumped to my nose. Things couldn't have changed that much. I had been waiting for the old sparkle to jump back into his eyes, the way it used to when he looked at me. When it hadn't I figured it was because I looked real bad. But Tom's used to be the gang's hang-out anytime we were in New York. Mama had always said: "It ain't what a person looks like, it's what's inside what counts." I had thrown that out as garbage. Still, I had expected the me that Tom knew to always be tops.

"You mean I got to be passed on by some snot-nosed chippy before I can stay?"

"Well—it ain't that, exactly. . . ." Twisting, turning his heaviness like a fat walrus in the old chair. "Sure—you can stay—you know that. Till you find yourself a place." My head burned. "Book me a room at the Theresa Hotel," I said. But I kept staring to keep him wiggling, uncomfortable, feeling his guilt. When he looked about to fall out of that old chair from it, I said: "Don't feel bad,

Tom. I had changed my mind when I saw this old building. If I was a piece of shit, I'd stop up a feller's asshole before I'd slip out into this shithouse. Tom, how you let this elegant building turn into a fucking sewer?"

"Me? Why me? Ask the man what owns it."

"But you're the one living in it," I said. "He ain't." I had moved all over Harlem, gone to jail since giving up my apartment. But there Tom sat. Stuck. Trapped by his junk.

"What you expect me to do?"

"Anything. Everything. Kill the motherfucker, but don't let him have you live like this."

"There you go with your bad-mouth self. Neither jail nor being a preacher changed you. Same as you went in."

"But sitting in this shit changed you, old nigger. You look tired, worn out, goddamn old. . . ." I liked to think I was hitting him in tender meat. "You need to get off your fat ass and get to work. Staying in that chair got both you and your junk overgrown with mold."

"Dorine, these feet—"

"Never mind them feet, Tom. I been waiting a long time to feel rubber rolling beneath me, to see trees spreading out and away over highways. Hell, I'm ready for serious work."

Only one part of my needs. More than anything I wanted the feel of a dress soft on my skin. I wanted to click down the avenue—Seventh Avenue—on spiked heels. I wanted to see my reflection—looking pretty—through the light of a stud's eyes. Five years. I ached all over to look at something more interesting than tits and pussy. I wanted to feel the stretch of something harder in my hands than time had been on my mind.

"Things ain't what they used to be out here, Dorine," Tom said. His whining voice made me notice how his mouth had shrunk around those golden teeth, turning down at the corners. "This war done messed up with things something terrible."

"Something's always messing up things. When I went in, it was Depression. I come out, it's war. But people lives on, Tom. . . ."

The war broke out while I was in prison. I heard about Pearl Harbor. I had never heard of Pearl Harbor before. Now Tom was saying it had changed our lives.

"Things is just different, Dorine. Ain't you noticed? Ain't lots of cats hanging the streets. Everybody's working—defense plants, factories. . . . Even got black folks in department stores."

"Had them when I went in."

"These folks ain't sweeping floors, honey. They salesladies and stuff."

"You don't say? If that kind of money's around, we ought to be able to touch some of it."

"How—working in defense plants?"

"Getting goods to them that does."

"Don't work that way, Dorine. This war done unleashed a new breed. The hoods is gone in for hijacking at a rate. Furs—storesful. They hit jewelry stores like they was toy boxes. Guys comes away with a department store full of stuff. . . . We was specialists, Dorine. Out there's a marketplace."

"If there's a marketplace, there should be room for us," I said.

"Out on the road like some fucking sales folks? Fences laugh at the price we ask. Last time I went to my fence, I tole him: 'Man,' I said, 'I known you all these years; if you wants a present from me, just ask.' I give him the day's haul and walked out. . . . Naw, ain't nothing out there for us."

The room had grown more and more familiar as I sat there. It had grown around Tom like a skin, sinking him in the muck of his misery. What he was telling me was that he was tired, had retired. "What about the gang? They go along with your thinking?"

"What gang? Ain't no more gang, Dorine. That's what I'm try-ing to tell you, things is changed. Grace"—he softened his voice to keep it between us—"got herself in a lot of trouble. Big trouble—if the law ever catches her. FBI. Fool woman done kidnapped a baby—neighbor's kid she was supposed to be minding. Took off, she did. Disappeared. Nobody knows where—not even her old man. Two years now. Hell, if she wanted a baby that bad, you'd think she wanted it for both of 'em."

"That'll get her the chair," I said.

"Yep. . . ."

"What about Sally?"

"Sally's here in New York. Buddy done thrown her out. . . . Girl"—Tom got to sounding like an old woman with a basketful of goodies—"she called me, give me her address, but . . . Hey, baby," he shouted loud enough to be heard down the hall. "I never did get around to seeing her. . . .

"Dorine, these feet, they been talking to me. They say things like: 'Old Red, we done give you some good years and you been treating us like we your niggers. We ain't gonna take no mo.'

"Sally's daughter—I hear—she about to marry some high-class stud. . . . Buddy Jr.? He's a big-time Washington doctor. You know them Washington Negroes. . . ."

The chick high-stepped into the room. Dressed now, her dress as short as fashion could possibly allow, hitting her just beneath her pointy ass. Clicking into the room, skinny legs looking like stilts, on ankle-strapped platform shoes. "You call me, Daddy?"

"Yes, baby doll, look in my top drawer and get me my address book." Then as she started out of the room, "Yes, and call up the Theresa and book Dorine a room." Baby Doll cut her eyes at me like who did I think I was, looked away because I wasn't worth her time, then clicked out of the room, her short dress fanning her butt. At the look in Tom's eyes as they followed her, I was tempted to jump up, shout: All that chick's got on me is youth!

"My baby takes good care of me," Tom said, smiling. "She's the one somebody I knows that I can trust."

I looked away from Tom to stare at an old hag staring at me from her place on the wall. Between Tom's feet and his young lady, the feel of old age started creeping down on me. I shook my head, keeping my thoughts straight. Age had never been a big thing between us. But hell, Tom had to be damn near sixty to my thirty-six.

"What's with Bessie?" I asked.

"Bessie—she stays in Chicago. She ain't been doing much since you got hauled in."

"And Albert?"

"He's around New York somewhere, getting drunk, acting the damn fool, playing the li'l boy to any old woman what wants him. . . . You know Bessie run him out."

"So he's drinking a lot. . . ."

"Yeah, he's about shot. . . ."

"And Ann?"

"She's gone—to one of them islands."

"Ann!"

"Yeah—got married. Girl, that woman sure had gone to the dogs. Looked ba-ad. Drinking, laying around, first one pimp, then another. Then she meets up with this old West Indian. He picked her up, cleaned her up, married her—and took her on home."

"And so . . ." I stared at the picture of the old hag. That left only Sally and Bessie to work with. Sad. I looked at my dry, hard hands, waiting for the clicking heels to come back down the hall, for Gladys to give Tom his address book. Then I waited for her to go back before I asked:

"What about the girls, Tom?"

"They gone," he said.

Waves of blood rose from my feet to my head. "What the hell do you mean, gone?"

"Gone," he repeated, then seeing my face, said: "Dorine, I declare I done all you tole me. I paid a few months' rent for the room I got them. I put your things in storage, your car in the garage. By the time I got back to see what they was about, they had cut out."

"How long before you got back?"

"Couple of months. They had my address—telephone. I waited to hear from them—not a word."

Tears jumped to my eyes. (God knows, I cry at the prick of a pin.) Five years of worry. I had had to be locked up to understand Gogi. A strange girl, but strangeness was no sin. Shy, locked in with her books—reading had become her life. School her ambition. She had not forgiven him those beatings. She hadn't forgiven me not understanding—she hadn't forgiven me leaving. . . .

"Dorine, they weren't babies." Tom's voice took on an edge, an apology. "Hell, you was their age when you got out on your own. They full-grown by now."

Which didn't check my tears or keep that space prison had dug out of my life from spreading.

"What about Sonny?" To Sonny I had entrusted the family. Left them to him to see to because he owed me—more, he owed them.

"Sonny's in partnership with some Eyetalians. They got themselves a bar and grill—in the Bronx."

"The who? What the hell is Sonny doing in the Bronx?"

"Lots of black folks done moved up to the Bronx. Started even before the war. Been a stampede since. Hear tell them Jews looked up, seen them niggers coming, and said: 'You want the Bronx, niggers? Here, take it—it's yours.' They started running—cutting out. . . . For Christ's sake, woman, what you sitting there bawling about?"

"I ain't bawling, Tom." I blew my nose. "It's just that I'm missing things. What the hell is Sonny doing in the Bronx? Seems like I come home—to nothing. . . ."

"Nothing? Woman, you got your vault in the bank, full. You got a warehouse stuffed with furniture. An almost brand-new Buick greased and waiting. Who you ever know to come out of the clink in a better way?"

And that was as near as he managed to caring. I stared at him, my red-from-crying eyes showing him how empty I thought he had come out of it all. A guilty, knowing look forced his eyes to his aching, tender-looking feet: A kindly, freckled old feller, gone soft from lack of use, sharpness dulled. The one thing to brighten lack-luster eyes a young, pointy ass.

"Dorine," Tom said, "there's a lot you can do. You got money. Hell, what you think you can do setting on it? Hatch it? Get into business—buy a house—do something. You ain't getting younger, you know."

That brought me to my feet. "Old age is a disease you done caught, old nigger. I best get the hell on out before I catches it too. No no"—I pushed him down in his chair when he fumbled to stand. "You'll have a hard time keeping up with me making it to the door. . . ."

My first thought—to make it over to Sally's, then go off to Bessie's in Chicago and get right back into working—I put off until I pulled myself together. But getting the girl out of prison turned out to be a damn sight easier than getting prison out of the girl: scrubbing with hard brushes to scrub off dead skin; soaking in oil to bring life and shine back to faded brown; rubbing scales off rough feet, forcing them to softness with heavy socks worn night and day; hours of oil treatment at the hairdresser's; soaking rough hands, creaming them, keeping them in gloves to coax them back to presentable hardness—the manicurist, the pedicurist—all took its own time. Then: shopping for silks to baby the body, clothes to fit the extra pounds I was determined to shed in weeks, high heels to throw the best of fleshy hips forward when I finally clicked up the avenue. But instead of Sally's, I made my first stop Sonny's.

Sonny's Place—a combination delicatessen-cafeteria in bygone days—started in the middle of one block, downstairs from some el tracks of an IRT station, turned the corner, and went almost mid-block of a main street. Inside, the bar tried to take up the length of the big, sprawling room—a room decorated with chandeliers bright enough to light up Times Square. Silver-and-blue wallpaper (gaudy!) tried to hold the barnlike openness of the place together. Small lamps on tables tried to add atmosphere. Nothing worked. It still looked and felt like a delicatessen-cafeteria.

I stood at the end of the long bar, waiting for Sonny to look up and see me as he moved toward me. Laughing, joking, greeting customers standing three-deep at the bar, not missing one. Smoking a long cigar, playing with the outsized diamond on his pinky for the glitter that the chandeliers picked up, he belonged to every inch of the place. In his lifetime, Sonny had one thing going for him: style. He had only needed a stage. Now he had one.

He had tackled the years, too, but had come off the winner: His added jowls went with his buck-eyes. The gray at his temples did a lot for his black skin. The furrows deepening his face softened some of the slickness off it. His smile, his manner, spoke of a mellowing.

"Hey, buddy, how you doin'?" he called out to a customer. And to another: "Hey, old-timer, you looking good!" "Have a taste on me, my man. Set my man here up." And the admirers: "Whatcha know, Sonny? No, let this one be on me." "Howya doing, Mr. Boss Man?" And Sonny soaking it all in, loving it.

Still being able to read him gave me the good feeling of being on familiar turf. A feeling I sorely needed to bring my parts together.

His hooded eyes kept sweeping the bar: How many people had he missed? How many more to go? His eyes swept over me, and back. He stopped to talk. They swept over me again, going to sort out, count. I waited. Once more they looked to the end of the bar and, in swinging away, blinked and swung back.

The cigar stuck on the dry bottom lip of his open mouth. His head stuck out of his collar. He squinted (needed eyeglasses, too proud to wear them). "Dorine. . . ?" He took a few steps, then stopped to make sure he wasn't mistaking. "Dorine! Girl, what you doing here?" He rushed up to me, pounded me on my shoulders, squeezed my arms. "When did you get out?"

"Been a couple of weeks now."

"What? And you just getting here? Where you staying?"

"Theresa. But I'm looking for a place. I see they opened up them apartments on the park side. That's where I want. . . ." I wanted to be in my old neighborhood, the neighborhood where I had lived in family life.

"I know of one, around the corner from the park—with an elevator man. Want a look-see?"

"It can't hurt. But I always did want to live where I can look clear over to the other side of Central Park. But tell me, Mr. Harlem, what you doing up here—in the Bronx?"

"Dorine baby, the whole world done opened up to us. It is ours. So wherever . . ."

"You finally made it."

"You know I always been wanting a legal place, Dorine. This here's still in partnership—but goddamn, it's coming."

Up and down the bar, eyes looked in respect at Sonny, in admiration at me. I smiled, feeling good. Glad to have chosen the beige flannel suit, the wide, brown Milan straw hat, the brown-and-white spectators to help out my heavy legs.

"What about the folks?" I asked.

"What folks?" The question forced the smile away until we got ourselves dead-center on the same course. "What folks would I be talking about, Sonny?"

"Oh, you talking about them back home. They okay, I guess. . . ."

"Guessing ain't good enough." I spoke as though I had a gun aimed at his head. He had known what he had to do. He owed me. Fooling around when I was home was one thing, but when I was helpless? And he knew—excuses just were not allowed.

"I been looking out, Dorine. It ain't been easy, you know? That Sugar—remember the chick? She turned out to be a real bitch, man.

291

Got the law in on me. It took some doing to get out of that. But I been doing. . . . Of course, when your brother-in-law passed—"

"Joseph? He died?"

"Ain't you got the letter I wrote?" He blinked, once, twice, three times. A damn lie. I let that go. I hadn't expected letters. Folks I knew weren't writing folks. Tom had sent on letters Lil and Brother had written. But those had stopped when I didn't answer.

"You go to the burial?"

"No."

"No! Then how you know how they was doing? Sonny, did you ever go down?"

"No." Sonny was the one somebody I knew who meant it when he said he was *from* the South. Still, at a time like that. . . . Didn't any feeling ever go deeper than the way his eyes fit into their sockets? "Sonny, that money I give you to save your place from them cumsuckers wasn't for free. What the hell you done to earn it?"

"I sent money—when I could. I swear, Dorine. Ask Lil. I talked to Lil regular. Talked to Jennie Mae, to Brother. . . . Brother called when Son went to the service—wanted me to get word to you."

"Son! He ain't old enough!"

"He volunteered."

God, I had spent a lifetime—a goddamn lifetime out of the world! It had become a totally different place! What in the hell did that hardheaded, plump, stubborn rascal have to do with a place called Pearl Harbor?

". . . the army," Sonny said. "Dorine, it ain't no sense in you coming out faulting me. They ain't babies. Nobody is. . . ." His echoing Tom's words tore into the different parts of me, damn near shattering what was left of me. "They all working—that is, except Bud."

"Bud? . . ."

"Yeah—the youngest. And the reason he's still in school, Jennie Mae says, is that he thinks he's too pretty to study. But all the rest—they're working."

"Working? Doing what?"

"Well, Lil and Jennie Mae?—they teaching. The one called Jane plays the organ—and is secretary in church. Ruth is off to school, studying."

"What about Brother?"

"He's teaching. He got married, you know."

"How you expect me to if you ain't told me?"

"Bought himself a house. His kid must be almost three . . . a girl." Sonny's face lifted in a broad smile. "See—I ain't let you down."

Because he hadn't—because the threads of our lives had been woven so close—a sudden need for Sonny came rushing over me. Hell, we had gone through some times. . . .

"But Dorine girl, you sure looks good," he said. "Gained a li'l, but it makes you even prettier." His eyes teased, which made the need bubble and flow like a goddamn fountain. I teased back. Why not? Why the hell not? What was wrong with testing whatever had been left over between us?

"Baby—so sorry to be late. . . ."

The words came as clear as though whispered into my ear. They had been spoken with just such intention. I knew when I saw this tall, skinny blonde leaning against Sonny's back, whispering in his ear—and looking past my cheeks, pretending he stood alone.

The teasing in Sonny's eyes eased. From bullshit, they went to lovingly serious without a blink. "Hey, sweet lady," he said, turning to her. "Been wondering what was keeping you. Wait there, Dorine," he called over his shoulder, walking away. Seating her at a table, he stood bending over her so that their heads touched.

Eyes from up and down the bar turning from me caused a sweating—it messed with the makeup on my face, stuck my silk underwear to my skin, itched my legs beneath my silk stockings. My eyes narrowed, my nostrils widened.

Lousy son of a bitch; his son in the army—right in the mouth of the motherfucking cannons—and there he stands, drooling over the very one who put him there. A man like that didn't deserve a son. What he deserved was a good ass-kicking. And seeing I had spent too much time and money getting to look cool, I had no intentions of being the one to do it. I walked out.

A bicycle-repair shop had replaced the shop of the best butcher I ever had. The doormen around my old neighborhood had all gone. So had the elevator men—except in the apartment that Sonny had lined up for me (and he went when I had been there a couple of years). All other elevators were self-service. Folks I used to greet during my family days had all moved away. Everything had changed. Pulling my parts together was coming hard.

I took my things from storage, threw out the broken and the worn, spent weeks shopping for good antiques. When I had finished, the place still didn't belong to me—or me to it. I had always fitted into the bigness of my apartments. Their grandness supported my style. These seven rooms with a view of the park—which kept a crook in my neck from having to admire from the side of my window—looked over Seventh Avenue. Yet I rattled around all seven rooms—a dried-out pea in a drier pod.

Pulling the thought of Sally and work out again, I set out to find her. And through Harlem I drove slow, keeping my big eyes searching for someone, anybody to say hello to. I covered half of Harlem, but it didn't happen.

I kept driving slow down Sally's street. Then, seeing this sign swinging in the breeze, I braked the car and swung over to the curb. The Club. Surprised to see it still there, I jumped out of the car and headed up to the old brownstone.

"Don't you go in there. Don't you dare." A voice from behind made me turn. A young stud—he had been shining the Lincoln I had parked behind—kept frowning, letting his eyes travel over me. "Not without giving me one good look." He smiled. "Yeah—just the way I likes 'em. Heal-thy. Plenty meat on dem dere bones."

Zoot suit—that, too, was new. Pants narrow at the ankles and blousing from the ankles up. Jackets reaching the knees, and this young turkey had a gold chain hanging beneath his. I laughed. Shook my head. "This meat's been around, lover-boy. You ain't got the heat to cook it."

"Ain't no tellin' 'less you do some tryin'." I walked on up the steps still shaking my head.

Ringing the bell, I strained to hear those familiar sounds—laughing, music, chips. But supposed the still-hanging sign to have been an oversight of new owners. "Yes?" A tall, lean, kindly gray-haired man opened the door smiling.

"I know I made a mistake," I said. "But I took the chance. This club used to belong to a friend—Big H?" He moved aside. I stepped into the once glamorous club.

294

It struck me—its need for light. Daylight came shining through. Yet the place needed light the way some plants—even when washed in daylight—had need for the direct rays of sun. I stood waiting for the rush of machine sounds upstairs, the clicking of chips hitting against chips downstairs. No—the drab, lackluster room gave back a deafening quiet despite people sitting at tables in groups, talking. No white-jacketed waiters moved around tables. The heads raised and turned to me were few—men, old-timers.

They stared for a time then looked away. And with the turning of their heads, visions rose from around them—memories—of ball players, the respectable, the slicksters, the numbers kings and queens—the educated, high-bred world-changers—they all let out one terrible roar and came stampeding toward me. The babble of their voices filled my head, forcing me to spin back into time. A time when we had breathed into each other, raised our eyebrows acting out this or that, throwing around high-sounding words. . . . What had happened? So much time, so many people pushing in between, leaving gaps—emptiness. . . .

"Dorine? Dorine Davis? Well—as I live and breathe. . . ." I turned to the voice and my face began to glow. I know it glowed because of the tight pull of skin over my cheeks—a purring from the back of my throat. He looked the same. Thank God, he looked the same. His hand grabbed mine, and I felt the strength beneath its softness as I remembered. The smile, the smooth, round, brown face, the serious look from smiling eyes. "God, how good to see you. I can't believe this. . . ."

"I was driving by—saw the sign."

He kept holding my hands. We grinned, kept grinning, bringing back that other time, forcing the in-between years to slip to the background, to disappear. "What can I get for you?" he asked.

"A Coke." We laughed, long, loud at times gone. And sitting at a table, we held hands and looked at each other, kept looking.

"You look exactly the same," Big H said. "Lovelier."

"I put on the pounds," I said. "Been in jail."

"I know—Tom told me."

"Yep. I got to be the chief chef."

"You? A cook?"

"Didn't do me no good," I said, patting my hips.

"Weight suits you."

"The slop they used to serve at first made me vomit. And did I lose weight! Didn't know when I was lucky."

"And then you got the job as chef. . . ."

"Begged for it." I laughed. "It was going on to Christmas, and seeing I was the bigmouth around, some of the girls pushed me into going to talk to the warden. I did. 'Madam Warden,' I said, 'we sinners'—see, I was supposed to be a preacher. And this woman, an old, sweet woman—we called her Juneat—one of my angels, went with me, so I had to act as though talking in the Lord's Name. 'We sinners in this joint accept that we all are justly here to pay for the wrong we did. And we paying for it—dearly, Madam Warden. It's right that we do.

" 'But Madam Warden, killin' is a sin. Now, they done killed them poor animals. And them cooks is killing the Lord's lovingly grown vegetables. Now when they takes and throws all that dead shit together, Madam Warden, it's about to kill us.

" 'Them animals got souls, Madam Warden,' I said. 'And all the souls of them poor animals cry out to us at night, begging for retribution. "Kill them cooks," they tell us, " 'fore they kills you all. . . ."

" 'Madam Warden, we begs you. Leave us cook our own Christmas dinner to save our own Christian souls, and to rest the souls of them poor dead creatures.' Nothing she could do but laugh. And I ended up with job as chef."

We laughed. "Dorine, Dorine, you never change. It's so good to hear your voice."

"You did some time too, I hear."

"One year. For banking numbers—years after I had stopped."

"Tom said it was because of some of the big boys in Washington being sore."

"You mean because the navy had to leave the islands?" He hunched his shoulders. "Who knows? Dewey was after me, you know. And Dewey's a very ambitious man."

"But the navy did leave?" I asked.

"Quite some time ago. The army is there now." He laughed. "The army is everywhere. This war, you know. Small islands, small countries, are destined to be pawns of the big. Our history. Our destiny."

"All that struggle—for nothing?" I asked.

"No—no. People are being treated with more respect," he said. "We're not forced into labor. Not being killed and forgotten. Some crimes against us, even by whites, are being punished. We are still poor, but people must feel they have dignity. That isn't much to ask for. But that is all we expect."

I looked over to the corner table. "And Monica. . . ?" Given the place, its memories, the question asked itself.

"Monica? She's dead, you know. She went back home—died there."

That beautiful lady? That smooth-skinned beauty with the thick black hair—lying in some grave? That high-yeller, intelligent woman, who only needed a frame to last forever in that corner—dead? Why hadn't he married her? She had been in his corner—sitting in that goddamn corner, at his side—all the way.

In his sudden seriousness, the skin that had held Big H's smile slackened. Two soft pockets hung on each side of his chin. His eyes were faded at the edges. The hands holding mine—were they shaking from remembering? From old age? How old was Big H, anyway?

"Cancer," he said.

"Yes—of course . . . ." What else? It had to be cancer! All that waiting for one man—for him. All those juices flowing from being overanxious. Juices squeezed out of glands, spurting over the insides of stomach, draining away from breasts, leaving glands empty, ready for the goddamn cancer. Juices like lye eating away bit by bit, destroying the best of a woman, her generousness, her youth. What else? It had to be cancer! All that suffering endured—sitting in corners. What a shame, that gorgeous woman with the full red mouth had to go home to sit and wait for cancer to carry her out.

I pulled my hand from his and looked around the room, fragile with its ghosts of bygone days. Death clung to its walls like funk. I wanted suddenly to get up, run, go to Sally's, get out of the emptiness of this time, go on to Chicago. . . .

"What happened to Odel?" I asked.

"Odel turned against me. He was chief prosecution witness."

"Bastard."

"He thought to gain an empire. But those days are gone. He got his hands on some valuable property—I had trusted him. But Odel never had the head for business. He lost everything."

"And you? How are you doing?"

"All right—I suppose. I still have this. . . ." He waved his hands to indicate the room, the house. "A bit of real estate upstate. But I'm no longer wealthy." He laughed as though at a joke. "Money dwindles, you know. It takes so much time and effort . . . and when the will ebbs. . . ."

But why did his will ebb? Why did he no longer care? He had been in the driver's seat. "Do you ever go back to the islands?" I asked, remembering how many times I had waited, those juices running, while he went dashing off to far-off places.

"No—not often," he said. "I don't often feel like it. . . ."

His soft hand covered mine. He smiled—a promise. The brown skin smoothed out. The laughter forced out the faded parts from his eyes. His eyes said: We are friends. Old friends. We shared some good years. I'm alone. You're alone. What can we do to salvage moments. . . ?

But Big H's life was over! Mine was about to begin. Big H, like Harry, like Tom, had become a part of another time. Back then, he had pleased me. Men in the fullness of their lives had pleased me. Men in the fullness of their lives still pleased me. I was young!

Seeing me reach for my purse, his hand tightened over mine. "You will come again?"

"I just got out," I said. "I'm looking around for something to do."

"Like what, Dorine?" He spoke as though he was ready to help, as though he thought my need was to share the last of somebody's years. . . .

"Something exciting," I said. "Something like—maybe blasting away to the moon."

"Great!" He threw back his head laughing, and I got a good look at his flabby underchin. "I like the feel of that, Dorine. I really do. . . ." His eyes said he wanted me, wanted to do whatever. Wasn't he used to making a woman's wish come true? "Come back and let's talk."

"Soon's I get settled." I know a lie when I hear one—even when I'm doing the telling. What Big H wanted was to piddle and talk. What I wanted was to move and fuck.

Outside, I sat in the car, staring. The meeting had disappointed me. Frightened me. It had showed up my lonely self.

God, I had been so young. Young, and loving them all. Young and anxious to please. I had done everything I knew to please. Used my body as a toolbox. Ooohed and aahed over gifts, pretending I thought they were given me through love—hiding from myself that I was a fool. I sure hadn't hid it from them. I had been around for their pleasure. In return, I had wanted to be near them, touch them, feel them, say they belonged to me. All the while they knew it was a lie. They got their kicks. I said thanks. . . .

I started up the car. "Hey, pretty brown thing, you change your mind?"

The zoot-suiter stood posing against the Lincoln. He looked good. So young. . . . Prison sure changed folks. It had changed me enough to even sit looking at that—wishing. But had it changed my style all the way? I had to think about that. What I wanted to do was to drive across the avenue to see Sally. What I did was turn the car and drive back home.

2

"The President's dead," the man said. I looked around to see if another car had pulled up alongside of me. None had.

"Talking to me, mister?"

"The President's dead," he repeated, his white face chalky; then he staggered off the curb like a drunk and zigzagged in front of my car, crossing the avenue.

My habit of going down to the tip of Manhattan late mornings, parking at Battery Park, walking around eating hot dogs and sauerkraut from carts, then driving back just before the late afternoon, took me through the jewelry exchange, the stock exchange, past City Hall, the court area, then on up Broadway: feeling the beat of the city, seeing the crowds—how different crowds in different sections dressed a different way. A different kind of walk, the different way folks thought of themselves—styles—veins pouring into the belly of the city. . . .

I kept on up Broadway, going through the garment center, maneuvering around the loudmouthed, shouting, rough-and-ready workers pushing carts along the streets and adding to the congestion of the traffic. At Times Square a bigger-than-ever crowd stood, unmoving, gazing up at the electric sign flashing around the Times Building. On the corners, the jostling, pushing at the corner newsstands—folks staring, reading over one another's shoulders. Shock chalking out of white folks' faces made me think of the short white man talking into my car window. Then I heard him: He had said, the President—Roosevelt—was dead!

Wanting to jump out, join in with those walking around stunned, waiting for the fullness of their grief to fall, I sat instead, frozen at the wheel. I had to talk to somebody. The honking of horns behind forced me to move on. I drove up to Harlem.

White folks grieve silent. Black folks lets it all hang out. "My President—my President. He dead, he dead, he dead. . . ."

A crying and bawling hit me from all sides as I drove up the avenue. Folks just crying, falling out on the sidewalks. Folks being comforted by crying folks. Death had hit Harlem about as hard as when Joe Louis had been knocked down by Max Schmeling. "Lord, Lord, Lord, my President is gone, gone, gone. . . ." I had to have some one person to talk to!

In my lifetime, I had known but one President. Roosevelt. Sure, I knew of Hoover, and that others came before. But I only knew Hoover's name after Roosevelt had been elected—his name being one and the same with Depression. Before Roosevelt, life to me had meant that folks were born, ate, or starved to death trying to make it. Those who didn't prayed to God for salvation. I had made it. But I knew that to lots of folks, Roosevelt had put a new meaning to the word President. I appreciated that. He might even have been able to help Harry. I just had to talk to somebody! I drove on to Garvey's corner.

They sometimes cleared my thinking. But the folks out there were not talking. A bunch of silence. A giant hand had struck. It had pushed meaning out of words. The most they could express was silence. But I had been silent long enough. I needed words.

Then I thought of Son. We were at war. Son was in the army—

over in some foreign land—and the man responsible had dropped dead. I started up the car and headed for Sally's.

Up to that second, I had sworn out that my feelings for Son equaled what I had for the rest—no more, a little less than for Lil. In one second the big lie had been exposed. The fat little black child clung to my heart the same as its casings.

Helpless. The first time I admitted to the feeling of ordinary folks. What did a woman do when her borned child was off in some strange land, and the one who knew how to bring him back had just up and dropped dead?

I drove up to the sign of The Club, slowed down. Big H knew about Washington—back then. I sped on. If a hincty Washington Negro with a son didn't know what to do, nobody did.

Then I pulled up in front of Sally's door. And all thoughts of Son, of the President, took a place in the back of my mind. Never in my life had I imagined Sally living in such a place. When Tom had given me her address, I thought Sally lived in the basement of a brownstone like the ones on the next block. But this broken-down hovel had never been swank. It had had no better days. What in the hell was that hincty woman doing in this crappy hole?

Forcing myself to climb down those rickety wooden steps to the entrance beneath the stoop, I knew something was wrong. This scene fitted no pattern I knew. Climbing down into the difference brought on a foreboding (that spiritualism I had practiced in prison had tuned me in, no matter what Tom Rumley said). At the entrance I looked into a whitewashed, gray-with-soot stone passage leading back to the boiler room. Nearer the entrance an electric bulb, hanging from the ceiling by a cord, threw a dim light on two facing apartments. One had the word "Super" marked on it. I knocked on the other.

In the quiet behind the door, a rustle of paper, a scurrying of tiny feet made my suspicion grow. I knocked again. This time the silence—deep, unsettling—cut a path through the door. It entered me. Suspicion turned into sure knowledge with the smell of rot seeping out beneath the door. From the apartment marked "Super" the radio, over and over: "President Roosevelt is dead . . . he died. . . ."

I knocked again, a hand squeezing my stomach. I had been there before. I had been like this—on the outside of somewhere, trying to get in. . . . A nightmare? The smell of rot grew. I stepped outside to breathe, going back to knock at the super's door. My first knock brought the door open. The big, gaunt man—colored as dull as the gray stones of the sooty corridor—had been listening.

"The lady that lives here"—I pointed to the door—"the tall, light-skinned lady with a head full of hair?" I described Sally to make sure I hadn't been mistaken. He nodded at my description, but his mind was still on the radio. "When did you see her last?" He shook his head—he hadn't. The radio behind him said:

"Roosevelt has been in office longer than . . ."

"Yesterday? The day before. . . ?" He kept shaking his head. "Anyone been here to see her lately?" He hunched his shoulders, looking at me from one side of his face. "You living here, right, mister?"

"Ain't seen nobody." He moved to shut the door, but I had read that move and had put my foot on the doorsill.

"Look, mister, I'm a friend—how about opening up the door for me?"

"Ain't got keys," he said.

I took out five bucks. His attention snapped away from the radio. "Something ain't right in there," I said. "I ain't leaving unless I know what it is."

"Look, lady, what happens in that apartment ain't my business." But his tone got softer, his eyes stayed on the bill.

"Got to be," I said. "That smell makes it your business. If you can't smell it, you needs a doctor. If you can, you needs the police."

"I ain't done no wrong," he said.

"I don't know that," I answered. If he had never done one earthly wrong, living poor held him to guilt. The law kept poor black folks to that thought. Mama always had said: "Live in shit and you got to smell of it." "If you ain't done no wrong, how come you scared to open the door?"

He kept staring at the money. So I made as though to put it in my bag. His hand reached out. "Now lady," he said. "This is your doin'."

One kick, the door opened. The smell leaped at us. Rats, mice, and roaches scurried beneath scattered newspapers. Some roaches crunched beneath my shoes when I went in, handkerchief over my face.

Clothes were strewn everywhere: high on the bed, the dresser, the floor. The kitchenette had an icebox, an electric burner on a table. I went to stand between bedroom and kitchenette to look around. Water had overflowed from the pan beneath the icebox. It had covered the floor, dried, and left mud puddles in the grooves of the worn, whelped linoleum. Two mice, frightened by our coming, squeezed into a corner, fighting over a hole that wasn't there. Roaches crawled up the walls, over the icebox and stove, in droves. I looked back into the bedroom at the piled-high bed—and saw her.

She lay beneath the pile. Her long, coarse hair, like a mop, spread out over the pillow. Her face looked small, almost tiny. I went to her, but stopped before I reached the bed: Bedbugs were marching—over her face, into her hair. Bedbugs marching up the wall at the side of the bed. I kept my distance (nothing I hated worse than chinches).

"She's dead," the super whispered. "See for yourself. Lying in her own bed—dead—right?"

"Got a phone?" I asked. And to his nod, "I got this man I want you to call—and then the police." I gave him Tom's number. When he had gone, I stood at Sally's bedside, looking at her aristocratic mouth still turned down, the hincty nose turned up. And it hurt. Guilt for not having come. I had had no reason. I had been alone— needing company. She had been alone—needing a friend. . . .

The stink of piss, of shit, reached out. I turned from it, going back into the kitchenette, opening the icebox to the smell of rotten meat, milk that had soured and dried, vegetables rotted and turned to slime still dripping from the top shelves to the shelves below. I slammed it shut. The two mice still trembled in the corner. "I'm with you"—I spoke to hear my own voice. "If this ain't the dirtiest, funkiest, goddamndest place I ever seen, I sure don't know what is." Then I walked back into the bedroom and jumped from fright. I looked right into Sally's open eyes.

"Sally?" I called, to make sure she was still dead. Her eyes flickered. I moved from side to side. Her eyes moved with me. Then I went to her. "Hey, partner, what's ailing you?" She stared at me.

But her eyes were calm. Whatever had happened—and I supposed right off she had had a stroke—Sally had faced death and had accepted it. Her forehead, cool, almost to the feel of death; her hand, its long fingers pale to its fingernails. I tried to raise her. But the skin draped over my arm. The feel of bones, loose, disjointed, forced me to lay her back down. I bundled the piled-high clothes off the bed, pulled back the bed sheets. Pee stains formed circles around her. Shit, soft and dried, clung to her, caked on her.

In the kitchenette I looked around for the mice. They had gone. I looked for a basin, settled for a pot. I looked for soap, settled for Rinso. With warm water I started to scrub her clean. Her flabby skin kept folding. To get between its folds I had to stretch it. I scrubbed the dried shit from her buttocks. Skin kept washing off. I stopped. Did I leave the shit and save the skin? But folks weren't meant to live in shit. I scrubbed all the skin off her poor buttocks. Then I dusted her with starch and put on a half-clean gown I found in the pile on the floor.

Sally's being so hincty had always kept her from the rest of us. Her pride in her home, her kids, that red-lipped, whiskey-head, "good-haired" husband had kept us from pity—even when he had started going upside her head. Her eyes still held that same pride. So although my heart hurt, I kept pity to myself. But it was a god-damn shame. Proud Sally had no business dying alone in a Harlem basement, lying in shit.

The police came, and then the ambulance. Tom caught up with me at the hospital. "I called Buddy," he said. "Told him Sally was dead."

"What he say?"

"Too bad. . . ."

"Call him back. Tell him Sally ain't dead—at least not yet. . . ."

Buddy never came. Tom and I sat with Sally those last days. We took turns. Sometimes we came together. When we did, Sally's eyes went from one to the other of us. Grateful? Happy? She had never asked for pity. Her eyes didn't ask now. I didn't give her any.

I was grateful. Happy. Happy that He had seen fit to let me get to her before she died. To let me be with her at the end. When her eyes closed for the last time, she had to know the folks she had worked with were caring folks.

Tom and I gave Sally a decent burial. Tom had even kept out of his stuffed chair long enough to drive around town, tracking down Albert. And Albert, looking like a runaway from a whiskey bottle, his face nicked from shaving too close with shaky hands, had come, his wide grayish eyes still holding the look of surprise as though he had lost out on a good thing and didn't know why.

The three of us stood at one side of Sally's grave with the preacher-undertaker. Buddy Jr. stood at the other side—a handsome six-footer with broad shoulders, Sally's coarse skin and hair, and his father's full lips. Dressed in a dark blue suit, Buddy looked the young educated gentleman. We stood looking down as the coffin was being lowered into the grave. When the first shovel of dirt hit, he lit out, racing to his car.

"Buddy, wait up," I called. But when he kept moving, I went after him. Running, jumping over graves, even stepping on the heads of some poor sinners, trying to catch up. I did as he opened the door to his blue Oldsmobile.

"Feller," I said, catching hold of his arm. "I don't ask you to say hello." I hadn't seen him in over seven years, but I doubted that he had forgotten me. "Personally, I give less than a damn what you think. But that woman we done buried happened to be your mother—the closest somebody to you. You can say thanks to us for having given her a decent burial."

The handsome, broad-shouldered, educated-looking man looked down at the arm I was holding as though my touch might have rubbed dirt off on it. I tightened my hand. "Why did you?" he asked.

"Because your daddy didn't," I said, remembering him as a little boy. Remembering how Sally had fussed over him, changing lights to make sure he didn't get eyestrain. Buying cashmere sweaters, knowing full well he had to outgrow them.

"He didn't have to," this nice-looking, well-spoken young doctor said. "They obviously have places to dispose of people of her caliber."

"What the fuck does that mean?" I asked. "Sally done scuffled like a dog to get you the education to use them big words. It's a goddamn shame you got to use them over her poor dead bones."

"Of course, you would take it personally, wouldn't you, Dorine?"

Seeing his Sally-looking face over his Buddy-looking red lips, and the way he looked down on me, got me mad. The D.C. look. Sally had used it on us—her friends.

"You talk as though your mother was a whore," I said.

"Is that what I talk as?"

"But your father was the whore," I said.

"Leave my father out of this." Buddy Jr. looked as though if he lowered himself to touch me it would be to sock me. I kept hoping he'd try.

"Why should I leave him out? Because he ain't here? That's proof he's a goddamn whore."

"What do you know about my father."

"I know he wouldn't have married your ma if she scrubbed floors," I said. "He married her because she was the biggest money-maker he ever known. He wanted a big house, he wanted servants and big-name whiskey in his cupboards. And he wanted his kids in fancy schools. All them things took money."

"My father—"

"Fucked," I said, and Tom, coming up behind me, grabbed my arm and half pulled, half pushed me in beside Albert in the limousine, then sat next to me boxing me in.

"Dorine, why you got to be so hard on the boy?" he asked.

"I ain't had the time to be hard. I was just coming—"

"It ain't his fault. Who knows what his old man done told him?"

"There he goes," Albert said. I looked out of the back window to see the sleek blue Olds tearing up the road.

"Buddy Jr. is a man, Tom. A doctor. What good did all of Sally's money do if he can't think for hisself?"

"Educating a feller don't mean he got to think the way you wants him to—that ain't progress."

"Whatever that bastard thinks, Tom, his grandma scrubbed floors, his mama was a booster, and his papa a low-down whore. He can't get away from that."

"He can try, can't he?"

"How? By knocking his mama?"

"No, by moving on."

"To where?"

"Who the hell knows? Maybe to the moon. . . ."

That sounding like some simple thing I might think up kept me quiet. I looked out—past Albert, huddled in his corner, not yet caught up with himself since Tom had pried him loose from his bottle—to the green velvet lawn spreading out behind and around us. Here and there trees clustered, trying to give the feel of woods that flowers piled high on mounds, crosses, monuments standing at heads of graves, gave the lie to. Here and there folks standing, as we had just stood, over open graves; preachers praying, families crying, friends looking on in sorry silence. Here and there bouquets of flowers—pure in their whiteness, calm in the mixture of blues, pinks—moved over the green lawn in hands of visitors going to visit family plots. And as we headed for the gates, all seemed to be spinning out, around: a wheel of dying things—a wheel of time. . . .

"Kids," Tom said, sighing deep. "They got so much to go through."

"More than we did, Tom? More than me? Hell no. I tell you, if Son, or Lil, or any of my family was to talk to me the way Buddy just talked about his mother . . ." A shiver, as though a feller had walked on my grave, kept me still an instant. But I went on: ". . . may the Lord strike him—them—dead, wherever they may be."

"Dorine, these kids is coming up at a different time, under different sets of pressures. No matter what we wants, kids ain't as much a measure of their folks as they the measure of their own time."

"What you got a home for if you don't ever use it?" Tom's complaining voice came over the telephone he had ordered to keep me company, after Sally's burial. A piss-poor substitute for folks, although folks were using phones for just that reason since the war.

"This apartment and this fucking phone ain't doing one damn thing but driving me out of my mind." I looked around at the room as I spoke—the wooden venetian blinds, clean because I cleaned them every day, to have something to do. I looked at the picture of Dr. Du Bois and the one of Booker T. that I had picked up from Richard B. Moore's 125th Street bookstore, the heavy antique sideboard I had picked up at an auction, the graceful crystal decanter sitting on it. All the time, the money spent, and it had done nothing to bridge those five missing years, or stop the loneliness caused by Sally's dying alone.

"Where you been?" Tom asked. "Still taking them simple drives through town?"

307

"That's me," I said, then admitting that driving through the busiest city in the world hadn't been the answer, added:

"But I'm shaking this town—making it on to Chicago. . . ."

Once Sally had been put in the ground, my first thought had been to rush off to Chicago. I hadn't. And the longer I stayed without going, the less likely I was to get there. Being lonely is the same as being crippled—it took away the strength I needed to push myself.

"What you want to do that for?" Tom asked.

I tried to think up a better answer than checking up, looked out into the hot summer day, and said: "Got to see if I can move Bessie off her rear end, and into some real action."

"Like what?" Tom said. "Y'all gone in for acting? You gonna act as Bessie's cane—keep her from hobbling while she's gonna act as your pusher—push your fat butt out of them doors you get stuck in trying to make y' all's getaway? Dorine, that's old stuff. Get yourself into something legal. Settle down. Buy yourself into some kind of business—or else, them GIs coming out of service with that mustering-out pay'll beat you to it."

Tom's idea had merit. Seeing him sitting in his rocking chair, playing big daddy to his pointy-assed chick while money kept coming in, got me downright jealous. But Tom had started back in the twenties—with the first black-owned bars around Harlem, the black leagues. There were not that many new black-owned bars around. Whites might have moved out of Harlem, but they still had business life locked up.

"I'll look into something when I get back."

"Study long and you study wrong, Dorine. Look into it first and then go."

I held still. If I was able to muster the strength to get out and get to Chicago, there was nothing in the world he could say to stop me. "Anyway," he said. "I just called to tell you that's Sonny's been trying to get hold of you. Says your brother is in a jam in Montgomery. He's in hiding—some such thing."

I came to life with a rush of blood to my head. It brightened my eyes. "Then I had better be getting on down there," I said.

"He said to call—not go."

"Ain't no sense in calling—if I'm going."

"Dorine, for God's sake—if you got to go someplace, go on down to Bessie."

"What I'm gonna do at Bessie's?"

"What the hell you gonna do in Montgomery—fool." I heard that last as I hung up.

In less than an hour I had thrown clothes in a bag, stopped to pick up a loaf of Silvercup bread and a pound of sliced ham, filled the tank with gas, and was on my way.

The tingling feeling of being alive again! What a ball! In jail, thinking of the South, exaggerating all that had happened to me there, I just knew that if ever I went back something more had to come about. God, to be ready to take that on! All fears of the South gone. Yeah—better to die in the South, helping Brother out, than to dry out from being lonely in New York.

My first time on the road in years. The number of cars out there impressed the hell out of me. Women drivers impressed me—white women and black women too! Once upon a time, with a week of driving I rarely saw women—hardly ever a black one. Things had sure changed.

I dug it. No longer to be an odd sight out there. No staring eyes reading me, no crazy son of a bitch ready to do me in. No more to be singled out because I was black—and a woman, and some evil cracker happened to be poor and jealous.

The war being over, lots of soldiers and sailors, duffel bags slung over their backs, were thumbing their way. White soldiers and sailors looked in at me, hoping. Black sailors and soldiers looked in at me, expecting. But things hadn't changed that much. This black woman, alone in her big, black Buick, saw the Whites Only, Coloreds Only signs still along the way, so wanted no one sitting beside her with such damn fool notions of maybe getting hungry, or a crazy-assed need of shitting. I drove right on by.

But the feel of the road beneath me—miles of it—revived me. The fact of myself, a woman, going down south again, willing, ready, and damn able to take on whatever. The world might be about a lot of things. One sure wasn't being lonely and sitting in an apartment dying from it. Making things happen—all kinds of things—that had to be what it was about. Energy flowing, I drove the rest of the day and all night. When my body nudged me that it mightn't be as young as it once was, I pulled into a wooded spot on the side of the road and went to sleep—my determination still strong.

Midafternoon, driving through the pine forests that stretched along both sides of the highway between Georgia and Alabama, I remembered Ann—way back then, a hundred years ago—and slowed down. We had been something! So trim, so pretty—and from the distance in time—so damn young. We had arrived there at dawn. Then, the smell of pines fresh-opened by dew had hit hard at our nostrils. We had been so tired. Nonetheless we had been getting to a real understanding when that evil old cracker had driven up and begun tailgating us. What had Ann said to him to make him take off? I had kept forgetting to ask. Even in jail, thinking about it had given me deep regret, not knowing.

Smells sure can pull out sadness. Made me want to cry about times past. Not because they had been sad, or dangerous, or stupid—just because they had passed. Stopping the car at the side of the road with motor idling, I looked at the woods. I listened to sounds—birds singing, or flying, their wings brushing at branches. Squirrels, opossums, other wild things, rustling dry leaves.

When I drove on I found that my mood had changed. Why? Thinking and thinking, it came to me it had to do with the ivy. Ivy climbing those giant pines. Ivy winding around the long trunks, twisting around their branches, strapping their needles out of sight of the sun—squeezing them even as a snake wrapping around a man might squeeze him of his breath. And having curled to the very tops of the trees, their creepers, finding no more room at the top, draped down. Miles and miles of leaves, curtains—delicate green, beautiful to the eyes—deliberately hiding the fact that they were hell-bent on squeezing the life out of those once magnificent pines! A lesson on life that I had seen over and over again without ever knowing—and still didn't—what I had been looking at. Depressing. Damn depressing.

Late afternoon of that too-hot day, I drove into Montgomery. Seeing the large new swimming pool near the edge of town, spreading out to the side of me, I was tempted to stop the car and go in—

until I saw that only white men and women were stretched out on the tiles around it, sunbathing. Nevertheless the sight of the white children scampering about, jumping into the cool-looking water, the sound of them shouting, screaming, tugged a smile of pure jealousy from me—until I saw one little boy being lifted out of the pool by a laughing woman, being hugged, kissed, and wrapped into an over-sized towel at the same time. I noticed black boys stood on the other side of the high wire fence locking in the pool, their fingers laced into the mesh, their noses pressed against it, their eyes stretching out of sweaty heads, pouring their pain through the wiring. My depression took a deep plunge.

And as I drove on into the city, memories of times past reached out; forcing me to drive slow, keeping my eyes dead on the road while they took in all things happening around and to the back of me: old crackers, looking at my license plate, spitting when I passed; blacks, eyes slipping and sliding from sides of heads, pre-tending not to see me. What in the hell was happening in the god-damn town this time? I got to sighing—deep, real deep, trying hard to keep my sagging courage high. Why had I come? Why in the hell had I? To save Brother. . . !

Dusk had gone to settling when I pulled up in front of the old house. I sounded my horn—once . . . twice. No one. Getting out of the car, I went around to the side and looked the house over. It had an empty feel. An empty look. I turned to walk away but saw a shutter shake. Someone peeping. Going up to the front, I climbed the stairs to the porch and was about to knock when a voice whispered:

"Get your car around the back."

I ran down the steps, jumped into the car, drove around the house, and walked up to the back door. It opened. Inside I was about to go through to the parlor when someone grabbed my arm. "Dor-ine, what in the world are you doing in Montgomery?"

I could just barely make out the figure of a tall woman—a fa-miliar one—hovering head and shoulders over me. "Coming home—I thought," I said.

"Lord, Lord, Lord. Folks around here been thinking that Broth-er's with you in New York. Your coming sure messes things up."

Whatever I had expected, after my years away from home, this sure wasn't it. The emptiness that I had been driving away from since I left New York caught up and pushed right back into me. "Messed what up?" I asked. "What the hell's going on here?"

"Brother—he's got lots of folks around here mad. They suspect he's still here—so we been letting it out that he was with you up north."

"Where's Brother now?"

"Reckon over Miss Jessica's way. Dorine, anybody see you come in?"

"How the hell do I. . . . Yeah, come to think—seems a woman *was* standing across the way. . . ."

Going through the parlor to the window, I peeked through the shutters. Even through the dusk I recognized Sister Janie's simple white friend, Sarah—simpleness having preserved her in time. "Yeah—that's ole Sarah," I said.

"Lordy. . . ." She looked over my shoulder, her heart thumping so hard against my back, forcing my decision.

"Head her off," I said. "I'll get out."

I waited while she walked out of the house, until she went up to Sarah, stopping her in the middle of the road on the way to the house. Their shadows met, their heads touched. For minutes they talked before walking off. When they had disappeared behind a row of houses farther down, I went out the back, got into the car, and with lights out drove onto the road. Cutting off the engine I coasted until reaching the shading woods where Ann and I had played that simple game of hide-and-seek a long while back. I parked.

And sitting in the dark, staring out at the tiresome darkness, I felt a weight fall over my shoulders. Goddamn. As quick a visit as I had ever made—anywhere. Two days driving, then in and out of my own home—in less time than it takes to tell it—and Janie (I had finally put a name to my tall niece gone fleshy about the hips and tits) had not even had the grace to greet me proper. They had gone past the time of needing me or my money. Sally all over again.

Knowing that I sat twisting the picture to feed my pain didn't lessen the pain. I wanted to cry. But lonely folks are empty folks. They have no business crying. They need to be mad. So instead of going on to Mildred's (the Lord knows, I wasn't about to support being pushed around one more time—whatever the reasons), I started up the car and drove over Miss Jessica's way.

The darkness was as firm and black as coal when I turned down the road I thought I wanted. Hard to tell. My headlights made mountains out of small mounds of mud, forests out of clumps of trees, deserts I swear I had never before seen out of patches of open spaces.

Bumping along the gutted mud road, the car rocked. All its parts rattled, forcing me to drive slow while I peered beyond to lights shining here and there through the darkness. Not too many. Country folks believed in getting out of bed with the sun, working along with the sun, and going to bed when the sun got tired. But as I drove, wondering if perhaps I had turned wrong, shadows got to detaching themselves from shadows to fall in the path of my headlights, only to disappear. Then out of the dark my perked-up ears commenced to pick up words:

"Yeah—that her. I swear it is."

Expecting the worst thing possible, and being too tired to give a damn, I kept rolling, until the shadows got busier, slipping out of darkness, slipping out of darkness. Then I stopped.

"Miss Dorine. . . ?" A shadow walked into my headlights—a broad-shouldered, gentle-voiced shadow—came to stand alongside.

"Yeah—that's me."

"Ma'am . . . I think you'd best wait right here. Turn the car round. You won't be able to go further."

"You know Mr. Davis?" I asked.

"Yes'm. Mast' Davis back at Old Man Johnson—down near the creek."

I opened the door to get out. He closed me back inside. "Don't you worry none, ma'am," he said. "Just go on—turn the car around. We'll fetch him. . . ."

He disappeared while I was turning the car. I sat looking at cigarettes glowing out of the dark, not too far from me, trying to make out the forms around them. So—they had expected me? How? Janie? Hardly. More likely some of those slipping and sliding eyes had recognized me when I drove through town. But how to tell I'd end up here?

"Ma'am, can I have your key?" The big feller reappeared at my side. I handed him the car keys then sat stone-faced, staring out at the glowing cigarettes, feeling movements at the back of the car, hearing whispers. . . . The trunk of the car slammed shut and the voice spoke again in my ear:

"Here your keys, ma'am. Don't you worry none. I'll be following right behind."

I started the car and drove off. A truck about to fall to splinters as it hit the bumps on the muddy road rattled behind, following. We drove without lights, leaving the dark country behind, then leaving the sleeping town behind, then the swimming pool at the edge of town, its waters still, shining under the bright lights around it. We drove for almost one half-hour and were already deep in the pine forest when the lights of the truck went on. I pulled over.

"Ma'am, can I have your key?" The big man appeared at the window. Once again I handed him the key. And sitting there I looked out trying to see the draping vines again—trying to imagine the way they had looked earlier. But in the dark the ivy had lost substance—and so meaning. What I did feel in the darkness was the overpowering strength of the tall pines. Their sharp, clean fragrance ladened the air. I closed my eyes, breathing deep, remembering how they were long before.

My eyes were still closed when the door opened to my right and someone slipped into the seat beside me. The gentle voice spoke from my left.

"Ma'am, I'll be stopping off here. Good journeying to you."

I took the keys and drove off. But I kept watching his big frame at the open door of his truck; and I kept looking at the lights of his truck until they were but pinpricks in my rearview mirror.

Only then did I notice how hot and clammy my hands were on the wheel, how cold and thick sweat stood out on my brow, and how my foot pressing hard on the gas kept the nerves of my knees from jumping. I had seen no sheriff, no lynching; no gun had been pointed my way, no one had even threatened me—not by a look or sworn word. Yet I had seen the last of Montgomery. My heart ached with that knowledge.

Scared? There might have been reason for fear. But fear I was used to. I had always had the courage to deal with fear. Something else had happened to me back there. The house? Janie? I had been a stranger. The smells of the house had changed. More than the fear, the silence, the smells had not caught me to it. They had pushed me away—a stranger. Had the time I spent in jail put that kind of distance between me and my home? I had to think it out. But even without thinking, I knew the distance would take more than a car ride to bridge.

"Damn, Brother." I spoke without looking at the man beside me, needing the familiar sound of my own voice. "I expected a short trip home. But not this damn short, not this goddamn final."

3

I woke and stared at the hand on the wheel of the car—long, clean, well cared for—doctor-looking hands. The gold wedding band and gold watch made it look like anything but belonging to a man making a getaway in the trunk of a car. I moved. Every muscle of my body put up a squawk. I opened and closed my hands to get them to working, wiggled my toes to force my sleeping legs awake, twisted my shoulders to work out the kinks (had I actually come to this?). My neck refused to turn. I cocked my head to the side to get my first look at Brother. I had to have been damn near dead to give over the car and not remember.

I waited for the blood to start waking up my limbs before saying: "Now Brother, you gonna tell me what that was all about?"

"What all?"

"All that damn finagling and shit going on back there," I said.

"Nothing. I hadn't expected you to come down when I called Sonny. Seeing you did—it was as good a time as any to get going." He smiled, exposing gold-crowned teeth curving out. They made him look brassy. His natural white ones had given such a look of sweetness.

"But you did call. . . ."

"So that you would be expecting me—sometime. Hungry?" He pointed to the back. I turned to see a big brown bag on the seat. I wanted to ask where he had stopped, but seeing we hadn't come to D.C. yet, decided against it. He had probably done the "right" thing and waited at the back of some cracker joint to get served. "Like a dog," I answered.

He pulled the bag to the front. For the next few minutes, biting into a roast pork sandwich kept me quiet. Then seeing he wasn't about to offer any explanations on his own, I had to ask. "Brother, why'd they chase you out of Montgomery?"

"I wasn't chased, Dorine," he said. "I left. I decided it was better to leave—unnoticed, that's all. Your coming made it easy. No hard feelings, no questions asked. . . ."

I know a lie when I hear one—at least the stretching of things to sound the way it ain't. And when he had given it a little thought, he saw too: "The sheriff's been wanting to have words with me—I didn't think it wise right now."

All that secretiveness? All them scared folks? The whispering—just to get out unnoticed? "Disappearing in the trunk of a car's the same as being chased, to me, Brother." Brother only smiled like he was playing school, with him being the teacher and me the child. So I said: "Thought you was all set with your big-time teacher job."

He hesitated a bit too long before saying: "I lost my job, Dorine."

"Lost your job? With all that education you done got?"

"Kicked out."

"But Brother, wasn't that job supposed to last you for life?" I kept looking at his hands on the wheel, thinking about the education that ought to have made him a doctor.

"Well—it didn't. . . ." The long fingers tapped the wheel. I sure liked the look of his hands. "I—I—the president of the college and I didn't agree. He didn't take to the idea of my organizing sharecroppers."

"You? Organizing sharecroppers? To do what, Brother?"

"To vote."

"To vote? He kicked you out of your good-paying teaching job on account of that?"

"Yes."

316

"But I thought that president of your college was a black man."

"He is. But the white directors control. They didn't think I was doing a wise thing."

"Me neither," I said. "If you had to organize, it ought to be for some act of mercy—like tracking down crackers and putting them out of their misery." Brother laughed the clear, healthy laugh of an honest man.

"That kind of thinking comes from living too long in the North, Dorine. Always jumping to violent solutions for problems which can be thought out."

"And was you thinking them out, Brother?"

"Yes."

"Then how come none of those I left behind is near being solved? And how come you hot-tailing it out of 'Bama? Sure all you was doing was thinking?"

"I'm a very cautious man, Dorine."

"Like that black president of your school."

"He had his job to think about," Brother said, in a pleasant, forgiving voice.

"You mean if *you* had his job—you'd have been only thinking about the job?"

"I *don't* have his job, Dorine. At any rate, I can't see shaking a tree if its fruit aren't ripe."

"But you ain't shook no trees, Brother. All you did was think and here you are sitting next to me. . . . What if you had organized them sharecroppers? You'd think them into the polling place expecting crackers to think them welcome. . . ?"

"I didn't realize how upset the white folks were. I guess they thought I'd rile up the farmers—getting them to act like those northern black soldiers who used to be stationed down here raising hell."

"What do black soldiers have to do with it, Brother?"

"They used to come into Montgomery, during the war—go into restaurants, knowing they wouldn't be served—then trying to start a riot when they weren't. They'd try to go into the front door of places, knowing they were supposed to be going through the back. They thought they could change things—just because they wore a uniform."

"I reckon most of those black soldiers stationed down here was born here—least their mamas were. Why shouldn't they try to change things?"

"They forgot what the South is about, Dorine." Brother puckered his brow at the road. "They conjure up some strange notion that living in the North makes them bigger than they are. But they're still nothing but black men."

"How you mean, nothing but, Brother?"

"What I said, Dorine," he answered in a calm, soft voice. "Nothing but black men—niggers trying to act bad."

For seconds I held still, a real thrill of anger going through me. Hell, even Brother must have heard about the black soldiers who had gone back home and had had their eyes gouged out with hot irons—even been lynched for trying to sit on the front seat of a bus— and they had been from the *South*.

I looked at his hands again. I really liked those hands. I glanced down at his tweed jacket, which had shed its wrinkles from time in the trunk. He looked proper. His face, all calm—yeah, he actually looked intelligent. "Brother," I said, "you so worried about how them crackers feel. You sure you had the time to worry about them sharecroppers?"

"Do you know how many sharecroppers there are, Dorine? Can you imagine the power we can wield, if we had the vote?"

"That sounds like you might be trying to change things, Brother."

"The South has its own tempo, Dorine. Things will change. We will change it—in our time."

"Seems we done give it a lot of time, Brother. Our lifetime."

"You didn't." He spoke calm, smiling superior. "You left."

Blackmail! Folks down home liked to beat those of us who left with that, trying to shame with those words. "Goddamn right I left," I snapped. Then remembering how he had tried to stop me from leaving the house the night of Big Willie, I turned spiteful: "Guess I never did believe that the safest place is the darkest, Brother." Then we both gave our attention to the road.

After a few minutes had passed he said, "That's what worries me about Son." His soft tone told me he hadn't thought enough of our disagreement to be mad. I doubted he had even heard what I said.

318

"What about Son?" I should have stayed around to find out. But that quiet old house had told me he wasn't there.

"His bull-headedness. God knows what new notions he'll be coming home with."

"The war's been over more than a year, Brother. Why ain't he home?"

"He had a special detail after the war. But he's on state side now. Guess he's bumming around trying to get things together. I'm glad. Better than him rushing home with new ideas, trying to raise hell. Those northern boys—"

"Tell me one thing, Brother." Seemed we had one disagreement an hour. "Is it because black soldiers didn't go in the back door of stores, is it because I left home when I was real young, or is it because Son might go back and start a li'l hell-raising that that black president of your college kicked *your* butt out of your high-paying-supposed-to-last-a-lifetime job?"

Then we were home. I opened the door, Brother stepped into the apartment, and right away it looked like it was supposed to. It had only needed a man to make it work out—a tall, quiet-spoken man, no matter he was only a brother or that he looked intelligent and talked like a fool.

I took him from one room to the next, showing off the place, priding myself on how good my taste. "So, you're home now," I said. "What do you think?"

"Nice view." He squinted out of the side of the window to see the park.

"It's grand from the roof," I said, liking the way the sun came slicing between the blinds, changing the color of the crystal vase on the lovely old antique sideboard.

"Which room is mine?" he asked.

"Which one do you want?"

"What about the studio, in the back?"

"Any one but that one," I surprised myself by saying. "That one's been spoken for."

He shrugged. "The one next to it will do."

He had begun to walk around the room, all restless. Fingering things. Then he stopped in front of the pictures of Dr. Du Bois and Booker T. He laughed. "Did you put these two together to bring their points of view closer?" he asked. "You do know they disagreed," he said. "Violently."

Not wanting him to start my back to raising again with his tone of knowing all, I stopped him in my best sugary voice. "Brother, this man"—I pointed to the picture of Dr. Du Bois—"is a good friend of mine. We used to hang out together in The Club, uptown. And you know I just had to have old Booker T., him coming from 'Bama. And talking about 'Bama—I sure went a long way not to meet your wife."

"You'll be crazy about her." He started walking around again. "She's real good people."

"And your daughter?"

"Ellen?" His eyes brightened behind his gold-framed glasses. "A smart child. Wait until you meet her. . . ." Knowing I had paid my absolute last visit to the South, I started wondering which might be the best room for her.

Brother sat down, clasping his hands behind his head, and leaned back against the couch. "I'll be staying a spell, Dorine." But I had already figured that one out. "That is if you don't mind." I had just gone down to bring his skinny butt north. He had to know I wanted him. He crossed, then uncrossed his thin, long legs. "And while I'm here—I-I-I thought I'd like to take a few courses—in law . . . at Columbia. That is, if you can stand it, Dorine."

If I could stand it! Brother had been working at his high-paying school job for years. I looked at his expensive tweed, then at the gold watch. I opened my mouth to question him, then closed it. Asking had to bring on the small talk—his new house; family expenses. . . .

"I know I took more advantage of our agreement than was originally intended," he said.

"A-men," I agreed. He hurried to add:

"But these courses are important to me." In less time than it had taken him to walk through the house, it had begun to matter that he was there. I nodded okay. I had paid for a lot more in life, and got a lot less. Still I had to let him know—he was no trickster and I was no sucker.

"Columbia?" I said. "That will mean you'd have gone to every school there is, and learned just about everything taught, won't it, Brother?" He roared laughing—I right along with him.

A schoolteacher. That's what Brother had made himself into. I suppose in a classroom he was a damn good one. He believed in what he said. It made the house a better place to live in when I agreed with him. So I did—until the day he came home late from his classes to let me know: "Dorine, I never met Sonny before."

I looked up from my cooking to see him, hands behind his back, head bowed, walking around the kitchen.

"How'd you know where to find him?"

"Telephone. I always called him when you were away."

"Yes—so you did," I said. He sat down and his face had become so serious, I decided to sit across from him to see what was ailing him. I just hoped Sonny hadn't been simple enough to tell him I had done time. Brother tapped the table with his long, pure-looking fingers.

"He's quite a man, that Sonny," he said. "I like him."

"Do tell."

"He's the one—isn't he, Dorine?"

"The one? What one, Brother?"

I kept looking at Brother looking at me. Then I heard him. My eyes popped wide to warn him: change that subject. But Brother took his teaching damn serious. He kept tapping the table (that must have been the way he drummed things into his students' heads), peering from those eyes—small behind their thick-lensed, gold-framed glasses.

I had spent so many years supporting Brother—years when he moved around in the background, all quiet, studying—I kept forgetting that he was of my generation, not Jennie Mae's and Lil's. But remembering, my eyes went cold to give him the message: a feller whose ass I had cared for, was still taking damn good care of, had as much right to question me as he had of questioning the workings of the Almighty.

"I had never actually met Sonny," he repeated.

"So Brother," I snapped at him. "You met him, so what?"

"Don't you think he ought to know, Dorine?" He took off his glasses, wiped them, put them on as though to see me better.

"Know what, Brother?" I bassed my voice to street. Even Brother had to understand that language. But damn the sucker was brave, for all his skinny schoolteacher-looking self.

"That he has a son, Dorine."

I thought of the last time I saw Son, the round butter-ball. I wondered if I'd ever see him again. If I didn't why cross tongues with Brother? But my habit was secrecy. Son, as far as I was concerned, had been Janie's baby since I left him with her. She had accepted it. Joseph had wanted it that way. The girls, Son, didn't know any better. Even Mildred with her half-crazy self had seen fit to accept the arrangement. Now Brother with his know-it-all self. What if Son did come home? I saw Brother as good as anything saying: You know, Son, your sisters are not your sisters. . . .

I kept my eyes steady on Brother. "Who has a son? Sonny? Do tell."

"Oh come off it, Dorine. Anyone seeing those two would know. I have never seen any two people who look more alike. What if Son comes here?"

"If he ain't been here all this time, he ain't about to."

"I wouldn't be too sure." He kept tapping his fingers on the table, trying to drum his understanding through my head. "Folks will talk, Dorine. I think it best for you to talk to Sonny and—"

"Talk, talk, talk. That's all you do, Brother. What's folks talking got to do with what you're saying? Talking don't make things so if they ain't."

"But it is so, Dorine," Brother insisted. "It will help if you do explain—"

"Brother, all your talking ever got you was to have your black ass chased out of Montgomery."

"We're talking about different things, Dorine."

"No, we ain't. We talking about talking," I said. "And right now we talking about your black ass being chased out of the one place you want the most to be—because of talking—even though you stood as much chance of being listened to as a tear in the eye of a hurricane stood of being seen." It got to me. I never agreed with Brother. I pretended to—he being so educated. But if his next words weren't to my liking, he had had the best of my acting.

The doorbell rang. I left him tapping his finger on the table and fumbling in his simple mind for the right words to dispute me—words for which I could have no come-back—he thought. Going to the door, I yanked it open. Then for the longest time I just stood. Frog-eyes stared into frog-eyes. The man before me was not so tall as Brother, nor near as thin—and a hell of a lot younger. Round black

322

face, with shining cheeks pushed up in a grin that started beneath a bushy mustache. Finally I moved my eyes away from his face, to examine his body—a soldier's uniform.

"Son. . . ?"

4

I guess I always loved him more than the rest, without actually acknowledging it. I understood him more. He didn't have to explain to me why he hadn't gone right home, or why once he got there he hadn't stayed. I knew. But Brother didn't. Every time they talked Brother kept after him:

"Straggling, Son. That's what they call it. After that special detail that kept you in service after the war, why didn't you get home?"

"Like I said, Brother. I was trying to think things out."

"That's a lot of thinking, Son. Over a year? All that time to make up your mind?"

"I still haven't made it up," Son said.

"Then you go home and just leave?"

"I know I was wrong to cut out without saying something to the folks," Son said, looking across the kitchen table at Brother. His big eyes young in their blue-whiteness bulged, not blinking. "But Brother, I keep telling you, if I had stayed in 'Bama, I'd have been dead—and more'n likely taken a mess of crackers along with me."

"That kind of talk comes from spending too much time with northern boys." Brother drummed the table with his fingertips.

"Why northern boys?" Son said. "Southern boys got feelings too." I guess my feeling for Son kept growing because we shared the burden of Brother's backwardness. "You tell him about it," I said. "I been trying to."

"Deep feelings," Brother nodded, agreeing. "But we Southerners learn to use our feelings and not let them get out of hand and use us."

"Don't know about that, Bro." Son shook his head. "Everything's inside us to use—when the time comes." His open face, his smile carried as much weight as Brother's drumming fingers.

"Remember Sylvester Willis?" he asked. "Boy used to box in the back of the dry-goods store to please them crackers?"

"He got killed over there, didn't he?" Brother said.

"I was with Syl when it happened." Son's smile showed pain. "We were out in this field talking—about Montgomery. Syl had just said: 'Man, ah used to let them mu' fuckers rub mah head for good luck, then ah'd try to kill mah best buddy to give it to them. When ah gits back,' he said, 'ah'm gonna shave off all this hair, walk down the middle of Main, and say to dem crackers: Step up for one good rub. The first one to touch this head will get real good luck—right between the eyes.' "

"Then Sylvester Willis was due to die, wasn't he?" Brother asked. But before Son could answer, the telephone rang and I went out into the hall to answer.

"Dorine." It was Tom. "Look, got a call from this woman Dot—one what stays with Bessie? Says Bessie's gone to the sanatorium—TB. I'd go in a minute, Dorine, but these feets. . . ."

Since Brother and Son had come I had pushed all thoughts of Chicago and Bessie out of my mind. But whether Tom went or not, I had to. Bessie was my best buddy.

I went back to the kitchen and stood in the doorway hearing Son say: ". . . and we heard the planes. We both dived for our foxhole. I made it. And squinching there, listening to bombs exploding, I kept feeling drip, drip, drip on my helmet. When the planes had gone I looked up. . . . Syl hadn't made it. He lay over me on the bank, his brains spattered every whichaway. . . . It was his blood dripping on my head."

I wanted to go to him, pull his head to my chest, comfort him. But his arms lay on the table, the black skin pulled smooth over its hard muscles. His shirt, open at the neck, exposed ropes of veins—and his eyes. . . . He didn't need me. It came to me then that when I got back he might be gone. My apartment would seem empty again. I'd be alone again. I couldn't stand that. I searched my mind to find

words—the right ones—to make *him* responsible for my well-being—
for my *life*.

"Seeing Syl's brains spattered like that," Son said, "cured me
of fear. Before, I'd be too scared to date a white chick, in Paris—
scared some cracker might not like it. My back always felt as wide
as the side of a barn—exposed. After Syl got his, I went wherever I
wanted and with whoever I damn pleased. I quit looking over my
shoulder, my back stopped quivering. That, Brother, was when I
knew I had lived my entire life afraid.

"What a feeling, Brother, to walk down a street without a
prayer locked in my brain. What a great thing not to have to put my
fate in the hands of some God, that he keep a white sucker's intentions pure.

"Dorine." Son looked at me. "Just think, not to walk around
chained to the whim of some unknown God. Then, Brother—I
stepped off that train in Montgomery, took two steps, and voom—
right back on my back—fear. . . ."

I stilled the fear of Son's having blasphemed to say: "Them
crackers can squeeze it outa you like you was a beet."

"Worse," Son kept on. "Because I was scared, I wanted to prove
I wasn't. I felt the need of taking a gun and start to blasting.
So I left."

"Then you did the right thing, Son," Brother said. "But I think
that what you're doing is mistaking caution for fear."

"Brother, I was *scared*. We were born scared. We grew up
scared. You got to lose something before you can miss it. I lost fear
on the battlefield—and found it back in Montgomery."

"Brother's scared too," I said, waving Brother still. "That thing
he calls caution is nothing but plain old-fashioned rabbit-ass scared.
Anyway, Son, it was best that you did come. They'd have kept their
eyes on you knowing you had been over there killing up crackers."

"I wasn't killing crackers, Dorine. I was fighting Germans,"
Son said. "They were the enemy."

"Do tell."

"Yes, you got to have heard about the Germans, invading Europe." His eyes slid from mine, ashamed of my ignorance. "You got
to have heard about them killing the Jews."

But that had been happening long before I got locked up. I

wanted to tell him that Bilbo and Talmage had been my enemies when I went in and Bilbo and Talmage were my enemies when I got out.

"But Son," I said, "ain't it the Japs they done drop that atom bomb on?"

"They were the enemy too, Dorine," Son said. "They attacked us, remember?"

I held back from telling him that I had never heard of Pearl Harbor before going to jail and I could lay him odds that he hadn't either. "But Son," I said, real gentle. "If the Germans and Japs were the enemy—how come you was so scared to stay home?"

Son's head jerked up. He snatched my hand and squeezed. Seeing his face so shiny and pleased with me, it came to me: I might have hugged him, but I had never kissed that pretty round face on my visits home. I missed not having kissed him.

The telephone rang. Brother stood up to answer. He was already at the door when Son said, "But I intend to go back."

"When?" Brother spun around in the doorway.

"Dunno." Son shrugged. "When I makes a heap of money—and when folks like you start throwing caution to the wind."

"That," Brother said, "is not likely."

Someone had tried to change Bessie's style, I noticed when I walked into her living room. The curtains blowing in at the windows were the popular see-through white. Bessie had always had loud eye-catching curtains, printed fruits and flowers dancing at the windows when the wind blew at them. Her blood-red, mohair couch and stuffed chairs had withstood the years of use, though. And her bright-colored silk flowers remained still in their vases, unbending, promising their intention of being around after folks like us had long gone.

"You remember me?" the woman Dot asked. I should have. She remembered me. Plump, brown-skinned, ordinary—and looking as though she had always looked ordinary. Most unlikely kind to stay on my mind.

"Sure, I remember," I said. Then on a hunch: "You're from Bessie's hometown, ain't you?"

"Yeah—sure you remember."

"So, tell me about Bessie."

"Well—you know Bessie," she said. "She been sick, and just hanging around. Wouldn't see a doctor till she got to spitting blood. He sent her right off."

Sitting on the blood-red couch, eyes closed, I kept listening to the front door open and close, to footsteps going up and down the steps, to footsteps over my head, promising to wear holes in Bessie's never-to-be-worn-out rugs.

"How long since Bessie's been taking in roomers?" I asked.

"Oh, been years now—three, maybe even four."

Loneliness—that's why Bessie had opened up her house to strangers. She hadn't needed money. And why not? I, who had loved living alone when we had first met—except for my next bed partner—had just about died from loneliness. Why not loud-talking, loud-laughing, gay Bessie? She had always liked a roomful of folks around.

"That feller—Albert?" The tone of her voice caused my eyes to pop, trying to stop her. Whatever she had to say, she was out of line. She had no right talking about folks she had only known through Bessie's charity. "He hung around for a time. But you know how wild Bessie be sometimes, hee-hee."

Goddamn ordinary son of a bitch, wouldn't know a dirty look if it was hot piss in her eyes. ". . . Bessie took a pistol one day, she cocked it at old Albert's head. Man took off—must be running still, hee-hee. . . ."

I turned from her to look into the dead fireplace, and memories—loud, gay memories—leaped out to dance over the walls. Fingers jumped to the piano; a boater, bow tie, and walking stick moved around the floor doing the soft shoe. . . .

Albert. My chest heaved. That pistol had been cocked at his head the day he had chosen to stay with Bessie—the day he had thought he was big enough to fill Bill's shoes. And weren't we all to blame? Rushing, rushing, rushing back to Harlem—scared that it might sink into the sea. But Harlem had outlasted a-many and was due to outlast what was left of us. Albert—those dead-giveaway eyes. He might have fooled himself about his intentions, he sure hadn't fooled us. I pushed the picture of him huddled in the

327

corner of the limousine at Sally's funeral from my mind.

"Got a place to put me up?" I asked.

"Sure do. Bessie always keeps rooms ready for you—and that feller, Tom."

The sanatorium on the outskirts of the city had the drab look of cleanliness, with its white marble floors and white walls, and the smell of disinfectant. Worse, the doctors and nurses, the attendants had their uniforms covered with antiseptic gowns. They wore masks hanging around their necks, or covering their noses, forcing thoughts of germs, of infections, of death, to jump to mind. So did the patients shuffling around corridors in disposable gowns and robes, padding soft as kittens. Condemned to death by that king of all diseases: TB.

Outfitted in a gown and mask too, I got out of the elevator and set out to find Bessie's room. I searched through long wards, where patients lay in a stillness akin to death. I lost my way along corridors that branched into other corridors leading to other wards, walking past folks, their bodies bent, holding themselves up along the walls—and it seemed to me after a spell that half the black population of Chicago had been confined to that sanatorium. Whites were there too—there being more white folks in Chicago than blacks. But I do declare, if it was a race, blacks sure were the clear winners. But all—blacks and whites—wore the mark of waiting, of marking time on their faces, their wasted bodies.

When I had just about given up on ever finding Bessie, I came to the room that bore the number on my card, opened the door, stood in the doorway, and burst out laughing:

Bessie had to be the blackest and brightest somebody that hospital had ever seen. She sat up in bed, a royal blue quilt drawn up over her legs, wearing a bright orange-yellow gown, and around her head she had tied an orange-yellow satin bow. "Goddamn, mama," I said, still laughing as I walked up to her. "If you ain't the damndest, prettiest sight ever. Do you know I damn near wrecked my car getting out here? Thought you was ready to breathe your last—and just look at you."

"Honey, I'm just about ready for Freddy," she said. "Just been holding him off waiting for you."

"For me?"

328

"Yeah, you—or Tom—or the both of you. Got to have somebody to bury me."

I sat next to the bed and took off the mask to show her anything that might take her off could have me too. "That ain't why I come, to sit here with you, waiting on Freddy. I come to take you out of here and home."

"No, baby doll," she said, shaking her head. "Home for me is that li'l piece of ground I bought next to Bill in the cemetery."

"That why you got yourself up so fancy, mama? To be put in the ground?"

"Might as well go purty," she said. "Lived purty all my life. . . ." We laughed and she said: "Hell, Dorine, I made me enough dough in this life to pay somebody to keep me looking this good while I wait for the undertaker man."

"I see you still talking on account you loves the sound of your voice," I said.

Bessie had shrunk even to her titties. Sitting up in bed she looked as slight as a fourteen-year-old. Her cheeks had sunk, and despite her years, the skin had pulled beneath her cheekbones to smoothness. Her eyes, feverish bright, were still full of mischief. Her hair, except for the few strands pulled loose to tie with the ribbon, had matted to her head (nurses think they get burrs in their fingers if they comb black patients' hair).

Seeing me looking at her head, Bessie shook it. "No, ain't nothing you can do about these naps except cut them off. And I ain't got the strength to hold still to let you. I'm too near the end."

"A hell of a way to greet a feller who come this far to say hello."

"I known you'd come, Dorine. I was just praying you'd hurry."

"Keep on talking. Before you know it, I might even believe you," I said.

"I thought first of getting laid in the same hole—right on top of Bill," she said. "But then that sure wouldn't be decent in the face of the Lord. . . ."

We laughed. Bessie started coughing. Her body shook. She spat blood into the basin on the table at her bedside. Any hope I had that she might come out of it died then. I believed her, even before she lay back on her bright, royal blue pillow, her face gray, as she waited for breath to push back through her body.

The other women—there were three of them in that room, two of them black, one white—had turned from us because of Bessie's coughing. And as they lay, backs exposed to us in their open-backed hospital gowns, staring into their own futures, I knew that my coming had robbed them of Bessie. Miserable creatures. They had to be glad to have Bessie. Bright, happy Bessie, she made being with her worth the trip—even that last one. Out of the window, sea gulls floated in the distance, circling, circling, ready to land somewhere on Lake Michigan. Did sea gulls catch TB?

". . . Any old who," Bessie said, her face brightening, "that ain't the way Bill and me did it. We weren't no freaks. We went in for straight up-and-down fucking. We loved it that way. . . .

"Ain't it a bitch, Dorine?" She grinned, winked. "That pretty, big thing, all shriveled and waiting between that man's legs— and I ain't gonna get none. . . . Putting all that ground between, on account of I'm a religious woman. . . . Got to opt for them gates. . . ."

She laughed. But she had set the tone for the days I had to spend with her (short moments because she didn't have strength for long talks). But it had been her tone. She had lived by it. I had known her that way. Why change? Why cry? Why moan? Why damn things that neither one of us knew what to do about? We had never been that kind of women. I tried to make sure that we kept on being the kind of women we had always been. . . .

"What's Tom doing these days?" Bessie asked, after the matter of business had been put behind us.

"Tom? He's getting old, girl. Simple. He's done made his stuffed chair into his rocking chair. Cranky! Fretting. All hepped up since this young feller—Jackie Robinson—signed up to play with the Dodgers."

"What he got against colored boys making money?"

"Swears the boy's a sellout to the race."

"Seems like Tom would be proud of having a colored boy show up them whites."

"Honey, Tom gets so mad when he thinks of it, gets right blue in the face. He declares it's the end of our colored baseball leagues."

"Because of one colored boy?"

"To hear Tom tell it. Girl, I pays Tom no mind. All he's doing is sitting in that ole rocking chair getting old, evil, grumbling of the past, while this young thing—I declare, Bessie, she's young 'nough to be his gran—goes through his money like a maggot going through a pile of shit."

"Who? Cheap Tom?"

"The one and the same."

"What 'bout you, Dorine. Been working?"

"More or less. Family started dropping in—first Brother, then Son."

"Lordy, Dorine you and them kids—after all these years. . . ."

"Ain't no better way to get them than when you ain't got to change shitty drawers," I joked. "Anyhow, I'm having a natural ball."

"Who'd have thought it?" Bessie shook her head. "Kitchen mechanic at your age."

"Yeah—I'm rattling them pots," I said. "But only for a while. I'm thinking of looking around for something legal—know what I mean? Son—remember Sister's oldest boy? Well, he calls himself wanting to study engineering—under the GI Bill. Ever heard of a black boy being an engineer?"

"I sure ain't," Bessie said, trying to tie the bow that had become untied. Seeing how her hands were shaking, I took over, tied it, then held on to her dried-out, cold hands.

"Way I sees it," I said, "I got to get on to something before Son finishes school. I'd hate for him to finish and then find that even a war ain't made engineering work for blacks."

"He's got to find that out hisself, don't he?"

"And blow his brains out? He ain't like Brother, you know. Brother don't like nothing better than a blackboard and ruler—not even pussy."

"But Son's damn near grown, ain't he, Dorine? Got to be at the very least twenty-two."

"That don't make him grown, Bessie."

"Hon-ey," Bessie said, trying not to look serious. "In my country men thinks they's grown even when they eighteen. Bet Son's even got hisself a chick," she said. "Chicks don't go for in-laws doing the planning for their men."

Laughter dried on my face. Heat flooded it. Surprised that I got mad, Bessie pulled her hands from mine.

"Dorine, the kind of planning you're thinking of is the kind of planning women do with their *men*. Time you ought to have got all the way behind a guy was behind Harry. You was young then. You all could have had one hell of a life. Know what I mean?"

I didn't. Neither did I like her tone. "I went all the way with Harry, Bessie. He was my man."

"Did you for real, Dorine?"

"You got to know that, Bessie. I loved Harry same's you loved Bill."

"No you ain't." Her hot eyes flashed at me. "I ain't never had no limits when it come to Bill."

I didn't believe my hearing. All those years? She had been wearing laughter like a mask, to hide her true feelings? Then why had I left my home—Son—to sit at the bedside of a stranger?

"Bessie." Fighting to keep from shouting kept my voice at a whisper. "I couldn't stop Harry's dying. He was dying when I met him."

"Ain't we all dying, Dorine?" Bessie's chest heaved. I sat back out of reach of the breath, fanning my face, and raised my eyes to the window. In the distance sea gulls, wings flapping, floated, and as I looked at them Bessie's voice reached me where I stood, outside of myself, at the door of Harry's slum apartment. Once again I walked through the old house, its half-empty rooms, its run-down kitchen. But I didn't want to stay. I had to get out, to run, keep running. Only Linda's smile blocked me. Sass oozing out of Gogi's flat Chinese-looking eyes blocked me. . . . No, I had never been a mother. Not the kind you wanted—no more than to my own family. Maybe I didn't do the best I could by you. But I did what I knew how! I cared. Somebody had to care and I cared. Goddamit I had cared, cared, cared. . . .

". . . and it seems to me," Bessie said, breathing hard, "that you had tied your life to that man. So instead of spreading your money so thin—"

"Bessie, that ain't never been in my hands to decide. I did what I had to do—put my bets on *this* side of life."

"So now it's payback time—Son?"

Hadn't she heard me? Why didn't she want to understand? A

red mist rose before my eyes, blotting her out. Clown! Fucking clown: Had she looked into Linda's golden eyes, into Gogi's flat eyes, and seen only a goddamn rod? An underpaid cock? My hands tingled. I floated weightless toward her. No, fool! Son's no payback! Son's mine!

"Dorine." Bessie's laugh reached inside my head and turned off my switch. I saw her again, felt the sweat streaming down my face. "Lordy," she said. "We sounds like we 'bout ready to take off on one another. Girl, you got to know I loves you. What you done—a man couldn't—"

"Oh stop it, mama," I said, trying to laugh. "I ain't strong—"

"Sure you is, baby. A strong woman. How long was you and Harry together? Six years? It ought to have been longer—that's all. Made no sense for a pretty brown thing like you to be doing so much—and to be alone—know what I mean?"

Back at Bessie's that night, I felt as though I had taken one hell of a beating and had cried a week. I put a call through to New York: "Tom, you best be pulling them old bones together," I said. "Bessie ain't got long."

"How long you figger she got, Dorine?"

"Can't say. But she's into true confessions. Whenever you gets here won't be none too soon." Falling back on the bed, I got to wondering: What in the hell was all that about? Why had I got so hot with poor, black Bessie. After all, most things about myself had become clear to me—just then, and there.

When I got to the hospital the next day, the attendant was changing Bessie's bed sheets—moving her first to one side, then to the other. "My friend here." Bessie jerked her head at the woman. "She's a good Irish. I don't think she likes us much. But I pays her good money to keep your best friend smelling sweet, looking bright." Bessie wore red—gown and matching ribbon. The woman was making up the bed with yellow sheets. "Don't I?" Bessie winked. The woman went from white to red to white. "I pays her real good. And every day she takes my pretty things and washes them sweet. A natural doll." The woman patted Bessie's bow before leaving—a substitute for whatever expression she hid beneath her mask.

"The Lord don't like ugly," Bessie said. "So He seen to it I had me enough money to prepare the way I goes to meet Him."

I handed her the long green feather boa I had dug up from her closet. She took it smiling. I smiled. We burst out laughing.

"Dorine, weren't we something!" she said.

"A team," I agreed.

"*The* team. Class—nothing but class. . . ."

"Yeah—me with my highfaluting British accent. . . ."

"And me being fed to them whites. They thought niggers were all supposed to look like me—they'd be so busy laughing. They sure loves to laugh at us."

"Don't they though. . . ."

Our tone was light, determined that our last serious moments had been the last. "Times sure have changed, Dorine."

"Sure has, Bessie. I do believe that atomic bomb—"

"Ain't it the truth. Girl, I do declare the sun farted in the face of a full moon that year—turned everything upside down."

She wrapped the bright green boa around her neck and commenced to stroking it. "Yeah, something definitely happened that year—not for the good."

"Things sure ain't never gonna be the same."

"Hon-ey," Bessie said. "You ought to see the way folks celebrated that bomb—laughing, hugging, kissing. One bomb, millions dead, and folks just a-hugging and a-kissing. Blacks as well as whites, honey. Even that old simple Dot, coming in talking about how *we* control the world.

"Ordinary folks!" she said. "I ain't never one who likes ordinary folks, Dorine. Can't stand 'em. They is all killers—every one of 'em." She got quiet for a while, then: "One goddamn thing about us—all we ever was was some goddamn fine boosters." We cracked up laughing.

If laughing rushed Bessie along, I helped her on the way. I was anxious to get it over with. Since our argument, I had a real need to get back. To see Son. But I hid my need seeing her get weaker and weaker with all the laughing, the joking.

"What's old Sonny doing?" she asked. "Bet he's making it good."

"Yeah. I hear he's about to open up a new bar in Harlem. Harlem's where that fool belongs."

"I known he'd make it." Bessie said. "Dorine, maybe that's the man you should have hooked up with, after all. That Sonny, he never gives up."

"Bessie," I said. "You sure you wants me to bury you? Or do you want me to take you outa here and put you in a fucking nuthouse?"

She fell back laughing. When she tried to sit up this time, she didn't make it. Seeing her tired, I got up to leave. But she grabbed my hand and pulled herself up so that her face came next to mine, her gut-smell of sickness fanning my nose. "Dorine, I don't want none of them ordinary folks having nothing to do with burying me, you hear? Just you and Tom. Ordinary folks—they ain't got no understanding. . . ."

"You wants me to put one a them audacious hats on your head, too?" I joked.

"Girl, how else you gonna cover up this nappy head. . . ?" She fell back against her pillow, closed her eyes, and slipped into a coma.

I went to meet the plane Tom came out on (his first airplane ride). "I declare," he said, getting in beside me in the car. "Why ain't nobody ever tole me about this here flying? Beats trains—might even beat the hell outa driving. Easy on the mind and a damn sight easier on the feets. Dorine, you ought to try it."

"If God had meant me to fly He would have give me wings," I said.

"He sure the hell meant for me to walk, so how come He give me these bad feets. . . ?"

Bessie stayed in a coma for most of the time Tom stood at her bedside. I went around making her funeral preparations. We were both standing beside her when she opened her eyes and looked about her, wild-like, not knowing where she was. Then she saw us, winked, closed her eyes, and died.

We stood dry-eyed at her graveside. Her ordinary friends stood all around us, crying. We waited until they had gone, until her grave had been filled. Then we spread the flowers brought for Bessie to cover Bill's grave, making the two as much alike as circumstance allowed. When we left, I put my foot down on the gas, tearing through the distance.

And as we drove, the quiet in the car grew heavy. Wondering why Tom hadn't spoken, I glanced at him, sitting next to me, and surprised him eyeing me all evil, suspicious. Right away I saw into his simple mind:

Tom and I had been burying our friends so regular that it had become habit. Now there he sat, trying to figure out which one of us might be next. So deciding the time had come to hold a mirror to his rusty-assed, bad-footed self and put him in his place I said:

"Damn, Tom Rumley, ain't no sense in you sitting there, with your mouth poked out trying to give me no evil eye. You got to remember I was a lot younger than the youngest one a y'all when I got started. Hell, old red nigger, compared to you I'm damn near a baby." Then *I* got quiet feeding that Buick. Going home—getting back to my family.

5

Homekeeping. Years gliding into one another without confusion or crisis had never happened to me. That, I reckon, might be the reason I thought a lot about going into business yet never seriously made an effort—until the morning the doorbell woke me. I looked to the window. Dark. Thinking I had been dreaming I snuggled down beneath the covers. The bell rang again. I listened to hear footsteps—Son's or Brother's—in the hall. When I didn't, I turned on the bed light, looked at the clock. Four o'clock! The bell really got to ringing this time. I jumped out of bed and rushed to the door. "Who the hell is it?" I asked, bassing my voice.

"Dorine, it's me—Sonny."

"Sonny?"

I cracked open the door and peeped out. Sure enough, Sonny stood there looking as bad as I had ever seen him. It was snowing. His overcoat was wet and looked slept in. His usually smooth-shaven face had a two days' growth. "What the hell done happen to you?" I asked.

"Got to talk." He pushed by me into the apartment. "It's important."

"What's so damn important it can't wait till the light of day?" I said, but led him on into the bedroom. Getting into bed, I sat looking at him as he stood at the foot of the bed, hands in his pockets, jowls hanging loose from a face that had gone ash-gray. Sonny almost looked his age. "Dorine, I got to have ten grand—bad."

"What do I look like to you?" I asked. "Your mama?" I hadn't seen Sonny since I had first come out of jail. "Here I ain't seen you in all this time, and you come to be begging, as though I'm your fool."

"Dorine, it's my bar. I borrowed money from some loan sharks to open it. I ain't able to pay back. I'm in trouble, Dorine. Big trouble."

But I had heard the bar was jumping. Doing a big business. He had a live band. The place was called "the hottest spot on the avenue." "Why come to me? Why ain't you asked your ofay broad?"

"What ofay?"

"The one I seen you with in the Bronx."

"The Bronx?" It took him minutes of recall. "Woman, I ain't seen that broad in years. I swear. . . ."

"You got to have seen her since you seen me, old sucker."

"Look, Dorine, I ain't here to talk about no woman. I got to have some loot—and fast. . . ."

Desperate. If he had borrowed from loan sharks, that's what he had to be. Those popping eyes had bloodshot veins going every whichaway. "How much you owe the man?"

"He wants ten grand tonight." Ten minutes after four—that gave him time.

"I ain't asked how much he wants tonight. I wants to know how much you owe the man."

"Thirty grand. I borrowed twenty—but the interest. . . ."

Loan sharks had no friends. They didn't play. All Sonny's slipping and sliding, his fleshy smiles, blinking eyes, slick ways, didn't count. He had to deal with the slickest. I knew that. Sonny ought to have, too—before he went to borrow from them. "I'll give you the full thirty grand," I said. "Pay them slicksters off—get them off your butt for good."

"You will. . . ?" Right away, fifty pounds of weight slipped off his back; his wrinkles smoothed out, his gray face went to black again. "I'll pay you back, Dorine. I swear it. Every week I'll give something on it, until it's all paid up. You the one person in the world I can trust. I always known that." His fleshy smile came back, his big eyes teasing. . . .

"You don't have to pay me nothing by the week, Sonny, nor by the month." I smiled, teasing him back. "I'll give you all of two years—then I wants the whole thirty thousand."

"You sure you can stand it, Dorine?" he asked, reaching for my hand, holding it, rubbing his thumb over the back, tender-like.

"Sure, I'm sure."

"You know you the greatest woman I know? If there's something you ever want from me. . . ."

"No." I shook my head. "I don't want a thing, except the agreement you sign, saying you'll give me my money in two years, or I gets the bar."

"The bar! My bar!" His face went slack. "Woman, you got to be joking."

"You don't see me laughing."

"What makes you think I'm gonna sign my place over to you? I ain't asked you to give me nothing. I asked you to lend me."

"That's what I'm doing, Sonny." We went into staring at one another. "I ain't like them suckers what loaned you, either. I ain't asking for no interest."

"Dorine, you think you slick." Spittle sprinkled from his mouth. "But do I look your kind of damn fool? Those crooks ain't getting my place and you ain't either."

"You both crazy and a damn fool to wake me up in the middle of the night and ask me to hand you over ten grand."

Sonny waved his hand, knocking over the clock on the dresser. "Don't give me a thing," he said. "Keep your goddamn money!" He slammed out of the room. A second later I heard him slam out of the house. Picking up the clock, I turned it on the dresser to keep my eyes on it, then got back in bed.

"Who was that?" Brother said, coming into my room. "Sounded like Sonny."

"That's who it was."

"What was all the shouting about?"

338

"The first step in a business arrangement," I said.

"What kind of business?"

"Family business," I laughed. "Never know. You might get tired of school—one day."

"Don't get anything set up on my account," he said. "I'm going home."

"Home, Brother? When's this supposed to be happening?"

"My last day of school was today, Dorine. I'll be leaving for Montgomery next week."

"And it's now you telling me?"

"I was going to tell you tomorrow," he said. "But I guess this is just as good a time as any." Then seeing how upset I was, he added, "I thought you'd be happy, Dorine. Haven't I been living off you long enough?"

That he had. At forty, with a family (they had come to pay visits; his wife was damn near as big as me), and him staying in school taking from me to give to her, he had caused me resentment. But he didn't have to shock the hell out of me by ending it.

Forty-two years old, two men in my house, not one man in my bed, and happy. I had been happy. Brother saying he was leaving ought to have made me happy. It made me sad. It spoke of the beginning of an end. School was out, or about to be—for both of them. How much longer did Son have?

"However." I shrugged. "Whatever setting up I do, I'm taking you into account. School's out for good. You getting too damn old."

Without his gold-rimmed glasses to hide behind, Brother's eyes looked sunken, the skin around them dark, wrinkled. Standing there in his bathrobe without his tweeds, he looked just another tall, skinny, elderly man. He seemed ordinary . . . forgetful. Two years younger, he looked ten years older than me. He sounded older, too: "Dorine, you know how I hate to meddle," he said in the voice he used when he decided to meddle. "But I'm asking you again. Tell Sonny about Son—they're bound to meet, you know. For all you know, Dorine, they might take to each other."

"What has that got to do with me?" I snapped at him. "And what's it got to do with you?"

"What will you do—if they do meet?"

"Living life one step at a time has always stood me in good with the Lord, Brother."

He wanted to say more, so to stop him I said: "I never knew your neck was so skinny, Brother. It sure will look sad in a noose. . . ." He left to go back to his room and I settled down to get some sleep.

The bell rang again. I opened my eyes, looked at the clock. I had expected to get two hours' sleep—it had been only a little over an hour. I went to let Sonny in.

"Okay, Dorine," he said, following me into the bedroom. "I'll sign your ole piece of paper. But I still don't see why you got to be this hard on me."

"I ain't hard on you, Sonny. The man you owe that money to is the hard one."

"But you and me, Dorine. We friends—been friends."

"Friends, Sonny, we ain't been—not since you put me to jail and left me there to rot."

"What!" His eyes pushed out from not believing. "Dorine Davis, you ain't still talking about way back then?"

"I ain't never stopped thinking about way back then."

"Hell, that's been way over twenty years. We been buddies ever since. . . ."

"No we ain't, Sonny. We been a convenience to one another, never buddies."

He stared at me a long time before hunching his shoulders: "Okay, if I got to sign, I got to. Where's the paper?"

"Sonny, my lawyers got paper down at their office. We can use theirs when we gets there—later this morning."

"Lawyers! What damn lawyers?" His hands clinched and unclinched.

"I hope you ain't thought I'd just hand over thirty grand to you without my lawyers drawing up the papers. What you think I pays them for?"

"Since when you been having lawyers, Dorine?"

"Since I talked to you a li'l while ago, old nigger. I knew you'd be back. . . ."

It's all in knowing a feller. All I had to do was sit back and wait. . . .

Son went with me to see Brother off. Driving to Penn Station we were quiet for a long time, locked in with our thoughts. And then

Son said: "Well, Brother, staying with Dorine wasn't half bad, was it? Sure wasn't like when she'd come down home."

"No indeed," Brother said, teasing. "We wouldn't see Dorine for years, then there she'd be. Brown soap and lye in one hand, broomstick in the other, pointing, directing—do this, do that—work the hell out of us."

"Didn't she, though?" Son said, giggling. "She'd have folks run themselves dizzy—got the place so clean, we'd need sunglasses to find our way around, then wheeee," he whistled. "She'd be gone."

Both of them got to laughing at a joke I didn't see funny. "You ought to be glad I made you," I said. "Cleanliness is next to Godliness. I declare if I had let you live in the shit you all wanted, you'd never have made it."

"Dorine," Brother said, "I think we'd have managed."

"Oh, but we did," Son said. "The day Jennie Mae sold that old stove—remember how we all celebrated with Doctor Pepper?"

"My God," I said. "You all done sold that old stove!"

"Sure thing." Son kept laughing. "With all them newfangled gas and electric easy-to-clean ones on the market who was going to mess over that old grease catcher?"

So those smells in the old house, those smells that had nothing to do with Mama, with Janie, smells that had nothing to do with me, closing me out of my old home. They had sold the old stove.

Tears sprang to my eyes (I cry at the prick of a pin and they had broken my heart). "Dorine—what on earth would you have done with that old stove up here?" Brother asked, seeing my tears.

Didn't he understand? Didn't Son? We were close, Son and me. I thought we were.

We stood in that drafty old Penn Station, which offered only memories. Folks came, folks went their way, lived happy, unhappy, died, and the old Penn stayed big, ugly, and drafty. But the trains always came. Brother's did.

"Dorine. . . ." Brother's small eyes twinkled at me from behind his glasses—he sure would have made a good doctor; barring that, he would have made a good old teacher. An organizer. . . ? Those gentle, kindly eyes. . . . "You know I'm grateful—always will be. We might not always agree on things, but one thing we do- we are a loving family. . . ."

"That we do," I said. "Because Brother, if I could live forever,

I'd damn sure see to it that you stayed in school forever. But, you see, that ain't promised. . . ."

We all laughed. I hated to see him go. Whatever else, Brother was intelligent. I had always liked rubbing elbows with intelligent folks. "But you still got a chance, Brother. Go on back and grab your family and run. . . ."

"Dorine"—he pulled me to him, sweet, tender, loving. "I'm not leaving Montgomery, my wife's not leaving Montgomery, and my daughter's not leaving Montgomery. They might end up killing us, but they can't chase us. . . ."

"They're more likely to kill than chase you," I said. And as the train started moving off, I shouted: "But go to it. And if you got a second to spare before they tighten that noose, just let out one holler and we'll make it down in time to grab you and run. . . ."

"Don't you worry," he shouted back. "Always remember—your brother is a very cautious man. . . ."

"That he is," Son said as we walked back to the car. "A very cautious man. I'll never forget the night he kept you from opening up the shutters—the night of Big Willie? You went out of the door anyway—you and Ann. . . ."

"You can't remember that, Son. Somebody must have told you," I said. "You were just a li'l bit of a thing."

"That's actually my first remembrance," Son said. "I remember Jennie Mae and Janie, with me in the middle, squeezed into the same bed. Scared. When Miss Jessica ran out after you, I tried to get up. I wanted to go to Papa. But those girls just kept on squeezing and squeezing—liked to squeeze the life out of me. And I kept thinking of you—of the others, too, but mostly of you—out there getting killed. . . .

"I declare—thinking of that night always gives me a chill—excites me. Years later—overseas, advancing, in a dangerous situation—I'd think of you two out there, and I'd square my shoulders, stiffen up my spine. . . ."

Pain caused by boys is different from pain caused by men. It goes as deep and it's sharper. But their sweetness is so many times more sweet. Blood bubbled, flushing my cheeks.

". . . Sometimes awaiting an attack, I'd force myself to think up the bravest people I knew. And no matter what—and some of the men out there did some damn brave things—you always came out ahead—you and Ann.

"I often wondered if y'all were as scared out there as I was out there waiting. Were y'all just naturally brave, Dorine? Were y'all scared?"

Words jumped to mind to say that I agreed that, being born in the South, a day never passed without my being scared. Being always tensed up prepared me for my kind of work, or for heart trouble, or high blood. Then I thought of Ann running through strips of moonlight. I remembered how we walked arm in arm, feeling brave. And how the sound of Miss Jessica's running made her whip out that little pistol. . . .

"Well, Son," I said. "If we weren't scared when we set out, when we hit that old house coming back we were moving. Not a living soul heard from us that day. And that night when we lit out of town? Ain't nothing seen us but the wind, the moon, and them shading trees."

"A-men," Son said, and we shouted together, laughing.

The day my new car—a Lincoln Continental—was delivered I decided to drive by and give the "hottest spot in town" a look-see. The time had long gone when Sonny was supposed to have paid me back. I was in no rush: the reputation of Sonny's Bar on Seventh Avenue kept building, and Son still had school to finish.

The spot was hot—jumping, no question. Parking the car three-deep from the curb, I felt the ground rock beneath my feet. The place was so jammed, mashed potatoes had nothing on the folks squeezing in. I changed my mind about going in, then couldn't get out as folks behind me kept packing me into the smoke of that smoke-filled room. So I worked my way to the bar and called to the bartender: "Tell Sonny Dorine Davis is here and waiting." I managed to be heard after I had said it four times.

Then I leaned against the bar, listening to the musicians—a quartet: drummer, piano, bass, and saxophone—on a stand at the other end. Progressive jazz. A new beat for me. But for the customers packing the room from wall to bar, it had another effect, another tone, to judge from their heads nodding, their closed eyes, the movement of the crowd as one. Freaky. A room filled with men and women standing side by side, just listening. That close and no one hugging, no squeezing? But in that hot, sweaty room, with waitresses shouting out orders over the heads of customers, bartenders handing out drinks over the heads of customers clear to the other side of the room, no one fussed and no one fought. Just a roomful of grooving niggers.

And from the look on Sonny's face as he came pushing through to me, the scene had done good by him, too. Never had I seen that face looking so sure, so full of itself. Shaking hands over the heads of the crowd, nodding his sweaty head, Sonny had the look of a man who had made it—or thought he had. . . .

"Hey, Dorine—Dorine, come on back here. Girl, it sure is good to see you." Grabbing my arms, he pushed me through the crowd. I got a buzz: even in the best of times, no one ought to be glad to see a feller he owed money to—especially when the bill was so long due. . . .

Sonny pushed me on into the back room—a small eating room. He led me to a table where four expensive-looking gents sat, adding to the smoke with big cigars. "I wants you to meet one fabulous woman," Sonny bragged, proud to be presenting me. "Dorine Davis—the original self-made millionaire. . . ."

That was some strong shit. Without appearing to, I looked the gents over. They were doing likewise: Dorine Davis—too much on the heavy side. Ground-grippers instead of spikes, plain, dark below-the-knee clothes that had no relation to the "new look." (I had come to sport my car, not my clothes.) Dorine Davis, the woman no longer of interest to men (young ones) and one who men no longer interested (old ones). Only the diamonds I wore on my thick-jointed fingers spoke of any possibility of propositions—not cheap ones.

"Yeah," Sonny said. "Dorine's been around. She's known some men—I mean the biggest. . . ." Flashing his teeth, forcing me to flash mine, nonetheless it nettled me, him trying to picture himself a little boy looking up to me from the distance of his youth.

"She's still a mighty pretty woman," one of the men (older one) said. "You got to be blind to see that she needs no makeup on that smooth brown skin—and just look at them big, pretty teeth. . . ."

"You should have seen her back then. . . ." Sonny said, and I thought it time to break up his little-boy worship.

"I got some talk for you, Sonny-Boy."

"What about, Dorine?"

"We got to be alone. . . ."

"These here's my friends," he bragged. "You can talk in front of 'em."

"If you say. . . . Are you about ready to—"

"Anyway," he broke in, sort of timely, "I'll be here tomorrow. I gets here after two every day."

"See you then. . . ." Getting right up, I pushed on out.

The next afternoon, I came early and had to wait for Sonny. The day crew—one waitress, along with the bartender—stood at the cash registers, counting the day's receipts. The cook sat at a back table, looking over the night menu. I sat at the almost empty bar, looking out onto the avenue.

Daylight had never been Harlem's best time. But now, the days when sandblasting had sparkled old buildings to newness had long gone. The buildings carried years of dirt and grime heavy into their stones. Drabness had taken over even in the people walking around: men in shirt-sleeves and slacks, women in loose dresses, wearing slippers or worn-down-in-the-back shoes making them into slippers. Numbers runners, slick-looking like outdated small-time cons, went in and out of shops and stores along the avenue. Petty hustlers, pushing cheap goods in paper bags, or protected like crown jewels beneath jackets that they opened up to flash when they popped into bars.

The sun lit up the drabness, took away its secrets. Its pulse-tickling mysteries. Everything wide open, exposed to the glare: winos bunched on stoops, sharing pints of Sneaky Pete; drunks standing in front of bars, talking loud, outpointing one another, saying nothing. Here and there a kid, doped up from the stuff being pushed by white gangs around Harlem. . . .

But across the avenue from the bar—the funeral parlor with its long line of limousines, its palace-decorated white front, added a touch of elegance. Pallbearers, ushers, in cutaway suits, rushing in and rushing out, kept the high-tone quality of the home going. Messengers of death, I had just thought, when Sonny's Cadillac pulled up.

He stopped in the doorway as though shocked when he saw me. "Hey—Dorine, what you doing here so early?"

"Ain't you the one who's late?"

He slipped onto the stool next to mine, studying my face. I studied his, finding pleasure in the signs of old age—at last. More than the heaviness around his face, the thickness of his middle, Sonny had the look of a man who had come a long way and had a willingness to settle.

"You know we got things to talk about, Sonny."

"How do I know if you ain't said. . . ?" I waited for his eyes to blink. When they did I said:

"Thought you might be anxious to get me off your back."

"How's that?"

Even if I had been born the very same day, I would have known there was no way in the world for Sonny to forget that kind of money. I hadn't heard that he had developed any strange disease. He didn't act as though he had had a complete breakdown. I had to get tough. "I know it ain't news, mister. You ain't funny and I ain't here to play games. It's collection time."

"What? Is it that time sure 'nough?" He blinked, once, twice, three times. Back to the old days. "Who'd have thought times goes by that quick. . . ?"

Going to the back, he started fumbling around with something in the cash register—to gain time, from the way the waitress and bartender stood back looking at him, wanting him to finish.

"Well . . . ain't neither one of us getting any younger, is we?" he called to me.

"Never thought you'd admit to that," I called back.

"Yeah—yeah—time sure does move. . . ."

All that stalling rang my buzzer again. Whatever his reason, Sonny thought he had one-upped me. I had only come to check up, make sure that Sonny had the place in hand. As far as the business, I had to deal from his hand. If he sold out from under me, there was no way for me to get the place—or to squeeze my money out of him.

Seeing the expensive-looking men sitting bored at the back table, and Sonny doing his best to impress them with his boy act, got me naturally suspicious. So whatever my good intentions when I came, I now had to push Sonny to show his hand. "And you know this lady"—I threw him a teasing, flirty look, laughing—"she still thinks she can move along with the time."

Two men coming into the bar held Sonny's attention. "Hey

man," he called. "What about one on me? Set 'em up," he said to the bartender, then came to stand opposite me—behind the bar.

"Now, tell me what this is all about?" he asked.

"No, you tell me," I said, grinning, simple as I was supposed to be.

"You talking about that li'l money you lent me, Dorine?"

"Uh-huh. . . ."

"I'm good for it," he said.

"Then pay it," I said.

"What's the hurry? You sure can wait a couple of months."

"How much you asking for the place?" I said, careless-like.

"What! How you sound, girl?" So selling wasn't what he was about.

"I don't mean nothing except I want my money—now. Today."

"You can wait a couple more weeks."

"I waited for more than six months, I can't wait no more," I said. "You got to know I ain't hit a lick of work in years. . . ."

"A little more time can't hurt. It might even be for the good."

"If you ain't hung on to a li'l money in a couple of years, how you figuring on coming up with it in a li'l while?"

"Dorine, times is hard." He kept his smile going, and I kept waiting for the joker at the back of his tongue.

"For the both of us, Sonny. But you ain't got no worries, I'm sure. Jam-packed as this place was last night."

"Bay-bee, you got to know things ain't what they seem—ever. Things is tough. . . ."

"That's why I need my money—right now," I said, then sat back for him to hit me with his joker-trump.

"Bay-bee. . . ." To hear an old feller use old methods is a back-crawling experience. "I'm good for it. You knows that. . . ." I kept looking at him, waiting. His eyes shifted to the bartender, at the men drinking at the bar. I guessed he was figuring the best way to run, when he hit me: "I just ain't got it right now. What you gonna do about it? Kill me?"

"No, I ain't gonna kill you, Sonny. But like the paper we signed says—I'm ready to move you out."

"What good is this bar gonna do for you, Dorine? You can't run it."

347

"I run damn near every joint you ever had."

"Joints," he said. "Illegal joints. But this here place is legal. A legal *public* place. Dorine, folks what got police records can't get license to run no public place."

He had to have it straight to play it that way. I looked into his eyes, and clear as anything, I saw he had thought that one out a long time ago. All that floor show. . . . Sweat jumped to my nose.

"Sonny," I said, real quiet. "There you go with that fist again—jerking off. But that's a pleasure you can't share, bay-bee. If you got any other cheap tricks on your mind—don't tell it to me. Tell my lawyer.

"But before I leave outa here, know this, lover-boy. You made one big mistake, thinking that your butt tied a woman to you for life. The man ain't yet born what tricks this woman called Dorine Davis—and gets away with it. And it don't matter if his thing is one-hundred-carat gold, tipped with a ninety-carat diamond."

Even in my wildest dreams I hadn't thought of running a place without Sonny. Sonny and Son, in partnership, had been stuck somewhere in my mind. Sonny had the know-how, and the following. He had lots to teach Son—but damn—to just stand still while a low-down mother measured my butt for a kick? He and all the mothers' children like him had to paint new thoughts to even think that.

I made it home in less than five minutes by the clock and went to Son's room. I stood in the doorway looking at him studying. An engineer? Who in the fuck had ever heard of a black engineer? "What you want to be an engineer for anyway?" I asked, interrupting his study.

Son looked up, eyes heavy with needing sleep. "Dorine, I'm sure we went over that one before."

"Ain't no future in it," I said.

"Well why don't we wait to find out," he said, anxious for me to leave him to his work.

"Wasting goddamn years—best ones you'll ever know," I said. "What you got against getting rich anyhow?"

"Who said I got something against being rich? But how you figure I'll just walk out of a door and get that way?"

"What about owning a bar in the middle of Harlem?"

"Dorine, where am I going to get a bar in the middle of Harlem?"

"You got one."

I walked in on them the day Son took over. Son and Sonny were standing near the cash register when I came in. Looking up, they jerked their heads in greeting, then went on talking.

Three men sat at the quiet bar—a let-down lifeless feeling after a night of blaring music—talking to the bartender. "Coke," I called out, and when the bartender brought it, I sat at the far end to wait.

The hot air coming in through the open door from the streets, where folks stood puffing, sweating, fanning, stifled the room so that the men's voices sounded thick, muffled. Once or twice, Sonny's voice rose, explaining: "You dig what I'm saying? That's the trick, man. . . ." Then dropped back to below hearing. Sonny kept his head and hands moving, trying to impress Son with his seriousness, and Son, eyes wide, nodding his head, looked impressed.

Dogged, determined, I had stayed in the background while they were going through the transactions. I had left them to themselves wanting them to get to know each other without my weight. Son had been quick in learning. Sonny didn't seem to mind teaching. I had no hard feelings. For me, getting hold of the bar had wiped out the past—for good. That's what I had come around to tell Sonny— not expecting him to appreciate it until he got over being peeved.

Sitting at the end of the bar looking down at them, I felt real good about myself—and them. Then they forced themselves into my eyes: Lordy, but that was something! I almost thought it out loud. The surprise. Once upon a time, a thought had drifted in that maybe one day we might all be together; but it had drifted out—had faded in importance, even before my need for the old buzzard had. Only now and then had I admitted to the fact that they actually were related—or that it mattered. Seeing them together now, their heads bowed close, their likeness to one another struck me with the force of a blow.

The same round heads—except Sonny's hair had grayed at the temples; the same height and thick frames—except that the years had filled out Sonny's; the same black complexion—except that the shine had been powdered out—or had faded out—of Sonny's face, and Son took his mustache real serious. Their clothes were different. Son, having thrown style out the window, wore baggy pants and shirt-sleeves, the shirt wide open at the neck. And Sonny—was forever Sonny. . . .

The men at the bar kept glancing at me, thinking I might get around to a light flirtation. When I looked past them—kept looking past them—to the two at the other end, they turned to look too. I felt their interest bound. Their whispers took on a note of excitement. I tried to think them still, to blind them to what they were looking at, prevent them from repeating their whispers out loud. Knowing it to be impossible tempted me to get up, to get the hell on out. But I stayed there, hypnotized, as if forced to sit to the end of a suspense picture I hated, wanted no part of, yet couldn't tear myself away from.

Already I imagined them pointing accusing fingers at me, finding me guilty—of a silence from which the two had been benefiting all these years. So what might have been panic I turned to hard-cutting anger, even before the man, having waited as long as curiosity could stand, called: "Hey Sonny, I been knowing you a lotta years, man. How come you been holding out on me? How come you ain't ever let on you had a son?"

"Yeah," the other man echoed. "How come, man? It's sure ain't no woman on this earth had nothing to do with that boy. Ain't you done spit him outa your very own mouth?"

Their heads snapped up as one—Sonny's and Son's. They stared at the men, turned to stare at each other. But where Son bowed his head back over the work, Sonny looked over to me, then walked on past the men, past me, and on out the door. I got the message: Sonny had stopped speaking to me.

He never spoke to me again. I heard of him, though—through Son. Sonny took every occasion to visit the bar that still bore his name. He went there to give Son tips, on this or that. He hung around just to talk. . . . And it was through Son I knew when Sonny had opened up his new place on Lenox Avenue: a dance hall. I drove by on the day men were hoisting its name: S-O-N-N-Y-'s in big neon lights that took up almost the entire block.

Sonny intended to light up the avenue for miles around, I knew that before Son told me. Sonny had planned to make his ballroom

350

replace two—the Savoy and the Golden Gate—ballrooms torn down to make room for housing projects. Generations to come would be dancing from early evening to dawn, to big-name bands playing at this place called: S-O-N-N-Y-'S.

Broke, he didn't have enough to pay the asking bribes needed to get his liquor license. But knowing Sonny, he would think up something—like selling what was left of his soul. . . .

Conclusion

The Supreme Court decision of 1954, desegregating schools, had black folks grinning and handshaking on back and front pages of all the newspapers. Folks congratulating themselves for winning a victory. Fools. I sat back waiting. And just what I knew would happen, happened: crackers got to bombing black folks' homes, and bombing even the white school that let black kids in. Lord, it was enough to drive the devil out of his mind seeing his messengers—grown-assed women—spitting on kids, their faces all twisted and ugly like they had caught leprosy. And those kids, starched and pretty, heads all proud, just a-marching. It made my heart weep. I went to Garvey corner, and parking the car, listened to this Black Muslim preacher, Malcolm X, shouting and pointing his finger: "Men, real men, would never let children go to the front to do their fighting for them," he said. "We can't call these men. . . . We call them nig-gers!"

Rushing home, I put a call through to Montgomery. When Brother answered I lit right into him: "Brother, just tell me what is going on when grown-assed men put poor little kids out there to take on those low-life murdering crackers?"

"Dorine." Brother spoke in his best supposed-to-be-patient

353

voice. "President Eisenhower has called up the troops to protect the children."

"Yeah, I seen a picture in the *Daily News* with these blacks standing with guns, supposed to be upholding some little girl's dignity," I said. "What if them troops were crackers, Brother?"

"Even cracker soldiers are trained to obey their commanders, Dorine."

"What if the commanders had ordered them soldiers to kill the kids and protect the crackers?" I said.

"But they didn't, Dorine. They won't."

Brother could kill me swearing about what white folks would and wouldn't do. I held quiet. Even by telephone you can force a feller to listen to himself if you hold still long enough.

When the quiet should have been about to bust his eardrums, I said, "Anyway, Brother, how are them stiffs you get paid to look after?" A million years of schooling and the only job he could find was sticking fluid up the ass of corpses!

"I'm managing, Dorine. Managing. I had been moving ahead, talking with sharecroppers, though—until this school decision. You know how these whites in Montgomery get when they hear about things changing. I'm taking it easy right around in here. . . ."

"Why?" I never understood why Brother bothered, if he hadn't the nerve to be bold. "One thing sure, you don't have to worry none about your li'l girl being sent to the front line. There won't be no front line in 'Bama. . . ."

"How is Son making out with the bar?" Brother said to change the subject.

"Hon-ey." I tried to make pictures of my words. "Son and me? We doing fine. We're up here trying to make all the money there is."

"I'm glad he's up there with you," Brother said. "As tense as things are down here I was afraid he might get the silly notion in his hard head of coming down."

"Who? Son? You gotta be outa your mind, Brother. Nooo, honey. Son's as happy as a punk in a YMCA steam room, making all this loot. He ain't thinking of leaving."

Of course I had no way of seeing inside Son's head, it being as closed to me as a Brazil nut. Making money had become his one living thought. We saw little of each other and spoke less. Working ought not to have been a reason.

But we did work hard. So hard that we told one time from the next by the change of seasons. Son worked from early evenings to early mornings. Son had kept Sonny's old bartender, who managed the bar days. I did my cleaning while Son slept, then went around Harlem the rest of the day, looking into deals.

Black folks were coming into bars in Harlem now (the drugs the mobs let loose in Harlem had changed youth gangs, fighting over their turf, into desperate addicts fighting and killing over any and everybody's). Whites were selling and cutting out.

I had just closed a deal for a bar on 125th Street when, on my way home, I switched on the radio in the car to hear an announcer saying: ". . . Montgomery, for refusing to leave the front seat. . . ." Montgomery!

By the time I got to listening the program had changed back to music. I kept twisting the dial searching for a news station, but had to wait to hear about Rosa Parks until I got home. ". . . A middle-aged seamstress, arrested in Montgomery, for refusing to move from the front seat of a bus after being asked. . . ." I turned off the radio and reached for the phone. I put a call through to Brother. But no one answered. I called Lil: "Lil, Dorine."

"Dorine, you heard about what's happening down here?" Her voice sounded high-pitched from excitement. "Folks down here are mad, Dorine."

"All on account of some woman not able to sit in the front of a bus?"

"All on account of that, Dorine," Lil said. "We down here are just about tired. We aim to do something about it," she said.

"Like what?"

"Like what we have to, Dorine." She spoke in a quiet voice. I shouted:

"Don't you be no fool and get yourself all involved, Lil. Them crackers'll kill y'all."

"We're not scared, Dorine."

But I was scared—for them. They were no longer little things that would be overlooked when the going got tough. "Look Lil, before things get worse, pack up y'all's things. I ain't got nothing here but some rooms."

"Dorine," she said. "You don't seem to understand. We're mad—and we're ready." I heard her then. Saw her long, lean body, her octopus arms, and remembered her standing by her mother.

Hanging up the phone, I turned to find Son standing in the doorway. "Talking to Lil?" he asked. "What's happening with this woman Rosa Parks?"

Gut instinct brought out a lie: "Oh, they're getting ready to do something or the other. . . ." But he knew—or could find out, by just turning on the radio. "Lil sounds as though she's expecting all hell to break loose," I said. Then wondered why I had felt the need to lie.

"Don't say." Son moved past me to turn on the radio. He smiled and I prayed the silence that we had been living in was about to break.

In a way it did. Now Son found the time to sit in the living room with me—around the television, the radio, the telephone—looking, listening, waiting for news.

"What's with Brother these days?" Son asked one evening before going off to the bar.

"Making it with them stiffs, I reckon." Then wanting to press on to our old closeness, I added: "You know Brother. He ain't about to have white folks link him to no hell-raising."

"Cautious Uncle," Son laughed. "His heart's straight. It's his spine that don't go along. But then who are we sitting up here to talk?" I hated his meaning but feared to question his reasoning. His big eyes—red and looking more like Sonny's from working in the smoke-filled bar—sent me a message. Fear spread like mist and quivered my insides.

Lil called with more news: she had joined a committee, Jennie Mae and Lil had turned their cars over to the committee; Jane, Jennie Mae, and Lil were driving folks to and from work. Ruth, Mildred's youngest, was coming home from studying medicine in Canada to join them. "Dorine, this Montgomery bus boycott is going to be the biggest thing that ever happened in these parts."

"It'll take more than a boycott to change things down there," I said to Son. "Montgomery's evil so deep down, it needs a atomic bomb to uproot."

"No, all it takes are enough folks willing to try," he said quietly, and a knowledge seeped through his pores, settling in the room, the apartment. I wanted to shout: Never you mind Montgomery. That bus boycott's black folks' simple dream. Montgomery ain't gonna change. Your place is here, in New York, with me! But as he only sat there quiet. . . .

That night a fit of sadness took hold of my heart. Reaching for the phone next to the bed, I called Tom. "Tom Rumley," I said. "Seems to me that I ain't done something right in this life. After all these hundreds of years, a fool woman sits in the front of a bus in Montgomery and it's about to mess the hell outa my life."

"How's that, Dorine?"

"Son. I keeps getting the feeling he's thinking of leaving—maybe going down home."

"Dorine," Tom said in his patient voice. "If a woman sitting in the front of a bus all the way down in Montgomery is gonna mess with your life, it ain't because you ain't lived right. It's that you ain't been thinking right."

"I tell you Son—"

"—is grown. Now, you taken care of things you had to in your time. Leave the young folks to take care of that they wants in theirs—" I slammed down the phone. Then for the life of me, I twisted and turned in bed, and got wider awake.

I went to the toilet. I came back and stood staring out the window. What had I done wrong? I flipped through the pages of my life: everything or nothing! Folks oughtn't to search their lives for faults like searching through pubic hairs for lice. At my age? No, goddamit, the big part of my life had already been lived.

I turned toward the bed. But a stirring outside the window held me. A disquiet in the dark held me. The feel of something—almost familiar—out there, keeping itself invisible but busy. . . . The wind whistled around the corner. It hit against the window. A restless soul trying to find shelter? That thought brought an even stronger gust racing around the corner. It rattled the window, and the rattling caused icy lines to be drawn along my spine. I shivered, shivered, shivered.

Son came in at dawn and I was still awake. His key in the lock brought me out of bed. By the time I stepped out in the hall his door had closed. I went to his room and knocked. He opened the door and stood in the doorway, a polite smile frozen on his face. What hadn't I done right?

Looking into my face caused his smile to fade. His eyes slid over my shoulder. So instead of having out the talk, which I didn't know how to start anyway, I said: "Son, I just closed the deal on this new bar. I want you to come with me later to look the place over."

"Dorine, are you sure you want another bar?" he asked.

"What? All the time and trouble I've put into this deal? Now you ask?"

"I know you want it, Dorine," he said. "But won't it be hard on you?"

And there we were, on the brink of the talk I had thought we needed. Which I didn't want—no part of it. Yet I was forced to say: "On us, you mean, don't you, Son?"

"Not on us, Dorine. I'm going back home."

"Home? I don't understand. . . ."

"Yes you do, Dorine." He locked eyes with me. And it had been so long since I looked into his, I didn't know how to read them anymore.

"But this is your home, Son. . . ."

"I'm talking about Montgomery, Dorine." He spoke in that patient voice he liked to use with me.

"I don't believe it," I said, glad, suddenly, that we were having it out, putting it out in the open where it belonged. "New York is your home. You have roots here."

"You always knew I intended to go back, didn't you, Dorine?"

"Knew? How would I know a thing like that. . . ?"

A feeling is only a feeling. But we should have talked. We should have had this talk long before. "After all, we never talked about it."

"I told you when I first came."

"That's been years. . . ."

"If it took a hundred. . . ."

"And the bar? You a businessman now, Son. You not the simple soldier that you were when you came to my doorstep seven years ago, talking about being an engineer. You a man, Son. A successful businessman. Not every feller can have a business dropped into his lap, one he never asked for. . . ."

"That's right, Dorine. I never asked."

"You ain't done so bad—for all that."

He walked away from me. I followed up the hall and into the living room. Putting on the light, he sat, expecting, it seemed, the long talk I had wanted.

"And so you think you can just drop everything and leave?"

"Yes."

"On account of some woman you don't even know sat down in the front seat of a fucking bus?"

"Is that all what's happening back home means to you, Dorine?" He searched through my eyes as though looking for something he had lost there.

"Whatever it means, one thing it don't is that you can pull up the way you think and run off, leaving me alone."

"Bud will come up and run it for you."

"Bud!" I said, then remembered the nephew I kept forgetting.

"Yes. Bud has always wanted to come to New York. He can manage the bar for you—it *is* your bar, Dorine, no matter whose name it's in—or who you have fronting for you." He looked long at me, waiting for me to dispute him. When I didn't, he said:

"I didn't know what I was getting into, you know, Dorine." He spoke slowly. He had given it a lot of thought. "And when I found out, I didn't appreciate being used—against Sonny." He waited for me to answer. But I had no intention of going back into a time he didn't know, wouldn't appreciate, and damn sure would never understand. "Anyway, Bud is a good man—handsome. He will draw a damn sight better crowd than me. . . . I'm leaving. I'm so tired of New York."

"Tired of New York!"

"Goddamn tired," he said. "It's been a hard load to carry, Dorine."

"If it's hard, you can hire more help," I said. His head snapped up. His eyes tried to bulge into mine. "You're not hearing me, Dorine. . . . Why?"

"If I'm not hearing, it ain't because of me not listening," I said. "You been working good, spending money." I moved to get away from those bullet-eyes. "I ain't heard you complaining."

"I'm not complaining now, Dorine." He spoke softly. "I'm just leaving."

The calm way he overlooked my needs burned a thin thread of heat through my brain. "Like hell you are," I almost shouted. "After all I done for you, you can't just stand there and tell me, just like that, you leaving. . . ."

"Please don't get mad, Dorine." He reached for my hand. I snatched away from his reach. "Look," he said. "We know you did a lot for us. There's no way in the world we can repay all you've done."

"What we, they, us crap you talking about? Talk about you!"

"Me, then. I know you worked hard. . . ."

"Nigger, you don't know what that word means!"

Annoyed at my shouting, he walked to the door. I ran to block his way: "Yes, nigger. Every bit of food that ever crossed your mouth cost me plenty! Shoes for your feet cost me these fallen arches! I roamed this damn country from one coast to the other to make sure you had! What the hell do you know about hard work?"

Rage. I had seen rage. Harry had had rage. At last I understood: Helplessness. Standing by as life passed and helpless to do one damn thing about it. Shout loud, lie, playact, cry out that you would die if you were lonely: nothing made a damn bit of difference.

"Hanging on to that legless old man." I kept shouting. "Papa. Papa shit! He lived so long on account of I spoon-fed the bastard. What the hell do you know?"

"That legless hunk of man happened to be my father, Dorine." He had put steel in his voice, thinking to quiet me. "Papa never talked, never spoke one word since I remembered. His hand on my head spoke of love. He loved me, Dorine."

"A hand on your head or all the kissing and hugging in the world couldn't bring you from there to here—"

"I'm going back—"

"—and back," I said.

"Dorine, I'm not trying to hurt you," Son said. "You more than most must know that being together don't mean being tied together. . . ."

"I spent my life tied to you!" I said. "Every thought I ever thought, every step I ever took, I took chained to you. You can't go and leave me—"

"Me, Dorine. . . ?" His eyes peeled out to look into mine, to force me quiet. Questioning eyes, listening deep, deep, daring me to speak, to say those words that would turn my pain into the pain he would be forced to bear.

And I thought of that day, with him standing at the bar next to Sonny, of Sonny looking at him, then looking at me—of Sonny walking out, never to speak to me—while Son, his head bowed, remained still . . . so goddamn still, refusing to look up—refusing to look up. The image stuck a pin in my rage. I lowered my voice:

"I done give you a dream, fool."

"Your dream?"

"How many people you know can come to New York, to Harlem, and make it into the big time?"

"Yours and Sonny's dream."

"Everybody's goddamn dream," I said.

"Not everybody's," Son said. "I never thought to live a dream. I only wanted to live life. I wanted to make money, then go home to Montgomery and walk down the middle of any street with my head shaved and give the sucker who rubs it for luck one between the eyes."

"That's a goddamn hallucination," I said.

"But it ain't a dream, Dorine—it's a promise," he said, and the telephone rang.

We both stared at it, kept staring. Finally Son walked over and picked it up. He said, "Yes?" He listened in the receiver, then replacing it, turned to me. "Dorine, that was Tom Rumley. He called to tell you—Sonny had a heart attack last night—dropped dead—in his ballroom."

I stood at the bar that still bore his name, looking through the window, across the avenue to the funeral parlor where he lay. Son had gone to see him. Now he stood at the far end of the bar going over the books he had to turn over to the bartender. He was leaving. Friends went in and went out of the funeral parlor. Friends drove up in big cars, rushed in. Friends, squinching down from the cold wind, walked from up or down the avenue to go in. Crowds: the Sugar Hill bunch; the musicians. White friends. Black sporting-life friends.

Mr. Harlem, they had called him. Mr. Harlem. He had known

every corner, gone down every street, slipped into all its dives. He had sported his big cars on its avenues—folks knew him, pointed to him: There goes Mr. Harlem. . . .

The grim cold winds had swept the streets clean. Winos hovered in doorways. On the corner, across the street from the parlor, one lone figure, dressed in an old black fur, a large black shawl pulled over her head and shoulders, hawked numbers books from her cart to passersby.

I saw Albert. He turned onto the avenue, shoulders squinched together, hands gripping the collar of his coat as he hurried up to the funeral home and dashed in. In less than one minute he rushed out and scurried up the block, frightened—I suppose of the nightmares he might be taking back to mix in with his drinks.

Tom drove up and I left the bar. I wanted to go into the parlor with him. But traffic stopped me. The wind, blowing in my face, held me to the island in the middle of the avenue. And although Tom took a long time getting out of his car and shuffled slowly to the door, by the time I crossed the avenue, he had gone into the parlor. When I got in, he had just walked up to the bier, where he stood looking down. Seeing him up there, alone, looking at his old Baltimore buddy, I left him this last moment and, sitting behind him in the front pew of the chapel, waited.

Hundreds of flowers—wreaths, bouquets, baskets filled with all types of blossoms—stifled the air with the sweet, heavy smell of death—a roomful of dead and dying things. But Sonny's friends had not played him cheap: among the flowers, a large wreath of lily of the valley, one of roses—yellow, red, pink, and white. And a wreath of purple orchids.

Tom sighed, a big sigh. In the last few years, sighs took the place of his deep belly laugh. His broad back heaved. It had happened again and still not to him. He still had to wait and worry about its happening. How many friends had we looked down on? How many funerals had we attended to look across a room and see Sonny's face among the faces of moaners: Bessie Smith, Chick Webb, Jimmie Lunceford—and even more recently, Big H. God, we went like flowers—handpicked and packaged.

Tom sighed again. So many years of friendship had to be worth those sighs—lapping, lapping a giant tide of sadness that took the place of tears. . . . Tom turned, started up the aisle, and seeing me, came to stand beside me. He sighed again. What to say? We had said it all. He shuffled up the aisle on his poor aching feet. . . .

And then it was my turn. My turn to look down at those bulging eyes forced shut, the gloved hands holding each other. His diamond ring was missing. They ought to have left him that—his pride. It had seen the years with him. But his face looked clear of struggle—anger, hate, even its slickness had been smoothed out. Only the fleshy smile—no, *a* fleshy smile—curved up the black, powdered face. No more thoughts to think, none of those driving thoughts that had filled his every life-filled moment. His force. To have quelled that force had to have killed the man. . . .

Ahh—but Sonny had been one hell of a man. He had lived one hell of a life. He had worked to make his every dream come true. Yet he had never been successful. His dreams had always been too big for him to handle. He had been slick but never clever. . . .

I hated leaving him. I had known him so long—longer than anyone in the city. I had known him well. Better than any had ever known him—better than I had known anyone. I wanted to stretch those last minutes with him—to stretch and stretch them. . . . Someone came to stand beside me. I walked up the aisle and out the door.

Outside, I stood looking around through a haze. Cars raced down the avenue. I heard the screech of brakes, the blowing of car horns. I stood, hearing them all crashing together through my ears. I looked across the street—the woman had moved her cart closer to the shelter of the building and had settled down next to it—a hulk of darkness. Leaning against the building—near to the white palace of death—two junkies, knees bending and straightening like puppets on a string.

A cold gust of wind blew through my coat. I thought of crossing the avenue to my car parked in front of the bar, of driving away. Laughter pouring out of a nearby hallway claimed my attention. Winos, huddled together for warmth, sharing a pint of wine, claimed my attention. The junkies—bobbing and weaving, never feeling the cold—let themselves finally sink to the sidewalk and sat nodding, sleeping.

I looked around to the once lovely buildings that took up the corners, saw the windows—newspapers stuffed in broken panes to keep out the wind. Hunks of bricks missing here and there, leaving big gaping patches of darkness. . . .

We had come to Harlem, Sonny and I. We had pushed some ugly things out of our way—the taste of lost youth, too quickly spent, too soon used up. Pioneers? Settlers? We had taken a stand in a place we loved. We had lived, worked hard to add to its shine. We had survived in a world that had thought to decide our fate, had joined up with others who shared a dream.

Women. Men. People of substance. World-changers. They had walked up and down this avenue in their cutaways, their top hats, vests, twirling their canes like batons of gold. Big-timers. Big dreamers.

Only their ghosts remained—memories slinking around the slums, gliding in and out of broken-down buildings, floating over the fallen bodies of junkies, winos. Great men. Big men. Who would tell their tales when those buildings finally crashed down to bury their memories?

Who would tell the tale of a buck-eyed slickster who had struggled—underhanded at times—to rise, a star in this city of his dreams—Mr. Harlem. And who would tell the story of a big black man with the yellow-brown eyes who had tied his dreams to the United States of America, through a place he called The Rising Sun, but had ended up with his head beaten in on the concrete sidewalks of his dreamland? Would someone ever think with pride of a smooth-faced West Indian—a millionaire—who raged from Washington to his island, demanding something he called dignity for his people? The beggars were out in full force. Did any of them give a damn?

"Pancakes! Sons a bitches. . . !" The dream-book lady had risen. She stood staring out on the avenue, pointing as though to a parade of marching ghosts. ". . . Dey kick all-you ass outa Greenwich Village. You take it! Dey kick all-you ass outa de Tenderloin. All-you take it! And your blood did flow, like fire, in de streets a San Juan Hill! You take it! Now dey wipin' up de streets a Harlem wit all-you ass. . . . Pancakes! Sons a bitches!"

I crossed the avenue to my Lincoln Continental and opened the door just as Son came rushing out of the bar, excited. "Dorine," he said, reaching the car as I slipped into the seat. "Brother just phoned from Montgomery. . . ." Big eyes bright, staring only at tomorrow's promises, he put his head up to the window as I got set to turn the wheels into the traffic. ". . . Told me to tell you he's thrown caution to the wind. . . . Says he's joining up with Reverend Martin Luther King."

"Martin Luther King?" I snapped. "Who in the fuck is Martin Luther King?" Then pushing my foot down on the gas, I roared up the avenue—Seventh Avenue—once the grandest, damndest avenue in all of New York City.